If I Should Wake Before I Die

The Complete Horror Short Fiction

Eric B. Olsen

authorHOUSE®

AuthorHouse™
1663 Liberty Drive
Bloomington, IN 47403
www.authorhouse.com
Phone: 1 (800) 839-8640

© 1994, 2016 Eric B. Olsen. All rights reserved.

No part of this book may be reproduced, stored in a retrieval system, or transmitted by any means without the written permission of the author.

Published by AuthorHouse 06/30/2016

ISBN: 978-1-5246-1131-6 (sc)
ISBN: 978-1-5246-1130-9 (e)

Print information available on the last page.

Any people depicted in stock imagery provided by Thinkstock are models, and such images are being used for illustrative purposes only. Certain stock imagery © Thinkstock.

This book is printed on acid-free paper.

Because of the dynamic nature of the Internet, any web addresses or links contained in this book may have changed since publication and may no longer be valid. The views expressed in this work are solely those of the author and do not necessarily reflect the views of the publisher, and the publisher hereby disclaims any responsibility for them.

For Patrick

Contents

If I Should Wake Before I Die

Other Stories

Blood Feast

Bride of Blood Feast

Introduction

If I Should Wake Before I Die is the first of a series of unpublished manuscripts that I have had stored in a box in the garage for twenty years. Prior to the advent of on-demand printing of books, self-publishing was indeed a pursuit that deserved the name "vanity publishing" as it was extremely expensive, publishers kept the author's rights to their book, and usually left the author with only a one-time run of several hundred books that usually wound up . . . in a box in the garage. While there is certainly a degree of vanity that goes into much of the self-publishing world today, especially in the e-book market, these particular manuscripts have been looked at by numerous editors and agents and received a lot of positive criticism. Most blamed their inability to publish these works on the vagaries of the publishing world at the time rather than any inherent flaw in my writing, though I suspect some of them were being kind. Still, all of these works have been seen by a number of editors and read through rather than rejected out of hand, which makes me feel justified in bringing them to print, both physically and electronically, for the purpose they were always intended for: to be read by an audience.

The stories in this book are the first writings that I ever attempted. They are not quite juvenilia—as I was already in my late twenties—but certainly lack the depth and confidence that I would exhibit in my later writing. Nevertheless, they do contain a young writer's excitement at learning a new craft, and the verve that goes along with it, trying out ideas and modes that might be dismissed out of hand by a more seasoned author. My original intent was to go through and revise them for publication in book form, but as I began to read through them I realized that they are a product of their time and would somehow be diminished in being retooled too much. My wife at the time helped me edit all of the stories, and I owe her a tremendous debt of gratitude. She was a wonderful editor and proofreader, and a lot of her punctuation choices are quite unique, things I would never think to do even today and so those remain as well. I fixed obvious errors and places where the text was confusing, but for the most part the writing remains intact, essentially as I first imagined it.

All of the stories, with the exception of the two novellas at the end of the book, were written between 1986 and 1992. They are horror stories of the simplest kind, usually dealing with some form of karmic revenge on an unlikable protagonist. My primary literary inspiration at that time was Stephen King, and while I never set out to emulate him in content or style, I certainly felt his powerful influence exerted on me as I attempted to write my own tales of the macabre. The other major influence on this book was, interestingly, Ernest Hemingway. As I was putting this collection together, back around 1990 or so, I had been reading Hemingway's first set of short stories, *In Our Time*. Each of his stories in that collection was preceded by a short vignette, not really a story in itself, and not even obviously connected to the story that followed it, but it was something that left an impression on me in terms of the book as a whole.

It was only later that I had the idea to write a something in second person, as a lark, and that's how the story "The Funeral" came about. I sent it out to a small California horror magazine in 1991, and to my complete surprise they bought it and published it. I already had eight other horror stories that I had written and submitted to magazines small and large, one of which had been picked up for publication, and so I decided to write seven other second-person stories and put the whole collection together in the manner of Hemingway's first book. That's how *If I Should Wake*

Before I Die came about. I thought it was a great title for a book of horror stories and for the last twenty-five years I've been waiting for someone else to use it, but it hasn't happened yet.

All of the second-person stories deal with isolation in one form or another. This could be the complete isolation of something like outer space, or the social isolation that comes from being shunned by family, and while not strictly supernatural horror I felt they did mesh well with my other works. I also tried to relate each in some way to the story that follows it. The only story that doesn't have an attendant second person short-short is the first, as I wanted the collection to begin with a complete story rather than just a vignette. In the meantime I had completed my first novel and by the time I embarked on a second I had really lost interest in the form itself. Two other stories followed and there was really no way to shoehorn them into this collection and so they have been left separate. The two horror novellas were written to meet the demands of a small press publisher who soon went out of business and left me with no real avenue to publish them and so they sat, unread, like the rest of these works, until now.

The first story I ever completed was "One More for the Road" in the summer of 1987. I was naturally excited about my accomplishment and showed it to all of my friends, especially Patrick, and this encouraged me to pursue writing with the aim of becoming a published author. But that goal couldn't have even been considered if not for a man named Jaime O'Neill. When I graduated from high school I had no idea what I wanted to do with my life. One thing I did know, however, was that I didn't want a regular job. As a result, I attended community college and promptly flunked out in my second semester. Then I began playing music and my father was incredibly generous in allowing me to stay at home while I pursued this avocation for the next four years. After four years of playing music, however, I realized I did not have the temperament to pursue any artistic endeavor that involved a dependence on other people. So I decided to go back to school with goal of getting an actual degree. I was during my first semester back at a new community college, in English 101, that I had the privilege of being taught by Mr. Jaime O'Neill.

I had passed my high school English courses by copying the papers of other students and plagiarizing my essays, and so when I entered college I had absolutely no idea how to write. But Professor O'Neill loved everything I wrote for him. It was a revelation to say the least, and it made me think that perhaps writing was something I should explore in a serious way. Since those first papers I wrote were essentially non-fiction, that is what I thought I should pursue, and since horror films were one of my passions I though a history of the genre would be fun and profitable to write. At that time there were very few serious books on horror films and so I felt that I was working in an area that was fairly uncrowded. That kind of book, however, entailed a tremendous amount of research, and while that was going on very little writing was done.

The next significant event in my writing career was reading. I hadn't really done much other than the required reading in college. But with the idea of the book on horror films I thought I should begin reading some of the original novels as part of my research. I began with *Dracula*, by Bram Stoker, but found it heavy going. I had barely begun when my friend Patrick saw me with the book in hand and said, "Re-reading the classics?" When I confessed that I had never read a horror novel he quickly told me that Stoker was not the place to begin, and the next day he loaned me his copy of *Ghost Story* by Peter Straub. That was one of the two or three transformative moments in my life. I had never known this type of completely absorbing fiction before. Well-written, intricately plotted, and infinitely believable, Straub's fiction quickly became a staple for me. Next I read *Floating Dragon* and *If You Could See Me Now* in quick succession, and I can remember being so enraptured with *Julia* that I brought it to school with me and continued to read it through my lectures.

I'm sure I read some Stephen King around this time— probably starting with *The Talisman* because Straub had co-written it—but his work wasn't nearly as memorable for me in terms of my early reading in the genre. I also remember going on a road trip one weekend with a bunch of friends and seeing someone's copy of Anne Rice's *Interview with the Vampire* lying casually on the dashboard of the van. I picked it up and began reading, and for the next two days I was so completely absorbed that my friends began making fun of me, in a very good-natured way. One night we had to sleep in a grange hall where a bat was also in residence, and while he flew over our heads that night Patrick cracked me up by calling him Louis. It was around this time that I began flirting with the idea of writing my own horror stories, and the book on horror films sort of slipped into oblivion.

One of the things I had a lot of fun with in writing these stories was coming up with the titles. I was drawn to clichés and idioms that would convey the meaning of the story only after it was read. Of course most titles do that, but these particular titles gave nothing away and I enjoyed that particular challenge. In terms of the writing itself, it's difficult to imagine being able to come up with stories like these today. I would certainly be using longer paragraphs of narration than I did back then. Still, I like the dialogue and the overall unpretentiousness of the writing. Even back then I believed in what I call "transparent writing" where the writer's style stays out of the way of the story and allows it to stand on its own without self-conscious artistry that draws attention to itself. A lot of the characters and ideas are derivative of the movies I was watching at the time and heavily influenced by much of the reading I was doing in the horror genre. But I'm not sure that this really detracts from their artistic merit considering the reader would have to be as familiar with those specific films as I was in order to spot the borrowing I did.

Another noticeable aspect of my writing then was a willingness to deal explicitly with sex. Following the injunction to write what you know, I felt that sex was as much a part of life as anything else and that to leave it out would be somehow cheating the reader out of a true experience. But I can also remember talking with a writer at the time that I respected greatly. He said that he didn't generally care to read about other people having sex. I thought that was a rather silly idea then, but I was still in my early thirties. Twenty years later I tend to agree with him, and this is yet another way that these stories would be very different if I were to attempt them today. Nevertheless, some of the more graphic descriptions have been toned down or eliminated in order to keep the emphasis on the story itself. I also did a good bit of deliberation in reviewing the scenes in *Blood Feast* where my characters refer to Native Americans as Indians. Ultimately, the characters are operating in a less sensitive time period, and their comments were not meant for the general public, so I decided to leave it as is.

I continued to write after these stories were completed, but very little of it was short fiction. After writing a horror novel in 1993 I devoted myself to writing mystery novels. In 2004 I wrote two mystery short stories, one of which was published in *Alfred Hitchcock's Mystery Magazine.* Another mystery novel followed, but since 2009 I have devoted myself entirely to writing non-fiction, which is a bit ironic considering that this is the kind of writing I always imagined myself doing from the very beginning. Though my days of fiction writing are over, it is my hope that readers will get some measure of enjoyment from these works and that they will at last reach an audience, however small, who can discover in them the joy I had in creating them.

Eric B. Olsen
April 30, 2016

If I Should Wake
Before I Die

Men fear death, as children fear to go in the dark; and as that natural fear in children is increased with tales, so is the other.

Sir Francis Bacon
Essays, "Of Death"

I do believe in spooks. I do believe in spooks. I do, I do, I do, I do, I do, I do believe in spooks.

Bert Lahr
The Wizard of Oz, 1939

"The Wrong Side of the Bed" is the second short story I ever wrote and the first story I ever sold . . . though that didn't actually result in its publication. I completed the story in 1988 and immediately sent it to Twilight Zone *magazine, but they had already gone out of business by then. I didn't get around to submitting it to another magazine until it went to* Thin Ice *in 1991. The editor, Kathleen Jurgens, liked the idea but not the ending. She asked me to do a revision and when I submitted it again she accepted it "for either issue 18 or 19 . . . I can't be more specific until closer to deadline." That was in early 1992. But it was just my luck that issue number seventeen was the last one published before the magazine folded in 1995 and so my story never actually made it into print. I'm honestly not sure how I came up with the idea, though the last man on Earth trope is certainly not an original one. My idea was to make the story personal, dealing with the psychology of the protagonist in a way that the films I'd seen on the subject couldn't really do. I don't think I actually revised the ending, either. What I did was to add the last section of the story to the original ending and in the process created a much more satisfying version thanks to Ms. Jurgens. A couple of the character names are straight out of Universal's* The Wolf Man *from 1941, specifically the last name of Talbot for the protagonist, and Gwen for his wife.*

The Wrong Side of the Bed

The first thing Evan Talbot saw when he opened his eyes was his wife's bra dropped precariously over the arm of the chair in their bedroom.

He smiled.

The rest of her clothes, as well as his, were strewn haphazardly across the floor.

He sighed.

Last night had been the most intense lovemaking of their marriage.

He smiled again.

It was Saturday morning and as he lay in bed reminiscing, Evan's thoughts turned reluctantly to other matters. The grass needed cutting and he would have to borrow Doyle's lawn mower. Then there was the inevitable garage cleaning. Good God, the drudgery of it all. But it was going to have to wait a few hours; the first thing on the agenda was the Sonics game on TV.

He was about to hop out of bed when he turned to his wife. Gwen was sleeping quietly with her back toward him, long brown hair gently feathered across the pillow that cradled her head. He leaned over and smelled the lingering scent of her shampoo and then patted her naked behind, but when his hand touched her skin he recoiled instantly as if from an accidental brush with a hot stove. Beads of sweat emerged on his forehead and his breath quickened as he inched his hand toward her a second time. She was cold. Jesus, everywhere he touched her was cold!

Evan flung the covers off and bolted out of bed like a frightened animal, nearly collapsing as his feet hit the floor, his body shaking uncontrollably. He reached out to brace himself against the wall, eventually traversing around to the other side of the bed, his eyes, unblinking, never leaving Gwen's motionless body.

As Evan stood next to his wife in silence he used all of his powers of concentration, staring at the cataleptic form beneath the sheets in a vain attempt to detect movement, a breath, a twitch, anything that would tell him she was okay.

But there was nothing.

The sheet was hiding her face and he reached out a trembling hand to lift it away. His heart nearly stopped as he unveiled two glassy eyes, staring back at him from beneath the covers.

Evan slumped to the floor and wept, waves of grief building into seizures that gripped his body and shook it by the spine. His weeping soon turned to wailing as he took his dead wife in his arms and held her close, pressing her lifeless face to his, tears, mucus and saliva mingling against her cold cheek as he cried out in anguish.

Nothing could have prepared him for this. Both of his parents were still alive. Christ, all of his grandparents were still kicking. No one close to him had ever died, and now the one person he loved more than any other was gone.

Finally, he was able to pull himself away from her body, and he gently laid the sheet over her head and walked numbly downstairs. For a while he just sat, trying not to think, wishing it was all a dream and yet knowing it was true. Then he would get up and travel around the room, looking at and touching everything she had touched, seeing Gwen everywhere. For the next several hours Evan paced the front room of their modest suburban home, alternating between fits of rage and despair, crying all the while until his body collapsed on the couch in shock, numb from the inside out.

By the time he had recovered enough to think about telling someone what had happened it was nearly five o'clock. Something had to be done, so he pushed himself up and went to the door. He would go over to the Webers'. Doyle would know what to do. In the midst of his tragedy Evan was certain of only one thing: he did not want to face it alone.

He turned the knob and pushed but the door wouldn't budge. At first he thought he must have forgotten the deadbolt, but no, it was open. He pushed a little harder and the door opened a crack. Something was blocking it from outside—something heavy.

He put his shoulder to the door this time and pushed with all his might, but suddenly his grief-stricken body began to quiver and they had to sit back down. After a couple of deep breaths he shook himself out of his stupor and viciously attacked the door. What he saw as he burst out of the house nearly made him relapse. Jones, the mailman, was lying in a heap on the front stoop.

Evan quickly placed his hand around the man's throat to feel for a pulse, but he knew as soon as he touched the cold, clammy skin that Jones was dead. It was when he turned his head away, giving his brain time to make sense of what was happening, that he looked across the street and saw the rear end of a green station wagon sticking out of the Spencers' kitchen.

"Jesus Christ," he muttered, and unconsciously he began to run across the street. He pounded on the Spencers' door but there was no answer. And then he saw the dead bodies in the car. Evan was frantic as he raced back toward his house. In the middle of the street he veered off toward Doyle's house. He needed help in a big way. There was no way in hell he could deal with this kind of shit on his own.

He was in a state of near frenzy as he approached his next-door neighbors' house. He beat on the door with both fists until, dissolving into tears, he slumped to the ground. No one answered.

Minutes later—it could have been two or twenty—Evan had calmed down somewhat and he took a look around. Both of the Webers' cars were in the driveway. Someone had to be home. He stood back up and rang the doorbell several times with no success and then, getting to his feet, he walked around to the front window. He peered in and could see Doyle asleep on the couch but just as he raised his hand to tap on the window he became paralyzed with fear.

Doyle wasn't asleep. His eyes were wide open and they had that same glassy-eyed stare as Gwen's.

"No!" Evan screamed at the top of his lungs. He turned around and ran back to his own home now, not wanting to give his thoughts time to register. Evan was thirty-eight, and at two-twenty, a bit on the heavy side. He had never seemed to get around to exercising off his excess weight and wheezed terribly. But he kept pushing himself. He was out of control.

As he cut his way through Doyle's lawn, wet grass stuck to his bare feet and for the first time he realized he was still in his bathrobe. On the way inside he caught his foot on foot on Jones' mailbag and tumbled headlong into the house.

II

When Evan came to, his head was swimming and he felt nauseated. Before he could even move he began to retch, his stomach muscles burning with every contraction. After nearly passing out again he finally managed to stop, a glistening strand of drool stretching to the floor the only thing to show for his efforts.

A soft light diffused through the room. It was hard to tell if it was dawn or dusk. Maybe it had all been a dream, he thought, but as he sat up he could see the faint outline of Jones' body through the still open door.

He looked at the clock. It was ten after five. It must be morning. Evan pushed his tired body up off the floor and sat on the back of the couch. His head was clear, and thoughts of yesterday began to filter into questions. What's happening? Is everyone in the neighborhood dead?

He picked up the phone and dialed 911. "Come on! Answer, damn it!" But no one did. He slammed the phone down in disgust and dragged out the phone book. He dialed the number for the police: no answer. He dialed the fire department: no answer. Ambulance: no answer. Evan could feel his chest tighten. No repeat performance of yesterday, he told himself.

He called his parents, his neighbors, friends, relatives: plenty of answering machines, but no people. He tried the operator, businesses, long distance: same thing. Then an inconceivable thought rolled around in his head for a moment before he dismissed it completely.

Is everyone dead?

Evan flipped on the TV. Black-and-white snow hissed back at him from every channel. Nothing on the radio either. Maybe the phone was out, too. There had to be some rational explanation for all of this. Nuclear war was his first thought but that didn't jibe with the facts, namely, that he felt fine.

His gaze fell on the stairs and Evan looked up. He couldn't go back to the bedroom. Fresh tears began to roll down his cheeks when a rumbling in his stomach made him realize that he hadn't eaten since Friday night. And today must be . . . Sunday. I'll just go rustle up some chow, he thought, and then drive down to the police station.

Scrambling up some eggs in the kitchen he thought that was probably what his brain had looked like yesterday. He allowed himself a smile. Then the inconceivable thought rolled back into his mind.

What the hell am I gonna do? What if I'm the only one alive?

While the eggs cooked he threw on some dirty clothes that were in the laundry room. Then he wolfed down his breakfast, grabbed the car keys, and headed outside.

Everything was the same as it had been yesterday evening. Everything was also very different. His senses had been practically nonexistent the day before but today the horrible reality was in clear focus. The sky was yellow and the air was tinged with fine smoke. It smelled like a mixture of burning rubber and wood. He could also hear the sound of sirens and alarms wailing in the distance. Undoubtedly fires had started, but no one had bothered to put them out. And though Evan had no idea what it was, he was certain that something terrible had happened.

He climbed slowly into his car and began to drive toward town. It was a holocaust. Hundreds of houses had virtually burned to the ground and he was very thankful that his neighborhood had escaped the flames. He winced as he passed the smoldering remains of a diner, several cars still idling in the parking lot, dead drivers hunched over the steering wheels. The freeway was littered with the charred wreckage of thousands of cars, most on the side of the road, but a few turned every which way in the middle. And as he drove through the city—bodies. Everywhere there were dead bodies.

Evan worked his way through town to the police station. He could hear ringing and buzzing from inside the building, but there was no movement outside at all. Empty police cruisers sat like stone gargoyles and Evan walked past them and inside. What he saw made him more confused than horrified. All of them were dead. Men in blue littered the building—the desk sergeant, the other officers, the prisoners in the cells: they were all dead.

He stumbled back to the door and tried to think of what to do next. Work—the office—maybe on familiar ground he would be able to think more clearly. Still somewhat stupefied, he hoisted himself back into his car and drove to work. The building was empty save for the night watchmen and the janitor, both quite dead of course. He couldn't understand why no one else was here; the police station had been full. Then it dawned on him. All of this must have happened on Friday night. No one *would* be here, he thought, and almost laughed.

In the middle of town several buildings were still in flames, and the din of alarms that had been set off was almost deafening.

Next, Evans pulled into an all-night grocery store, forcing open the electric doors to get inside. Much of the downtown area seemed to have lost electricity. Evan walked through the aisles, looking for anyone still alive. He stepped over a few corpses in produce, and even thought he recognized a couple of people in the frozen-food section, but they were lying facedown in the frozen

peas and he didn't want to know that badly. Evan fought back another laugh.

He ripped open a bag of potato chips, grabbed a can of beer and was about to leave when the bank of cash registers caught his eye on the way out. This time he did laugh, releasing all the nervous frustration he had been building up all morning. His eyes were watering he laughed so hard, and he had to wipe them with the sleeve of his shirt. What possible use could money be to him now?

He was finally starting to believe that the inconceivable had happened. It would be amazing, really: to be the only man alive. The thought sobered him and he set down the beer and chips. Wasn't there something he should be doing? Then it came to him. What if it was just here? He had to find a phone. He had to know if this had happened everywhere. The library seemed a good enough place to start; they would have phone books from all over. But when he ran up the front steps and tried the door it was locked.

After looking around for a large stone near the building, Evan picked one up and hefted it through the glass door in front, setting off another alarm in the process. Damn it, he said to himself. Inside, he hunted down a few out-of-state phone books and even lucked across a book with a bunch of international numbers on it.

He wouldn't be able to talk very well with that damn alarm ringing, so he found a ladder, pulled the cover off the wall and began yanking out wires until it stopped. After disconnecting the alarm Evan spent the next hour on the phone, but he never spoke to a single soul. Either everyone *was* dead or nobody in the world was home.

Evan knew at that moment that *he* would never go home again. He couldn't. Just the thought of his wife, her eyes glazed over, was enough to bring on another crying jag. He decided he would spend the night in a department store.

As it turned out, Sears was the only store around that still had electricity. Evan had to break in and kill the alarm first, then he took the stairs up to the second floor. He rolled up a big-screen TV next to a deluxe king-sized bed, and hooked up a VCR in

7

preparation for the two videos he had brought from the grocery store. Tonight's selections were *The Day After* and *Omega Man.*

He sighed as the first film began to roll. "I guess I'm going to find out what it's like to *really* be single."

III

After several long days, life in the city became uncomfortable. The stench of thousands of rotting corpses permeated everything, and there was no place to hide.

Even though all humans were dead, other animals did not seem to be affected. It wasn't long before packs of dogs were roaming the streets, gnawing at the decaying flesh just to survive. After a while, even they had to compete with swarms of flies that nearly blotted out the sun. But Evan knew that he had to leave. There was still the possibility that something was wrong with the phones. He had to know if anyone else was alive. So, taking his cue from Charlton Heston, he filled up a brand-new Porsche at the nearest gas station and headed off down the giant obstacle course that the highway had become. But town after town was the same. That smell. The same bloated bodies everywhere. No one was alive.

Traveling across the country, Evan found that he could do anything he wanted to. Stay anywhere. Eat anywhere. The best hotels, the finest restaurants—of course he had to do his own cooking, but at least he didn't have to wait for a table—it was all his.

By the time the bodies had reached their ripest stage, however, going into cities became out of the question. The stench was unbearable. But that was all right by Evan. If he had to take a piss he just stopped the car in the middle of the interstate and pissed. When he felt like a shower he could just stop at the nearest house—only if it was vacant—break in, freshen up, grab a bite to eat, sleep, anything.

But it wasn't long before the novelty wore off and Evan stopped doing much of anything. He didn't shower or shave anymore, and after a while he virtually stopped sleeping. Soon he wasn't even eating. He would just drive endlessly down the highway, mesmerized by the pulse of the white lines, sometimes going by at 150 miles per hour. Evan was dying inside, and he knew it.

All his life Evan had needed to be around people. He needed their warmth and companionship, their validation of his existence. If no one was left to acknowledge him, was he really alive? He cranked up the volume on the stereo, stomped down on the gas pedal and felt himself sink back into the leather seat of the Porsche.

One thing he had stopped doing long ago was thinking. Evan always had the tape deck blaring in his car, or in the houses he stayed at. As long as he kept his mind occupied he was okay, but every time he thought about his wife, his will to live capitulated to serious contemplation of suicide. He tried to banish the thoughts from his mind and sometimes it worked. Most of the time it didn't. A month later he could think of little else.

IV

Evan paced anxiously around the small gun shop in yet another city that was . . . Hell, he didn't even know what state he was in, much less what city. He had dropped forty pounds during the last two weeks and looked better than he had since high school, weighing in at a trim one-eighty. But at this moment he looked more like a visitor from another planet than the last man on Earth. Wearing a full beekeeper's suit to protect him from the clouds of insects and a gas mask to combat the stench, he paced around the gun shop with a loaded pistol in his hand.

He didn't know what kind of gun it was, and spent nearly an hour going through the shop trying bullets in the thing before he found some that fit. He only managed to get one into the chamber, but he knew that one would do the trick just fine. The loneliness was killing him and he couldn't take it anymore.

Every day the memories of life as he had once known it dripped in his brain like a Chinese water torture. And every night he suffered horrible nightmares, the picture of his dead wife flashing over and over in his mind until all he wanted to do was die, just so he wouldn't have to see her anymore. Evan was losing his mind, and he knew it.

After several hours, Evan stopped pacing. He whipped off his hood and the gas mask, ignoring the smell completely. He suddenly felt better than he had in weeks. He sat down in an overstuffed chair in the center of the gun shop and breathed a sigh of relief. It was finally going to be over, and as he stuck the barrel of the pistol into his mouth he couldn't help by smile. Then Evan closed his eyes, breathed the last breath of his life and squeezed the trigger.

V

A small group of people quietly milled about the homey living room. Off to one side of the room, seated on a brown tweed couch, was a woman dressed entirely in black. She was approached by another woman in black who took her by the hand and said: "If there's anything we can do for you, dear, please don't hesitate to ask, okay?"

The woman on the couch lifted up a handkerchief to dab way the tears that had rolled down her reddened cheeks. She nodded.

In the adjoining dining room was a large table laden with food. Two men had sidled up to it with plates in their hands. They, too, were dressed in black. One man began carefully surveying stalks of celery which had cream cheese spread down the centers. The other was spooning up a dollop of potato salad when their eyes met. Both nodded their acknowledgement.

"I don't believe we've met," said the man with the celery, returning one of the stalks and selecting one with peanut butter instead. 'I'm Dick Stratton. I worked with Evan down at the office."

"Doyle Webber," offered the man with the potato salad. "I'm Evan and Gwen's next-door neighbor."

Both continued dishing up in silence.

"Tell me . . . Dale, was it?"

"Doyle."

"Doyle. I don't know if I should be asking you this. I mean, I don't want to be rude but . . . Well, I never did hear exactly what happened. Do you think you could fill me in?"

"Sure, I guess so," said Webber, staring intently at the Jell-O mold. "I was sitting in the front room at home last Saturday watching the Sonics game when the phone rings. I figured it was probably Evan calling up to borrow my lawn mower or something—he was always doing that—but instead it's Gwen. I could tell she was crying and that's about it. I couldn't make out anything she was trying to tell me, so I went over there right away. I guess I was the first one she called. God, what a shock, you know?"

Stratton raised his eyebrows.

"I mean, at first we thought it was suicide. When I came in the door she was covered in blood and pointing upstairs to the bedroom, so I went up. Evan was lying in bed, still with covers on, only it looked like the top of his head had been blown apart—everything . . . all over the wall above the headboard. His mouth was wide open and he had his hand up to it. The weird thing was, nothing woke Gwen up during the night. Said she even slept late. I'd never seen anything like it before, but it sure looked like he'd killed himself to me."

Someone else came up to the table and the two of them walked to an empty corner of the room. Stratton licked his lips nervously. "Then it wasn't suicide?"

"No," said Weber, head shaking, eyes on his plate. He picked up a Buffalo wing and took a bite, then, still chewing, looked back up at Stratton. "They never found a gun."

"Murder?"

Weber shook his head again and took another bite of chicken. "They couldn't find a bullet either."

The Void

It wasn't supposed to happen like this. You distinctly remember checking and rechecking your equipment. You always have. Your brain is churning, frantic to recall even the tiniest inconsistency, and yet you keep coming up with the same answer: it just couldn't have happened. But at this point the exercise is entirely pointless, because it has.

It's been twenty-nine hours now and the only bright spot you can think of is at least the panic is gone. Only fear and frustration remain to keep you company, for you are utterly alone. You haven't seen them since yesterday. Did you really expect them to come and save you? Yes, damn it! But in reality, you have always been painfully aware that they wouldn't.

The silence is unbearable. At times you talk out loud just to hear something other than the maddening rhythm of your own breathing roaring in your ears. You close your eyes every once in a while, but only for a moment. You are afraid of falling asleep. And then you laugh when you realize why: you're afraid they'll come back and you'll have missed them. But you know that won't happen. You'll be dead long before then.

The ship was low on fuel in the first place, heading for home, and a crack in the starboard engine fuel line was threatening to break wide open. The captain said that the line would hold as long as the engine wasn't operating on full, but you didn't believe him. You wanted to make sure, so you volunteered to go out and repair the line yourself.

You could see the relief in the captain's face as you told him, confirming your suspicion that even *he* hadn't thought the line would hold. And now come the incessant memories. You know you checked the fuel level on your jet-pack. You know it as sure as you know that you are adrift in space at this very moment.

Your suit was in perfect condition—you distinctly remember checking the jet-pack's fuel level—and the crew was thanking you profusely. You acted like it was nothing. Routine, you recall yourself saying. Then the air-lock was opened. You thrusted gently out into the eternal night and—

You remember suddenly how you used to love the stars, the feeling of weightlessness, of scurrying around the outside of the ship. Though the pay was terrific, you remember thinking you would have done it for free. Just the chance to strap on a jet-pack and fly, that was the only pay you ever needed. But that was then and this is now, and those memories seem as foreign to you as if they were someone else's. Because the only thing you feel for space right now is loathing.

The air-lock was on the other side of the ship, and once you had cleared the port you maneuvered up and away. You were showing off, even as the ship was in danger. You pulled out and away so that you could thrust on full and come roaring up to the starboard side, swing around to a screeching halt like a hero. Only that screeching halt never came.

You hadn't even eased back yet on the thruster when you felt your pack run out of fuel. You were twenty feet above the ship with nothing to hold on to, nothing to keep your momentum from taking you to the end of the universe. There was a scramble as you announced the emergency. Williamson was the best in a jet-pack next to you, but you were already a good half-mile away. You remember seeing her come toward you, stop, and then turn back around.

When the captain finally got you to stop screaming he told you, in that arrogant tone of his, that there wasn't enough fuel in any of the jet-packs to reach you and still get back. Pathetic. He said they would send word back to home and get a rescue ship out as soon as possible. Who did he think he was kidding?

So for the last twenty-nine hours you have drifted, the empty jet-pack jettisoned long ago. For a while you were able to keep an eye on the ship, but now you don't even know which direction home is. You have no idea where you are heading, or how fast. You could be going ten miles an hour or a thousand. There is no sense of motion other then what you can see, as the stars subtly shift around you. There is enough oxygen in your suit to last about another hour. After that . . .

Thirty hours now. You shouldn't have to die this way; no one should. It wasn't supposed to happen like this. But before you go there is one last thing you must do, for your other self, the one who was in love with space. You have visited other planets, other moons, and swam among the stars. More than any other being, you were at one with universe. But you have never *seen* it.

Always through glass, whether the windows in the ship, or this bubble over your head now, you have been forced to view the cosmos. You refuse to suffocate. If you are to die in space, then space itself will have to kill you. And so, in the final seconds, as your oxygen supply becomes exhausted, you remove your helmet.

And in that one brief moment, before your own internal Earth-pressure has burst every cell in your body, you finally look into the void.

The genesis of "It's Only Skin Deep" began with the novel Star Time, *written by entertainment lawyer Joseph Amiel in 1991. I was working in a bookstore at the time and, while usually repulsed by novels that rely solely on insider status in order to sell books, I had recently read the mystery novel* Killed in the Ratings *by William DeAndrea and enjoyed it a lot. But that novel had been written in 1978, and this was a new book. In fact, one of the things I remember most about it was the price. At that time prices of books always ended in ninety-five cents, and the price of most hardback novels had plateaued at $14.95 with publishers reluctant to break the fifteen dollar mark for a couple of years. In the course of about a week, however, several books came in at fifteen and sixteen ninety-five, and with the dam suddenly broken, this novel came in priced at a whopping $19.99. I was really aghast. The guy wasn't even a real writer as far as I was concerned. He was a lawyer trying to cash in on his entertainment experience by writing a rather tepid power-play romance-drama that took place behind the scenes at a TV network. I read it, and I thought it was bad. But the story gave me the idea to combine those kinds of characters and setting with something like* Coma *and create a plausible post-apocalyptic science-fiction story around it. In preparing this collection for publication I thought the name Christine Parkins might be a variation on the name of Robin Douglass's character Carly Perkins from the TV movie* Her Life as a Man, *but when I went back and looked at Amiel's novel, his protagonist is named Christine Paskins and her former boyfriend is Greg Lyall, so it's pretty clear I lifted the names directly from the novel.*

It's Only Skin Deep

Roderick Bartlett sat in front of the TV and scowled. He didn't like what he was seeing, didn't like it at all. He punched in seven digits on the console directly beneath his hand and watched as a small insert appeared on the bottom right-hand corner of the screen. A second later, Graham Lydell walked into view.

"Yes, sir?" he said, his image only two square feet of Bartlett's giant screen.

"What the hell happened to Parkins?"

"What do you mean, sir?"

"Her skin! It looks like leather!"

Lydell gave a quick glance over his shoulder at the studio monitor and Bartlett glanced up at his own. Christine Parkins was The Network's lead anchor on their nightly news program. Her presence onscreen and her ability to ferret out stories were the main reasons the program was first in the ratings, and Bartlett knew it. But the woman simply did not know how to stay out of the sun.

"I'll get some more makeup on her right after the break, sir."

"What the hell's wrong with her?"

Lydell looked nervously over his shoulder again, but Bartlett didn't take his eyes off him. "She doesn't like to wear the suit, sir," he said, turning back around.

"I don't give a good goddamn what she likes! This network is riding on her and we can't afford to look unprofessional, not with sweeps weeks only a month away. See that she has an epidermal this weekend."

Lydell hesitated. "I don't know, sir—"

"You're not paid to know, Lydell. You're paid to follow orders. Understand?"

"Yes, sir."

"Then see it's done. She's still an employee here—I don't care how popular she is. You tell her she isn't going back on the air Monday without it. Understand?"

"Yes, sir."

Bartlett pushed the disconnect button on the console and Lydell's image disappeared. When Parkins came back on after the break she didn't look any better so he fumed for a while and then turned the set off.

".   .   . three, two, one, and clear." Lydell pulled off his headphones and ran out of the control room in time to catch Christine as she came off the set. Bartlett had had the studio gutted and lined with lead two years ago, so there was no need for them to wear suits inside. Christine was wearing a blue blazer over a white blouse and a matching blue skirt.

"So, what do you think, Mr. Producer?" Christine stood facing him as a studio technician removed her earpiece.

"I thought it was good," said Lydell.

"Good? Jesus, Graham, you're really overflowing with compliments today. Justin!" she yelled across the room to one of the techs. "The teleprompter is going to have to go back to where it was before."

"Aw, Christine, gimme a break." Justin was holding out his hands, but she was already ignoring him. Then she brushed by Lydell, heading toward her dressing room, script in hand. He had to run to catch up with her.

"Look, Christine. I think we'd better talk."

"About what?"

"About the show tonight."

She stopped dead in her tracks and Lydell almost ran her over. "I thought you said you liked the show."

'Well . . . *I* did, but . . ."

"Oh, Jesus, Graham, spit it out."

"I got a call from Bartlett tonight."

"*During* the show?" Her face looked like it might have gone ashen, though he couldn't tell under all the makeup. "Is that what the little touch-up was all about?"

"Yeah."

She turned slowly to walk back to her dressing room and he followed her, both of them silent until they reached to door. After a quick glance around to see if anyone was watching she told him to come inside.

"What did he say?" She was sitting in front of a large mirror and began to remove her wig.

"He wants you to have another epidermal."

Lydell could see her in the mirror's reflection but she stopped and turned around to look at him anyway. "Are you kidding me?"

Lydell shook his head.

"I just had one six months ago. Does he know what a royal pain in the ass one of those things is?"

"I don't think he really cares."

Resigned, she turned back to the mirror and removed her wig. Her bald head glistened with sweat from the hot lights and she rubbed it dry with a towel. Next, she peeled off her false eyelashes and popped out her dentures, slipping them into a glass on the counter. The she stood and walked over to the sink and washed her face, penciled eyebrows and rosy cheeks swirling down the drain. When she was finished she walked back over and checked herself in the mirror again.

There were only three or four sores on her cheeks, a couple on her neck and one on her forehead, but not one of them was running yet. Her skin, somewhat youthful-looking on camera, was now yellowed and cracked like old parchment.

"Hell," she said, after putting her plates back in. 'I'm good for another three or four months yet. When does he want it done?"

"By Monday."

She didn't bother to turn to him this time, but he could see the pain in her eyes reflected back at him. "Oh, Graham. Not *this* weekend?"

"Yeah. I already called and canceled our reservations."

They had been planning to fly up to Denver for the weekend. The radiation levels were remarkably low up there and they were going to stay at one of the six lead-lined hotels that were already in operation. Rumor had it that three more were in the works.

He stood up and walked over to her, placing his hands on her shoulders. "You're going to have to get a hold of the clinic and make an appointment."

"I wonder if they're even open on a Saturday."

"They will be for you."

Lydell started at their two hairless faces in the mirror. They could be twins, he thought, but then so could practically everyone else. The war, if you could even call it that, had been a speedy affair, over in a couple of days, but the repercussions from the fallout were still being felt. Lydell's hair had been the first to go, beginning with wisps and ending with great clumps. By the time he was completely bald his teeth were so loose that he couldn't eat solid food. A quick trip to the dentist fixed that problem, and now he never went anywhere without his Poligrip.

For most of the men he knew it had been simple enough to let it go at that. You saved money on shampoo, and you could get your head bone-dry with a towel. For the women, though, the beauty industry resurged with a vengeance. Wigs, makeup, plastic surgery—business was indeed booming. Cosmetics stocks had gone through the roof, and you could always identify plastic surgeons on the road by their hermetically-sealed Mercedes with lead windows.

And now Christine would be going to one of them instead of spending the weekend with him. Oh, well, he thought, life—such as it was—goes on.

"If I can't have you this weekend," he said, squeezing her shoulders, "how about dinner tonight?"

She reached up and patted his hand, a smile on her face. "You got it."

They stepped through the pneumatic doors of the studio building into the California sunshine, the deadly California sunshine. One of the more devastating effects of the week-long nuclear exchange two years ago was the nearly complete loss of the ozone layer. The experts, it seemed, had been way off in their estimates as to just how thin that layer really was. Now they knew.

During the first few days after the war, third-degree burns had been fairly common. These days, everyone wore suits to protect them from the ultraviolet light as well as the radiation, yet another invention born of necessity that had stockholders jumping with glee. The suits were a reflective silver, lead-lined and water-cooled, each with its own electronic communication circuitry built in to the hood.

He and Christine held silver gloved-gloved hands as they walked to the new Mexican place that had just opened near the studio, but neither said much. When they reached the front door and pressed the buzzer, they were quickly scanned to make sure they were both wearing suits; some of the older places had been contaminated as a result of slipshod security. The door opened automatically and closed once they were inside.

The tiny enclosure they were standing in was then flushed of radioactive air and replaced with fresh, from the restaurant's own generators. They were instructed to remove their suits and Geigered before another door opened and they were ushered inside. There were plants everywhere to help with the oxygenation, and as they were shown to their table they passed a frothing, man-made brook running the length of the room to further aerate the building. Christine ordered the tofu taco salad, and Lydell had the bean enchiladas and rice. Smart people these days avoided meat, not because of fat or cholesterol, but because of radioactivity.

In the United States alone, ten million people had been killed outright as a direct result of the bombings. Two hundred million were lost in the next few weeks due to airborne radiation, and of the remaining population, roughly half died over the following

Eric B. Olsen

six months from radiation in the food supply. But things were improving every day. Most of the better restaurants grew their own food indoors, for those who could afford it, and the government housed gigantic indoor farms for the masses. Raising animals as food was simply not economically feasible.

"Did Bartlett say anything else?"

Lydell shook his head.

Instead of her wig, Christine was wearing a scarf wrapped up like a turban. She had her false eyelashes on as well as her painted eyebrows, but no makeup. Even though millions of people watched and revered her every night on the evening news, she was totally anonymous tonight.

"Are you sure you can't come with me tomorrow?" she asked.

"I wish I could, but I think I should stay and oversee the special segment for the weekend news."

"You were going to have to miss it if we went to Denver."

"I know, but things have changed now. Besides, you'll probably be using some of the footage on Monday night."

"The summit meeting in Moscow?"

Lydell nodded as their food was served. Christine took her Geiger out of her purse and gave their plates each a pass. The levels were low enough, so they dug in.

"I was talking to one of replacement lighting techs today," Christine said between mouthfuls. "You know, the one who took Maureen's job?"

"Sure, the old guy."

"Right. Before the show he was asking me about the time I covered the war. Then, after we had been talking awhile he starts telling me about watching the news when the Berlin Wall came down."

Lydell whistled, "That was what, fifty years ago?"

"Forty-eight."

The war had made a lot of careers, including Christine's. She had already managed to work her way up to a spot as The Network's Washington correspondent when the bombing started. Thank God the wind had been blowing west that day. The attack had come from such an unlikely source that looking back two years now it still seemed unbelievable: Cuba.

After Castro's death things in Cuba had never really stabilized. Factions were fighting each other in the streets for control of the government. The U.S. and the Soviet Union were too busy with each other to notice who was in power during any particular week. Star Wars satellites had been placed in orbit around the Earth by half a dozen countries and yet all the technology in the world couldn't stop the Cubans.

They had been asking the U.S. for aid ever since the Soviets abandoned them, but the U.S. wasn't giving handouts anymore. So they dug their hidden missiles out of the ground, dirty ones from the last century, loaded up eight passenger planes, flew into U.S. airspace on autopilot, and ejected. The planes crashed, wiping out Miami, Jacksonville, Atlanta, and Charlotte with direct hits. The other four were misses, falling into unpopulated areas of South Carolina, Tennessee, Kentucky and as far north as Indiana.

Retaliation was swift and efficient and all that remained of Cuba today was a charred, black rock sitting in the middle of the Caribbean. The East Coast, as well as the rest of the world, had time to prepare for the blanket of radiation that rolled across the planet, but the rest of the U.S., Western Canada, and Mexico were turned for a while into no man's land.

After finishing the last of his margarita and paying for their meal, Lydell walked Christine home to her lead-lined apartment building and made love to her before falling asleep in each other's arms.

Graham had dropped Christine off at the clinic and now she stood in the reception room waiting for the doctor.

"Ms. Parkins?" A surgical assistant, the one with the bad toupee, was sticking his head through the door. "Right this way."

Radiation levels were extremely low today and so she had brought her suit along for the trip home, but she hadn't worn it down here. Graham was angry with her, but she just didn't see the point. She looked down at her arm; it was already beginning to blister.

"Been out in the sun today, have we?"

Christine looked up and smiled. It was Dr. Mercheson. "Hello, Edward."

"You've been a very naughty girl, Chrissy."

She slipped her arm through his as they walked down the corridor toward her room, the assistant dismissed by their conversation. Dr. Edward Mercheson looked the picture of health, wearing an immaculately sculptured hairpiece, very subtle lashes and brows, and a pencil-thin false mustache. His dentures had simulated dental work to look more natural, and the skin grafts on his face were almost undetectable.

"And how is Graham?"

"Fine. He's taping a special today."

"I saw your show yesterday. I thought you looked fabulous. How come you're back here so soon?"

"The head of The Network doesn't agree with your assessment."

"Well, don't you worry about a thing, dear. We'll have that dirty old man drooling over you again in no time."

Christine laughed as they turned in to her room. She liked Edward's bedside manner and they had become friends over the course of her last two epidermals. He closed the door once they were inside, and she began to undress, lying down naked on the table when she had finished as Edward moved in to examine her.

Expectedly, he spent the first few minutes on her right leg. Since he had last seen her, the skin there had turned hard and nearly opaque and she could see the veins and muscle clearly beneath it. "I guess I didn't do a very good job here," he said.

"As long as I don't do the broadcast below the waist I'm not going to complain."

"You're such a sweet girl. Now let's see how I did on those seams."

She spread her legs and he examined the skin on her inner thigh and around her vulva.

"Well," he said. "My work seems to be holding its own, but that's more than I can say for the standard equipment. You know, dear, you really should consider a genital reconstruction."

"Oh, no, Edward. We've talked about that before."

"I know, I know. But you should at least think about it. Just imagine how absolutely delicious it would look."

"Graham likes me just fine. And besides, what about the loss of sensation? That doesn't seem like a very attractive incentive."

"The price we pay for beauty, my dear," he said with a wave of his hand. "Now, over you go."

She turned to lie on her stomach and he finished the examination by looking at her back. "Okay," he said when he was through, "get dressed and we'll pick out something wonderful for you."

They walked past the glass-enclosed operatory, where two dozen people in white were busily making preparations for the procedure, and then into the selection room. It was extremely warm when she stepped inside, as big as a football field with nearly every inch of floor space occupied. The room was dimly lit, and undulating waves of shadow danced around the walls from the fluid-filled tanks where each selection was kept pink and perfect. Then Edward turned on the harsh overhead lights and led her through a jungle of tubes and wires that descended from the ceiling and over to one of the shallow tanks.

"This is the one I thought of as soon as I got your call."

A long corrugated tube ran down from above, into the water and to the selection's mouth; she thought it looked funny breathing under water. Food lines snaked into the tank as well as lines for removal of waste products.

"It still has hair," she said, obviously pleased.

"Of course. Only the best for my Chrissy."

"I'm a little worried about the breast, though, Edward. They look kind of small."

"I measured them myself this morning before you arrived: 36 B."

"Well . . . If you're sure."

"Then it's settled."

"Wherever did you find her?"

"They come from Maine, I hear. Whole towns of them. Perfect skin."

"How's the radiation?"

"Check it yourself."

He handed her a Geiger and she passed it over the tank. The needle barley moved. "Okay. Let's do it."

Mercheson was hard at work removing the skin of the donor when Christine was wheeled in on a gurney. Before the war he had been an average plastic surgeon, doing face-lifts and breast implants and making five hundred thousand dollars a year. But afterward, with the new technology and the rich clientele, he was grossing three to five million.

He didn't know exactly where the donors came from, only that they were acquired by the company that owned the clinic, and he knew enough about them not to ask questions. The bodies were delivered to him unconscious and he fed them carbon monoxide until they were brain dead. After that, the life-supports systems were hooked up and they were submerged into a pH-balance solution that kept the water content perfect. By the time the patient received the transplant, the skin was as smooth as a newborn baby's.

He'd finished the most crucial part of the removal, the head, and let his assistants finish the rest while he prepped Chrissy. She was anesthetized and a topical ointment was applied that dried her skin out and pulled it away from her body. She was then turned over and he made the dorsal incision, beginning at the apex of the skull and continuing down to the anus. He finished the incision by cutting around the vulva and down the back of her legs.

Now she was turned over. Three other assistants quickly removed her dead skin, applying a coagulant to her exposed muscle as they went along to prevent her from bleeding to death.

"We're finished over here, Doctor."

"Good. Start applying the regenerate. I'm almost finished with the head."

They began applying the ointment to the inside of the sheath of skin that would be slipped onto Chrissy's body. The regenerant, originally developed by the military for use on the battlefield, was now widely used in hospitals. It totally eliminated rejection of the donor tissue and quickly aided in the formation and connection of new blood vessels to the donated skin. Mercheson finished with Chrissy's face and called for the new tissue. It was carefully wheeled over and he held onto the fine, thin facial skin while his assistants began the transplant. First Chrissy's raw legs were slipped inside of the new skin. Her toes were seated and then a slight adjustment was made around the genitals. Two slits were made just below the kidneys and the torso was seated. Until the regenerant dissolved the coagulant and began stimulating attachment of the vessels, guide stitched were made at the heel, kneecap, genitals, bellybutton, and nipples to keep her new skin in place.

Next, her arms were slipped in, a stitch going in at her wrist, elbows, and shoulders. And at last the face. Mercheson delicately pulled the mask of skin over Chrissy's head, and using regenerative concentrate, connected it around her lips, nostrils, and eyes. Stitches were used behind the ears and then she was turned over.

While the assistants went to work closing up her back, Mercheson went to work on her genitals. Too much of her own skin had deteriorated and it was obviously from the amount of work he was going to have to do that she would not be able to undergo another epidermal without genital reconstruction.

Six hours after the operation had begun, Christine Parkins was wheeled back to the recovery room. When she was alert enough, she would then be taken to her room, where Graham Lydell was waiting for her.

Monday evening, Roderick Bartlett took his seat in front of the giant screen as he did every night at six. He turned on the TV and sat through a few commercials with the sound off and then turned it back up when the program came on.

"Good evening. I'm Christine Perkins, and this is The Network News . . ."

She had a pink, radiant glow tonight. Bartlett knew her age was thirty-five, but on screen she looked like she had the skin of a twenty-year-old. Then Bartlett laughed, a loud booming laugh, and said aloud, "She quite possibly does."

The Trenches

"Got a light?" you ask the soldier next to you.

"Sorry," answers your partner, "My matches are wet."

This is all that the war means to you now. You stand knee-deep in mud, you don't have enough to eat, your clothes are wet, and now you can't even smoke a cigarette for warmth.

The weather is the worst you can remember since the beginning of the fighting. The rain is almost constant. The battlefield, once a large meadow bordered by woods, has been transformed by an endless deluge of precipitation and artillery fire into a vast quagmire punctuated by splintered branches and uprooted trees. The streets and roads are nearly impassable from a thick covering of slimy mud. And running through this morass are the trenches: a meandering mass of shelters and dugouts surrounded by gun emplacements and barbed-wire barricades, communication ditches and land mines. You put the unlit cigarette to your lips and look over at your men. It is 5:00 a.m., November 11, 1918, and most of them are still asleep. They are nearly all replacements. Soldiers like yourself, who have survived the past four years of carnage to continue fighting, are few. Nights like this are also few. The enemy usually saturates the area with artillery fire at night, but this morning the bombing doesn't start until just before dawn.

Shrapnel hisses overhead and you cover your head as the first shells explode. Your helmet in one hand and your rifle in the other, you brace yourself against the forward wall and wait. Soon, men from the front-line trenches come tumbling in one after another speaking excitedly of the enemy who has gone on the offensive and will soon be continuing its march forward.

You are digging in further, mud raining down on you all the while from the artillery barrage, when an order comes down the line for you to mount a counterattack. Battle-weary, you begin to assemble your meager forces for assault. The bombardment slackens now and you can hear the ominous sound of enemy soldiers in the trenches beyond. Overhead comes the drone of planes, followed by the crash of more bombs. In addition there is the constant threat of gas and you remember sometimes having to keep that suffocating mask on for twenty-four hours at a stretch.

When the bombing ebbs again, you give the command to move forward; a command that will send most of your men to their deaths. You have long ago ceased to question the orders of your superiors. There are no decisions for you to make, only orders for you to follow. You are materiel—no more, no less—something to be used up and thrown away. For you, there is no such thing as death with honor, no glory in dying for your country; your only reward is survival. Perhaps that is why you have lasted so long.

You lead your men over the top. The enemy trenches are only a few hundred yards away and as soon as you are detected the area is sprayed with machine-gun fire. Those of your men who are not killed instantly hit the ground of their own volition. You watch, frozen, as some continue on their stomachs while others run for cover. As they cower in watery shell holes and ditches, the artillery fire begins anew. Shells explode, hurling clouds of stones, earth and sand into the air, choking you with an acrid yellow steam that pierces your nostrils and waters your eyes.

Though you pray for a respite the shelling continues unabated. The counterattack has stalled and your men are looking to you for answers but you have none to offer; you can only provide an example. And so, in the face of certain death, dodging shell and shot every step of the way, you emerge from a crater to lead your men forward.

Before you can reach a sheltered position, however, the concussion of a nearby explosion sends you and your partner reeling. You both remain motionless for several minutes until you finally crawl through the mud to see if your friend is all right. But as you roll his body over you can see at once that he is dead, his face contorted into a perverted imitation of life. And staring at the inanimate mass of flesh that had once been your friend, a sight you have seen a thousand times before, you truly wonder which one of you is luckier.

Suddenly your attention is drawn elsewhere. Your ears are ringing but you can still detect an unmistakable sound: silence. The air is quiet. The shooting and shelling stopped.

You loosen the buttons on your coat and lift the watch from your breast pocket. You press down on the release, lift the cover and note the time: 11:00 a.m. No sooner do you replace the watch than you get to your feet in the middle of the battlefield and begin to walk slowly back to the trenches that you left only hours before. Your men get up as well, following you in peace just as they did in battle.

The fighting is over. Armistice. After four years of attrition the guns are silent. But the silence will last only twenty years. For on this very ground, history will repeat itself like a malevolent *Doppelgänger* wresting peace from the world, and your children will be left helpless to finish what you could only begin.

Eric B. Olsen

I'm pretty sure the inspiration for this story was "The Most Dangerous Game," by Richard Connell. While I had read the story in high school, I had probably only recently watched for the first time the classic film version by RKO starring Fay Wray and Leslie Banks. I wrote "Old Soldiers Never Die" in 1988. It was my third short story and I sent it to Weird Tales *and* Amazing Stories *a couple of years later and received standard form rejections from both. What gave me the idea for my story, however, was another short story by Stephen King, "Battleground," from his* Night Shift *collection. I sort of combined the idea of both and set it in the remote wilderness of northern Canada. The character of the old man was an amalgam of two characters from the film* Never Cry Wolf, *the old Inuit named Ootek, and his grandson Mike, who was missing his front teeth. Brian Dennehy, from the same film, was the model for the main character, and the film was also the inspiration for the setting. The name of the protagonist, however, came from my father. When I was still in grade school I received a G.I. Joe for Christmas—the one with a real beard and hair— complete with a footlocker, a sea sled, and an orange wetsuit. On the front of the footlocker was a place for the soldier's name and rank. I had no idea what name to give him and so I asked my dad. He said I should call him Master Sergeant Lance Sterling.*

Old Soldiers Never Die

"How much longer?" Lance Sterling had to shout over the noise in the tiny cockpit, but the steady drone of the Cessna's twin engines was like music to his ears. In fact, he could hardly contain his excitement during the flight and finally had to surrender the controls to his co-pilot.

"There it is," the co-pilot yelled back. He was pointing to the flat stretch of ground where they would land. Sterling gave him the thumbs up and took control, touching down a few minutes later on the hard Canadian tundra.

Stepping off the plane Sterling gazed out over the miles of rolling hills to the north. It was early in the summer and melting snow and ice made the ground glitter like a billion tiny shards of broken glass on the shrubbed and grassy terrain.

Sterling then turned his attention to the south. He was on the edge of what was called the North Woods, a seemingly endless expanse of evergreens whose ragged silhouettes stretched across the sky from Alaska to the Hudson Bay. The air was awash with the scent of pine and the smell of decaying compost on the forest floor.

Sterling looked masterful as he stood on the threshold of the woods. He was a very large man, nearly six feet tall with a barrel chest, thick, hairy arms and stocky legs. His short-cropped blond hair reflected every gust of the cool summer breeze, and two rosy cheeks poked out over a thick red beard.

With no apparent effort he hoisted a hundred-pound backpack over his shoulder and disappeared into the woods. Sterling had eschewed any suggestion that he should take along a guide. He meticulously planned every detail of the trip himself, decades of experience had taught him to depend on no one *but* himself. His co-pilot had instructions to meet him back here in exactly two weeks.

As he marched between the trees, through the sparse undergrowth, Sterling reflected on his situation. From the four corners of the globe he had brought back nearly every animal imaginable. Sterling had hunted everything from big game in Africa to tiger in Asia, crocodile in Australia, grizzly bear in Canada, and alligator in Louisiana, as well as smaller game in Europe, South America and the South Pacific. He had even hunted humans, in a way.

As a young man Sterling had fought in the infantry in Africa and Italy during World War II. He was wounded at Anzio and still walked with a slight limp. After the war he became a mercenary, fighting in Africa, the Middle East, and Central America. In the process Sterling had become a very wealthy man.

But Lance Sterling was bored. After hunting nearly every kind of animal on the earth, what could he do for an encore? It was quite understandable then why he had become so obsessed with an article he had run across in an obscure hunting magazine.

Somewhere in northern Canada, the article claimed, lived a man who knew where to find the most challenging hunting in all the world. He was quoted as saying that the area was abundant with wildlife but that he had never seen a hunter yet who had returned with a kill.

"Oh, yeah?" Sterling had muttered, his eyes devouring every word.

Just reading the article had infused new life into his tired blood. It had been at least ten years since he had really enjoyed himself on a hunting trip. This looked promising. The man supposedly lived in a remote part of the Northwest Territories and Sterling had immediately put out the word. With the help of some high-powered friends, he was able to pinpoint the exact location in Canada where this man lived. And now he was here.

It was a three-day hike over the hills to the south and after setting up camp the first night Sterling had trouble sleeping. He tossed and turned all night, but it didn't really bother him. It felt great to be excited about hunting again, and trying to imagine what type of game could be so challenging.

Perhaps it was some sort of rare animal that only inhabited this small area of Canada. Maybe it was an area so densely forested that a hunter couldn't get close enough to get off a shot. But he knew ways around that. The more he thought, the more relaxed he became and before long Sterling nodded off into a restful sleep.

The next two days passed uneventfully as he became more accustomed to his new surroundings. The area was indeed thick with trees and abundant with game, but his fixation with on this new and supposedly elusive prey caused him to overlook more mundane quarry completely.

As dusk approached on the third day, Sterling was drawn into a small clearing by the smells of burning wood and cooking food that mingled in his nostrils. Tucked away neatly into one corner of the glade was a tiny log cabin. It had no windows and if it hadn't been for the chimney pipe releasing a thin wisp of smoke into the air, Sterling might have missed it.

He pushed open the door without knocking and was immediately enveloped in a cloud of suffocating heat. As soon as he stepped inside, a grizzled old man in a tattered flannel shirt, dirty Levi's and a leather vest turned around slowly to glare at him. The man had long flowing hair, white with streaks of grey, and a beard of the same color.

Before Sterling could state his business the corners of the old man's mouth turned up in a toothless grin. For some reason Sterling suddenly felt a chill. He slammed the door and said, "What the hell are you grinnin' at?"

"Pardon me," said the old man; "It's just that I've seen so many of your kind up here that I am able to recognize you by sight." He had a thick French accent. His back was slightly hunched but he approached Sterling with a powerful stride.

"What do you mean, *my kind*?"

"You're a hunter, no? And you've no doubt heard that this is where you might find the most challenging game in all the world?"

Sterling rubbed his beard and puzzled over this curious creature.

"Come, sit. We have a long day of hunting ahead of us."

Sterling cast another wary glance at the old man.

"Pardon my presumption, *Monsieur*. Would you prefer to rest a day?"

"Hell, no. Let's get right to it."

The old man grinned again.

"Now cut that out!" said Sterling, peeved but slightly apprehensive.

The old man motioned to his guest and Sterling took a seat at the small table in the center of the one-room cabin. The man then dished up a bowl of strange-smelling stew from a kettle in the fireplace.

"So tell me, old man, what type of game is this that's so tough to bag?"

"All in good time," he replied, looking like he might grin again. "My name is Claude Chevalier. I have lived here for the last fifty years." He handed Sterling the bowl.

"So, you hunt, fish? How do you survive way out here?"

The old man was shaking his head. "Let us say that I have many friends with whom I barter. I provide them with certain items, and they in turn provide me with all the food I need."

Sterling grunted his understanding while chewing on a strange-tasting piece of meat. "Say, what is this stuff? I never tasted anything like it before. I'll bet it's that animal I'll be hunting tomorrow, huh?"

The old man's smile was wide this time. "Possibly," was the last word he spoke all night.

Trudging behind the old man early the next morning Sterling was glad to be out of that claustrophobic hotbox of a cabin. His day had finally come. He just hoped that it wasn't all for nothing. Many was the time that he had gone on what was promised to be a great hunting trip only to be disappointed.

The old man was a real mystery, though; he didn't carry a gun. As far as Sterling could tell he had never even fired one before. There was nothing in his cabin to suggest that the hunting was as good as promised: no skins, no antlers, nothing.

After about an hour of plodding along behind in silence Sterling spoke up.

"Are you going to tell me what the hell we're supposed to be hunting?"

The old man stopped abruptly and Sterling nearly ran him over.

"Oh, I will not be hunting with you today, *Monsieur.*"

Sterling couldn't have been happier; he didn't fancy having the old fart tagging along once he'd caught the trail of something. But that still didn't answer his question.

"If you will go just beyond that ridge," said the old man pointing off into the distance, "in the valley you will find what you are looking for." Then he started to set up a small camp.

"What gives? Are you staying here? I can find my way back just fine," griped Sterling.

"Of course, *Monsieur.* I'm just going to rest here for a few moments before I return." Another grin of glistening gums erupted from his face.

Sterling marched away toward the ridge. It only took a few minutes before he forgot all about the old man and began to mentally prepare for the hunt. Since the old man had refused to tell him what he was hunting for, he decided to bring all the weapons he had with him. For this trip he brought along his preferred weapon, a crossbow, as well as two rifles, and a Luger that had wrested from a German soldier in hand-to-hand combat. He would set up a sort of camp on the ridge where he could leave his pack and then proceed down into the valley.

When he finally reached the ridge the view was breathtaking. The valley was a lake of green spruce and fir trees, and from the opposite side a good-sized river carved a path through the vast expanse of foliage. Sterling took a deep breath and every reservation he had since arriving was exhaled along with the spent air. He set down his pack in a secluded but carefully marked spot and began his preparations. Once he had assembled the crossbow and stowed the two rifles, he headed down into combat.

After descending only a short distance into the valley he had the feeling that something was wrong and he stopped. He hadn't really noticed it before because he had been so excited, but there didn't seem to be any sounds. Of course he could hear the breeze stirring the tree branches and the distant rushing of the river, but nothing else. There were no bird calls or animal noises, no sounds of rustling in the sparse undergrowth; it was almost as if he were the only thing living in the forest.

His thoughts once again turned maddeningly back to the old man. What was he trying to pull? But Sterling forged ahead, even more determined than before. What did he expect, after all? His prey wasn't going to run up to him and wave. Or maybe no hunter had come back with a kill because there was nothing here to hunt.

A half-hour later he was near the center of the valley. He hadn't seen or heard anything and it was beginning to annoy him. But he didn't have long to wait.

Suddenly a series of loud popping noises broke the silence. Sterling was in the process of turning around to see what was going on when something hit him hard on the left arm, forcing him to drop the crossbow. The noise, like the uncorking of champagne bottles, continued to echo across the valley.

Looking at his arm he could see an ever-expanding circle of blood being absorbed by the khaki jacket he was wearing. "Jesus Christ!" he yelled, realizing that the popping noise was gunfire. Sterling leapt for cover behind the nearest tree but by then the shooting had stopped.

That son of a bitch is shooting at me, he thought. That son-of-a-bitchin' old man has got my guns and he's tryin' to kill me!

He reached out with his good arm and retrieved the crossbow amid a new round of gunfire. Sterling's military mind instantly clicked into gear. He completely blocked out the pain in his arm and began planning his attack on the enemy.

The old man has taken his best shot, thought Sterling; the next one's mine. While checking his ammunition during the respite, thoughts of the old man with an arrow in his forehead drifted through Sterling's mind. He began to chuckle and was soon heartily laughing out loud. This was going to be a great hunting trip after all.

Still smiling, he took up the binoculars that dangled from his neck and looked in the direction of the gunfire. But the smile vanished and his face went absolutely white as he snapped the field glasses down in front of him. Sterling rolled his body back behind the tree and began to pant, his eyes wide with fear.

He took out a handkerchief and wiped off the lenses. His heart was nearly beating out of his chest and he put his hand up against it as if to force the pounding to cease. Then he looked again.

There was no mistaking it this time. Two grey squirrels in a tree about fifty yards away had a .22-caliber automatic pistol. One was sitting on its haunches, two tiny arms wrapped around the barrel, while the other, with all its might, was forcing a loaded clip into the handle.

For the first time since being shot, Sterling really noticed his wound. His mind, in an effort to avoid analyzing the vision his eyes had brought before it, concentrated instead on the dull throb just above his elbow. It didn't appear to be too serious as he still had almost full use of the arm.

He stripped off his jacket and in trying to stop the bleeding with a handkerchief saw that his hands were shaking terribly. Pull yourself together, he ordered.

Once the shooting started again, his instincts took over. First he would kill those two fucking squirrels, then he was going to get the hell out of there. But before he left he promised himself that he would put an arrow right between that old son of a bitch's eyes.

He pulled out the Luger, released the safety and barrel-rolled out into the open, his right hand on the trigger, the butt of the handle seated firmly in his left palm. He took aim and squeezed off two rounds, the first decapitating the squirrel holding the .22 and the second catching the other square in the chest.

Sterling hooted with delight as the dead animals tumbled to the ground. During his celebration the searing pain in his left arm bubbled up to his consciousness. In executing the barrel roll he had landed directly on his wounded elbow.

But no sooner had he taken his eyes off the dead squirrels than he heard a rustling coming from the same direction. He looked on in horror as two or more squirrels busily hoisted the pistol back up the tree.

Slowly, as if in a dream, he brought the Luger back into firing position. Stoically he squeezed the trigger twice, a pair of bright-red splotches on the tree trunk indicating two or more direct hits. No celebration this time. He could only stare, glassy-eyed as two or more of the grey creatures scurried out to take the place of their fallen comrades.

It was definitely time to get the hell out of there.

Sterling ran as fast as he could through the forest, gaining speed with every step. He was not out of control, but the vision of the squirrels had sent his mind into a tailspin. It had to be a dream, he thought, some kind of a hallucination. The wound on his left arm was no illusion, though.

He was rapidly approaching a clearing when he lost this footing on a patch of mud, sprawling face-first into the soft loam. Sterling was lucky. In his confusion he hadn't heard the roar of gunfire that was echoing across the valley—gunfire that was coming from the clearing right in font of him.

The noise worked on his mind like a drug. Once again instinct took over and Sterling crept through the underbrush to reconnoiter the area. What he saw caused his body to convulse with fear, a fear that he had never felt before in his life: the fear of being hunted.

In the oblong meadow, no more than fifty yards across and eighty yards wide, were hundreds of animals, most of which had guns. There were deer, elk, a few moose, a myriad of small animals from raccoon to opossum, and even a couple of wolves.

From what he could make out in his consternation, it appeared that they were having some sort of bizarre target practice. Two or three of the smaller animals would climb up onto the backs of the deer and elk. Then they would charge twenty yards or so down the meadow, lowering their heads while the smaller animals braced the gun, usually a rifle of some sort, on the antlers and fired. The wolves trotted along beside carrying boxes of ammunition in their mouths.

The raccoons, he observed, did fairly well and could usually hold on to the guns after firing, but the recoil of the weapons almost always sent the squirrels tumbling to the ground. He would have laughed if he hadn't been so terrified. He knew they were after him.

Sterling could only stare in disbelief at a sight that disobeyed all the laws of nature. He wanted to stay and fight—at least he thought he did—but he had only his crossbow and a few rounds left in the Luger. He was no match for hundreds of . . . freak animals. He had hardly begun to retreat from the area when he heard a deafening squall from above. Sterling rolled over on his back and felt his stomach rush up to his throat.

Hundreds of birds—hawks, crows, ducks, geese, and many smaller varieties—were amassed in the air above him making an ear-piercing racket. Soon bullets began whizzing around him and he knew that he had been discovered. Panic-stricken, Sterling bolted up and raced wildly through the woods, spurred on by the squawking above him and the thunder of the animals behind him.

Branches scratched at his face as he plowed through the brush, uprooting small bushes with his legs rather than letting them trip him up. By using an evasive technique of changing directions often and staying in overgrown areas he began to pull away from the herd of gun-toting game. He risked a look up. The flock of birds had already lost sight of him.

Sterling kept running, his chest burning with every breath, until his legs collapsed on him and he tumbled in a heap into a small thicket. No more than five minutes later he had the sensation of waking up. Like a hammer-blow to his body the pain came back and, along with it, the recollection of all that had gone on before.

Sterling didn't move. He doubted if he could have had he wanted to, and he definitely didn't want to. He must have pulled far enough ahead of the animals that they hadn't seen him fall. He could hear them in the brush close to where he was concealed, but they appeared to be heading further away.

For the first time in what seemed like hours, but had actually elapsed in a few minutes, Sterling had time to calm down and think through the situation. Though he had faced greater odds before, he had never been this rattled. All the rules of combat were out the window. It was a case of sheer survival: his.

He listened. It was quiet. Putting himself in the classic mind-set of thinking like the enemy, he figured that they were waiting for him to move so that they could flush him out and finish him off. The thought wasn't very reassuring. He didn't have much time, either. At any moment one of those damned squirrels could run across him and then he'd have had it.

Rattled as he was, through it all Lance Sterling had remained the consummate soldier: firmly gripped in his right hand, even amid this tumult, was his crossbow. He pushed himself up, his breathing still labored and his body one giant throb. The longer he sat with a clear head, the angrier he became. He was furious that he'd let the situation get out of his control.

Then something he hadn't noticed before made his ears prick up: running water. The river was obviously close by. Slowly, careful not to make any noise, he pulled out his compass and got his bearings. He was in luck. If he could make it to the river undetected he would be downwind of the animals. And he knew the current would take him farther away from them and closer to his rifles and pack.

That was one way to go, but if he broke one branch, snapped one twig, the whole menagerie would descend upon him. He would be discovered and killed in the process and it would all be for nothing. No, he had a better idea. Lance Sterling was not going to give up without a fight. If he was going to die here, he was damn well going to take some of them with him.

Judging the river to be about twenty or thirty yards away at the most, he pulled the cache of arrows from beneath the handle of the crossbow—silent death—and loaded the weapon. It was extremely quiet as he lay down and readied himself for action. Well hidden by the bushes he had fallen in, he thought himself lucky.

Sterling picked up a large twig that lay in front of him and snapped it. He listened. Nothing. Using his feet he shook the foliage around him for a second. He listened. Nothing . . . Wait! He could hear them coming closer now. That was all it had taken. The hair on the back of his neck stood up as he readied for the confrontation.

The first thing to come in sight was a large caribou with an opossum dangling from its antlers, the muzzle of a shotgun wrapped in the animal's arms. A raccoon on the caribou's back stood ready at the trigger as the trio stopped to study the terrain. Sterling took aim and released the first arrow. The shaft pierced the raccoon's skull just below the ear, sending the animal flailing to the ground. As the raccoon fell, the shotgun swung out of the opossum's grasp, discharging its load of buckshot as it hit the ground and launching the forest into turmoil.

Animals came pouring from behind the trees in waves. Sterling froze as the enemy rushed all around him. Cursing himself for that last bit of hubris, he decided to get to the river as fast as he could, hoping that in the confusion they might not see him. He turned to head toward the river. No such luck.

Ten yards in front of him stood a huge beaver with nothing less than an Uzi submachine gun in its paws. Rivulets of sweat streamed down Sterling's face as he watched the corpulent animal lean back on its large, flat tail, its mouth screwing up into a bucktoothed grin. The gun was aimed directly at him. It was too late.

Sterling hit the ground and buried his face in the soil beneath his arms as the beaver pulled the trigger. Bullets spewed forth wildly from the Uzi, sending the gun and the beaver spinning to the ground. Sterling pulled his head up and smiled. It had missed! He dropped everything and sprinted toward the river. Expertly weaving through the brush, the sound of the rushing water roaring in his ears, he reached the steep embankment on a dead run and dove into the icy current.

But just as his legs were leaving the ground a bullet penetrated his right hamstring, splintering his femur and exiting out the other side. The pain was excruciating, searing, a red-hot iron rod thrust into his leg. The scream that echoed across the valley made the frantic animals freeze momentarily.

As Sterling plunged into the frigid waters the impact forced out what little oxygen was left in his lungs. He knew that he had to stay under to avoid detection, but he couldn't. His head emerged from the froth amid a shower of bullets. His next breath was half water and half air but he submerged again.

His lungs were on fire but the current was swift and this time as his head pierced the surface there were fewer shots. He hacked to the point of near unconsciousness, gulped another breath and went under again.

His limbs were beginning to go numb, and his chest felt like a raging inferno. Finally he came up for the last time, sucking at the atmosphere for relief. It was slow in coming. No shots this time. His heart was pounding against his ribs, his head was throbbing, and he began to cry. Tears flowed down his cheeks and were swirled away by the rushing water.

He seemed to float on endlessly until the current slowed and he sensed his body dragging on the riverbed. He finally stopped, ebbing with the gentle motion of the water like a flotsam. He looked toward the banks in both directions and could see no movement. It was over. He must have drifted several miles downstream.

Sterling's near-hypothermic body, mangled from encounters with rocks in the river, masked the pain in his freshly wounded leg. As he lay in the water floundering, feeling lucky to be alive, one thought kept running through his mind: he had won. He could see the ridge above him and he knew that even if he couldn't walk, he could make it back to his rifles and his pack before the animals could find him. It was a hollow victory, but a victory nonetheless, and he was already thinking about a rematch.

He wiped the water from his face, embarrassed by the tears he had shed. Rolling his waterlogged frame over, he put all of his weight on his good leg and pushed himself up out of the water. His arms began to tingle and he gently lurched forward. A dull pain shot through his body and he was grateful for the numbness still left in his leg. He took another step, surprised that he could still walk at all, when the water began to roil. Though only two feet deep, it churned with such intensity that he couldn't tell what was causing it. His legs strained against the thickness in the water.

Suddenly, two translucent lines emerged from beneath the water and whipped like living tendril in a spiral, one around each leg. Sterling only caught the faintest glint of metal as two gigantic barbs sunk deep into the tops of his thighs. Then the lines jerked, pulling him flat on his ass, and his head went under the water as he was towed back upstream.

Five miles away, as the blood-chilling scream of a dying animal filled the afternoon sky, two smiling lips gradually parted to reveal a pink set of slimy gums.

A solemn figure boldly traveled a well-worn path through the valley. It was near dusk and the setting sun made his long, white hair glow like a seraphic halo. The path eventually led to the entrance of a cave. The old man took out a large chrome flashlight, the name Lance Sterling etched on the shaft, and entered.

From the floor to ceiling, skewered by wooden stakes embedded in the walls, were human skulls. The ones closest to the entrance were missing their jaws, few had teeth and a few looked like little more than thin shells. Further inside, the skulls were more complete. Soon bits of dried flesh could be seen dangling from the yellowed orbs of calcium. Still further, clumps of hair and shriveled stalks of eyes clung tenaciously to the skulls, and a wormy, gray goo covered the floor beneath them. By the time he had neared the back of the cave the flesh around the skulls was teeming with maggots.

Then the old man stopped, his flashlight trained on one particular skull with short-cropped blonde hair, a thick red beard, bulging eyes, and purplish-red blood still dripping from the neck. The old man turned and entered the back of the cave.

The acrid stench of burning torches, mingled with rotting flesh, made his nostril flare. Twenty-five, possibly thirty, small animals were furiously cleaning their guns. They barely noticed him as the old man threw two more rifles onto the pile of weapons against one wall. Off in one corner was a large brown canvas sack, a reddish-brown aureole oozing onto the cave floor from within.

"Is that it?" the old man questioned.

A raccoon threw down his rifle and mounted the sack, baring his teeth and screaming. None of the others even looked up from their work. After the raccoon returned to his gun, the old man slung the sack over his shoulder and disappeared into the darkness.

The Diver

The first time you see them your blood runs cold. Then you check your watch and see that you've been down here way too long. Damn! You look back again and begin to count them, losing track somewhere around twelve. Up above you to your left, through perhaps a hundred feet of water, is the shadow of your boat on the surface, and a quick look at the gauge on your air tanks confirms you have just a little under ten minutes to get there,

You pull yourself down behind the reef and hide while you try and figure the best course of action. All week long you've been down here collecting specimens and you haven't seen so much as dogfish. There must be a reason for all the commotion, and then you spot it: blood in the water. It looks like a wounded porpoise but you can't quite make it out in the murky distance. But it doesn't really matter what it is, only that it's directly under your boat.

As dangerous as it is in the water, if you surface more than a few strokes from the boat you'll be worse off. Your swimming will attract them and you'll have nowhere to go. It's too far to swim to shore, assuming you could get far enough away that you wouldn't be noticed.

So you begin stripping off your diving weights and anything else that isn't buoyant. You're going to have to float slowly to the surface, making as little movement as possible. Right now their attention is on the wounded porpoise, but that won't be for long; there are too many here to feed. You can feel yourself rising and you let go of the coral and begin your ascent.

47

It's all you can do to bring yourself to move toward the sharks, but you must get closer to the boat, so you take a few strokes in that direction. The boat has swung around toward you on the anchor line and you figure to be only about ten yards away from it when you surface. You breathe slowly, making as few bubbles as possible, but by the time you're halfway up you have company.

A fifteen-foot tiger shark cruises by on your right, then veers sharply away as two blues, each about seven feet long, race up on your left. The shadow up above you is getting closer, but you resist the urge to make a break for it. Then something brushes your leg, startling you. It's another blue racing by. The feeding frenzy has begun.

Whatever animal was in the water has now been reduced to a bloody pulp. Sharks are everywhere, darting at the scraps of flesh that have been torn away from the carcass. Three of them are writhing together, their jaws latched to the same piece of meat, until each has torn part of it away, making room for another. There are easily a hundred in the water around you.

You begin to kick now. You must get to the boat. Soon you're using your arms too, and a few seconds later your head breaks the surface. You spit out the regulator and push up your mask, and look in horror where the boat should be: it's not there. A dense island of kelp is bobbing in the swells in front of you. That was the shadow you saw. Frantically you whip your neck around and see the vessel fifty yards off behind you.

The tanks are empty so you strip them off, but before you can take a stroke you feel a violent pull on your leg and you're jerked under. You resurface instantly, coughing out the saltwater, and then look back down at your leg. The only thing you can see through the blood-streaked water is a stump where your foot should be, clean white bone protruding from the ragged muscle.

With the flipper on your good leg and with your arms, you begin churning up the water in an attempt to get to the boat. Your rhythm is strong and fast and you think you might make it when you feel the jaws grab your bad leg. Instantly you are flipped over and submerged. A five-foot blue has your stump firmly in its grasp and you reach down, just able to pry your leg out.

Then you are hit from behind and you notice your right arm gone at the elbow. And the feeding frenzy begins again. You're still underwater, thick and murky with your own blood, as you suffer one direct hit after another until the last thing you remember is taking a deep breath of the warm ocean water.

Eric B. Olsen

This is one of those stories that's completely over the top. "The Wombanizer" was written in 1992, about a year after I finished writing my first novel. I can't remember anymore what gave me the idea, but this was twenty years before the production of the film Hysteria. *There's also a certain resemblance to Cornell Woolrich's* The Bride Wore Black, *which I had read around that time. I do know that I had read something else, a novel or a story—it might even have been a film I had seen—in which a male gynecologist fulfilled his perversions though his medical practice. But I think in that story he liked to hurt his patients, and his satisfaction was more about sadism than sexual desire. I also know that I had recently rented* I Spit on Your Grave, *another variation on the Woolrich story, which is probably what gave me the idea for the revenge angle. The other influence was David Cronenberg. I'm pretty sure that* Dead Ringers *was still fresh in my memory, and there's also a scene in* Videodrome *with James Woods that may have led me down this particular path. From there, however, it's an easy step to the worst male Freudian nightmare ever. I tried both* Weird Tales *and* Cemetery Dance *for this one, but I'm not sure I really believed that anyone would want to publish it.*

The Wombanizer

Mrs. Philby whimpered slightly as the doctor inserted the speculum, but he continued with his work until it was properly seated. Only then did he ask, "Are you all right?"

"Oh, yes, I'm sorry for making a fuss."

The doctor smiled. They liked him. Even when he hurt them they apologized.

Surgical gloves pulled taut over his hands, his smooth fingers went about their business between Mrs. Philby's legs. The doctor is in, he thought with a barely suppressed snicker.

Gynecology. Quite simply, there was no other specialty Dr. Albert Praeger could have gone into—or even considered, for that matter. He had known what his calling was the minute he had stepped into gross anatomy lab in medical school back in 1958.

Most of the teams had been given shriveled male cadavers to work on, but his group had been fortunate enough to receive a young woman, looking so fresh he would have expected her to be warm to the touch. Secretly, he and the four other men in his group had drawn straws to see who would get the honor of dissecting the lady's genitals. Praeger had won, spending the better part of that particular week with a tremendous hard-on.

As far back as he could remember, Praeger had been obsessed with the female genitalia. It seemed as though the whole of his youth had been spent underneath bleachers, looking through knotholes, peeping in keyholes, or spying around doors to get a good look at a naked woman. And yet he had never succeeded.

Back when he was a kid it hadn't been so easy. You couldn't just walk over to the corner Seven-Eleven and plop down your allowance on a *Penthouse.*

Praeger had hoped things would improve after puberty but they didn't. During college he had scared off a series of potential girlfriends with his desire to "just look." Finally he decided that there was only one way he was going to be able to meet his needs: the professional approach.

It seemed ironic now. He knew of several colleagues in different specialties who used the services of prostitutes, actually paying women to strip down and spread their legs for him. Yet week in and week out, women steamed into Albert Praeger's office and paid *him* for the privilege of doing the very same thing.

He removed the speculum from Mrs. Philby and stripped off his rubber gloves, "You can go ahead and get dressed now. I'll be back in a few minutes, all right?"

"Thank you, Doctor."

Praeger walked to his office with the files under his arm. He didn't have any nurses to interfere with his patients, nor did he want any. Praeger had a small but devout following and handled his practice by himself, the receptionist, Miss Logan, his only employee. He tossed the buff-colored file on his desk and sat down.

After jotting a few notes, he leaned back, reflecting on his nearly thirty years of medical service to women. There was nothing more beautiful, he thought, than the female genitalia. Like snowflakes, no two were alike, each with its own unique personality and charm. Sure he had his favorites, but none had ever disappointed, and for this reason he always thought of himself as the Will Rogers of gynecology.

In fact, it wasn't until a few years into his career that he realized he had trouble recognizing his patients unless he was examining them. It had begun to cause him some embarrassment until Miss Logan suggested putting the patient files in a little holder *outside* the examining room. All Praeger had to do was take a peak at the file, and then come strolling in with it under his arm, patient name at the ready. It was a good system, refined even further by color coding—that had been Praeger's idea. Buff-colored files were for married women, green were for single. Single women under eighteen had red while those over sixty were grey. And one special category of files, containing only about two-dozen women, were aptly colored blue.

The blue files contained women from every category, and if there was any other link that connected the women Praeger was ignorant of it, blissfully ignorant. While most women visited their gynecologists once a year, the blue files visited Praeger once every three months. One of his examining rooms, in fact, was devoted entirely to them. It contained all of the standard equipment as well as a tent of green operating curtains that totally concealed him from the upper half of the women's body; they preferred it that way.

During these particular "examinations" Albert Praeger went way beyond merely looking, and many of the women had even begun a curious Pavlovian response to their visits: lubricating at the sound of his snapping gloves. Afterward, they thanked him and acted as if nothing abnormal had taken place, the flush on their cheeks the only evidence of their true reason for coming.

Could he trust them not to tell? The thought was laughable. Evidently, the only fear these women had in regard to him was that he would refuse to see them. They were very loyal. It had been this way throughout his entire practice, and was probably why he had never gotten married. While other men had hated their jobs, Praeger looked forward to work every day.

He imagined that when his women had sex with their husbands or boyfriends—if they did at all—they made sure that the lights were off, the covers on the bed were pulled chin-high, and they closed their eyes and thought about him. But of course that was a pure speculation, and he supposed it didn't really matter. In the end they continued to see him, and he continued to service them, and medical insurance covered everything. Praeger pushed himself away from his desk with a sigh and walked back to talk with Mrs. Philby.

"We'll send those to the lab right away and I'll call you next week to let you know the results, all right?"

"Oh, thank you, Doctor," she gushed.

Praeger escorted her back out to the waiting room and gave her file back to Miss Logan. The personal touch; it was what kept his patients coming back for more. They felt that he truly cared for them, and he proved it to them by calling them personally with their test results. It was surprising how little office time it took and how infinitely satisfying it was for his patients.

Miss Logan was good about keeping his appointments adequately spaced out during the day so that no one had to wait more than five or ten minutes. He had a total of three examining rooms, and insisted that only one be filled at a time. He'd had four buff files and two red today and was just thinking he could do with something special when he looked up and saw the blue file nestled neatly in the holder by the examining room door. Praeger smiled, his excitement already straining the material of his pants.

He took down the file, peeked at the name and the frowned. He didn't recognize it. That wasn't right. Lucy Caleb, it read, unmarried, twenty-six years old. Why couldn't he remember her? He decided not to take any chances and walked back to the reception desk.

"Miss Logan, will you come here, please?"

The receptionist stepped away from her desk, through the doorway, and back into the hall. "Yes, Doctor?"

"About this Caleb woman, are you sure it's a blue file?" Praeger knew that Miss Logan had no idea what the significance of the blue files was, only that he made all the color determinations.

"It was in with the others, Doctor. She called last month to set up an appointment. I remember it distinctly because her name didn't ring a bell as being one of your patients. I looked through all the other files and I was about to tell her that we had no record of her when, just to be thorough, I went through the blue files. And there it was. It says you've seen her once before, but the date is smudged and I couldn't read it. Was it not supposed to be there?"

"Oh, no," he said, not wanting to let on that he didn't have a clue who this woman was, or that he couldn't remember one of his blue files. "It's just that it's been awhile since I've seen her. Thought I'd ask, that's all."

Miss Logan smiled and nodded and went back to her desk, while Praeger made his way slowly back to the examining room, his mind a total blank. Finally he took a deep breath and entered.

A tent of green material hung over the examining table and he could see a coat on the rack in the corner and clothes folded neatly on the chair beside it.

"Hello, Miss Caleb. How are you feeling today?"

"Fine, Doctor," came the voice from beneath the curtain. "I'm just glad you could see me. I mean it's been so long since my last . . . well, you know, checkup."

He grinned as he washed his hands at the sink, but his smile was tempered by the fact that he didn't recognize her voice at all. It was clear, however, that she was indeed a blue file, and he supposed that once he took a look under the drapes, everything would come back to him.

"Are your feet in the stirrups?" he asked gently.

"Yes, Doctor."

"All right, then," he said, sitting down on the stool in front of her and snapping on his gloves. "Let's see what we can do for you."

Praeger lifted up the sheet and almost knew. The sight was indeed memorable, the folds the wrinkles, placement of hair—everything was familiar and then again it wasn't. He was sure he'd seen this woman, and yet . . . he couldn't remember where. The office? He didn't think so. He'd been in the same building for his entire career, but the two didn't seem to go together. He *did* recognize her, though, he was sure of it.

"Is anything wrong, Doctor?" the voice said.

"Oh, no, Miss Caleb," he said, trying to think quickly, "I was just adjusting my gloves. Are you ready to begin?"

"Very."

His heart rate and respiration increased immediately, and though he was unsure of himself for the first time in his career, he was urged ahead by the tension in his crotch, increasing with every moment he stared at Miss Caleb's. He began to palpate her externally and she reacted with low moans. But something drew his attention from his work for a moment and he squinted up at the overhead lights.

"When was the last time you had a general checkup?" he asked, his medical curiosity momentarily overriding his libido.

"I suppose it was just before my last visit with you."

He frowned. Since he couldn't read the chart, that didn't help him a bit, and he certainly wasn't going to admit to shoddy recordkeeping by asking when that had been. Her entire body from the waist up was covered by a green tent. He looked at what he could see and then back up at the light. Her legs had a decidedly yellow color to them and it worried him.

"Just to satisfy my own curiosity, did your doctor happen to mention anything about you having jaundice?"

"No," she said thoughtfully.

"Have you noticed your skin as having a yellow tint to it?"

"Not any more than usual. Why? Is something wrong?"

"No, no, just curious." But his face was burning with embarrassment. Was she Asian? How could he have forgotten to look on her chart?

"Doctor?" she said, snapping back to the present.

"Yes?"

"Well, I . . . I don't know exactly how to put this, but I *really* need this examination."

Typical blue filer, always impatient. There was no need to hesitate any longer and so he stripped off his gloves and began his patented internal palpation.

"Is this better?" he asked.

"Oh, yes."

But it wasn't two seconds later when he felt something sharp gouging one of his fingers. What the hell is that? he thought. Praeger had learned in medical school not to say things like

"Oops" or "Oh, no" while he was with a patient. They would lose their confidence in him if they thought he could be taken by surprise or that he could make mistakes. And he didn't make a sound now, but the pain was almost too much to bear.

When he tried, gently, to remove his finger, it only made the pain worse, so he pushed a little deeper to relieve pressure. Then something gouged his other finger. "Ouch!" he actually said aloud, unable to keep it in.

"Is something wrong?" the voice asked, and a small trickle of sweat ran down Praeger's face.

"No, nothing to worry ab—"

With a jarring yank, entire hand was suddenly inside the woman. He slipped off his stool before he could react and his knees made a resounding crack as they hit the floor.

"Jesus Christ!" he yelled, his chest heaving while his arm inched further and further inside of her. "What the hell's going on?"

'You've been a naughty boy haven't you, Albert?"

"What . . . Who are you?"

But the woman said nothing more. Praeger could see the muscles of her legs flexing beneath her yellow skin and, each time they did, more of his arm disappeared. He could hear the faint sounds of exertion behind the curtain and struggled to his feet just as his elbow reached the entry point. Pain shot through both legs as he stood, wobbly, above the green tent, and with his free hand tore the sheet away.

Albert Praeger's heart rate nearly tripled. His face was frozen in a screaming rictus, but he could utter no sound as his throat was still in shock. The only sound in the room was his chest, sucking in great gasps of air like a rapidly moving bellows.

Below him on the table was the naked body of a woman, or what was left of her. Her skin, yellowed and transparent, was cut down the entire length of her chest. The tissue was splayed open on both sides, exposing her internal organs, shriveled and brown and bloodless. Both of her arms were reaching deep into the white coils of her intestines and Praeger realized the pain he

Eric B. Olsen

had felt were her fingernails, even as his own hand emerged from her body cavity.

Then she yanked his elbow in and he fell again to his knees. She took her legs out of the stirrups now and sat up facing him, his bicep just slipping inside of her as she tugged again. Her face had been shorn away to the bone on one side and the top of her skull was cut off giving him glimpses of the white convolutions in her brain. The skin had been removed from her arms as well and he could only watch the naked bundles of muscle tissue, flexing as they pulled his own arm further inside of her.

He was up to his shoulder now, his arm protruding from her chest, wet and glistening. The stench of formaldehyde filled the room and he thought grimly that it was almost as if she had been . . . Then suddenly he had it. He remembered. It was the cadaver that he had dissected in medical school. And in that brief moment before his head was eventually pulled through, Albert Praeger finally found his voice.

When Jenny Logan heard the scream she was on the phone with a patient. The sound didn't come again and she tried to remain calm as she finished making the appointment and writing it in the calendar. She could see the lone patient in the waiting room staring at her, but she ignored the woman, and after hanging up the phone she hurried back to the examining rooms.

She knocked on the door where she had placed the last file. "Dr. Praeger? Is everything all right?"

There was no answer, and as she looked around she realized there was no one to help her, either. Praeger didn't believe in nurses and she was the only staff member here. She knocked again. "Dr. Praeger!"

Still no answer. She ran back to his office and looked in, then over to the other examining rooms: all of them were empty. After taking a deep breath at the door where she had started, Jenny Logan turned the knob and went inside. She screamed freely at what she saw.

Praeger was lying back on the examining table, his feet up in the stirrups, and twin jets of blood spurting across the room from the bloody hole in his crotch. In one hand was a scalpel and in the other, a bloody mass of tissue that had once been the good doctor's genitals.

When she was finally able to tear her eyes from the grisly scene, Miss Logan ran back into the hall and puked her lunch out on the wall-to-wall carpet. Still shaken, she walked out into the now-empty reception area and called the police.

Back inside the examining room Lucy Caleb finished dressing and put her coat on. The woman who had come in hadn't seen her—no one could unless she wanted them to, and that included five certain gentlemen of the medical profession who had drawn straws over her barely-cold body many years ago. Make that four now; one of them was dead.

She didn't even look at Praeger as she left the office. He had been the one to draw the short straw, and aptly had been the first one she had visited. She only had a brief time to finish her work, and a very busy schedule ahead of her. The next one on the list lived in New York City, a proctologist. Boy, was he in for a surprise.

The Vagrant

"I thought I told you never to come around here again."

At first you don't think he's talking to you but when you turn around you realize he is.

"I . . . I wasn't doing anything," you lie.

He says nothing.

"The door was open," you lie again.

He says nothing.

"Look," you explain, "I'll just leave, okay?" and you start to walk toward him, toward the door.

But he pulls a gun and you stop. Suddenly *you* don't feel much like saying anything.

"You mangy son of a bitch. I should have killed you years ago, 'cept *she* was still protectin' you."

He starts toward you and you begin to back away, not looking behind you, yet not bumping into anything. You've been here before.

"Well, *she's* gone now."

"I know . . . That's why I came back," you say, still moving away.

"Well you came back too fuckin' late!" he yells at you.

Now you've run out of room—you've backed into the corner—but he keeps coming closer. "Too fuckin' late!" he yells again. He's almost on top of you. The gun is shaking in his hand as he touches the barrel to your forehead. You don't move. You can smell yourself now, the sweat; you can smell it and it stinks.

But he just stands there looking at you through bloodshot eyes and a two-day beard. He just keeps standing there, pushing the gun harder and harder into your forehead. His breath stinks of beer and whisky and the rest of him of shit. Flecks of spit fly into your face as he yells, but you still don't move.

"Fuck you, you son of a bitch," he says, and smashes your face with the gun. You hit the wall and slide to the floor, your cracked, swollen lips bleeding profusely. Your mouth is numb but you can taste the metallic slickness of your own blood, and spit it out onto the floor.

He watches you get up and shakes his head. Then he lets the gun fall and hang by his side as he walks away, his back toward you, still shaking his head. He starts to say something but you're already lunging toward him, the knife cold and hard in your hand.

Would he have done it? Would he still do it? It doesn't matter now; you've almost reached him. Does he *want* to do it? Is he capable? He turns at the last second and you see the tears in his eyes. He tries to point the gun but instead it waves impotently in the air. You've already reached him.

It's not so much a stab as it is a push. The blade just sort of sinks into him. He tries to yell but only blood comes out of his mouth. You don't pull the knife out, either; he falls away from it, leaving the sharp metal warm and wet in your hand. His head hits the floor hard as he falls, but he never lets go of the gun.

You stand for a minute, maybe more, just looking at him. Then you wipe the blade clean on his pant leg and slip it back into your coat pocket.

You pull your trench coat, warm and malleable, stained and crusted with dirt, tight around your shoulders. You hitch up your pants, moist, stinking of urine, and tighten the rope that you use as a belt. Your beard is coarse, caked with filth as you reach up to scratch it, and you brush your hair, matted and lice-ridden, from your eyes.

Then you go back to looking and you keep looking until you find it: the picture. The one *she* wanted to give you the day you left, the last time you saw her before she died. When you find it you don't even look at it, you just put it into your coat pocket, right next to the knife.

You turn and stare blankly around the room for a while. You don't think, you don't reason; maybe you remember a little bit. After all, you know this place. As you leave, you step over the dead body. It moves, not alive, yet not quite dead. And you turn to look, one last time, at your father lying on the floor. Then you say good-bye.

Eric B. Olsen

This is one story that has a very clear and direct inspiration for me, Stephen King's "Apt Pupil" from his terrific quartet of novellas, Different Seasons. *My undergraduate degree in college was in history with a focus on the Holocaust and Nazi Germany, and my first novel was about a Nazi doctor after the war, so this was something that I had given a lot of thought to. One of the things that always made me curious was what kind of rationalizations former Nazis had to tell themselves after the war in order to live among the rest of us. The other influence, though not as pronounced, was probably the novel* Pursuit *by Robert L Fish, which was subsequently turned into a TV miniseries called* Twist of Fate. *"What Goes Around Comes Around" was the one story I never sent out for publication, so I'm not sure exactly when it was written. But because of the date that appears in the story it was most likely 1991. The main character's name was probably a variation on that of Christopher Walken, who I had been taken with ever since his performance in another Stephen King adaptation,* The Dead Zone.

What Goes Around
Comes Around

When eighty-four-year-old Karl-Heinz Wolken woke up he knew he was finally dead. He could tell because he had never felt this good when he was alive, and the end had come none too soon. Wracked with pain ever since his stroke, bedridden for the last year, in his own mind Wolken had been dead long before today. If he'd been a real man he would have killed himself—a bullet in the head, or a black capsule. But none of that mattered anymore; it was finally over.

Wolken slipped quietly out of his bed on legs that seemed to be those of a twenty-year-old. His room was subtly different but as he looked around it wasn't readily apparent in what way. Then he walked to the bathroom, not out of necessity, but to look at himself in the mirror. Staring back at him from the silvery glass was a face he could only remember from pictures: himself at twenty-two. He didn't know why he knew the exact age, only that he knew.

Wolken's face was smooth and unstubbled, and as he looked around him he noticed that the bathroom was different somehow, too. This time he realized what the difference was: there were no personal items of his anywhere. The electric razor was gone, there was no soap next to the sink, and the rack where his towels had hung was now just an empty aluminum rod. A sadness for the distinctly human things that he would never do again suddenly came over him, and Wolken walked back out into his bedroom.

This was the room he had lived in—had been imprisoned in—for the last year, but it was not *his* room anymore. The pictures on his dresser, the get-well cards, the magazines he used to read at night, and the dirty clothes hanging over the back of the chair—all of them were gone.

He pulled open the closet door and when he saw the single black suit and white shit hanging there, a pair of black shoes on the floor beneath them, he knew he had an appointment to keep. Wolken was not surprised to find a single pair of white briefs, a white T-shirt, and a pair of black socks in his dresser drawer. Methodically, he began to dress.

When he had finished knotting the tie, Wolken walked through the shell of what had once been his house. The kitchen had no food in it, the living room walls were barren of paintings; only impersonal furniture and appliances attested to the life he had once lived here. And now that life was through, the fact that nothing of his remained here somehow made it easier to leave, and Karl-Heinz Wolken walked to his front door for the last time.

He stepped out onto the stoop and into the bright morning sunshine. The air, crisp and fresh as he had never known it before, was only part of the change he witnessed in the neighborhood where he had spent the last forty years of his life. He could hear no cars, no birds, see no people or animals, and yet trees and plants flourished in abundance. It was as though he had entered a different dimension, a dimension where he was the only animal that existed.

From his left he saw a man coming up the sidewalk, but Wolken wasn't frightened, and he descended the stoop and walked out to meet him. The young man was dressed in red from head to foot—coat, shirt, tie, slacks, and shiny red leather boots. Wolken smiled, genuinely happy, as the young man in red approached him.

"Have you come for me?" Wolken ventured.

The young man's face was very relaxed and nonjudgmental. His mouth moved in an almost imperceptible smile and his head may have even nodded. Then he turned and began walking, and Wolken fell in step beside him.

For a while, Wolken was content to be silent. He was still marveling at the changes in his once-decrepit body. He was actually walking. The pain was gone, too. It was wonderful. As he examined his surroundings, he found everything around him was focused with crystal clarity, and instinctively he reached up his hand to adjust his glasses before he realized he wasn't wearing any.

He smiled again. The young man next to Wolken looked to be about thirty-five, lightly complected, with a touch of grey around the temples of his wavy brown hair. Walking next to him, Wolken was reminded of an old movie he had seen on the television after he had come to the United States. But Karl-Heinz Wolken knew he wasn't going to be meeting Mr. Jordan. No, he was expecting someone more along the lines of a Dr. Caligari or Count Orlock.

"Pardon me, sir," said Wolken finally. "Could you tell me where we are going?"

The man looked up at him and even though he didn't say a word and his expressionless face didn't change, the answer in his eyes was clearly no. But Wolken had expected as much. It wasn't as if he should merit any deferential treatment at this point. On the contrary, he knew in his heart what he had done and only now, it seemed, could he finally come to terms with it. After all, it was out of his hands; someone else would have to judge him now; he was through. There was no more need for justification, rationalization, or even plain repression. It was time to come clean.

"Do you know who I am, young man?" Even though Wolken now looked half the man's age, he still referred to him as "young."

The man turned to look at him, but said nothing.

"I'm a living oxymoron. Or at least I was—living, that is. War criminal. That's what they called me. Oh, it sounds all right if you don't think about it too much, but I was no more a criminal than any of them. I was a soldier, a warrior if you must, and we were at war."

He took a deep breath of the clean air. Oh, yes, it felt good to talk about it now. The years of hiding, the assumed names, the endless guilt—it was all over now. Wolken looked around, and though they couldn't have gone very far in the small town he had come to know so intimately over the last four decades, he found he didn't recognize the neighborhood they were in. No matter. He took another breath and continued.

"They said I was evil, but I never felt evil. They said I did evil things, but I was simply following orders."

The young man may have raised an eyebrow, but it was hard to tell.

"Yes, I know, I know how that sounds and I don't care. It was the truth and I feel no shame about it. But that's what they wanted us to feel: shame. I don't understand it at all. I never did. If we were evil, why didn't they just kill us? Why didn't they put us before a firing squad and let us die with honor?

"I'll tell you why, because that wasn't good enough for them. They wanted to rub our noses in it first. Kill us without a trial? That would be barbaric, lowering themselves to our level. *Scheisse!* We'd had our trial; we lost the war. Shouldn't that have been enough? Well, it wasn't for them. They wanted to publicly humiliate us. They didn't want us to die like soldiers—they wanted is to die like criminals. If they want to call me evil, fine, but I was never a criminal."

As the two men passed over a bridge that Wolken had never seen before, he fell silent. He suddenly realized that never in his life had he told his story to anyone. The years of silence, the years of suppression, were finally over. It was liberating. He only hoped that he would be able to finish by the time they got to wherever they were going.

The young man seemed interested enough, and in a way, Wolken had the impression that this was the man's job, if there was such a thing in this dimension he was in.

"My father died in 1933," Wolken continued. "I was in medical school at the time and my mother was left alone to support me and my younger sister and younger brother. When I graduated I didn't have time, let alone the money, to set up a practice. My mother was working two jobs to support us and it broke my heart. That's when I joined the SS. Not only did they give me a job in a hospital, but I had a rank, a uniform, and, most importantly for my family, money. My mother was able to quit *both* of her jobs and take care of the younger children."

"There were, of course, tasks I was expected to perform in the hospital. The retarded, the incurably sick, the mentally ill were all allowed to die."

The younger man turned again, but Wolken returned his stare as steely-eyed as ever.

"That does not make me a monster. I was once as they were, sick and bedridden, and I can tell you here and now, with God as my witness, that I would have welcomed that end, either by my own hand or someone else's. I was not afraid to die, and neither, I believe, were they. We helped deformed infants and the old and infirm as well. That was only right.

"Forty-five years ago they called me evil for doing that, and yet people in this very country, even as we speak, are attempting to pass laws that will allow them to do the same thing. Death with dignity, they call it. I say, what is the difference?

"I worked in the hospital until 1943, ten years of service to the Fatherland, ten years of service to the Furher. I don't think people realize how much he did for us. He wasn't perfect—he wasn't a god. I know that now, and I knew it at the time. And some of the things he did toward the end—well frankly, I think they were wrong. But to say we should have stood up against him? *Gott in Himmel!*

"Before Hitler came to power we were an oppressed people. We were outcast. Politically oppressed, economically oppressed, intellectually oppressed—we were hated by the world. But Hitler changed all that. I couldn't have done it. No one I knew could have done it. I don't think there was anyone else in the world who could have done what he did. He gave us back our pride. People were working again. Things were good. For the first time in twenty years we were a proud nation again. And for that I should have rebelled against him? No, not me. The man who did all that, in my mind, had earned the right to make a few mistakes. So when I was ordered to Poland in 1943, I went."

The two men had rounded corners and walked down sidewalks as Wolken narrated, and now they were entering a built-up city center, one such as Wolken had never seen before. The town he had lived in had no buildings taller than four or five stories. But the place they were in now looked like a metropolis, only cleaner. The streets were lined with grass and shrubs, the pavement was clean, and the buildings spaced to throw more light on the area than he possibly could have imagined. It was in stark contrast to the stinking, muddy camps he remembered at Auschwitz.

"We were all doctors—all of us there—who made the selections. But it wasn't medicine we were practicing; that much I can assure you. It was the closest thing to hell on earth that I know of. We had to make life and death decisions all day long. We would drink ourselves blind just to cope, to numb ourselves from the pain that was going on all around us. It was a wonder we were able to maintain our sanity, or our humanity, but we did.

"I remember one time—it was early in the morning. One of the guards came to tell me that a train had arrived and that I was to perform the selections that day. I was angry and irritated, but I was also a soldier, as much at war as the men on the Russian front. Toward the end of the day my patience was wearing thin. An old man had fallen down next to me and he wouldn't stand up. I was furious and without thinking I reared up to kick him. Well, he looked at me with such hatred in his eyes, such pain, that I stopped myself immediately. I did not hate them, and I refused to allow myself such an inappropriate emotion in the course of carrying out my duties. I walked away after that and did no more selections that day.

"I do not believe it was the Fuhrer's wish that the problem be solved in the way it was. I know it was not mine. The situation was such that we were forced into taking whatever measures we saw fit. It was left entirely up to us. I mean, it's not as though they never had a chance to leave. They were encouraged to go, told that they were unwelcome and yet many elected to stay. And the ones who wanted to go couldn't. No other country would take them. What does that tell you about how much the world valued their lives? The world did nothing. These days they are called the homeless, vagrants, bums. We called them subhuman. The words may be different but the meaning is the same.

"We were at war, for God's sake, and people die during war. That has never changed. Why should we have been singled out for humiliation, simply on the basis of whom we decided to call 'the enemy?' For one country the enemy was Japanese living in Hiroshima and Nagasaki. For another country it was the Jews."

Wolken had finished just as the young man in red turned toward the front doors of a giant high-rise office building. He followed. The man held the door open and Wolken walked through and into a large foyer. It was spacious and well-lit, with marble floors and white walls and ceiling. Directly in front of him was a wide descending staircase and for the first time that day, Wolken felt uneasy.

He followed the man down the stairs as they narrowed to a set of double wooden doors. Once again, the young man held the door for Wolken as he entered a large waiting room. With a subtle turn of the man's head, Wolken understood that he was to sit on one of the long couches and wait. As he did, the young man took a seat behind a desk across the room, and began to enter data into a computer.

There was another door to Wolken's right and he knew at some point he would be going in beyond them. What was in there? He had a pretty good idea. The room around him was black, and even though the only light appeared to be coming from the young man's computer screen, Wolken could see perfectly well. That, along with the red suit and his descent into this room, made it obvious. Karl-Heinz Wolken was going to hell.

Disappointing? Yes. But it came as no surprise to Wolken. Why should death be any different from life? Perhaps if he hadn't gone to Poland he wouldn't have ended up like this, or perhaps all of Nazi Germany had been damned and what he did or didn't do was immaterial. Any further speculation certainly was. There was nothing left to do but wait. In a strange way he believed he had been waiting for this moment all his life. At last, he was ready.

As if reading his thoughts, the young man in red stood up and walked to the inner door. His look prompted Wolken from his seat, and he was ushered into a large, black office. The door was shut behind him, and he walked forward to the large desk in the center of the room. Another man, also wearing red, was busily typing on a computer and Wolken stood silently watching him beside the single chair in front of the desk.

After a few moments the man stopped and turned to Wolken. "Please," he said, motioning with his hand, "sit down."

Wolken did as ordered and watched as the man opened a slim file and leafed through the two or three sheets of paper it contained. He was a big man, strong and powerful; Wolken could tell just by looking at him. He had thick, black hair, a full close-cut beard and piercing black eyes. The man was an imposing figure, but Wolken liked him at once. It had been a very long time since he had been addressed in German.

"Let's see, now, you're Wolken, Karl-Heinz. Is that correct?"

"Yes."

"Born, Germany, 1908. Died, United States, 1991. Is that correct?"

"Yes."

"Well, Herr Wolken, I see here you've led quite an industrious life."

Industrious? Wolken thought. Was that supposed to be some kind of joke? "I suppose so."

"Very good," he said, and smiled warmly. "Our information here says you were directly responsible for 138,459 deaths, and indirectly responsible for some two million more. Is that correct?"

Wolken hesitated. "What do you mean by 'directly responsible?'"

"Come, come, Herr Wolken. I'm not here to judge you. The facts speak for themselves. If you think they are in error, this is your chance to be heard, nothing more." There was compassion in the man's voice and though he didn't want to, Wolken believed him.

"I already told the gentleman who brought me here—"

The man held out his hand and Wolken stopped. "Yes, you did. And he is transcribing your words right now. Your . . . fate, you might call it, has already been determined, Herr Wolken."

"By whom?"

"By yourself, of course." Wolken made it clear by his facial expression that he didn't understand, and the man continued. "All of the decisions you have made during your lifetime have been entered into the computer. A formula, which I barely understand myself, computes your placement subsequent to death. Your actions, not ours, determine your fate."

It was as he had feared, but he had to know for sure. "Then I am going to hell?"

The man chuckled. "Ah, Christianity. As ye sow, so shall ye reap? No, nothing as dramatic as that, I'm afraid."

"But I am an atheist."

"Is that so? You know, I had a gentleman tell me once, from that very chair where you're sitting, that the mere denial of God presupposes his existence. I'm no philosopher, but I must say that I do find the religions of man fascinating. But of course they bear little on the reality of death, wouldn't you say?"

Wolken nodded.

"Now, if you would be good enough to tell me whether our figures are correct we'll be all through here."

"Please, what is going to happen to me?"

The man's look suddenly went stern. "It wouldn't be a good idea for you to know, Herr Wolken."

"But you didn't say I *couldn't* know."

"That is correct."

"Good, then I demand you tell me."

The man rubbed his whiskered chin and pushed himself back from the desk, fingers steepled in front of him. "Very well, I will tell you all that I am allowed. It is a very complex procedure that you are going through, Herr Wolken. I doubt if you would understand it, but I will try to tell you in a way that will make sense to you.

"I said before that man's religions were fascinating to me. I suppose that is because so many have elements of the truth in them. It is interesting to see the explanations people have invented to explain that atavistic knowledge that is within all of them and how close they have come to actuality.

"The world, Herr Wolken, your world, your universe, is cyclical. That's not saying much, I know, but that's as specific as I can make it for you. There is no beginning and there is no ending. Your science, your philosophy, your history, as well as your religion, contain elements of what you would call the truth, but there is ever so much more, that as a human being you have not yet begun to understand. The human souls, as you might call them, that come through here all have vastly differing destinies. Yours, Herr Wolken, is to return."

"Reincarnation?"

The man smiled sardonically. "In a way. But as nothing so peculiar as a plant or a bird or an animal. Merely as another human being."

Wolken's heart was beating faster. Reincarnation. That was good, wasn't it? At least he thought so. "Will I know who I am, or who I was?"

"That I cannot answer, for no one really knows. As I said before, everyone has a different destiny." For a moment the man was silent, and then sat up to his desk again. "Now, what do you say we clear up the matter of these figures?"

"Yes," said Wolken, unhesitatingly. "They sound about right."

"Good," said the man. "Then I see no reason to detain you any further. If you will just go back through the doors by which you entered, someone will be waiting for you."

With things suddenly at an end, Wolken stood up and walked back toward the door. He turned around to take one more look, and perhaps thank him, but the man was once again busily entering data into his computer. When he turned back, the door in front of Karl-Heinz Wolken was opened upon an entirely new existence.

◆ ◆ ◆ ◆ ◆ ◆

Six days without food. Gregor Theopoulos had eaten his last meal on Thursday evening and he could remember every bite distinctly. And now suddenly, nearly a week later, he regretted not having that second helping of dessert: baklava, with fresh honey on top. He had wanted to save a piece for the next night, but the next night had never come. The thought of that lone piece of baklava, moldering in a tin, was maddening.

Six days without water. The hunger came and went, but the itch in his throat for water never left him. Gregor didn't salivate anymore, and he had stopped pissing after the second day. His lips were cracked and scabbed, and he breathed with his mouth open because they would stick together if he didn't. Every time he pried them apart they split and bled anew.

Six days of standing. The boxcar had been packed to capacity with everyone standing up. One corner was used for a toilet and even though no one had used it for three days, the smell of defecation permeated the entire car—during the heat of midday, it was nearly suffocating. There was virtually no room to move around, and though most of the woman and children had collapsed on the floor, standing was still preferable.

The boxcar let in very little light during the day, and it was like a tomb at night. Many had already died, including the infant boy of a couple standing near him. The mother's milk had dried up and yet she clung desperately to the body of the dead infant. She hadn't allowed anybody to put it with the others. At night he could hear the couple having sex against the wall next to him, and yet all his mind could conjure up was the image of her gripping the dead child while they did.

Relocation to the North, they said. Well, they were right about that. He guessed that they were somewhere in Poland but he couldn't be sure. Gregor had been rousted from his bed around midnight, the taste of baklava—with fresh honey—still very much on his tongue, and taken to the train station along with his family. Somehow they had become separated at the train station and he had been forced into a boxcar with nearly one hundred others, locked in and moved out. It was the morning of the sixth day before the door was finally opened.

The light was blinding at first. People nearest the door simply fell out onto the ground, while others were hauled out. Those in the back where he was were able to step forward on wobbly legs and jump out. All of this activity was set to the chorus of uniformed men shouting *"Juden, raus!"*

Thousands of people, most of them crying out in Greek for their lost loved ones, were herded forward toward the gates. Those who didn't follow orders were clubbed with rifle butts; those who tried to get away were shot. Gregor followed orders, his neck craned behind him, looking for his family. Then he heard a shout from in front of him that he recognized. It was his daughter Georgia, and his little grandson Nikolos in her arms.

He ran toward her and also saw his two sons and their wives. Gregor's wife had died before the war and as he walked forward holding his grandchild, he was almost glad. She would not have to endure whatever private hell the Germans had in store for them. Cosima had been a good woman. She deserved better than this.

When the line finally stopped, they moved slowly for several hours through the gates. It was only then that Gregor noticed the smell. Thick clouds of stinking smoke rolled up into the sky from somewhere inside of the fenced camp, smelling of burning meat. Above them was a sign in German: *Arbeit Macht Frei.* It was a few hours later before he saw what the wait was for.

A uniformed man in black stood at the head of the line, pointing his thumb in different directions, some of the people going to the right, and some of them to the left. Every so often he would stop to examine them, asking questions. All around him German guards were shouting in Greek for twins to step forward, for doctors to step forward. His family, as far as he could remember, had always been farmers. They stayed in line.

When they finally reached the front, the sun was beginning to set. Powerful banks of light flooded the dirt grounds. Suddenly, little Nicky was torn from Georgia's arms and thrust into Gregor's. She was pushed to the right with his sons and Gregor was pushed to the left. Georgia and Nicky were both crying and he thought there must have been some mistake for a mother and her child to be separated like that. But when he moved out of line to give his grandson back to his daughter, he was clubbed in the back of the head with a rifle butt.

Gregor fell, sprawled onto the ground while little Nicky tumbled out of his arms. Guards were all around him screaming now, but when he looked up into his little grandson's puzzled face, he couldn't move. Maybe it had been the long trip, no food, or standing in line, but Gregor Theopoulos did not have the strength to stand.

The man in black, from the head of the line, walked over to him. He barked out something in German, but Gregor wasn't listening. His eyes were riveted on the man's face. Surely he did not recognize the man in black; Gregor had never been out of Greece before. But he did.

Dirty Jew. That's what the man was thinking. It was impossible, but it was as though he could read the man's thoughts. And what thoughts! Jew? Why he was no more Jew than . . .

The man in black suddenly reared a boot above his face, and then Gregor knew what was happening, what was *really* happening. "You," he said, and the man in black froze. Their eyes locked. Gregor couldn't believe what they were going to do to him, what they were going to do to his family. As the German slowly lowered his boot, Gregor whispered the name that was on his lips, the name of the man who was standing before him: "Wolken."

The fear in the other man's eyes went almost unnoticed as Gregor tried to cope with fear of his own. The German tore his eyes from Gregor and stormed away, leaving him helpless on the dirt floor of the camp.

"Wait," Gregor yelled. "You can't do this." He wanted to run, knowing that if he tried to escape, the guards would shoot him; then it would all be over. But he still couldn't move, and he began to cry. Two men finally picked him up by the arms and carried him down the cement stairs to the showers. Showers that a soul once named Karl-Heinz Wolken knew were really gas chambers.

The Chair

The first time you knew it would really happen was when you felt the cold steel clamp around your wrists. You were standing, back turned, sirens still ringing in your ears, closing your eyes because you thought it might help. That's when you knew.

But in reality, you knew it even sooner. Despite the impending trial and the appeals that would follow, the stays and calls to the governor, somehow it all seemed preordained. You knew it as soon as you pulled the trigger.

The sound of the shots had roared in your ears, blacking out everything else, overpowering the screams that tried in vain to reach you. You'd heard the bullets tearing through clothing, sinking into flesh, mangling bones and organs in their path. And that was when you really knew.

It was in the smell of your sweat, beading up at first but then merging, each tiny droplet flowing into the next, from your forehead, your upper lip, your temples. You caught a whiff of it coming from your armpits as you raised the gun, and you smelled the acrid stench of sulfur wafting up to your nostrils after it was over. You could practically taste it: death. Waiting for you. It was only a matter of time.

And you remembered the flames, flames that nearly blinded you as they jumped from the end of the barrel, licking at the darkness in search of a victim. And the blood, his blood, oozing from his chest in bright red circles, telling you it would happen.

You remember feeling the shock waves ripple through your body as you fired each round, rattling your bones to the marrow, all your muscles holding tight, clinging to your vibrating skeleton. And afterward you felt life rushing to escape from the body on the floor, leaving behind its husk of humanity. That was when you really knew.

But then you forgot.

As the days passed so did the memory. And it took the cold steel around your wrists one last time to bring it all back again: the days turning into months, the months turning into years, grey cement walls and green painted bars inching toward you from all sides. It's all coming back to haunt you now and you can think of little else.

That is, until you take the first step, and suddenly the past doesn't seem so important. Only thoughts of what lies ahead fill your mind. Adrenaline secretes into your bloodstream and your heart begins to race. Your mouth is dry and hanging open, sucking in air.

Many footsteps echo down the hall but you only hear your own, each step ticking off another second of your life, taking you closer and closer to the black room that awaits you.

Keys jangle in the lock as the door is pushed open. The sight of the chair makes your bowels liquefy. Fear wells up inside you and you weep, softly, not caring that they can see you. Then they sit you down.

You smell the leather straps as they bind first one leg, then the other. Straps around your chest allow the back of the chair to grab hold of your spine. It knows; you feel it. And it will never let you go.

The tendrils of the wire reach around from behind you and attach to the skin on your arms and legs, warming, expanding as they draw out your body heat. They wait, patiently, to return to that heat an immeasurable-fold.

Then you feel the sponge against your bare, shaven head, tiny rivulets of water running down your face, mingling with sweat and tears, dripping from the tip of your nose and from your chin as the metal bowl is strapped to your head.

For the first time now, you actually hear them. They are speaking to you but you don't understand. You shake your head and they go away. Behind the mirrored glass you know they are watching. Eyes, *their* eyes, burning through to the back of your skull as the hood comes down around your face.

You shake, you cry, you plead to any being who will listen to your anguished prayers. And then, without warning, it comes.

The first jolt stops your heart mid-beat, the next, in an instant, freezes your muscles solid. You feel the warmth between your legs as your bowels burst. You smell your own burning flesh and fouled clothing as the current courses through your body.

You convulse, your eyes bulging and your brain exploding, your genitals shriveling and your lungs collapsing, your tongue swelling and your limbs twisting, your ears ringing and your bones melting, your blood boiling until finally . . .

Blackness.

Eric B. Olsen

This is another story with a clear inspiration for me. The segment of Creepshow *called "They're Creeping up on You" with E.G. Marshall, was a real jaw dropper for me when I first saw it in the theater. Bugs and spiders have always creeped me out, and I certainly felt for old E.G. up there on the big screen. I had been to Hawaii a couple of times and had seen some big cockroaches scurrying around the sidewalks in Honolulu, skinny and a couple of inches long. But it wasn't until I moved to Los Angeles briefly in 1983 that I saw a gigantic cockroach about four inches long and an inch across, big and fat, lumbering across the wall one night, and moved out of that house shortly after. "Bugged" was written in 1991 and I sent it to a couple of small horror magazines and received the standard rejections. The last names of the two characters, Harvey and Ted, came from teachers I had in grade school, and the name of the chemical plant was the last name of my junior high P.E. teacher.*

Bugged

"Goddamn, it's cold out there," said Harvey Slater as he brushed a few snowflakes from the wispy strands of grey hair still left on his head.

Harvey's partner, Ted Dassell, laughed as he shrugged on his coat. "At least you don't have to worry about bugs."

"Damn straight."

Harvey walked over to the counter in front of the small bank of closed-circuit monitors and set down his black lunch pail. Then he took the cushion from under his left arm, tossed it on the swivel chair, and began to shed his winter clothing.

When Ted had finished with his hat, gloves and scarf, he headed for the door. "Night, Harv."

"Night, Ted."

"Have a good one."

"You, too."

Harvey hesitated with his jacket until the door had opened and shut with Ted on the other side. The space heater on the floor hadn't come on yet, so he kicked it, and the familiar hum and pings, combined with the orange glow of the elements, finally induced him to remove his coat.

Harvey Slater worked the night shift at the gatehouse of Lacroix Chemical's Tacoma plant. The day shift ended at five, with a skeleton crew working the plant at night to handle the deliveries that continued around the clock. Harvey came on at six—the gatehouse shift was staggered back an hour so they wouldn't be changing during the end of the plant's regular shift. Anywhere from three to twelve empty tanker trucks rolled in through the gates every night, and rolled back out again filled to the brim with Lacroix chemicals.

Lacroix had a lot of products on the market but the ones Harvey was familiar with were their insecticides. With the other company's products, you could spray until the can was empty and the damn bugs acted like you were giving them a bath. But not with Raticate. Raticate was Lacroix's best-selling bug spray, and when you hit one of those six-legged suckers with that stuff, they knew they were dead. Harvey even kept a can of Raticate on the shelf above the coat rack for the occasional insect that strayed into the gatehouse.

Harvey pulled a clipboard out of the drawer under the monitors and filled in the date, January fifteenth, and his start time, six, on a fresh sheet of paper. Then he proceeded to record the movements of the plant on each of the eight monitors. Only two showed anything, the loading dock, where currently there were four tankers waiting to be filled, and the parking lot, where Ted was heading out to his car.

The workers all wore white, chemically treated coveralls to protect them from spills, and the ones who were directly responsible for filling the trucks sported white masks to protect against inhaling fumes. Crappy work, Harvey thought. He liked his job as a security guard just fine. When he was finished jotting notes on the clipboard, he adjusted the cushion on the swivel chair and fished his thermos out of his lunch pail.

After pouring the red thermos-top full of steaming joe, he leaned back in his chair and took a sip. Harvey always liked to start out his shift with coffee, especially on a frigid bitch of a night like this one. There had been a couple of snow flurries earlier, like the one he'd been caught in just as he arrived, but there was no snow on the ground yet. That was just as well; he hadn't gotten around to putting the studded tires on his Pontiac station wagon this fall.

Most winters were fairly mild in the Northwest and it was usually a surprise when there was snow. The rest of the year was chilly and wet and that was the way Harvey liked it; it kept the bugs away. Harvey was closing in on fifty-five. Lacroix didn't have a mandatory retirement age and that was good, too. Harvey wasn't sure what the hell he would do with himself if he had to retire.

He didn't have a wife or kids, and spent most of his free time down at the Ace of Spades Tavern near the port, watching sports with his buddies. On weekends Harvey drove north to Seattle to watch the Seahawks, the Mariners, or the Sonics, having season tickets for all three. And if nothing else was shaking, there was always the boob tube to keep him company. It wasn't the most exciting life a person could have, but he wasn't asking for a refund, either.

Harvey had plenty socked away in the bank and some of his buddies down at the Ace said he should think about retiring to Florida or California. No, sir. Who'd want to live in one of those cockroach-infested states with mosquitoes the size of small birds and horse flies the size of nickels? And any year them damn killer bees were going to be swarming across the Texas border. No, thank you, sir. Harvey Slater had been born in the Pacific Northwest and here was where he was going to die.

A half-hour later the phone rang: one of the trucks would be coming through any minute. When the tanker truck rolled up to the gate the driver jumped out and ran up to the gatehouse for Harvey to sign him out. There had been a time, years ago, when the drivers expected the security guard to leave the warmth of his office to sign his manifest. Harvey had put a stop to that. New drivers helped; he hadn't given them a chance to pick up the bad habits of their predecessors. They were all trained now.

Harvey slid open the window in the door, signed the driver out and handed the paperwork back to him, then opened the gate and sent him on his merry way. He did another check on the monitors—everything was fine—before pouring himself some more coffee and perusing the latest issue of *Sports Illustrated.*

Suddenly something buzzed in front of Harvey's face. His body instantly stiffened, a whimper escaping his throat as the chair began to coast backward and hot coffee sloshed all over his pant leg. Then it buzzed him again and Harvey was out of his chair like a shot. The plastic thermos cup hit the floor with a splat and Harvey was waving his hands in front of his face with fright, his head bobbing and weaving to avoid contact with the thing.

Harvey stood in the center of the gatehouse, his body quivering and his heart racing. He could feel the blood pumping through his neck at a surprising velocity as his eyes frantically searched for the intruder. At last he saw it: a moth. A huge, white moth, goddamn it, at least two inches long and as big around as his pinky.

"Why you son of a bitch," he said angrily, at the same time trying to keep his knees from knocking together. "You're gonnna be sorry you ever came in here."

Slowly Harvey made his way toward the coat rack, his eyes never leaving the fat, sleek body of the moth. When he reached the shelf, his arm snaked up and his hand wrapped around a large, 16-oz can of Raticate. On top was a big red button with a cone on the end to aim the death spray.

The moth hadn't moved since alighting on the ceiling near the naked bulb of the gatehouse. Harvey shook that can and placed his right index finger on the trigger and aimed. But as soon as he had depressed the button, the moth had taken off.

The can of Raticate produced a five-foot stream of concentrated pesticide. The side of the can was clearly posted with a skull and crossbones, and directions to seek medical attention immediately upon contact with skin or eyes, or if consumed. But as the giant moth fluttered around the gatehouse, Harvey's fingers never left the button on top of the can. He trailed the insect with a stream of Raticate that hosed down everything from the monitors and his clipboard to the windows and the door; it was dripping from the ceiling onto the bare wooden floor, onto the counter, the seat, and into Harvey's coffee cup. One particularly vigorous jet of Raticate had splashed the inside lid of Harvey's lunch pail and, as he chased the moth around, was being sponged up by the Wonder Bread in Harvey's baloney-and-mustard sandwich.

Finally Harvey had the thing trapped in the back corner of the gatehouse, and if the Raticate hadn't killed it, it most certainly would have drowned. When at last he stopped spraying, the can was nearly empty. His finger, which had been white as he compressed the button, was now red and tingling. The can was cold from the release of its contents and he dropped it to the floor.

Harvey had no idea how long he'd been standing there staring at the dead moth, when the bleat of an air horn made him scream. He clamped his hand over his mouth but it was too late; the scream had escaped. Now he took a quick look over at the counter and saw that at some point during his little dance with the moth, he had knocked the receiver off of the phone.

He walked over and replaced it, then walked out the door to sign the driver's manifest without remembering that he didn't do that anymore.

"Hey," said the driver over the idle of the truck's diesel engine, "Sorry about that."

"What?" said a bewildered Harvey as he scrawled his name on the papers.

"Didn't mean to scare you like that. We tried to call but there was no answer. Foreman told me to go on ahead."

The cold air had started to revive Harvey. "No problem." He said. "I was just taking a sit, if you know what I mean." The driver nodded his understanding. Harvey waved as he headed back into the gatehouse. "Have a good one."

Taking a sit; that was a laugh. The last thing Harvey would ever do was squat down in that outhouse of a chemical toilet in the back of the gatehouse, pants around his ankles, exposed to flies and mosquitoes and God only knew what else. No, sir. He did his business before he left for work, and if something came up during, and he had to hold it until he got home again, so be it.

The cloying scent of bug spray assaulted him as he opened the door, but Harvey went right to the control panel and opened the gate. The truck pulled put and then he closed it again. First things first. Now he could turn his attention back to that damnable bug. He picked his coffee cup off of the floor and set it on the counter, then fished out a couple of rags from the drawer to wipe off his cushion.

When the space heater came on he immediately shut it off. He sure as hell didn't want to be fumigated and opened the two windows to air the place out. But none of that took care of the moth. It was all Harvey could do to take a piece of cardboard and scoop up the dead insect. He didn't want to look at it, but if he wasn't watching and the thing rolled down onto his hand, he was pretty sure he would vomit. He flung it out the window and, after a moment's hesitation, tossed the cardboard out after it.

When he glanced at the clock on the wall, he couldn't believe it was already time to take another reading. Harvey walked over and sat in his chair, then pulled himself up to the counter and poured himself another cup of coffee from his thermos. It had cooled off some in the past few hours but he took a long pull, refilled, and sipped the rest while he jotted down his observations. Damn, this place is a mess he thought, and wiped what he could from the screens with a rag.

After the reading, Harvey went over every inch of the gatehouse, and when he had assured himself that there were no more bugs lying in wait for him, he shut the windows and kicked on the space heater. He was hungry from all his exertion and gobbled down his baloney sandwich, even though the smell in the gatehouse made it taste like bug spray. Then he topped off his cup with the last of the coffee and for the first time that night, had a chance to relax.

Absent-mindedly he looked at the monitors and watched the men in their white suits buzzing around the tanker trucks as they filled them with various Lacroix chemicals. He was still shivering, even after finishing the coffee, and he turned to see if the heater had shut off, but it was still glowing orange. Harvey stood up anyway and turned it on high. He didn't want it shutting off before the place had had a chance to heat up properly.

But a half-hour later he was still cold. Harvey had even gone so far as to move his chair over in front of the heater. It hadn't helped very much, though, He put his hands up to his cheeks and his face felt flushed and hot. Fever, he thought. He'd left the windows open too long and he'd caught a damn cold. The place was probably hot as an oven now, but Harvey was still shivering. And though he knew he should, he couldn't make himself turn down the heater.

Before long Harvey had something else to worry about: the tension in his bladder. The coffee had worked its way through his system right on schedule. Normally that wasn't a problem. There was a landscaped spot against the main building where a light bulb had been burnt out for as long as he'd been working here. Pissing outside was indefinitely preferable to unburdening himself in the outhouse. It was just that he was so cold. Putting the crimp in his bowels was no problem, but the bladder—that demanded immediate attention.

He mentally prepared himself for the trudge into the cold and then stood up and put on his jacket. But when Harvey Slater looked outside, his bladder took care of itself and a dark stain began to spread out from his crotch, temporarily warming his thighs.

What Harvey saw were moths, billions of them, swarming all over the gatehouse. "Jesus," he breathed, and stumbled away from the window. They were white, like the one he had killed earlier, only smaller, and when they flew against the glass they almost seemed to melt as more moved in to take their place.

Something clattered at his feet and when he looked down he instinctively grabbed the can of Raticate. He shook it, but it was almost empty, and besides, it wasn't going to do much good against the hordes of insects that were trying to get in, trying to poison him, kill him and then eat his flesh. He threw the can down and didn't notice when it rolled up against the space heater.

What the hell was he going to do? Harvey thought as he paced the tiny cabin, every now and then allowing his eyes to verify the swarms of moths on the other side of the glass. Would they attack all night long? Would anyone be able to get him out of here? Supposedly they were harmless, but you never knew with a goddamn bug. Besides, this could be a deadly new strain that no one had ever heard of. What the hell was he going to do?

He could call the foreman. But as soon as Harvey looked at the monitors he knew that it was too late. He sat down heavily in his chair and put his head in his hands; the sight on the screen was too horrifying to look at again. Giant white moths were fluttering over the tanker trucks. The loading crew was gone and Harvey didn't even want to think about what could have happened to them. The moths were gigantic, their bodies thick and segmented, nearly six feet tall, and they could barely keep themselves airborne.

Harvey looked outside and his heart began to dance in his chest. The swarm was gone now. He looked one more time at the monitor and saw that the smaller moths were flying around the giant ones at the loading dock. They must be preparing for an attack. The tiny ones are telling the giant ones where I am, he thought. He had to protect himself. He couldn't just sit here and let himself be eaten alive. He had to move and attack them first, before they could organize and descend upon him.

Harvey was going to need something much more powerful than a can of bug spray, though. He pulled open a drawer beneath the counter and eyed the revolver and the box of shells that were lying there innocently by themselves. The company didn't want their security guards carrying weapons—less chance of accidents that way—but they did recognize there might be a time when a guard would need to have one available, thus the revolver in the drawer.

Harvey picked up the gun and, with a flick of his wrist, swung out the chamber, giving it a playful spin with his other hand. Then he pulled out the box of shells and filled each empty hole with a bullet before snapping it shut. After slipping the box into his shirt pocket, Harvey stood and eased the gun into the waistband of his trousers, walked to the coat rack and put on his jacket, and then stepped out of the gatehouse into the frigid night air.

There were dead moths scattered across the pavement and on the shrubs and grass around the main building. Harvey looked furtively into the sky, but there was no sign of any more and he walked quickly to the three-story cinder block structure trying unsuccessfully to ignore the crunch of tiny white bug bodies beneath his feet. He cut through landscaping where he usually pissed not even noticing the frigid wetness in the fork of his crotch.

He was sweating heavily now. He had to take the long way around the building so that the giant moths wouldn't be able to see him coming. He adjusted the gun and smiled. "They shouldn't have left me," he muttered under the icy plume of his own breath. "It wasn't fair. They knew I couldn't get away." Harvey was speaking, of course, about his brother Troy and his buddies Julius and Mitch. Troy was two years older than Harvey and had been killed in Korea. As for the other two, he didn't know what had ever become of those particular juvenile delinquents.

It was supposed to have been a game, hide-and-seek, and Troy was going to let him join in with his friends, in the woods behind their house. Except that when Harvey had turned and closed his eyes against a tree to start counting, the three of them grabbed him instead. They sat him down in the dirt and tied him to a tree. They laughed at him for a while—Julius had even spit on him—and when they were bored of that they simply ran off and left him.

Harvey was only eight years old, and he remained tied up for six hours. During that time alone, trapped and tied up, bugs had crawled across his body. Ants, spiders, beetles, and potato bugs by the thousands, it seemed, paraded in and out, over and across his clothes and skin. He had cried at first, and pissed himself, but he hadn't started screaming until it got dark, and he could only feel them crawling on his body.

When Harvey hadn't shown up for dinner, his father had come looking for him. In response to his screams, his father finally found him in the woods. He untied him and tried for days to find out what had happened. Troy was quizzed unmercifully as well, but neither of them told. It had been forty-seven years since that little kid had emerged from the woods, snot crusted on his upper lip, in clothes he would never wear again . . . but he was back. Troy might be dead, but those bugs weren't, and it was time for revenge.

Harvey had only made it to the far side of the building from the gatehouse when a seizure hit him. He doubled over, holding his stomach, as white-hot pain raced through his body and sent him into the grass. The pain was intense, but he would not shout. No, sir. They would love to see him begging for mercy but he was damned if he would give them the satisfaction. His body seized again, infinitely painful, but smaller and more manageable this time.

It took a few minutes for Harvey's breathing to go from quick and shallow to slow and deep. Finally, he was able to stand up. But he could not straighten up. His spine, it seemed, was not going to cooperate. It didn't matter, though; he could still walk, and he could still make them pay. Harvey wasn't cold anymore, and shed his coat, pulling out his shirttail to cover the gun. He was almost there.

Harvey stopped at the far corner of the building, his body hunched over and sweating profusely, and looked around. There they were: half a dozen giant, mutated moths. The smaller ones were gone now, probably attacking the gatehouse, he thought. Well, they were welcome to it. He gently lifted the revolver from out of his waistband and checked the chambers. He had six shots, one for each of them. If he needed more, the heavy box in his front pocket ought to finish the job nicely.

As he was about to come around the corner and fire, he suddenly had doubts. Where the hell do you shoot a goddamn moth? He thought for a moment and then decided, head shot. If it was good enough for a man, it should easily work for a bug. Then Harvey hobbled around the corner, not realizing he had a limp. He aimed at the closest one, squeezed off a round and hit it right between its beady little eyes.

Even over the noise of trucks and machinery, the shot had clearly been heard. The other moths froze for a second, looking at the gore-soaked head of the one he had hit as it lay fluttering on the ground. Then they scattered.

Two times a month Harvey and Ted loaded up the Pontiac and drove out to the firing range to hone their skills with the revolver. Harvey was the better of the two by far, and long ago they had stopped betting on the results of their target practice. And now, severely hunched, his neck twisted and tongue lolling out of his mouth, Harvey went down on his good knee and squeezed off the other five shots.

His second kill came when one of them fluttered over to help the first and Harvey nailed him in the middle of his segmented chest. Number three got it in the back, right between the wings, as it was attempting to fly away. And four and five were considerate enough to flap out from behind one of the trucks, right into his line of fire: two more head shots.

Now Harvey sat back on his haunches and laughed. Oh, they had tried to play tricks on him. Every once in a while they had flickered in his vision and looked like men, but he wasn't fooled. Harvey had read how moths, even more than most insects, have camouflage to protect themselves. Some look like tree bark; one even has spots on its wings that look like eyes, and now these giant moths. They bore a strange resemblance to men.

Movement in the corner of his eye to the right silenced Harvey. There were more. Brown ones. They had looked at him and then disappeared around the corner. He took out the box of ammunition and shook the contents onto the pavement. Then he pushed out the chamber and dumped the empty shells, replacing each hole with a fresh bullet.

When Harvey tried to stand, he couldn't; his legs would not support his body. But he couldn't be stopped while there were still more of them, and he began to crawl. On hands and knees Harvey made his way around the loading dock on the end of the building. He could see the gatehouse now but no sign of the giant brown moths. The revolver was still in his hand and it skittered across the ground as he dragged the barrel against the cement.

He saw movement again and raised the gun high enough to get off a shot, but he had no idea if he'd hit anything. Harvey's pants had worn through in the knees, leaving twin wakes of blood behind him as he continued to crawl. He was looking in the windows of the side of the building when a sound like a gunshot went off in front of him.

Those bastards, he thought, those fucking bugs are shooting at me. What Harvey didn't see was the flames that began to engulf the inside of the gatehouse. By then his eyes had something new to focus on: the little moths were back. Everywhere they swirled around him darting and diving at his head. They were trying to confuse him so that he couldn't kill the giant brown ones.

They were loud, too, emitting a sound like high-pitched sirens. He tried to lift the gun from the cement but his hand wouldn't move. Red lights were flashing and the brown moths flew past him with large red egg sacs on their bellies and began to spray their eggs on the gatehouse.

He tried to move but the tiny moths kept coming. Then Harvey's body fell over onto the freezing cement and he began to scream as the white insects blanketed his body. Finally, mercifully, Harvey Slater curled up like a bug and died.

The Hostage

You push the door open gently and a soft breeze is there to greet you. In it you can smell the city: car exhaust, rotting garbage, dust, food from somewhere. And suddenly you remember how hungry you are.

It's been raining and there are puddles about and you consciously avoid stepping in them. You slip once but then catch yourself. Your stomach has jumped up to your throat and your whole body is jittery, so you stand for a moment to collect yourself, shaking off the fear of almost falling down.

The fresh air feels good in your nostrils; it's been a long time. Just then a bird flies overhead and you watch it until it is out of sight. Again you twist the rope that cuts into your wrists, and the raw skin beneath protests. The gun in your back is insistent so you continue on.

Tarpaper crunches underfoot as you walk and you wonder absent-mindedly if someone's roof will leak after this. Not too much farther now, but you continue the pace you have set. Once you reach the edge, you stop.

The gag is finally removed. You had intended to scream at this juncture but you are so stunned by the sensation of your mouth being able to close that you forget. You can almost taste the air now and for the moment that's all there is, until your hands are freed, and then all you want to do is hold your wrists, kneading them, working the blood back into your cold hands.

At this point, the push on your back is almost a surprise, but of course it's not; it's the reason you're here. You wave your arms in a futile attempt to catch your balance until your body, almost so weak that you weren't able to walk out here, resigns itself.

The sky whirls around you as gravity begins to pull and you become dizzy as you close your eyes. There's nothing in your stomach to vomit and it simply knots up instead. Your bowels, also void of anything, do the same. You're glad you can't see; you don't really want to know anyway. The end will come soon enough. You think about screaming but you're far too weak for that now. Perhaps you've even passed out. Your ankle snapping as you reach the pavement, though, convinces you that you haven't.

Before you have time to think your knee bends forward and shatters, driving your hip joint up out of its socket. Your body, however, continues its downward trajectory. Your arms reflexively reach out to break the fall and they, in turn, are broken.

When your chest finally hits, your ribs are snapped and driven through your lungs and heart. The whipping action of your torso has also ruptured several disks in your back and severed your spinal cord but it happened so fast that you didn't have time to feel the pain in the first place.

Your neck is bent backward, broken, and finally, centrifugal force lashes your head against the sidewalk, blood, brain and bone spattering in a starburst design across the pavement on a balmy August afternoon.

You are dead now, but some part of you continues to fall, deeper and deeper toward the earth's core. You open your eyes and you see nothing but a light, just a pinpoint at first, but becoming larger as you plunge toward it. Is it the center of the earth? Perhaps this is why they bury people when they die. But then another thought crowds that one out: perhaps this is why people live.

Eric B. Olsen

"Is It Live, or Is It Memorex?" is the one story in this collection that I genuinely have no idea what inspired me. If I had to guess, I would say that one of my favorite novels of all time, Replay *by Ken Grimwood, factors into the story in some way, especially the way in which the protagonist is unprepared for the disappearance of his daughter when his life replays again. But I've always been fascinated by video technology. I can remember vividly back in 1984, as a college student without two nickels to rub together, being obsessed with the idea of owning a VCR. When I finally bought one at Fred Meyer—on credit—I took it home and immediately set the thing up. I distinctly remember hitting record for a few seconds while a dog food commercial ran on the television. Then I hit rewind and there was the commercial again. For someone who used to record the audio tracks of movies onto a portable cassette deck to listen back to, videotape was like a miracle. Interestingly, while I used to make home movies when I was in high school, I never owned a video camera later in life. I was always much more interested in films and television than recording real life. The story was written in 1989 and was sent out to* Weird Tales *as well as a handful of small magazines. These days the only thing really similar is the movie* Click, *in which the protagonist can fast forward his life. Or possibly bits of* Groundhog Day, *where Bill Murray doesn't have to worry about breaking the law because his day will start over again at the beginning.*

Is It Live, or Is It Memorex?

"Attention, K-Mart shoppers," burst the nasal voice from the store PA system. It was the day after Thanksgiving and the store was jammed with people, but Joe Findley was on a mission.

Just last summer he'd bought himself a new video camera. This weekend his wife, Frances, was throwing a party at their home and, even though Joe hadn't used the camera since the day he'd bought it, she wanted him to record the event. Joe had used his last blank tape to record the colorized version of *Casablanca* and was here to replenish his supply.

After making his way through the crowd he emerged in front of the rows of blank videotapes. He sighed. All of the inexpensive ones were gone; the only tapes that remained were ridiculously overpriced. Joe had tried them all before and found that they were of only marginally better quality than the cheaper ones.

He was about to turn and head over to Fred Meyer when, down in the corner of the display, he spied an unwrapped cassette and stooped over to pick it up. It was obviously of extremely high quality—probably a ten- or fifteen-dollar tape—but the big red sticker on the front read ninety-nine cents.

He put the tape back. It must be defective, he thought, but then immediately reconsidered. It's got a price tag on it, so it must work. And, what the hell, it's not like I'm gonna be recording *Citizen Kane* or anything. So Joe took the tape to the checkout and stood in line.

Saturday night at the party Joe loaded the new tape into his video camera and began to record the festivities. At least forty people had shown up. Most were drinking heavily and the conversation was lively as Joe snaked his way through the house with the camera.

At the bar downstairs a couple of men whom Frances worked with were making like bartenders, mixing drinks for the whole crowd. They mugged for the camera and performed a lame imitation of Bryan Brown and Tom Cruise in *Cocktail.* A half bottle of gin lost its life for the cause.

After making his way back upstairs to the dining room, Joe came upon a dozen or so people dishing up plates at the buffet table. All of them smiled and waved, a friend of Joe's from the office told a dirty joke, and then Joe moved on to the living room.

A couple was kissing on the couch and Joe zoomed in for a close up; everyone laughed. Next to the couch a group of men were discussing why the Seahawks were having such a lousy season, and in another corner four people chose that moment to burst into spasms of laughter. Joe panned his camera to catch all the action. Next, it was out to the kitchen.

Frances was leaning over the sink, rinsing out a towel from the gin spill, while Carol and Anita were busy pulling trays from the refrigerator and off of the stove to restock the buffet table. They all served up obligatory smiles and Joe moved on to the den.

The big-screen television was glowing, playing one of the tapes in Joe's vast video collection. Fay Wray was being tied up between two poles by some fierce-looking natives and King Kong was about to make his entrance. But just as he did, Dave Howard, who was obnoxious even when he wasn't drunk, sloshed his drink on the projection console as he set it down and beat his chest in front of the screen in imitation of Kong. He stumbled on his way back to the couch, catching his foot on the power cord, and yanked the VCR off of the TV set. Several people reached out to save it, but it fell to the floor with a loud clang, instantly turning the screen to snow.

You asshole, Joe thought as he captured the whole scene on tape. He had always hated Dave but he usually put up a front for the sake of his wife; Frances was best friends with Dave's wife Anita. But now he let his hatred boil up to the surface.

"Goddamn it, Dave! Watch what you're doing."

"What the hell's up your ass, Findley?" Dave slurred.

The other guests in the room were visibly embarrassed by what had happened. Someone finally picked up the wounded VCR and put it back on top of the TV console.

"If it's fuckin' broke, bill me for it," Howard said as he pushed his way past Joe. From the hall he heard a belch.

After all the guests had left, Joe tinkered with the broken video recorder for about an hour. Frances was already in bed by the time he decided to give up. He finally hooked the video camera up to the television instead, so that he could play back his recording of the party.

Joe smiled broadly as he watched all of his friends having fun. It had been a great party, VCR breakage excluded, and Joe was soon laughing out loud at the antics of his friends. He sobered up when the camera entered the den in time to catch Fay Wray screaming in front of Kong. But the scene Joe remembered never happened.

Kong took Fay into the jungle, the camera pulled back to catch the group holding up its glasses in a toast, and then it swung around to capture more of the party. Joe jumped out of his seat and rewound the tape back to his entrance into the den. His mouth dropped open as he watched the scene a second time. He rewound it again, and again, and again. Dave Howard was gone!

Joe turned, heading for the bedroom to get Frances, when his eye caught the wounded VCR on top of the TV. He stopped for a second and scratched his head, considering the possibilities. His heart was beating a little faster now as he tentatively moved back toward the camera.

He rewound the tape and watched the scene again, this time keeping his eyes fixed on the VCR on the screen. Nothing happened to it because Dave Howard wasn't there to knock it off the TV console as he had earlier that evening.

Joe unhooked the camera from the TV and looked around for another tape. *Casablanca* was still on the coffee table and he pushed it into the broken VCR. He reconnected the leads to the machine and pressed the "play" button. Suddenly Claude Rains and Conrad Veidt materialized with crystal clarity.

Joe shuddered; it worked perfectly now. He watched for a while and then finally shut off the power. That's the weirdest thing I've ever seen, he thought. Still shaking his head, he slowly climbed the stairs to the bedroom.

The next morning Joe came down to the kitchen to find his wife putting away glasses out of the dishwasher. He grabbed a clean mug from the top of the rack and poured himself a cup of coffee.

"Damnedest thing happened last night," he said, leaning against the counter, still groggy with sleep.

"What's that?" said Frances.

"Well, I was watching the tape I made of the party—"

"Oh, how did it turn out?"

Joe chuckled as he remembered the gin bottle smashing on the floor, to the chagrin of the bartending team. "Fine, fine. It's just that in one spot . . . when I was taping the den . . ."

"Yes?" Frances stopped what she was doing and looked at Joe.

"Well . . . on the tape . . . Dave was gone."

"Dave who?" she said, pulling out a drawer to put away the silverware.

"Dave Howard," Joe said, but Frances blinked at him vacantly. "Dave Howard!" he repeated, almost shouting.

"Okay! I heard you the first time. I'm sorry I don't remember everyone you've introduced me to."

Anger bloomed quickly inside of Joe, but he just as quickly regained his composure. "I don't know what you thought I said, but I'm talking about Dave Howard."

Frances stopped with a fork halfway to the drawer and turned to Joe. "Why do you keep insisting I know this person?"

Joe slammed his mug down on the counter. Coffee sloshed over the side, burning his finger and making him even angrier. "Jesus Christ! Are you gonna stand there and pretend you don't know who Dave Howard is?"

"Don't get pissed off at me, Joe," she said as she ripped a paper towel from the roll and set the sheet under Joe's mug, "just because your *video* equipment doesn't work right."

Joe shook his head in exasperation. "I'm not talking about the *video* equipment, I'm talking about *Dave Howard.*"

"Well I'm sorry," she whined sarcastically, "but I don't know any *Dave Howard.*"

"You gotta be shittin' me!"

Frances whipped her head around to glare at Joe. He could tell that she would storm out of the room if he pushed her any further. Then he saw her leather-bound address book on the counter, still sitting out from when she had written the invitations two weeks before. "Okay, you wanna play games? That's fine with me."

He grabbed the book and began riffling through the pages, Frances looking on as though he had gone completely insane. He flipped once through the H's, and then a second time. "Where the hell is Anita's address?"

Frances nudged him out of the way, turned a head a few pages and said, "There."

"What's Anita's address doing in the J's?"

"That's where I normally put the Joneses."

"But her last name is Howard. She's married to *Dave Howard!*"

At this point Frances tipped her head back and let out a bray of laughter. "Well that's just wonderful. I was beginning to think Anita would never get married. Still, I'm a little hurt that she didn't invite me to the wedding." Then she frowned at him and snapped the address book shut. "Oh, honestly, Joe."

Tiny droplets of sweat appeared on Joe's upper lip as Frances went back to her dishes. He grabbed his mug of coffee, not saying another word, and went into the den.

He played the tape again. It was just like the night before: Fay Wray, Kong, glasses raised, and then out. He went over to his desk and pulled put the phone book. There was no Dave Howard listed. He flipped the pages ahead and there in bold, black print was the name Anita Jones, at the same address where he knew she had lived with her husband.

Joe sat at his desk in confusion. How could you make up a whole person? And if you did, why would you want to make up an asshole like Dave? Jesus, he thought he was going crazy. But he wasn't crazy; Dave Howard had been at the party last night and had broken his VCR. It had happened. Just like that. So why, all of a sudden, did it seem as though he had never existed? He picked up the phone and dialed Anita's number. It rang twice before she picked it up. "Hello?"

"Hello, is Dave there?" said Joe, trying his best to disguise his voice.

"I'm sorry, but you must have the wrong number. There's no one here by that—"

Joe hung up the phone. He sat dazed as his three-year old daughter, Linda, walked into the room and crawled up on his lap. Linda had two older brothers, Brian and Kevin, who were outside tossing a football around. "How's my girl today?"

"Fine," Linda said proudly.

Joe continued to stare across the room, trying to sort out in his mind everything he knew about what had happened to Dave. The most obvious thing was that he hadn't shown up on the videotape. He felt Linda's hand on his stubbled cheek and said, "How would you like to help Daddy with an experiment?"

Linda nodded vigorously. Joe picked her up and carried her across the room, set her down on the couch and grabbed his camera. He put the tape of the party in and ran it forward to the end of the party. For several minutes he made a recording of his daughter and when he was finished, he pulled out the tape and stuffed it into the VCR.

There was Linda waving to her daddy from the screen. He stopped the tape. *Something* had happened last night—it wasn't his imagination—but the camera seemed to be working fine now. He thought about it some more and then decided to try and re-create the atmosphere of the previous night. He dug out his tripod and set it up near the desk, attached the camera and began recording. The *King Kong* tape was once again playing on the big screen and Joe beat his chest, dancing around like and ape, to the delight of Linda who clapped and squealed.

He ran back to the camera, took out the tape, ejected *King Kong* from the VCR, and pushed in the newly recorded footage. There he was on the screen, dancing around like he had fleas in his armpits while Linda cheered him in the foreground. Nothing. Joe racked his brain trying to remember what else had happened the night before. He winced when it came to him: the VCR. He hated to do it but it was the only other thing that had happened with Dave on the tape.

He put the cassette back into the camera and started recording. This time after dancing around he hooked his toe on the power cord and yanked the VCR off the TV. He closed his eyes as it crashed to the floor, a loud hiss accompanying the snow on the screen. King Kong popped out of the wreckage with part of the mangled tape still hanging out of the front of the cassette.

He picked up the machine as if it were a sick animal and placed it back on the TV. Walking back to the camera he thought, Jesus, maybe I *am* nuts. But when he rounded his desk he caught a glimpse of Linda, a look of intense concentration on her face. She was diligently pulling out foot after foot of videotape from the broken cassette.

"Linda! Stop that!" He ran over to her and grabbed the tape from her industrious little hands. "You know better than to play with Daddy's videotapes!" he scolded her. "Now go out into the kitchen and see if you can help Mommy."

Linda hopped off the couch and skipped out of the room, seemingly unaffected by her father's harsh words.

"Ah, shit," Joe muttered to himself, strands of now-ruined videotape heaped at his feet. He picked up the pile and pushed it into the wastebasket at his desk.

He stopped the tape in the camera and rewound it. Now that the VCR was really broken he had to reconnect the camera to the TV in order to watch the recording. There he was, doing the now-famous monkey dance. He could have cried as he watched the VCR fly off the TV. He watched himself pick it up and replace it on the console, his head shaking in regret, then head back to turn off the camera.

Joe turned the tape off and was beginning to unplug the cords when his heart rushed up into his throat. He could hardly breathe now, and sweat began to trickle down his body as he fumbled to reconnect the leads. He rewound the tape. His hand trembled as he pressed the "play" button, and he watch in horror as the same scene played out before his eyes. Linda was gone!

The door to the den burst open and Joe ran wildly down the hall. "Linda! Linda!" he shouted throughout the house. He opened doors and turned on lights, still shouting her name. He was heading upstairs when he met his wife coming down. "Frances! Is Linda with you?" Frances scrunched up her face and said, "Linda? Who's Linda?"

"Oh, God!" Joe screamed, and ran past her up the stairs. Frances dropped the laundry she was holding and followed him as he ran through the hall to Linda's bedroom. He pushed open the door and through teary eyes he could see that the room was barren, the musty smell of disuse filling his nostrils. A neatly made guest bed was pushed up against one wall, with a small night table and a lamp next to it.

He ran to the dresser and pulled out all the drawers: empty. He rushed over to the closet and threw the doors open: empty.

"What the hell is going on, Joe?" asked Frances, her tone confused and a bit alarmed. But Joe ignored the question, pushing past her back into the hall. He ran into the library that overlooked the living room and threw open the cabinets that were underneath the bookshelves.

When Frances caught up to him he was going through their photo albums, nearly tearing the pages out in desperation. When he was finished with one, he would toss it aside and begin rooting through another.

"Oh, my God! Oh, my God!" he wailed over and over. Behind him, Frances just stood and watched. When he was through with the last one Joe rushed past his wife, this time nearly knocking her down, but as he reached the end of the hall he froze. Staring back at him from an eighteen-by-twenty-four-inch frame was the portrait his family had posed for the year before. Joe and Frances were sitting next to each other with stupid-looking smiles on their faces while the boys stood in the back. But Joe's lap, where Linda should have been, was empty. Linda was gone!

Joe fell to his knees sobbing. Frances rushed to her husband and put her arm around him. "Joe," she said, nearly crying herself, "what's wrong?" But he pushed her away and collapsed on the floor, crying uncontrollably. Frances ran downstairs in a panic and out the door to get the neighbors.

She was gone! Linda was gone! His little girl, his only daughter—she was gone and it was *his* fault.

A week later Joe was still grieving over the loss of his daughter, but he grieved alone. To the world, including his wife Frances, Linda had never existed. In the interim, Joe had figured out the link between the disappearances of Dave Howard and Linda.

Every night after work he would come home and go to his den. He locked the door and watched the tape over and over. He had been irritated at Dave for spilling his drink on the console, but when Dave had pulled the VCR off the TV, Joe had become positively hateful. The same thing must have happened to his daughter when he had scolded her for ruining *King Kong.*

What a waste, he thought. I lost my daughter over a worthless videotape. Sitting on his desk was the tape in question, looking just as it had when it had come out of the broken VCR. A small loop of shiny tape stuck out at him like a tongue from the front flap of the cassette.

Ever since his outburst on Sunday, Joe had become more reclusive, sometimes sleeping all night in his den. He had great bags under his eyes and he was beginning to miss work frequently. Frances had tried talking to him about it but he always waved her off. He wanted to be alone. Most of Joe's nights consisted of sitting at his desk and contemplating the ramifications of his discovery. By the start of next week he had a plan.

Driving to work, his magic video camera sitting bedside him in the front seat, Joe pulled into the parking lot of K-Mart. He went inside, plucked the most expensive tape from the shelf and threw a twenty on the counter, not really caring how much the tape cost. He stuffed the change into his pocket and without looking drove to work. After parking, he unwrapped the fresh cassette and loaded it into his camera, then took the elevator up to the fourth floor of the building where he worked. He passed right by his work station, heading for the office of his supervisor, Marcy McMillian. She was a bitch. If anyone deserved to disappear off the face of the earth, she did. I might as well get my money's worth out of this, he thought, and knocked lightly on the door before entering.

"What's with the movie camera, Joe?"

The stupid bitch doesn't even know the difference between a movie and a video camera. She deserves to die, or whatever the hell happens to them. "It's a video camera, Marcy. Mr. Tucker thought it would be a good idea if we each taped a little holiday message for the Christmas party next week."

Marcy looked puzzled, but Joe hoisted the camera onto his shoulder and started recording before she had a chance to question him. "Okay, we're rolling."

During the taping he thought over and over about how much he hated Marcy, how much he despised her for taking his promotion, for lording her position over him every chance she could get, and for always taking credit for his ideas. "Bitch," he blurted out under his breath, just in case he had to speak out loud for it to work.

"What did you say?" Marcy asked.

"I think that's enough, Marcy. Thanks for the contribution. Mr. Tucker will really appreciate this."

He left before she could say another word. Joe was all smiles as he walked to his station. He sat behind his desk and rewound the tape. "Good-bye, Marcy," he said as he pressed the "play" button and held the viewfinder to his eye. But, no, there she was giving her insipid message about the company loyalty and departmental togetherness.

"Shit!" He slammed down the camera. What had he done differently? Why hadn't it worked this time? He looked over the walls in his cubicle and saw Marcy coming out of her office. She shot him a dirty glance and turned down the hall toward Tucker's office. He looked back down at the camera and then it finally hit him. "The tape!"

Joe drove back home as fast as his Civic would take him. Leaving the front door open when he entered the house, he ran to the den and over to the huge bookcases that housed his video collection. He opened the glass doors and pulled out the tape. A plain white tag with the word "Party" scrawled on it was the only thing that adorned the cassette. He ripped off the tag and held the black rectangular case in his hand like an idol. "The tape," he said smiling, and drove back to work.

He reloaded his camera in the elevator and headed straight for Marcy's office. Either this thing was going to work or he was going to be looking for a new job. He pushed open her door without knocking. The tape was rolling as he swung the camera around to catch her startled reaction.

"You stupid bitch!" he shouted at her. "You told him, didn't you?"

"Get out of here, Findley! I don't have to take that kind of shit from you."

"You told Tucker, didn't you?"

Eric B. Olsen

"Get out!" she screamed, and Joe stopped recording. He walked out the door and she stormed out after him, slamming it on her way to Tucker's office.

Joe hurried back to his cubicle and rewound the tape. He held his breath as he put the viewfinder up to his eye and pressed "play." "Ha, hah," he cackled with delight, as the only thing in the scene was an empty desk. She was gone. He put down the camera and smiled. "Yeah," he said, balling up his fist and pumping it in front of him.

A tap on the shoulder nearly startled him to death. He looked up. It was Tucker. His chest tightened as he imagined Marcy waiting in Tucker's office to fire him.

"Joe, I need to talk to you right now," said Tucker in a voice that was almost impossible to read.

"Yes?" answered Joe meekly.

"Why don't we talk in your office?" Tucker motioned toward Marcy's door and went inside. As Joe followed, he looked at the plaque on the door and his face lit up. There in black letters, engraved on a gleaming metal surface, was Joseph Findley, Supervisor.

Joe didn't usually spend much time in the seedier sections of town but tonight was different. He was going to take his discovery one step further. Sitting in his car across the street from a tiny convenience store, aptly named "Mom & Pop's Grocery," he thought about his situation.

Even with the raise in pay at the office, it wasn't enough. Instead of being under Marcy's thumb he was kowtowing to the department manager. It was bullshit. No matter how high he rose in the company, there would still be Tucker, and he would still be *working* for a living. No, drastic times called for drastic measures.

He looked across the street at the little store again. The old couple at the counter must be none other than Mom and Pop, he thought. Joe placed his hand gently atop the camera beside him. Sure it was risky; anything could happen. He *could* make them disappear right now. But if Mom and Pop should suddenly cease to exist, would the store still be there? Or, more importantly, what about the money? He had to do this right.

Joe aimed his camera through the glass storefront and zoomed in close so that he would catch only the couple on the tape. The man was about sixty, a bit overweight and balding, but he was fairly husky, at least six feet tall and running two hundred pounds. The woman, on the other hand, looked another ten years older, wispy, not much over one-twenty.

He shot several minutes of footage, concentrating on the anger that had been building inside of him since the disappearance of his daughter and focusing it on each of them. He set the camera back down on the passenger seat, rewound the tape, and waited.

Joe sat patiently, alternately clenching his fists and releasing them, until the flow of customers slowed to a trickle. He wouldn't need a lot of time, just a moment when the store would be empty. As the last customer was leaving the store, Joe was already shutting his car door and walking across the street.

He stepped inside and quickly scanned the aisles; the place was empty. He checked for surveillance cameras; there were none. Joe smiled. Stuffed in the back of his pants was the revolver that had been kicking around for years in his closet. He reached behind his jacket, pulled out the gun and bounded over the counter, grabbing the old woman by the neck and pointing the gun at her head.

"Open the safe, Pops, or I'll blow her fuckin' head off."

The old man froze, apparently wondering if Joe would really pull the trigger. The woman screamed and Joe tightened his grip until she was choking, clawing at his arm for relief. With this the old man put his hands up to his face. "Just don't hurt her," he said. "Please, you can have the money."

"Do it, then," Joe said, pushing the tip of the barrel into the woman's temple. The man bent underneath the counter and began to spin the dial of the safe. As soon as he cracked the door open, Joe pointed to gun directly at the old man's head. "Let's go Pops. I'm in kind of a rush today."

He watched as the old man stuck his hand in the safe. But instead of pulling out money, the man pulled out a gun. Joe didn't hesitate—in fact, he had fully expected something like this to happen—and put two rounds into the old man's head. While Pops was twitching on the floor, Joe brought the gun back up in front if him, turned his head, and blew the old woman's brains out.

Blood and gray matter splattered everywhere and he let the body slip to the floor. Out of his back pocket he pulled a laundry bag, emptied the safe and cash register into it, and drew the strings tight. He had been lucky; no one had even walked by the store. He stuffed the gun back into his pants, adjusted his grip on the sack and ran back out to the car.

He threw the sack onto the backseat and with bloody hands grabbed the video camera. Taking a deep breath he put the viewfinder up to his eye and pressed the "play" button.

Joe had expected to see an empty counter in the store but the counter on the tape was bustling with customers. He closed his eyes, letting the tape run, and laid his head back on the seat. Something must have gone wrong. The busy screen flickered a couple of times and the he shut it off. Joe balled his fists, afraid to look up. His heart was racing with thoughts of what he had just done.

He brought a hand up to wipe away a tear that was making its way down his cheek. His hand was clean. He brought the other hand up and bathed them in the light that was streaming through the windshield. He noticed his clothes were spotless as well. There was no blood anywhere.

Joe looked across the street to the place where the little store had been, but the little store wasn't there anymore. It was now a shiny new 7-11. He turned and grabbed the sack from the backseat. The laundry bag was clean as well. He opened it up; the money was still there. It *had* worked!

Joe started up the civic and slammed it into gear. He squealed out of his parking space and headed for home. He was making good time, perhaps too good, when he passed a cop. A few seconds later the blue lights were flashing in his rearview mirror. As Joe watched the police officer get out of the patrol car he reached over for the camera, then thought better and pulled his hand away.

I've got nothing to worry about, he reassured himself; the store is gone; Mom and Pop are gone, too. And the cloth bag with a wad of money in one corner? Well, it's nobody else's goddamn business what I have in that bag, not even a cop's.

The officer reached Joe's car and tapped on the window. Joe was looking straight ahead when he heard the muffled voice: "Please roll down your window, sir."

He did as he was told and a gust of freezing wind tousled his hair and made him shiver.

"Sir, are you aware that you were doing sixty in a forty-five-mile-per-hour speed zone?" the officer asked politely.

"Uh, no."

"I also noticed that your registration tabs have expired. May I see your license and registration please?"

Joe flipped down his visor and pulled out the registration card, then fumbled in his wallet for his driver's license. The officer shone his flashlight on the two slips of paper and said, "I'll be back in just a moment. Please wait here."

This is bullshit, thought Joe. In a few minutes he's gonna sashay over here all sweet as pie and slap me with a couple-hundred-dollar ticket. Bullshit! I probably didn't get much more than that from the grocery store.

Joe grabbed the camera and whipped around. The cop was almost back to the patrol car. He recorded him for a couple of seconds, rewound, and then watched the in the viewfinder the empty street behind him.

He put the camera down and looked: the cop and his patrol car were both gone. He flipped down the visor: the registration was still there. Then he pulled out and opened his wallet to just to see the picture on his license smiling back at him through the clear plastic window.

For the first time since the party, Joe really believed in the power he possessed and in his ability to use it. He squinted his eyes in concentration. This is just the beginning, he thought. It's time for something big, something really big!

Christmas Eve, Joe was sitting at his desk in the den going over several charts and lists that he compiled during the week. He had a friend who worked at a large bank downtown and Joe had managed to get himself invited to their Christmas party the day before, on the pretext he would chronicle the event with his video camera.

After every couple of introductions, he had made some excuse to leave the room to jot down the names and positions of the bank employees he had recorded, as well as their order of appearance on the tape. Now he was going to use the tape to rob the bank. His task would not be an easy one.

The one thing in his favor was the efficiency of the tape. It seemed to have a black hole effect; people disappeared without any noticeable change in the people or places around him. There was none of the ripple effect that was evident in *It's a Wonderful Life*. It was all very neat.

He needed to be able to make enough people disappear so that he could enter the bank safely. But he also had to make sure that it was the right people; he didn't want the bank, as well as its money-laden vault, to disappear along with them.

It had seemed at first like too much trouble, but he couldn't keep knocking off Mom and Pop grocery stores for a living. Joe wanted to make one huge score, destroy the tape and live happily ever after. It was *definitely* worth the trouble.

A knock on the door didn't even so much as raise his head from the papers on the desk. It was Frances. "Joe, can I use the video camera? I want to tape the boys opening their presents."

"Yeah, sure, it's over on the couch."

Early on Joe had wondered whether or not anyone else would be able to achieve the same results with the videotape that he had, but he'd decided not to risk it, or perhaps he just didn't want to know. Anyway, he had hidden the tape after every use so that there would be no chance of finding out.

Still buried in his paperwork, he heard Frances rummaging among his tapes for a blank one. There were three right in front. Then she left without saying a word, leaving Joe to his plans.

Frances had never been shown how to operate the video camera and at first had trouble getting it to record. But she was not going to ask Joe. For the past few weeks, living with him had been like living with a stranger. He had always had a chip on his shoulder against the world in general, but now he was moody and belligerent to her and the boys, that is when he wasn't holed up in his den. They didn't sleep together anymore, and a few days ago, for the first time in their fifteen years of marriage, Joe had hit her.

Frances was finally able to get the camera started and began to record the boys as they each opened a single gift, a Christmas Eve tradition in the Findley home. Brian, the oldest at twelve, opened the wristwatch that his parents had bought for him. Kevin, the ten-year-old, unwrapped a G.I. Joe doll given to him by his brother.

As the two boys admired their gifts, Frances panned the camera around to the rest of the living room that she had tastefully decorated herself. She was proud of her work, even if Joe didn't notice. He hadn't even helped with the tree this year so she and the boys had had to set it up and trim it alone. She was pulling back to view the tree when the shouts of the two boys caused her to turn the camera around in time to catch them exchanging blows. Instinctively she yelled, "Stop that, you two!" before releasing the record mechanism.

Without bothering to find out why they'd been fighting she ordered them up to their rooms to put on their jackets. They were all going to her parents' house for Christmas dinner. She didn't yet know how, but she was also going to try and get Joe to come along with them.

Frances was about to knock on the door of the den when, on a whim, she started up the camera and eased open the door. Joe was still hard at work and didn't notice her. "Smile!" she yelled. "You're on *Candid Camera.*"

Joe whirled around in his chair. "What the . . . Jesus Christ, Frances! Can't you see I'm busy? Now get the fuck out of here!" And as if that weren't enough he added, "Now!"

"I just came in to see if you wanted to go with me and the boys to my parents' house. They invited us for dinner."

At this Joe bolted out of his chair and grabbed the camera out of her hands. "I said, get the fuck out of here, and I meant it!" He stared at her coldly for several seconds, and it was all Frances could do to keep the tears that were welling up in her eyes from rolling down her cheeks. Joe ran his hand through his greasy hair, set the camera on the desk and sat back down. Frances quickly removed the tape and left with the boys.

An hour or so later, in a rage of anger, Joe threw the papers on his desk into the garbage. It would never work. The vault would always be closed no matter who was in charge. And, just as he had moved into Marcy's place, someone would always take the place of the people he eliminated.

He only had one option left. The ninety-eight-year-old founder of the bank had been feeling spry on the night of the party, and Joe had recorded plenty of footage of the old geezer. It would have to be like the "Mom & Pop" robbery. He would hold up the bank at gunpoint, clean out the vault as best he could in the short time available, and, as soon as he was out the door, he'd make the place vanish right off the motherfuckin' planet. If the founder of the bank didn't exist, he reasoned, neither would the bank.

Resolute, he stood and walked over to the glass cases that housed his video collection. He opened the doors and eyed *The Invisible Man.* It was right behind that tape that he had hidden . . . It wasn't there! He pulled out a few more tapes. *The Hustler, Angels With Dirty Faces, 2001, The Blue Angel.* It was gone!

Soon tapes were flying out of the case as he pawed his way through every shelf. The cassettes came cascading down around his feet until he set his hand upon *The Lady Vanishes.* His heart nearly stopped, his chest tightened up and he could barely breathe. Frances! She must have taken it.

Joe lunged for the phone. He lost his footing wading through the videocassettes and fell forward, nailing his head on the edge of the desk. He quickly pulled himself up from the floor. Blood flowed down his face as he fumbled with the phone, his hands shaking as he tried to call his in-laws. Wrong number. He slammed the phone down and rummaged in his desk for the phone book. The blood was stinging his eyes now, matting strings of hair against his forehead.

When he found the number he pounded it out on the phone and waited. The phone seemed to ring interminably. Finally Frances picked it up. "Hello?"

"Frances! What tape did you use tonight?"

"Well, hello to you, too."

"Answer me goddamn it. What tape did you use?"

"How the hell should I know? I just grabbed one that didn't have any writing on it."

Oh, God, Joe thought, did I forget to hide it the last time? "I'm coming over right now to get it."

"Honestly, Joe, I don't know what's happened to you in the last few weeks, but I think it would be better if you didn't come over. I'll bring the tape home with me tonight after we're done watching it."

"You're not watching it now are you?"

"Yes, dad wanted to—"

Joe's body started to shudder and he screamed into the phone. "Stop it! Shut the tape off now!"

"Don't yell at—"

"SHUT THE FUCKING TAPE OFF!"

Joe was instantly drenched with sweat as blood-mingled sweat dripped from his chin, and he was sure he had pissed his pants. He heard his wife faintly over the phone: "Would you stop the tape for a second, dad?"

"Listen, Frances," Joe said as calmly as he could. "I want you to bring the tape over here right now."

"You bastard. You can't talk to me like that and expect—"

"I don't have time to explain this to you now, but you have to bring that tape home."

"I'm not going to the leave the kids here just to bring you your stupid tape."

"What . . ." There was a brief pause. He had almost said, "What kids?" Joe was becoming light-headed from the loss of blood. In a monotone he asked his wife, "Are you there alone?"

"Why the hell do you care, you son of a bitch?"

"Please, Francis, just answer the question. Are you alone?"

"Of course not. I brought the boys," she answered angrily. "I certainly wasn't going to leave them there with you."

Joe couldn't speak as the tears that were burning in his eyes rolled hotly down his cheeks. He couldn't remember any boys. He couldn't remember their names, how old they would have been, anything. He remembered Linda, though.

It took a moment for him to realize him to that they were now childless and it was all his fault. He couldn't imagine what her grief would be like, or her anger at him for the loss of two or more boys. "I'm sorry Frances," he said. "I'm sorry for the way I've been acting lately. I want to come over there. We need to talk—"

"I don't see why this can't wait until we get home."

"Please. Francis, please. I have to come over and talk, okay?"

It was a few moments before she spoke. "All right."

"Just don't play the tape."

"My God, Joe, I don't see what that stupid tape has to do with any of this."

"Look," he said, trying to keep from shouting. "I promise I'll explain everything to you when I get there, okay? Just don't play the tape, okay?"

There was no reply. "Frances?"

"Okay," she finally answered, and Joe breathed a huge sigh of relief.

As Frances was finishing the conversation, her mother came into the kitchen. "Dad couldn't wait any longer, honey, but he wants to watch it again anyway, so . . ."

Frances stared blankly at the receiver in her hand when she realized she wasn't wearing her wedding ring. That was odd. She could remember distinctly putting it on this morning. Even when she and Joe were at their worst, she had never stooped so low as to remove her ring.

"What's the matter, Fran?" her mother asked her, and Frances finally hung up the phone.

"Oh, it's nothing. Joe and I just had another fight, that's all. He's coming over to talk. I hope that's okay."

Suddenly her mother's face took on a strange, puzzled look.

"What is it, Mom?"

Frances's mother looked up at her and asked in all honesty: "Who's Joe?"

The Funeral

You arrive by limousine, dressed in black, matching the vehicle. You don't want to be here. Two men help you from the car but you don't thank them. Your family has been taken from you and you are angry. It's not fair.

Driving While Intoxicated, that's what the police report said. And though it's maddening, the reason is less important than the fact that you will never spend another Christmas with them again. The tiny faces of your children will be frozen in your memory, never growing older, until they gradually fade with the advancing years.

As you approach the gravesite a light mist begins to fall. It's unseasonably cool for July. A few umbrellas go up from the more prepared in the crowd. Like you, they are dressed in black. Some are crying, though you are not. You can't.

The disbelief, even now, is overwhelming. Here you are, only feet from them, and yet there is nothing so wide in all of human experience as the chasm that separates them from you now. You have tried not to let the thoughts of that day punish you—they cannot change what has happened—but in another way, there doesn't seem to be punishment enough.

Independence Day. It was just the four of you, a picnic by the river—that was your idea and the two girls had loved it. You remember having to take the old station wagon—the previous owner had removed the seat belts and they were still in the back on the floor—because there was a problem with the thermostat in the sedan.

The water was cool and the sun hot. It was a day filled with hot dogs and firecrackers, the squeals of delight that only little girls can make, and crying over skinned knees and lost marshmallows in the fire. The beach was an entirely secluded spot that only you had known about and, at one point, while the girls were napping in the car, the two of you stole off into the woods to make love.

But in the end, which all good things must come to, you threw dirt over the campfire, packed up the leftovers, and sent the girls on one last search for stray candy wrappers and lone sandals. It was a fine day and you remember looking at your nose in the rearview mirror as you backed out, wondering if it would peel the next day. Now you can't remember if it ever did.

The preacher begins to spout off his inane dogma about the afterlife being such a great place, and watching from on high, and smiling down on the bereaved, and such bullshit that you wished like hell you could strangle him with your own hands and throw *him* in a fucking hole in the ground. You can't believe you permitted this. But then some other people begin to talk and you tune them out.

You remember coming up to that corner by the railroad tracks, the one you were always reading about in the paper. It seemed like every weekend someone was killed on that damned corner. There were reflectorized signs, there were guardrails, they had even gone so far as to lower the speed limit a mile before and a mile after, although you could never see what the problem was. But then you'd never been drinking so much, either.

You'd been drinking for the better part of the day and it hadn't seemed to really affect you. You'd been sweating it out, snacking on junk food—hell you'd even been swimming and had felt fine. But after dinner, while the kids were roasting marshmallows and you were waiting for it to get dark enough to light up the sparklers, that was when you really started knocking them back. It just didn't seem like that big of a deal, until you got to that corner.

You remember letting out a big yawn just as you were turning into it. You were ignoring the speed limit change, and one of the girls was kicking the underside of your seat. You reached back without looking to give her a smack, and missed, so you turned to look the next time.

Things happened pretty fast after that. There was the scream, you felt the gravel of the shoulder under your right front tire, you overcorrected, and then there were the headlights. Head-on collision. It was fairly routine after that. Sirens, ride in the ambulance, visit to the hospital, the usual. Dead on arrival. They are gone from you forever and the knowledge that is was your fault doesn't seem like enough punishment, so there's always the fact that the guy driving the other car was killed too.

There is a lull in the ceremony and finally, mercifully, the casket is lowered. It's almost over. They might be back to talk to this plot of ground but you doubt you ever will. Pain like this, once in a lifetime seems more than enough. Then they all pick up handfuls of dirt and toss them down on top of the varnished lid of the box that cocoons your lifeless body.

The girls are crying now and so you decide to cut out early. You're not sure where you're going and you're not sure you care. Your family will leave this place in a few minutes, go back to school, the job. In a few years there will probably be a remarriage, somebody else sleeping on your side of the bed, a new stepparent to read bedtime stories. And though it's the worst punishment imaginable, to be out of their lives forever, it still doesn't seem like enough.

Though I can't remember precisely, after twenty-five years, I have a feeling that the idea for my first short story was inspired by Stephen King's "One for the Road" from his Night Shift *collection, an episode left over from the novel* Salem's Lot. *I always liked the idea of that because it reminded me of "Dracula's Guest" by Bram Stoker in the way that it had been a remnant of an early draft of* Dracula. *Going into the story I had been thinking about ghosts and their territoriality, and I began to wonder why they couldn't haunt any area instead of something specific like a house. In my early literary efforts I always found it easier to write characters if I could think of specific people to model them on. At this time I was enamored with Elizabeth McGovern after seeing* The Bedroom Window *for the first time, and had probably re-watched* Stake Out *recently, which gave me the idea of Richard Dreyfuss as a detective—though a character named Brody also shows up from Steven Spielberg's* Jaws. *I simply switched the last names and started writing. I have a feeling that Peter Straub's* Ghost Story *was one of my inspirations, but some pretty obvious imagery from the Spielberg produced* Poltergeist *is in there too. "One More for the Road" has what I call an E.C. Comics ending, with a laughing, rotting corpse, and in the first draft it was a malevolent road that lured people in and killed them. Why a road, I have absolutely no idea. It was probably to justify the title. Fortunately, a magazine editor from Chicago suggested I change the ending and the story is the better for it. In fact, I was given a lot of good advice by editors when I first started writing and I always followed it. The other thing I learned from that story was not to use a setting I'd never been to before, though I did keep the Chicago setting of this story because that same editor commended me for my description of the Illinois countryside.*

One More for the Road

"What the hell is this?" asked police detective Richard McGovern, half irritated and half curious.

The flatfoot who had just slapped down the dilapidated file on McGovern's desk continued on his way as he yelled back his reply. "I don't write the shit—I just deliver it."

McGovern again turned to the object of his query: a yellowed and coffee-stained file that was dated May 22, 1913. A Post-it note with his name on it was stuck to the front, but no indication as to who had sent it or why.

Before he even had a chance to lift the cover, his phone rang. A body had turned up over near the Calumet Expressway. He threw the file back on his desk, grabbed his worn sports coat and headed for the door.

Richard McGovern was a homicide detective working out of the 32nd Precinct on the south side of Chicago. He was a short man at five-five, and many people accused him of joining the police force to compensate for his lack of physical stature. Perhaps it was true.

He had just missed serving in Vietnam, enlisting in '74 to avoid being drafted. He was still in boot camp when troops were withdrawn, but unlike the draftees he still had three more years left to serve in the army. The structure and discipline of the military appealed to him, though, and after his discharge he enrolled in the police academy. In 1978 he joined the Chicago Police Department, and in 1986 he received his gold shield.

McGovern was a twenty-five-year-old rookie cop when he married a secretary from a downtown public relations firm. They had no children. By the spring of 1991 Richard McGovern, now 39, hated his life. His job was more drudgery than joy and he found himself looking forward to retirement. His marriage wasn't much better.

He and his wife had grown apart over the years, both involved in their separate careers. Somewhere along the way they had stopped having sex, though McGovern couldn't have said exactly when. For the most part they stayed out of each other's lives, the mutual living arrangements enough to keep them together.

With a job and a marriage that he despised, there wasn't much incentive for McGovern to keep going, but each day he waded through them both, as if somehow things would spontaneously change for the better.

The body turned out to be one Roberto Delgado. A Cuban from Florida, Delgado was into drugs, prostitution, guns, you name it. He had a healthy rap sheet and McGovern had busted him a couple of times on assault charges. The rest of his day was spent going door to door trying to find witnesses. He didn't have much luck, and shortly after 2:30 he choked down a cheeseburger and soda. By the time McGovern rolled back into the precinct it was well after six.

Filling out reports an hour later he began to realize just how hungry he was. He zipped the last report out of his typewriter, took his jacket off the back of the chair and was about to leave when something caught his eye: that file. He hadn't thought about it all day. He snatched it off the cluttered desk and went home.

McGovern's wife was out when he walked in. The note on the table said that she was having dinner with a client, a euphemism for fucking her brains out if ever he'd heard one. Not that he cared . . . or did he? He supposed he should leave her, but he just didn't have the energy. And besides, at least he didn't know the guy.

McGovern pulled off his tie, unbuttoned his shirt and began to forage in the refrigerator for something to eat. He managed to find some lunchmeat that was on the verge of going bad. The cheese had a layer of fuzzy, green mold on it, which he laboriously sliced off, and the two slices of bread he scavenged were stale. By the time he had slathered the concoction with mustard to disguise the taste, another burger actually seemed appetizing.

Carefully balancing the sandwich atop a can of beer, he retired to the front room, flipped on the TV and, as he ate, began to read through the file.

A young woman named Elizabeth Dreyfuss had been killed in 1913. There seemed to be a plethora of information in the file but little to do with the actual circumstances of her death. There were interviews with relatives, all manner of speculation as to what might have happened, but no evidence. The case was still unsolved.

Her body had been pulled from the Calumet River, an apparent victim of an accidental drowning. There were contusions on her head and no water in her lungs, which the coroner on the case said indicated that she had been killed first and then dumped in the water, but the police could find no suspects and the case was simply left open. This was all very interesting but there was nothing here that he thought should warrant his attention, or anyone else's, after 78 years.

That was why the last few pages of the file puzzled him. They were a series of illegible notes on the case made by a detective Joseph Wells in 1952. But even this revelation wasn't enough to overcome the fatigue of another grueling day. When Joanne McGovern came home she found the TV glowing, the kitchen light on, and her husband snoring contentedly on the couch.

The next morning McGovern couldn't remember coming to bed the night before. He could hear his wife in the shower as he awoke, then dragged himself out of bed and into the kitchen to make some coffee. While it brewed he sat down at the table. Leaning back, he ran his hand through his hair and stared out into the living room thinking of nothing in particular. When he finally looked down he noticed the file was on the table in front of him.

After the coffee was ready he stood up and poured himself a cup. His wife was toweling herself off when he came into the bedroom wearing only his boxer shorts, a mug in one hand and the file in the other.

Joanne McGovern was two years older than her husband, yet even at forty-one her body was still firm and inviting, though he couldn't remember the last time he had received an invitation. After carefully hanging up her towel she walked naked into the room. McGovern stared at her impassively from the end of the bed.

"You were asleep on the couch last night when I got home," she said. "How late did you work?"

"Till seven or eight, I guess. I don't really remember. How was your meeting?"

"It was dinner, and I think we got the account."

The obligatory small talk out of the way, she began to dress for work. He sat back on the bed and casually thumbed through the file, stopping now and then to sip his coffee.

At work that morning the death of Elizabeth Dreyfuss was the last thing on McGovern's mind. At the moment he was trying to sort through the case he had been investigating the day before. Delgado had been stabbed to death and tossed in a dumpster behind a run-down apartment building, the aptness of which was not lost on McGovern. Why anyone cared *who* had snuffed out trash like that was beyond him. Unfortunately, it was his job to find out. He glanced at his wristwatch. Only 9 a.m. and already the tedium was setting in.

The next step in the procedure was to take a look at the evidence. Like an automaton he went downstairs to check out the guy's personal effects. If he could get a lead on who Delgado had pissed off recently it might keep the captain off his back, for a few days anyway. There was little doubt in McGovern's mind that the killing had been quick, and that ending Delgado's life was the only motive.

Seated at the desk in the evidence room was Officer John Brody, a wiry man of about forty-five.

"Give me all you've got on four-three-eight, Jack."

"Sure, Rich. Isn't that the one that came in yesterday?"

"Yeah."

While waiting for Brody to get back with the evidence, McGovern unconsciously began to pat his pockets in search of a pack of cigarettes. Although it had been a year since he had quit smoking, he couldn't seem to rid himself of this hourly ritual. Finally Brody returned.

"Not much here, Rich. A wallet, handkerchief . . . watch, a couple of matchbooks. The usual stuff. Oh, and this." With a gleam in his eye he held it up. "A wad of cash that could choke a horse. Doesn't exactly look like your dime store-variety mugging, does it?"

McGovern barely managed the requisite you-can-say-that-again, while signing for the evidence. He was just about to leave when Brody called him back to the desk.

"Hold on a minute, Rich—I've got something else here for you. It came in yesterday, too. Looks like a book or something."

"Is there a case number on it?"

"Nope," said Brody, holding it up, "just your name."

"Okay, let's have it."

Once again Brody pushed a clipboard containing several pieces of paper, corners turned up at the bottom, at McGovern and once again McGovern signed it. He put the book with the other things and headed back to his desk.

Dumping the evidence amid the rest of the clutter, he leaned back in his chair to study the book. Same Post-it note with his name on it. Same handwriting. But when he opened up the front cover something he read made him sit bolt-upright in the chair.

Tom Millett, a young man of twenty-seven and McGovern's sometime partner, occupied the desk directly across from him. McGovern's reaction caused him to look up from his paperwork.

"What's up?"

"Do you know anything about this Dreyfuss case?"

"He was pretty good in *Jaws*, but I didn't care much for *Close Encounters*."

"Funny," said McGovern glaring at him wearily. "I was talking about this."

Millett laughed loudly as the file plopped on the desk in front of him, but stopped abruptly when he noticed the date.

"Where did this come from? I've never even seen a file this old."

"It just showed up on my desk yesterday."

"Looks to me like someone downstairs screwed up," said Millet, returning the file to McGovern's desk.

The day before McGovern would have agreed, but what had looked like a clerical error yesterday was about to become an all-consuming passion for him. The book he was holding in his hands was Elizabeth Dreyfuss's diary.

That night back at the apartment McGovern's wife was out again, which was just as well. Ever since finding that diary he hadn't been able to keep his mind on anything else. It was fascinating reading.

Elizabeth Dreyfuss had only been nineteen years old when she died. Her father had inherited nearly a million dollars from his father-in-law when Elizabeth was just a baby, and then promptly proceeded to lose most of it. A series of bad investments in falling stocks and failing businesses eventually reduced the Dreyfusses to a decidedly middle-class existence. The only problem was that somebody had forgotten to tell her parents.

They constantly paraded Elizabeth in front of the social elite of the day as if they were still living in the lap of luxury, only to be scoffed at and ridiculed by the other families. He could almost feel her crying as she recounted the constant humiliation she had endured. But through it all she never sounded bitter. She loved her parents and would have done anything they asked of her.

In one very interesting entry she told of a trust fund that her grandfather had set up for her, but there was no mention of how much money was in it or when she would receive it. Did Daddy try to get his hands on a little more seed money by killing off his daughter? The more he read, the more intrigued he became, and the more he wanted to know about her, especially the circumstances surrounding her death.

McGovern's wife looked surprised to find him up when she came through the door, but he simply hadn't been able to put the diary down since coming home that evening. Even after Joanne had gone to bed he continued to read.

It wasn't until about three o'clock that morning that he finally began to tire. McGovern set the book down on the couch for a moment, closed his eyes and laid his head back. Suddenly, just as he was about to doze off, his eyes popped open wide. He had heard someone whisper his name, or at least he thought he had. It hadn't really sounded like a human voice, but he had clearly heard his name.

He stood up at once and went into the bedroom. Joanne was sound asleep. He called to her quietly but it was clear that she was not awake. He told himself that it was probably just fatigue and that he better go to bed. He was going to need at least a few hours of sack time before work tomorrow. With little ceremony, he crawled into bed beside his wife and fell asleep.

The following day McGovern turned over all of his ongoing investigations to Tom Millett.

"You know the Captain's not gonna like this."

"Well, the Captain doesn't have to know anything about it, does he?"

"How long do you think it's gonna take before he finds out?"

"If he asks you, just tell him that I'm out questioning witnesses on the Delgado case."

"I thought you wrapped that up yesterday."

"I did—one of his girls killed him and skipped town. I just haven't filed the report yet. I'll be back this afternoon, okay?"

McGovern then stood up and lifted his jacket from its usual resting spot on the back of the chair.

"Does this have anything to do with that prehistoric file you showed me yesterday?"

McGovern hesitated slightly. He slipped on his jacket and the turned back to Millett. "Look, Tom, I'll be back this afternoon, okay?"

Millett nodded his head but said nothing as McGovern raced out the door. The file and the diary were already in the front seat of McGovern's '82 Buick. He couldn't rationally explain it, but something was compelling him to find out exactly what had happened to Elizabeth Dreyfuss. At this point in his lackluster career anything that took him away from the daily grind was a welcome relief, and to that end Richard McGovern gave himself up completely.

Driving through Chicago traffic he began to think through his plan. The first place he was going to check out was her house. If he was lucky enough to find someone still alive who remembered what had happened back then, he might get a better idea of how best to proceed. But in going over the file there was one thing he couldn't figure out. Someone had evidently gone through and scratched out every mention of the Dreyfuss's address. Why?

There was apparently no one he could question, either. He knew from the diary that Elizabeth had been an only child. Her mother and father couldn't possibly be alive. No, he would have to use other means at his disposal, so he turned the car in the direction of the Cook County Courthouse.

A separate office within the county records department was specially allocated for state and local police. It amounted to little more than an extra window and a couple of desks, but it sure sped up the process of digging for information. McGovern had been there many times before and walked right in.

"Nope. It's just not here. Are you sure the address is Cook County?"

McGovern was speaking with Ellen Nathanson, the buxom black woman who headed the department.

"It has to be," responded McGovern.

"Well, how about the mother? The property could have been in her maiden name."

"Don't have it."

She looked up at him, eyebrows arched over the top of her glasses, awaiting further instructions. None came. McGovern stood for a moment with a puzzled look on his face. He hadn't expected to reach a dead end so soon.

"Well, I guess that's it then. Thanks, Ellen. I appreciate your trying."

"Sorry I couldn't be of more help."

Driving back to the precinct, McGovern decided to skip lunch. He had one lead left: the police detective Joseph Wells. If that turned out to be a dead end, too, then the game was just about over.

Millett was gone when he walked into the squad room. McGovern plopped down in his chair and began to rack his brain, trying to come up with anything. Was there something that he had missed? Short of calling every Dreyfuss in the greater Chicago area, nothing came to him.

He sat up in a halfhearted attempt to get back to some actual police work but as he began to sift through the litter on his desk his blood ran cold. It was innocuous enough, in and of itself—just a small Manila envelope. On the front, however, was a Post-it note with his name written on it.

His senses dulled as his eyes fixed upon the object. In fact, he had not really even seen the envelope. What had commanded his complete attention was something he had not, could not have noticed until after reading the diary: the handwriting on the yellow square of paper was Elizabeth's.

He sat and stared at the envelope for several minutes before reaching for it. Then, with considerable trepidation, he opened it. It contained two items: both were very old photographs.

The first was of a beautiful, dark-haired young woman, dressed in white. He turned the picture over to see if there was any information on the other side. He didn't need to, though. He knew who it was. On the back was written "Elizabeth—1913." The other photograph was that of a house, nothing on the back. He figured it must have been the Dreyfuss' home.

McGovern did not pause to consider the implications of this latest discovery. It's time, he thought, to have a little talk with Joseph Wells. With renewed vigor he raced down to records in search of the whereabouts of the former Chicago police detective.

"Dead?"

"That's what I said," muttered the punctilious file clerk in the precinct records department.

"Are you sure?" questioned McGovern.

"It's right here in his file. Died: May 22, 1952."

The words rattled his skull like a cymbal crash. McGovern immediately looked at his watch. The date read May 22. And '52, that was the year that Wells was investigating the case. Things were getting stranger by the minute. He snatched the file from the hands of the now extremely irritated clerk and began poring over the information, keeping one eye on the other man. As soon as the clerk's back was turned McGovern bolted for the door.

"Hey! Come back here! You can't have that—"

His heart was racing as he hopped into his car. Wells had been killed in an auto accident—a head-on collision on a lonely stretch of road near Burnham, a suburb of Chicago. Wells had only been thirty-nine, single, and there was no next of kin listed in the file.

Something told him that Joseph Wells was the key to this whole thing. Why had he been on this case in 1952? Why had he died so suddenly, and, he had just realized, on the same date as Elizabeth's death? If only he could read those notes, he might be able to piece this thing together.

But the only thing he had to go on was the road where Wells had died. There just might be something out there, he thought, that can tell me what happened. Like a man possessed, he weaved in and out of rush-hour traffic toward the site of the accident.

The area in question was a three-mile stretch of road that began just off State Highway 83 and continued through the Burnham Woods, shadowing the Little Calumet River out to the Indiana border. As he turned onto the road, loose gravel flying up into the wheel wells created such a din that he had to slow the car to a crawl.

There was nothing exceptional about the area. It was heavily wooded on both sides with a dense undergrowth beneath the trees. Nothing else. No houses, no road signs, no litter, not even any noise. It was like driving through a ghost town without the tumbleweeds, and McGovern didn't like it.

How could Wells have been killed way out here? The road was narrow, yes, but he couldn't even imagine a reason for a head-on collision. The road was fairly straight, and though the woods on both sides made it rather dark, visibility was still good.

McGovern had gradually tuned out the shower of gravel against the undercarriage of the car and was moving at a good clip when out of nowhere a man appeared in the middle of the road in front of his car. By sheer reflex McGovern swerved to avoid hitting him. In doing so he ran off the road and straight into a group of small trees, the force of which sent him lurching forward, his head glancing off the steering wheel.

He threw open the door and hauled himself out. Nothing. There was no one there. He searched underneath the car and alongside the road. Still he saw no one. Before he had a chance to react he felt a drop of blood trickle down the side of his face.

"Damn it," he said, putting his hand up to the wound.

It wasn't until he took out his handkerchief to compress the small cut over his left eye that McGovern saw it. He turned away for a moment to clear his head and almost hesitated to look back again but there was it was: the Dreyfuss house. He reached into his breast pocket to compare it with the photograph, but there could be no mistake.

Through years of neglect the house had become nearly one with the woods. A few spots of peeling paint clung tenaciously to the sides of the decrepit structure. There was no glass left in the windows, and a forest of tall weeds now stood where once there had been a stately lawn.

McGovern took a deep breath. He felt nauseated. The whole experience was beginning to drain him. He climbed into his car and backed it onto the shoulder.

As he stepped out again, the old house loomed in front of him, almost daring him to enter. In slow motion he walked across the road, through the weeds and onto the front porch. There was no front door and McGovern stepped inside.

The house had a damp, loamy smell to it, and as McGovern made his way through each of the small rooms a certain calmness began to settle over him. He relaxed as he continued to look around but there was really nothing to see. The house was cool and dark, and also quite barren. That was why he was surprised to find a large, high-backed chair sitting right in the middle of what had probably once been the drawing room. By now his head was throbbing so badly that he dusted the chair off as best he could and sat down to rest.

It would soon be dark outside but he didn't feel compelled to leave. From where he sat he could see out a pair of French doors onto what seemed like an impenetrable wall of trees and bushes. Dusk was approaching and still McGovern sat, not knowing what he was waiting for. Then, just as the last rays of the sun streamed in through the foliage, something began to happen. Suddenly he wanted nothing more than to be away from there, but found he was unable to move.

At first the thickness of the air became almost palpable. It was as though waves of heat were emanating from a single point in the middle of the room, yet the air was still cool. Gradually the waves began to take shape. He could make out the faint outline of a human form. A woman.

She had long dark hair that was straight except for ringlets at the ends. She wore a thin, white cotton dress with many small buttons that went down the front to her waist. The longer he looked, the more distinct the image became.

He could now make out more details. The dress appeared to be damp, almost wet, and it was clear that she wore nothing underneath. It clung tightly around her breasts and he could see

136

the darkness of her nipples and the triangle of her pubic hair through the white fabric. Farther down, the dress hung loosely around her legs, and her bare feet hovered inches above the floor.

But McGovern was riveted to his seat by her eyes. They were the brightest, greenest eyes he had ever seen, pools of liquid phosphorescence set in her smooth, oval face.

It was Elizabeth, just as she had been in the photograph. But even though the details were clear, the image itself was strange, two-dimensional, as though it were being projected onto a cloud of fine mist. He was about to get up when she spoke.

"Richard," the image called to him.

He stopped. It was the same voice that he had heard in his apartment. Not any one voice, but a composite: indescribable.

"Come with me, Richard. Help me."

"What do you want?" he croaked.

"Help me, Richard.

"Why me?" he asked, not even realizing he was talking, but he really didn't care. An almost magnetic attraction was drawing him toward her, and he wanted to go. All he could think of was becoming a part of this sensuous vision. He never got the chance. The image that was Elizabeth began to waver, more and more violently with every passing second. Soon it was utterly unrecognizable.

Then everything changed. The room darkened and the air became thick with the smell of rotting flesh. McGovern fought back a gag, but not before he had to swallow down the splash of bile that had come up. Like a jolt of lightning a hideous figure materialized in front of him.

The image was of a man this time, and his clothes were covered with equal amounts of dirt and blood. His left arm had been torn off at the shoulder and congealed blood oozed from the mangled stump.

His face looked horrible. His right cheek flapped down, exposing the white of the bone. More blood ran along the curve of his jaw and dripped steadily from his chin. His watery eyes were set deep in his head, one of them clouded over, a murky grey, the other a brilliant, piercing blue. His lips were drawn back exposing his teeth, and his mouth gaped open in a death's-head rictus.

"Yes, come with us, Richard!" said the thing, mocking Elizabeth's words and erupting into an evil laugh. "You sap."

The image of his face and remaining hand appeared to be in motion. As the apparition came closer McGovern could see that the man's flesh was teeming with maggots.

With all his might McGovern wanted to run, but his body seemed incapable of responding to his brain's plea for flight. Sweat welled up from every pore as he realized that this was the man who had appeared earlier in front of his car.

The thing continued to move toward him until McGovern detected the decaying remnant of a shoulder holster and the glint of metal beneath the man's shabby jacket.

A badge? My God, could this be Wells?

The thing smiled knowingly at McGovern, as if it had heard his thoughts. "Did you figure it out yet detective?"

McGovern couldn't find a way to make his mouth work.

"A very interesting case, don't you think? It *haunted* me to my *dying* day." The thing laughed again and then leaned in close. McGovern smelled blood. "Don't make the same mistake I made, detective. She's a good-looking one, a real *killer*, if you know what I mean. Don't go off half-cocked or there'll be *hell* to pay. Heh, heh, heh."

The thing reached for him, but that was all McGovern could take. His fear finally overwhelmed him and he leapt up out of the chair. But the very instant he moved, the thing was gone. Nothing. The room was black dark and he left at once.

Detective Richard McGovern didn't go home that night. Instead, he headed straight for the nearest grocery store and bought himself a carton of Camels. His body finally stopped shaking as the first drag of warm smoke filled his lungs. He smoked half a pack while sitting in the store's parking lot.

Driving back into town he pulled over to the first bar he sighted, picked out an empty booth and didn't stop drinking until the last call. In front of him on the table was the spread out file containing Well's notes, as well as the diary and the pictures, and McGovern was more determined than ever to solve this case.

According to Elizabeth's father, he had come home late from work only to find Mrs. Dreyfuss in hysterics, and his daughter missing. He waited several more hours, and when she didn't show up, he phoned the police. Elizabeth's body was found floating in the river the next morning by a couple of kids on their way to school.

Why did he wait so long to report her disappearance? And just how much money would be coming his way if she turned up dead? Wells seemed to have been on the same track. After going over his notes for nearly an hour, the only words of Wells' scrawl that McGovern could decipher had also been underlined: FATHER and WILL.

There was only one place he could get the answer to what was in Elizabeth's will, and at 3 A.M., McGovern drove over to the Cook County Courthouse. He parked in front of the building, locked the doors to his car, and proceeded to pass out on the back seat.

Five hours later he was awakened by a loud tapping. Two uniformed police officers were peering in at him through the back windows.

"Would you please step out of the car, sir?"

McGovern emerged from his car still a bit drunk. "Thanks for the wake-up call, boys," he said, flashing his badge. "Official police business."

He breezed past the two uniforms and into the courthouse. Once inside he headed for the nearest toilet. After relieving himself of what felt like a gallon of alcohol and sprucing up a bit he tracked down Ellen Nathanson. She looked up at McGovern over her glasses as he strode up to her desk and promptly said, "Pardon me for saying so, Richard, but you look like shit."

"I haven't got time to exchange beauty tips right now, El. I'm looking for a will."

Eric B. Olsen

It took Ellen half an hour of searching through microfilm to track down the papers settling Elizabeth's estate. She hadn't had a will, but being next of kin everything had reverted to her parents upon her death—Mr. Dreyfuss certainly would have been aware of this—including a five hundred thousand dollar trust fund.

McGovern smiled to himself. It was so simple. Why hadn't anyone thought of it before? But of course Wells had, and now he was dead, but it was ridiculous to think that the two events were connected in any way. No, Detective Wells had run into a bit of bad luck, that was all.

Armed with the exact location of the Dreyfuss house, it was relatively easy to find out who the present owner was. The property had indeed been in Elizabeth's mother's name. The records indicated that the house had been sold only once. After the death of Elizabeth's parents, the property had been auctioned off to repay the debts of the estate; apparently Elizabeth's father hadn't done any better with his second inheritance than he had with his first. A man named Albert Praeger had purchased the lot in 1946.

The computer listed a Burnham address for Praeger. After his experience yesterday, McGovern wasn't sure he ever wanted to go near Burnham again, and why should he? He had ostensibly solved the case. But something kept nagging him, something seemed unfinished, and he was damned if he knew what it was. Talking to an old man couldn't hurt, though, and he finally decided to drive back out to Burnham.

In response to McGovern's incessant knocking, seventy-five-year-old Albert Praeger answer his door.

"Yeah?"

"Detective McGovern—Chicago Police," said a by-now hung over McGovern. "I'm looking for a Mr. Albert Praeger."

"That'll be me. What can I do for ya?" The old man eased out onto the porch to talk with McGovern but it was no use. Praeger was genial enough, but he had no knowledge of the people who had owned the property prior to him.

140

"After the war I came into a bit of money. Only reason I bought the place is because a developer friend of mine said it would be a good investment. Been tryin' to unload it ever since."

McGovern nodded politely.

"The only thing worth a damn on the whole place was the old tin lizzie I found out in the garage, 1909, before the assembly lines. The thing was all beat up to hell, but I had lots of fun fixing that ol' gal up."

Red flags were suddenly going up in McGovern's mind. Since both of Elizabeth's parents died in 1945—within a few months of each other—why would they have kept a beat up jalopy in their garage unless . . . McGovern winced at the thought. Could Dreyfuss really have run down his own daughter in cold blood? And what about Mrs. Dreyfuss? Did she know anything about it? Could she even have been involved?

"Do you still have it?" he asked the old man.

"Why? You like vintage cars?"

"Let's just say I have an interest in this particular car."

McGovern helped Praeger lift the garage door. There inside was an authentic 1909 Model T Ford, perfectly rebuilt.

"So, you say this belonged to the original owners of the house?"

"Far as I know."

"What was wrong with it?"

"Well, I don't think the think had been run in thirty years, had to tear the engine apart—"

"No," McGovern interrupted. "You said it was beat up."

"Oh, that," Praeger said, rubbing his chin. "You see the radiator in front there?"

McGovern looked at the shiny chrome and nodded.

"Well, they didn't have bumpers back in those days, and near as I can figure, somebody ran this ol' gal smack-dab into a tree. Smashed the hell out of her."

"How could you tell it was a tree?"

Praeger smiled at this. "There was twigs and bark still imbedded in the grill."

McGovern sighed. No more. As far as he was concerned, this case was closed. What point was there in continuing? He had no proof that Elizabeth had been killed for her money. It may have been a coincidence, but there was no crime in that. Besides, life with Elizabeth Dreyfuss was becoming increasingly traumatic. Dreary as it was, it was time to get back to *his* life. He smiled at the thought.

"How'd you like to take her for a spin?"

McGovern was caught off guard by the question, but after a moment's thought he said, "Sure, why not?"

"You'd better drive," said Praeger, pointing to his eyes. "Lost my license some time ago. Haven't had the old girl out on the road for years, but I fire up the engine every couple of weeks to make sure she still runs."

McGovern felt exhilarated as Praeger cranked up the engine. It idled roughly and the steering wheel vibrated in his hands. Then the old man climbed in beside him and motioned him on.

"Now take it easy on her. She only does about thirty at the top end."

"Don't worry," shouted McGovern above the noise of the engine. "I'll take good care of her."

Driving the open-air car felt amazingly good beneath the early morning sun. McGovern's decision to drop the case had made a new man out of him. Hell, he thought, if this keeps up I might even try to salvage my marriage. In his mind he was already chalking up the images he had seen in the old house to something he had dreamed up after the accident on that road. He laughed out loud as he ran his hand over the bump on his head.

They drove around for some time and occasionally McGovern would turn to look at the old man. Praeger spent the whole trip grinning from ear to ear, eyes squinted, and his wispy grey hair dancing in the breeze. But as the Model T Ford turned aimlessly onto a deserted gravel road, McGovern's cheerful mood subsided, followed by a look of terror that swept over his face.

"This is that road!" he shouted, and turned to Praeger. But Praeger was gone.

Immediately he slammed on the breaks, but the car continued to ramble on down the road. He tried turning around but the steering wheel wouldn't budge.

McGovern began to breathe faster. Paralyzed with fear, he could sense the presence of Joseph Wells beside him, and he turned his head slowly to behold the thing. The image of Wells, an animated corpse, rotting and putrid, laughed and taunted McGovern with its evil grin. McGovern could feel his chest tighten and his body tremble as he drove on.

In actuality, though, the car was driving itself. McGovern's hands were on the wheel, but he was powerless to control the vehicle. His foot was on the brake, but the car continued to accelerate.

"You stupid son of a bitch!" Wells yelled at him.

McGovern's throat felt no bigger than a pipe cleaner.

"You'd better turn this contraption around and get the hell outta here before it's too late."

"Why?" McGovern barely managed to squeak out.

"Jesus Christ, you're a stupid son of a bitch! Haven't you figured it out yet?"

When McGovern didn't answer, Wells threw his hand up in disgust, flinging a few maggots into the air in the process.

"Didn't you read the diary I sent you?"

"That was you?"

"Sure. I knew that you'd need some hard evidence to back up the notes I'd written. My theory turned out to be right, didn't it?"

"That her father killed her?"

Wells suddenly turned on him and the look in his eye was filled with more hatred than he had ever seen in a human. "That's not what I wrote in the file."

"I'm sorry. I couldn't read your handwriting."

Just as quickly Wells was laughing again, but for some reason McGovern felt even more scared. "Isn't that rich? At least you've still got both of your hands." Wells laughed again at his own joke. "She wants you, detective, just like she wanted me. Well, she got me, all right, and if you don't get the hell out of here she's gonna get you, too!"

McGovern had no idea who he was talking about. "I don't understand."

"Elizabeth, you stupid son of a bitch! Nobody killed that spoiled brat for her money. Didn't you read the diary? *She* was the one who hated *them*. That night when Daddy came home she tried to run him down, but she missed and hit a tree, accidentally killing herself dead. And Mommy? Well, she was far more concerned about a scandal than her little girl's corpse and she finally persuaded Daddy to dump it in the river."

"How did you know all—"

But Wells was already gone and the car had suddenly veered toward the side of the road. With all of his will McGovern tried to change its course, but it was as if he were frozen. Within seconds, the car had left the road and was descending a small embankment into a wooded area. McGovern, eventually regaining his bodily control, threw his hands in front of his face as the car careened toward a small stand of trees directly in front of him. But no sooner had he released his grip on the wheel than the car slowed to a stop.

When he opened his eyes he saw that a woman's hand was on the steering wheel, and when he looked up he beheld Elizabeth. But something was different this time. This was no apparition. She was flesh and blood. McGovern looked into her eyes and breathed deeply. As he took the air in, a rush of stimulation nearly overwhelmed him. It was as if he could feel every drop of adrenaline as it coursed through his veins.

She took his hand in hers and he marveled at the texture of her smooth, cool skin. Then she leaned over and kissed him full on the lips, and McGovern instantly became aroused.

Elizabeth opened her door, stepping out of the car, and McGovern followed her up to the gravel road. There he stopped with her and admired with her the beautiful mansion on the other side. Fresh white paint covered the smooth wooden siding, and the windows sparkled, accented by grey shutters. The Dreyfuss home looked exactly as it had in the picture.

The two of them walked hand in hand through the lush, dark-green grass and up to the polished oak door. Elizabeth let them in and then led McGovern through a maze of furnished rooms and up the stairs. At the end of the hall she opened the door of a bedroom that contained only one item: a brass bed dressed in crisp white linens. Elizabeth lay down on the bed and spoke to him. The unearthly voice he had heard before was replaced by one that was soft and breathy.

"Make love to me, Richard."

McGovern fell down beside her, his mind racing but not forming coherent thoughts. He had reverted to an animal state, his senses nearly overloading his brain with information. His mouth hungrily explored hers and his hands moved over her body as they slowly undressed. The sight of her nakedness nearly took his breath away. Her skin felt cool and wet next to his and he filled his nostrils with her musky odor as she spread her legs to accept him.

Richard McGovern was in ecstasy. Every fiber of his being was alive with sexuality. Never before had he experienced a more pure form of physical gratification. So great, in fact, was the intensity of his orgasm that as he reached his climax he blacked out.

A lonely black-and-white moved cautiously along the dark, deserted road. Only minutes before, the 32nd Precinct had received an anonymous phone call saying that there had been some sort of accident near the edge of town. The two officers who had responded to the call continued their search past the Chicago city limits and were soon nearing Burnham.

The moon was obscured by cloud cover and there were no lights to speak of. They were about to call it a night when a random pass of the searchlight reflected off something in the woods near the road.

The driver radioed back while the other man trained the light on what appeared to be an abandoned car. Both then took out their flashlights to investigate. As they approached the vehicle, the situation became clearer. A Buick Skylark had evidently driven off the road and smashed into a tree. The driver was still hunched over the steering wheel.

There was blood everywhere but as far as they could see, no one else had been involved. As quickly as possible they tried to ascertain the condition of the victim. When the first officer pulled the driver from the wheel, the second shouted.

"Oh, Christ! That's Detective McGovern from homicide."

"Are you sure?"

"Christ, yes! I worked with him on a case just last week. I'm going to radio for an ambulance."

"Well, you'd better radio the morgue, first. He's dead."

Other Stories

These final two stories were written without a thought of publication, and were never intended to be part of the previous collection. They were simply ideas that I had at a time when I still cared about realizing those ideas. "The Night Before" was inspired by an anthology called *100 Great Fantasy Short Short Stories* that was edited by Isaac Asimov. For the most part I don't usually read fantasy or science fiction, but I was intrigued by the idea of a "short short" story, usually anywhere from three to five pages. For the most part, I think of these kinds of stories as fictional puns. They have a twist in the O. Henry style that winds up being the entire point of the story. A couple of them had to do with an artist selling his soul to the devil, and I thought that I could put an interesting slant on it. The title of the story comes from a song title that plays into the way I always enjoyed naming my works of horror. "Special Delivery" is a different kind of work, but still in the playful vein of the previous one. It's the only vampire story I ever wrote, and I was only inspired to do that because of thinking about some of the more practical aspects of living in the modern world as one of the undead. It's fitting that in my last horror short story I named the main character after my friend Patrick who was really responsible for inspiring me to write horror fiction in the first place.

The Night Before

The stairs creaked as Johnny walked up to the old, second-floor office. The place looked as if it hadn't been used in years. When he had first come upon the London address that the man had given him, he thought for a moment that the building might be condemned. It wasn't. So he pushed open the decrepit front doors and ascended the stairs.

He reached the office and gave a tentative knock. The lettering on the opaque glass read, Nicholas Belial, Music Publisher. He knocked again and this time heard a shout from behind the door: "Come in!"

Johnny turned the brass knob and eased into the office. It was totally barren, save for a desk and a chair. From an adjoining room emerged the man. He was a heavyset man with dark hair and a thick beard, and he was dressed in black: black suit, black shirt, tie and shoes. He was wiping his hands with a towel, as if he had just washed them. Then he threw the towel on the desk beside a large book that Johnny hadn't noticed before.

"Good to see you again, Johnny. Please, have a seat." When Johnny looked around he saw that there was a chair behind him and promptly sat down. The man seated himself behind the desk, clasped his hands together and leaned forward. "Now, what can I do for you, lad?"

"Well, Mr. Belial—"

"Please, call me Nick."

"Yes, sir," Johnny replied. "You see, three other lads and myself have formed sort of a music group and we're looking for some songs that we might be able to record."

"I see," said the man, leaning back and locking his fingers behind his head. "And what type of songs were you thinking of?"

"Well, we've been trying to write our own songs, but the bloody things just sound so daft. Then I remembered you said you had sold popular songs, songs that people would buy if they were on a record."

"True," said the man, taking out a pouch from his breast pocket. "True enough." He unrolled the pouch and removed a pipe from another pocket, methodically filling the pipe and lighting it up. "I have had some previous success in that area. Let me show you the standard contract and you can decide for yourself."

Then the man pushed a sheet of paper toward Johnny. It must have been on the desk all along, but Johnny hadn't noticed it before. "I provide you with a predetermined number of songs in exchange for a price to be determined at a later date. Of course, this is the first group that I have dealt with. Most of my clients in the past have been individuals.

"The problem, as always, is with the payment; if you'll just direct your attention to paragraph four . . ." Johnny looked and read intently. It was pretty much what he had expected, but he was desperate. He and the boys were due to audition for a record producer tomorrow and as of yet they hadn't been able to come up with even one song on their own to record.

"Why is there a blank beside Date of Payment?"

"Good question, lad. That is to be filled in by me, personally, after the contract is signed."

"Then how will I know when to pay?"

"You won't. I will send out a collector at the appointed time, and then our business will be concluded."

Johnny thought about it some more. "According to the contract, you cant collect until all the songs have been recorded."

"True," the man answered, "But in a group situation, such as yours, the whole group must have access to the songs."

"But I'm the one who has to pay for them," Johnny frowned.

"As I said before, it's the standard contract."

"Okay, what if the group breaks up?"

"Then the songs, of course, would be your property alone. Just as long as you are aware that their popularity cannot be guaranteed beyond that point. But it's all right there in the contract: paragraph eight."

Johnny looked. Sure enough, there it was. "One more question," Johnny asked. The man nodded. "Suppose I just retire, quit, with one song to go. I would never have to pay, right?"

"Theoretically," then man answered, "if not for paragraph nine, which stipulates that the performer, you, may not remain inactive for a period of more than five years, after which, collection would be immediate."

"But if I worked it right, spaced out the recording, I might not have to pay for a long time, right?"

"The importance of success, I suppose, depends upon the individual."

"And you'll guarantee the songs?"

"As long as the group stays together."

"And I'll get writing credit on all the songs?"

"Of course."

There was nothing more to think about. Johnny signed the standard contract. He filled out the requested number of songs, leaving the Date Of Payment blank empty, and then handed it back to the man.

"An unusually high number of songs," said the man, more to himself than to Johnny, "but then I always try to accommodate new clients. Very well," he said, and countersigned the contract. "There, it's official." The man stood up, folded the contract, and placed it in his pocket. Then he handed Johnny the large, leather bound book that had been on the desk throughout the meeting.

"May I look at them?" Johnny asked.

"Please do," answered the man.

Johnny opened the book. They were beautiful. Oh, they didn't look like much on paper, but Johnny knew that they would be hits.

He just knew. Johnny stood up and prepared to leave the dingy office. "Thanks a lot, Mr. Beli—uh, I mean, Nick."

The man came around the desk and shook Johnny's hand. "My pleasure, lad. It always makes me feel good to help a struggling artist." The man opened the door and ushered Johnny out into the dark hall. "I wish you and your new group much success."

And with that he patted Johnny on the shoulder and sent him on his way. "Good luck, Mr. Lennon."

Special Delivery

Patrick looked at his wristwatch and thought he was going to die. His heart was thumping so hard against his chest he was sure it would burst through. In the entire year he had been working for the delivery service he had never been late before, never.

He wrenched the throttle of the moped unmercifully and the tiny engine whined its displeasure. "Goddamn it!" he yelled out loud. Patrick was doing top speed, thirty-five miles per hour, and was almost sure he could run faster than this stupid little bike could take him.

He took another look at his watch. Oh, yes, he was in for it this time. It was already four-thirty; he was supposed to have been there half an hour ago. Not only that, but he was miles from his destination because of a stupid mistake he had made on his last delivery.

Patrick's grades at the university had dipped below acceptable levels two quarters ago, and he had found himself unceremoniously frozen out of his financial aid. That was when he heard about the delivery job. It was nights, three days a week, and they even provided transportation—if you could call a beat-up moped transportation—so he had taken it. The pay was good enough to get him through that quarter, and now that his grades were up it kept him in beer money.

The first few nights had scared the shit out of him, but once he fell into the routine it became second nature. Traffic was practically nonexistent at night, and almost all of his customers

153

Eric B. Olsen

were regulars so he rarely had to look up an address. In fact, he
hardly ever looked at his route book anymore and that's why he
was in trouble tonight.

When he'd reached the second-to-last house on his route, old
man Barlow had looked at him kind of funny before inviting him
in. He didn't discover why until he tallied up his deliveries before
completing the run and realized he didn't have enough left. He
looked in horror at the route book when he saw that Barlow had
discontinued services. Now it was too late. He was forced to go
back to the depot for more supplies, and that presented him with
another problem.

The Barlow place, the depot, and his last stop formed a
triangle which put them as far away from each other as they could
get while still being within the city limits. He barely had enough
time to make it to his last stop from Barlow's house under normal
circumstances. Oftentimes Patrick had wondered what he would
do if he ever got a flat tire, but he had always figured he would
catch a cab or a thumb ride. He could have had a Lear jet tonight,
though, and he still wouldn't have been able to make it on time.

The rain that had been pelting down all evening had soaked
him to the skin, making him shiver, as if he didn't have enough
to shiver about already. When he first came back to the depot
the dispatcher marveled at how fast he had completed his run.
But when Patrick told him he hadn't, well, he thought that the
dispatcher would kill him long before his last customer would
get a chance to.

Standard procedure was to fill up on supplies at the depot and
then go out on the route, but there hadn't been time. He had to fill
up on the road tonight, and the burning throb in the crook of his
elbow as he drove reminded him that he still wasn't finished. Only
now he was almost there.

He reached the turnoff and skidded around the corner, the
moped fishtailing wildly and Patrick not caring. He stuck out his
foot as a brace, righted the bike and sped up the driveway. Once
he was at the front porch he dumped the bike in the lawn, threw

off his helmet and raced up the steps; then he rang the doorbell and waited.

Patrick glanced up at the sky and saw the stars were already gone. Oh, God, he prayed, please don't let me be too late. In answer, a hand with a grip like iron grabbed his neck from behind. Patrick tried to scream out, but the long slender fingers squeezed on his windpipe like a vise. From behind him another hand reached beneath is arm and opened the door, after which Patrick was thrown inside.

He lay on the floor choking and coughing, trying to catch his breath, as the door slammed shut. When Patrick looked up he was staring into the burning red eyes of Mr. Varney.

"You're late," the man said, in his deep, rich baritone.

"I know," Patrick managed to choke out, and then he coughed a couple more times. "The dispatcher told me to tell you no charge tonight."

With lightning speed the man was on him and he looked like he was ready to kill. "This isn't Domino's Pizza, boy. A freebie if you're late doesn't do me any fucking good after sunrise, does it?"

"No," said Patrick meekly.

"Then let's get going. I'm running out of time, and so are you."

Patrick stripped off his jacket and untaped the plastic IV bag from his chest—thank God it was empty—and removed the thin tube that connected it the vein in his arm. "All right," he said, standing up. "I'm ready."

"You're lucky, is what you are, boy," said Varney, and then Patrick felt the tear in his throat as the man latched on to his jugular vein. He was a little more vicious tonight than usual, and it was no wonder why. But Patrick didn't mind. Varney was one of Hemo-Serve's biggest customers and he tipped heavily. Patrick was lucky to have him on his route.

When he was finished Varney stepped back, drunk with blood, a satiated smile turning up the corners of his mouth. "I'm afraid I must retire now. The envelope is on the table next to the door as usual."

"I couldn't, Mr. Varney," said Patrick, a little lightheaded himself. "Not after everything—"

"Never mind," the old man said, waving his hand. "All's well, and so forth. I'll expect you the day after tomorrow, then?"

"Yes."

"Four o'clock?"

"On the dot."

When Patrick stepped out of the house and picked up his bike, the sky had begun to take on a gray tint as the night finally slipped away into morning. And as he drove through the empty streets, on his way back to drop off the moped at the Hemo-Serve depot, Patrick was already thinking about what he was going to do with the money on his day off.

Blood Feast

Blood Feast has an interesting history. It originally began as a short story called "2 a.m. Feeding" that I wrote in 1990, which I sent to *Weird Tales* and then promptly forgot about. But a year later I read in the Seattle newspaper about an entrepreneur in Portland who had started a publishing company called DimeNovels! His idea was to publish a series of short novels, each a hundred pages, from twelve different genres, as a way of emulating the dime novels of old. The novels were printed in a small format, about the size of a package of baseball cards, and came to stores in a prepackaged countertop display with each selling for $1.99. Every month stores would get a new box filled with copies of several different novels in various genres, horror, mystery, detective, adventure, science fiction, fantasy, western, and several sub-genres of romance. I immediately began writing a mystery novella to submit, but didn't know exactly where I was going to go with it. Then I looked around for something else that would work and realized it would be a lot easier to take an existing story and flesh it out rather than create something new. So that's exactly what I did.

It probably took no more than a few months to enlarge the story to ten chapters that would come out to a hundred pages. In the meantime the publisher had only put out one other group of novels. Apparently his plan of publishing twelve new books every month was a little too ambitious—probably because of the tremendous amount labor involved and the small initial sales he was getting back. I submitted a proposal at the end of August 1991, and they asked to look at the complete manuscript in November. In all that time, however, they hadn't put out a new set of novels, and by February of the next year I heard that the company had folded.

The name of the expanded work came, again, from my friend Patrick. I remember him telling me about how much he loved the titles of some of the old exploitation horror films of the fifties and sixties. One in particular he thought was great was *Blood Feast* by Herschell Gordon Lewis in 1963. As for the story itself, it looks like what I did was to combine elements of *The Wolf Man* from 1941 with *Alien* for the monster, and *Kolchak: The Night Stalker* for my detective. Finally, the name of the medical examiner was inspired by the former Los Angeles medical examiner, Thomas Noguchi, who had written two mystery novels that I read and enjoyed during the time I was writing these stories.

BLOOD FEAST

a horror novella

For John

If he were opened, and you find so much blood
in his liver as will clog the foot of a flea, I'll eat
the rest of the anatomy.

William Shakespeare
Twelfth Night

"Most serial killers keep some sort of trophies
from their victims."

"I didn't."

"No . . . No, you ate yours."

Jodie Foster and Anthony Hopkins
The Silence of the Lambs, 1991

PROLOGUE

Lisa sat bolt-upright in bed when she heard it: a strange noise that sounded as if it had come from somewhere in the house. Immediately she looked over at the baby. The crib was on her side of the bed, near the door, but she couldn't see him in the dark shadowy corner of the room. She wanted to get up and see if he was okay but all of the books said that you shouldn't do anything until they cried.

David had wanted her to get one of those electronic gadgets with a speaker so that they could hear the boy in the nursery—the one that he had spent all summer working on, he was quick to remind her. But Lisa had trundled the crib into their bedroom as soon as they had come home from the hospital, despite David's protest. Now she was grateful that she had.

She cocked her head slightly, trying to tune in, but the room was silent now. The only thing she could hear was the baby's quick and tiny breaths between David's long and deep ones, and, for some reason, the sound of her heart beating rapidly in her chest. She put a hand up to calm it, then turned and looked at David, still fast asleep beside her, and tried to relax. Over in the crib the baby seemed restless, too. I wonder if he heard the noise, she thought. She wanted desperately to go over and pick him up, but he wasn't crying, so she resisted.

She and David had been trying to have a baby for years, with no success. They had been patient, but once Lisa turned thirty she had begun to panic. It seemed that with every new fertility drug or technique she wanted to try, David's interest in the whole thing decreased. But at last . . . She looked over to the crib now and smiled. They had been so lucky. It would be their only child—she knew that—but that didn't make her sad. David was only thirty-five and she was thirty-two, and it was nice to know that they would still have lots of years left after the baby was grown up and living on his own.

Lisa was exhausted after hauling the baby around all day, first to David's parents' and then to hers. Once they had finally come home, David had passed out as soon as his head hit the pillow, but she was too keyed up to sleep. And now that sound . . . If she didn't get some shuteye she was going to be dead tomorrow. Lisa opened her eyes wide to take in the room, just to make sure everything was all right.

Then she heard it again. By now her thumping heart was accompanied by a thin layer of sweat beneath her nightgown. It was a strange kind of noise, distant and, if she was hearing correctly, wet. Now Lisa was really beginning to get scared.

Then it came to her: someone must be in the house. She knew it had been raining earlier, and the image of a masked gunman walking through the living room in wet shoes suddenly flashed in her mind. Lisa felt paralyzed with fear. The baby must be able to hear it, too, she thought, because she could hear him tossing and turning beneath his blankets.

"David," she said, giving her husband a hard shove. But he merely grunted and rolled over. Then she heard a muffled thump that sounded as if it were just outside the room, and her breath caught in her throat.

She reached out a hand to turn on the light. Maybe if he knew that someone was up, the intruder would leave. But before she touched the switch, she saw something move in the doorway and screamed. "David!" Her hand spasmed and knocked over the lamp. It shattered on the floor.

David's Head jerked up. "What the hell's going on?" He was still groggy with sleep as he reached over to turn on his own lamp.

She was about to tell him, but when Lisa turned and saw the empty crib she screamed again.

"Oh, my God! Someone took the baby! Someone took the baby! I heard him! Oh, God—"

She was vaguely aware of David's saying something to her and of glass cutting her feet as she ran from the bedroom, but she couldn't let someone get away with their baby. She and David waited so long—it wasn't fair. She had to save him.

David didn't come fully awake until Lisa was already out of the room, but he could have sworn he had heard her say something about the baby. Then he looked over at the empty crib. It must be sick or something, he thought. Damn, it was starting already. She'd just had to have it in the bedroom, and now it was going to be crying or puking or something every two hours and he was never going to get any sleep.

When they were first married, only a few weeks after graduating high school, having kids was all they had talked about. David couldn't wait to go to parent-teacher night and sit at his child's desk, put up finger paintings on the fridge and, if it was a boy, toss the football around and be able to pass on the family name. But as the years dragged on and Lisa never became pregnant, things had changed. The spontaneity was gone, sex became a drudgery, and making love began to take on an ominous significance. And now this kid.

He turned off the lamp and fell back heavily on his pillow. He was about to roll over and close his eyes when, from somewhere in the house, Lisa shrieked.

"Jesus Christ," he said under his breath, annoyance melting into a vague fear in the pit of his stomach. "Lisa?" he called out, but she didn't answer. "Lisa! Are you all right?"

Then he heard a crash in the front room. Instantly he turned on the lamp, but a scuttling noise on the bedroom floor made him pull his legs out of the covers and move his body away from the edge of the bed. He screamed this time. "Lisa!" But there was still no answer.

When he finally caught a glimpse of himself in the mirror of the vanity against the far wall, David realized how ridiculous he looked cowering in the middle of the bed in his boxer shorts. Jesus, something serious might have happened to Lisa, and here he was hiding in the bedroom because he thought he'd heard a weird noise.

He slapped his feet down on the cold floor and pushed himself up, but his first step sent him careening into the bookcase on his side of the room. The case tipped when he hit it, and a few dozen paperbacks came cascading down on top of his head.

"Fuck!" he yelled, throwing his arms over his head for protection after the last book had fallen. David began to pull his legs toward himself to stand when a bolt of electric pain raced up his right leg and made him cry out in agony. "What the hell?"

He froze, panting and sweating, and pushed himself up slowly to a sitting position, without moving his legs, in order to see what was wrong. His right leg looked fine in the dim light, all the way down to his . . . heel. David let out a whimper. The blood there looked blackish in the shadowed corner where he was sitting, and he shuddered but couldn't give voice to what he was seeing. He was frightened now, and his eyes were drawn to the bed, but the comforter was sagging down against the floor, obscuring the view beneath.

What was the crash he had heard in the front room? And why had Lisa screamed? Jesus, what if someone had Lisa and the baby? What if one or more of them was under the bed at this very minute? He looked at his leg again and the realization dawned on him that it couldn't be anything else. You didn't get a wound like this by accident. He thought about trying to move farther into the corner, but the memory of the pain stopped him.

He looked at his heel closely this time, and was about seventy percent sure . . . The straight thin line above, and the sagging bloody skin below—and then, of course, we wouldn't want to forget about our old pal Mr. Pain—made the odds better than even that his Achilles tendon had been sliced clean in two. The cut had to have been made with an extremely sharp object, a scalpel or knife. Christ, he hadn't even felt it. You didn't get this kind of injury from the head of a nail or rogue staple sticking out of the footboard.

There was no doubt in his mind that someone was in the house, maybe underneath the bed at this very minute, watching for him to make a move. But he would never know for sure, because his bloody heel was the last thing David ever saw.

CHAPTER ONE

It was late Sunday night and Jack was watching John Carpenter's remake of *The Thing*, a damn good movie in its own right, when the phone rang.

"Aw, Christ."

He groped for the remote control, found it, and froze Kurt Russell's hooded face on the screen. The phone was on a table next to the easy chair where he was sitting, and he picked up the receiver.

"Yeah."

"Hello. May I speak with Detective Ransom, please?"

"Who is this?" It sounded like some rookie who didn't realize that Ransom worked days. And it was now—he took a quick look at his watch—10:23 *p.m.* On top of which it was Sunday, and Ransom didn't work weekends, either.

"This is Officer Petosa from the University Precinct."

On the nose.

"Sir, is that you?"

"Yes. Listen, Petosa, they have detectives who work the night shift right down there at the station house. I'm sure if you gave them a call they would be glad to give you a hand."

"Yes, sir."

"Then I'll just say good night and get back to my movie—"

"Wait a minute, sir. I called the precinct like you said, and two detectives came out here right away."

"So why exactly are we talking?"

"Well . . . they told me to call you."

That was all that Ransom needed to hear. He didn't get called away at night unless it was pretty bad. He got the address from Petosa and then asked him how many officers were on the scene.

"Just me and my partner, and the two detectives."

"Good. I want you to run a crime-scene tape around the whole house," he said, "including the yard." Then as an afterthought he added, "Where are you, Petosa?"

"Fifty-second and—"

"No, I mean, where are you calling from?"

"The patrol car."

"Are your lights rolling?"

"Yes, sir."

"Why don't you shut them down? I don't want the whole neighborhood down there any sooner than necessary."

"Yes, sir."

"Has anyone called for an ambulance yet?"

"No, sir. The detectives wanted you to get here first."

"I'm on my way."

Ransom hung up the phone and turned off the TV and VCR before running into the bedroom to throw on some shoes. He grimaced into the mirror above the dresser as he tied his laces; it seemed as if he had more grey hair every day. At forty-six, Ransom didn't feel very old, but his body evidently had different views on aging. On the way out the door he shrugged a raincoat over his husky, six-foot-one-inch frame, still dressed in his sweatpants and sweatshirt.

"Aw, Christ!" he yelled as big drops of water began to fall from the sky. Ransom had to drive ten miles in the pouring rain to get to the crime scene. He cursed the worn set of wiper blades that smeared water against the windshield of his old Buick Skylark, and was about ready to stick his head out the window just to see where he was going.

Ransom hated the rain, despised it, and people laughed at him because of this. The fact that he had been born and raised in Washington State just seemed funny. When people asked him why he didn't move, all he could do was shrug and say, "This is home." As with many natives of the Pacific Northwest, his umbrella had become virtually another appendage.

By the time he arrived on the scene, though, a small one-story house north of the University of Washington, he was somewhat ambivalent toward the rain. At least it would help keep away the rubberneckers. The property had been cordoned off and was being guarded by two patrolmen in black slickers, the heavy rain beating down visibly through the yellow beams of their flashlights.

Ransom pulled in behind the blue and white squad car of the Seattle Police Department, and when he stepped out he had to pull the collar of his raincoat up over his head as Petosa led him to the front door: it was the first time he had ever forgotten to bring his umbrella.

But when Ransom laid eyes on the woman, covered in blood, her body splayed open and disemboweled, he turned and ran straight back out into the downpour. He doubled over on the front walk and Petosa ran up to him.

"Are you all right, sir?"

Detective Jim Razor, who had remembered *his* umbrella, was suddenly at his side. "He's okay."

Ransom felt a hand on his back and stood up beneath Razor's open umbrella. Once Petosa was out of earshot, Razor leaned in and whispered, "*Are* you okay, Jack?"

"Sure," said Ransom, and when Razor offered him a cigarette he gladly accepted it, even thought he didn't smoke.

Razor was one of the plainclothes detectives working the night shift out of the University Precinct. They had been partnered for a year when Razor was fresh out of the academy and Ransom was still in uniform. "Hell of a thing," said Razor. "Sorry to get you out here on a night like this." Ransom's adversity to the rain was well known in the department.

"That's okay. I'm glad I could see it before things got moved around."

"Well . . ." said Razor, visibly uncomfortable. "Things aren't exactly pristine."

"What?"

"Don't worry. We took these first."

Razor took a handful of Polaroids from the pocket of his beat-up letterman's jacket and handed them to Ransom. A three-sport athlete all the way through high school, Razor reveled in past glories. He was thirty-three and still looked like a jock: just under six feet and pure muscle, his blonde hair cropped short above a clean-shaven face. When a knee injury as a freshman football star in college had unceremoniously ended his sports career, he had been forced to make some alternate career plans. The jacket was just his way of coping with unrealized dreams.

"Aw, Christ! Is that a kid?" Ransom was looking at a picture of a baby, curled up in the hollowed-out body of the woman he had just seen.

"Yeah, I took some snaps and then I had to get him out of there. I got kids of my own, you know."

Ransom nodded and handed the pictures back. "Is it still alive?"

"Yeah, and apparently uninjured. We have him wrapped up in a blanket on the couch. He was fussy for a while before you got here, but he's asleep now." After a long silence, Razor continued. "Uh, listen, Jack. I was talking to Chet inside," he said, referring to his partner, Chet Burgher. "And if you don't have any objections, we'd just as soon hand this one off to you."

Ransom mulled the idea over while he listened to the rain beat on the umbrella and held his burning but unsmoked cigarette.

Razor was looking at the wet pavement and shaking his head. "Hell. I've been on the force fifteen years and I've never seen anything like this."

But Ransom had, seven years before, just about the time *The Terminator* was released. The newspapers had tabbed the killer the Decapitator because he had sliced the heads off all three of his victims, clean as a whistle, just like the photographer in *The Omen.* From the scrapings of Teflon under one of the victim's fingernails, Ransom had been able to trace the killer though a cookie sheet, honed razor sharp, that he was using as a sort of manually operated guillotine.

Ransom wasn't sure he wanted to deal with another case like that. "Let's go take another look," he said noncommittally. Then he dropped his cigarette to the ground, crushed it underfoot, and he and Razor walked back inside the house.

Chet Burgher, who had been on the force nearly as long as Ransom, had always reminded Ransom of a pudgy Don Knotts. Burgher was standing wide-eyed in the kitchen doorway at the far end of the house, looking intently at Ransom and Razor, and shifting his ample weight from one foot to the other.

Though the house was small, it was expensively furnished. Gleaming hardwood floors held up a couch and love seat, vases filled with dried flowers, potted plants, coffee and end tables, and a few strategically placed Persian rugs and runners. The eggshell-white walls were decorated minimally by a mirror above the mantel and a couple of paintings that Ransom recognized, but whose artists he couldn't remember.

Between Burgher in the kitchen, and Ransom and Razor at the front door, lay the body of the woman. Her age was difficult to judge because of all the blood: she was covered in it. The heat was still on, and it was obvious she had been dead for several days. Ransom reached for a handkerchief to cover his mouth, only to find he was still in his sweats.

Her throat was slit wide open, and the blood around her was dried and brown, matting her blonde hair and the tattered remnants of a nightgown, and surrounding her naked body on the floor like a dirty halo. The skin on her bloated face had taken on a transparent quality and was tinged with blue beneath. There were dried footprints of bare feet in the blood, and when he saw the cuts on her soles he was pretty sure that the footprints were hers.

There were also signs of a struggle: a turned-over coffee table, broken glass, the fact that her feet were cut, and the position of her body, which suggested that she may have been trying to reach the poker by the fireplace. Ransom finally had to look away

173

and when he raised his head he found Burgher's bugged-out eyes staring at him from the kitchen.

He circled the body of what he assumed to be the baby's mother, careful not to step on any of the blood, and he and Razor walked over to the couch. Ransom sighed. They were both looking at the child, approximately one year old, wrapped up in a blanket and peacefully sucking his thumb.

"There's another body," said Razor, and Ransom whipped his head around. He hadn't been informed of this. "The bedroom."

Ransom followed Razor down a small hallway to the right of the living room. The bedroom was lit by a dim lamp on the far side of the queen-size bed. The covers were in a heap on the floor. To his left was the baby's crib and directly in front of him, surrounded by a pile of blood-soaked paperbacks, was a man, throat slit open, body excavated the same way. He was brown-haired, fairly muscular, and on closer inspection Ransom found a nasty gash across the back of his foot. The tendon looked severed.

In the soft light Ransom could see the broken remnants of a lamp next to the crib and bloody footprints leading out of the bedroom. He could also see slivers of wood sticking up from the floor, and squatted down to examine them. They were uniform gouges that led in a path from the bed to the crib and out the door. The only explanation he could think of for marks like these was that the killer had worn track spikes.

The whole scene reminded him of something from a film by . . . David Cronenberg. He had almost thought George Romero, but Romero had never been this grisly, even on a good day. And this was real life. He and Razor walked back to the kitchen to talk with Burgher, but there was nowhere in the house that they could escape the stench of death.

"Let's go ahead and call the M.E. tonight on this one. I want an ambulance for the kid, too. Did anybody touch anything?"

"I had to kick the door in," said Burgher, his voice changing pitch like an adolescent's. "And I hit the wall switch for the overhead light. Nothing after that." Ransom looked to Razor and he shook his head. "Just the kid."

"Did you find the missing . . . uh, body parts?"

Razor shook his head again. "Are you gonna take the case?" he asked.

Though Ransom wouldn't have believed it possible, Burgher's eyes bugged out even further as he awaited the answer.

"Tell you what I'll do, fellas. You do the preliminary report tonight and leave it on Gorham's desk. He's my partner, and it's only fair that he have a say in this, too. We have a lot of other cases we're working on that we can't exactly drop. But if it's alright with him, I'd be glad to."

Burgher looked as though he had received a last-minute reprieve from the governor. "I'll go get things rolling," he said, racing for the front door.

"Thanks, Jack," said Razor, after they had stood silent for a minute or two. "I really appreciate this."

"Don't thank me yet. Gorham still has to say yes."

"Yeah, well, even if he says no, I appreciate your coming down here."

They stood silently again and Ransom waited until he heard the sirens of the ambulance and the evidence team before walking back out into the rain and heading home.

CHAPTER TWO

"Why are you afraid?"
"I'm not. I'm not. I've found release."
"That music doesn't speak of release."
"No . . . no . . . you're right."
"That music tells of the dark: evil things, shadowy places—"
"Stop! Stop! Stop!"

Ransom woke with a start, but it was only Gloria Holden trying to convince Irving Pichel that she wasn't a vampire. He hadn't been able to finish watching *The Thing* when he returned home the night before and had dropped *Dracula's Daughter* into his VCR instead. It was one of his favorites in his collection— beautifully atmospheric, a better plot than the original *Dracula* with Lugosi, but, more important last night, it was bloodless. He'd only watched about a half-hour before he had unwound enough to get some sleep.

Ransom owned about three hundred videotapes, all of them crammed front to back with movies, most of those horror. He had become real aficionado since the advent of video recorders, and his knowledge of the genre was extensive. Most people assumed that he would want to forget about violence when he wasn't working. But he agreed with the experts who said that people watched horror movies to escape the horrible realities of everyday life. And after all, who had more to escape from than a homicide detective?

But it was more than just a theory to Ransom; he knew it to be true. There was a reason he needed to escape reality that went far beyond his job, one that he never talked about, and one that very few other people knew of. Eighteen years ago Ransom's wife had committed suicide. Last night at the crime scene, for the first time in years, he'd had to run back out of the house because he was having a flashback.

The sound of a gunshot had awakened him in the middle of the night. Stacy wasn't in bed and when he got up to investigate he'd found her naked body on the bathroom floor. There was blood everywhere. She had put the barrel of the gun in her mouth and blown her head away with Ransom's own service revolver. She'd left no note.

He'd had dreams every night for years after that, and flashbacks during the day. The flashbacks were especially rough on him when was working. Then one night a friend had convinced him to come along with some of the guys and take in a horror film. That was the first night Ransom hadn't dreamed of her. The movies seemed to work like an appeasement to whatever god of nightmares was operating inside Ransom's head.

So now he watched horror films night and day. The VCR was hooked up to the TV in his bedroom as well as the one in the living room so that he could use it as an alarm clock. All he had to do was make sure the tab was removed from the videocassette so that when the power came on, the "play" mechanism would kick in. A timer plugged into the wall socket did the rest and Jack Ransom had a wake-up call from Hollywood every morning.

He hoped that last night wasn't an indication that the flashbacks were returning. The most likely explanation for what had happened was the initial similarity between the way he had found Stacy and how they had found the woman last night. In spite of the publicity, most homicides were not especially gruesome. There was blood, sure, but stab wounds and gunshots were the norm. The intensity of the scene last night had fired off something in Ransom's brain that had been dormant for a long time

His wife's name was Stacy Simpson. Ransom had met her during his first year of college, after a disillusioning breakup with his high-school sweetheart. He and Stacy were in a drama class together and wound up playing opposite each other in "Barefoot in the Park". The attraction was mutual, and two years later they were married.

Ransom had wanted to start a family right away, but Stacy was worried about his profession, worried for his life. She didn't want to end up a single parent; she wanted their children to have a father. Ransom was good at his job, though, and had no intention of quitting. Eventually he began to worry that she would never bear him the children he wanted so desperately. One of the worst shocks surrounding Stacy's suicide hadn't come until after the autopsy. It was when Ransom found out she had been three weeks pregnant.

He tried to date after Stacy but, as with a lot of cops, even the best of his relationships could rarely stand the sixty-plus hours a week that he had been putting in up until a few years ago. Now that he was tenured, so to speak, with twenty-five years of service under his belt, most of the long hours were behind him. Unfortunately, so was his youth. He was almost fifty, with graying hair and the beginnings of a belly, and though he'd had a few promising relationships, no one was exactly beating down his door to marry him.

Ransom pushed himself up out of bed just as Irving was helping Gloria into her casket, and headed wearily for the shower. The stinging spray revived him as he began to think about how his partner would react when he found the file on his desk. It wasn't going to be quite the hard sell that he had made out last night. In fact, he would be surprised if Gorham wasn't drooling over the case right now; the kid still came in early every damn day. It was the kind of case that made careers, though, provided you solved it. If you blew it, you could just as easily wind up busting hookers up on Aurora Avenue North. But Gorham was young enough not to know the difference, and eager enough not to care.

Back in the bedroom Ransom dressed, putting on his coat and tie while Gloria seduced a young waif into posing for a painting.

By the time he was sipping coffee in the kitchen, Gloria was snacking on the poor girl's neck. Ransom sighed. It was a great film. Shame he had to turn it off, but duty called. He checked for rain—none, thank God—then turned off the movie and headed for his car.

"I say we go for it, Jack."

As expected, Al Gorham had cornered Ransom the minute he walked into the squad room. At thirty-one, Gorham was one of the youngest detectives Ransom had ever worked with, as well as one of the best. He was sandy-haired and blue-eyed, and what he lacked in experience he made up for in enthusiasm. At the moment his youth was showing.

"Now, hold on just a minute, Al. You weren't there last night. You didn't see what those folks looked like."

"Sure, I did." Gorham dug into the Manila envelope he was holding and brought forth a handful of Polaroids. "They came with the prelim. The eight-by-tens should be ready this afternoon."

Ransom shook his head in disbelief and made his way through the maze of scarred wooden furniture and piles of papers toward his desk with Gorham in tow. "Yeah, I guess for someone who grew up with Freddy Krueger, this stuff seems pretty tame."

"Freddy who?"

Ransom stopped dead in his tracks and got that sinking feeling in his stomach again. Although the department usually did a good job of assigning partners, they didn't seem to factor in recreational compatibility. Ransom was sure that he had been teamed up with the only person on the Seattle Police Force—the only person in Seattle, for that matter—who had never seen a horror film.

Al Gorham, it seemed, was the product of an extremely conservative upbringing. Among other things his parents didn't believe in wasting money on, two of them were movies and television. Even while he was going to college, and afterward when he was on his own, he never watched them. It just wasn't something he was interested in, he said, and though Ransom could respect that it sometimes drove him crazy.

Tall and lean, with a mop of hair over his gaunt face, at first sight Gorham appeared awkward, but on the streets he was deceptively quick and agile. He was also incredibly smart. As far as the police work went, Ransom couldn't have asked for a better partner.

He had been working with Gorham for about two years, ever since his old partner retired. It was the department's policy to assign younger detectives to work with veterans. Ransom thought it was a good system. But now *he* was the senior member of the team, and things were different. Suddenly he began to feel responsible, not only for Al, but, ironically, for himself. Gorham was a quick learner, though, and didn't get defensive about criticism. He was a good cop even if he was a little obsessive.

Ransom hung up his coat when he reached his desk, and sat down. Gorham took the seat across from him. "Did you go see a movie this weekend like I told you to?"

"Come on, Jack. You know I wanted to look over that Adams file again—"

"That's not even our case. For Christ's sake, Al, you gotta loosen up a little. How do you ever expect to meet someone if you stay holed up in your apartment all the time?"

"We talk about this every Monday. You know I don't want anyone to become emotionally dependant on me when I might be killed in the line of duty."

"Okay, okay, I'll drop it," said Random, thinking it would do Gorham a world of good if *he* were to become emotionally dependant on someone. "What does the prelim say?"

"Two bodies, Caucasian, mid-thirties, one female, one male: a Mr. and Mrs. David Edison. The husband was found in the bedroom with his throat cut and all internal organs missing. The wife was in the front room, same condition, except that the baby was asleep in her body. The husband had his right Achilles tendon severed and the wife had cuts on her feet from the broken lamp."

"Did the internal organs ever turn up?"

"Nope."

"Okay. What about the kid?"

"Male, Caucasian—turns out the couple wasn't the real kid's parents. They were foster parents. We found papers in a desk drawer. The date on the papers is from last Wednesday, five days ago."

"Do you have those?"

"Sure."

Gorham handed Ransom the papers that gave the Edisons legal guardianship of their child. He checked them over and took special notice of the birth date. His guess was right on; the kid had been born last November, and was almost exactly a year old. "Do we know where the kid was before this?"

Gorham looked puzzled. "What do you mean?"

"I mean, where has he been for the last year?"

"He's only a week old, Jack."

"No, look, it's right here . . ." But it wasn't there. He had read it wrong. Now that he looked again, the birth date said that the child had indeed been born only a week ago. "Do you have a birth certificate?"

Gorham shook his head.

"There's no way that kid's only a week old. Is there a picture of him in there?"

While Gorham dug in the envelope, Ransom thought again about what he had seen the night before. The kid had looked older then—he was sure of it—but now he couldn't really say why. When Gorham handed the picture to him, he instantly realized what it was: the kid was lying on its side. He would have to check it out, but he was fairly sure that newborns slept on either their backs or stomachs.

"Where is he now?"

"Ambulance took him over to the Elliott Bay Medical Center. The adoption agency came and picked him up there early this morning."

"That was fast."

"Those people don't wait around."

Ransom left his seat and walked over to the window. The solid, gray mass of clouds was so oppressive that he turned around

Eric B. Olsen

and sat on the sill, purposely snubbing them. "How long were the bodies there? They smelled pretty ripe."

"Two to three days, most likely. The M.E. is doing the autopsies this morning and we should have the results by this afternoon."

His first thought was that a newborn kid who hadn't eaten in a few days should have been a little longer at the hospital. But if it was a year old, that was a different story. He was definitely going to want to look at a birth certificate to verify the date. There could easily have been a typo on the guardianship papers.

Ransom decided to move on. "So what do we know about the killer?"

"Okay, this is where it gets good," said Gorham, but when his eyes met Ransom's, his expression changed from gleeful to somber. "Or bad, depending on your point of view." Ransom shook his head and his partner continued. "Dusting for prints we came up negative. It's been raining, so the windows are locked up tight—no sign of forced entry. Doors were locked, too; the officers had to break into the house. A neighbor called 911, said she hadn't seen them in a week and was worried. A unit was sent around to take a look and that's how they found them."

"So maybe the killer knew them—maybe he had a key."

"Or maybe it was a woman."

"The real mother?" Ransom hadn't thought of that. "So why didn't she take the kid?"

Gorham shrugged. "Okay, what if they let the guy in and he locked up as he was leaving?"

"With his Hefty bag full of guts?"

"Sure. If you guys ask me, this guy's a complete psycho."

"Sometimes it's not as simple as that."

"What do you mean?"

"Well, what he did to the bodies—there could be any number of reasons for that, one of them being that this was a setup, that he's trying to throw us off track." Ransom looked out the window again and frowned. "But that's only part of it."

"Yeah?"

182

"There's also the kid. Why does this guy go to all the trouble of making sure there's no evidence, and then leave the kid in the woman's body?"

"You think he's trying to send us a message?"

"That's exactly what I'm thinking, and I don't like the things I've been coming up with so far. Motherhood, the baby in the womb—I've never been good with symbolism. I mean, is he trying to tell us where he's going to hit next, or just give us the reason why he's hitting? There has to be an explanation for what he did."

"Or didn't do." Gorham's face brightened. "Why didn't he kill the baby?"

"Exactly. He has to be sending us some kind of message."

"Jesus."

The two of them were silent for a moment and then Ransom looked at his watch. "Tell you what. I'm going to go down and talk to the M.E. this morning, maybe find out something that won't be on the report. I'd like you to see if you can find out where the kid's real mother is, then go over and talk to some of the neighbors again, okay?"

"Then we're taking the case?"

"Kind of looks that way."

"Great!" Gorham was up and out the door before Ransom was able to sit back down at his desk.

The fact that he could have misjudged the age of the kid was still bothering him. If he'd missed that, he wondered, how many other things had he missed? Was he getting slack? Was he losing it? Was that why he wasn't able to pick up on the killer's clues? Those were the questions a cop shouldn't have to ask himself. He'd never had to think about his job before, his instincts proving more than reliable. Maybe he just needed to concentrate more.

As he stood up, Ransom tried to shake off his self-doubts; they weren't doing anyone any good, least of all him. Besides, he had an appointment. It was time to call on his old friend Richard Nagumo, King County's chief medical examiner.

CHAPTER THREE

Ransom turned left off of 45th and goosed his Buick up to sixty as he eased, southbound, onto Interstate 5. Off to his right was Lake Union, and beyond that, looming up against the grey sky, was the Space Needle, a Seattle landmark left over from the 1962 World's Fair. Then Ransom turned his attention to the glut of skyscrapers dead ahead and, a minute later, took the Stewart Street exit. Midmorning traffic was light downtown and in five minutes he was pulling into the parking lot of Harborview Medical Center. Seattle's morgue was located in the basement there, and once inside, Ransom followed the familiar route to the offices of the county medical examiner.

He walked into Nagumo's office and was greeted by Katherine Sabin, Nagumo's secretary. "He's on his last case this morning, Jack," she said, barely glancing up from her typewriter. "You want me to call the autopsy suite and tell him you're coming down?"

"Uh, no thanks, Katherine," said Random, and quickly sat down. "I'll just wait here." Definitely.

Richard "Doc" Nagumo had been the county coroner since before Ransom had joined the force, and when the state finally changed over to the medical examiner system in 1969, Nagumo was the logical choice for chief. Though Ransom had worked with him before, the two had not become friends until the Decapitator case. Now they shared information liberally, and above all, they trusted each other.

There were no magazines in Nagumo's waiting room—he probably figures he doesn't need them, Ransom thought; all of his patients are dead—and Ransom had to content himself with listening to Katherine Sabin's rapid-fire typing. Twenty minutes later Nagumo breezed in the door, past Ransom, and over to his secretary's desk. "Hey Jack," he said, when they finally made eye contact. "What brings you down here?"

"The Edison case."

"I thought I saw Razor and Burgher's name on that one."

"Yeah, well, they asked if I'd take it over for them, what with my being the resident psycho-killer expert and all."

"I see what you mean," Nagumo said gravely. The man never did have a sense of humor.

Nagumo was a few years older than Ransom, but still had a full head of jet-black hair. His face was hard and round, with brown almond eyes behind his wire-framed glasses, and he was dressed in his standard uniform: crisp white shirt, tie, and blue slacks beneath his pristine-white lab coat. Nagumo ushered Ransom into his office and they both made themselves comfortable, Ransom taking his usual place on the couch against the wall, and Nagumo—at five-four, his rump just reaching over the top—sitting on the corner of his desk.

"So what can you tell me, Doc?"

"Cause of death was laceration of the carotid artery in both victims. They bled to death."

"How was it done?"

"Animal claw of some type—"

"Whoa, Doc, hold it right there. Are we talking about the same case?"

"If you're talking about the Edison case, we are."

Ransom was floored and took him a moment to catch his train of thought again. "I don't mean to tell you your business, but I was there. It looked like a clean cut, with a sharp knife or something."

"Yeah, that's what it looks like, all right, but that's not what did is. You see, the entry wounds are on the side of the neck, and the punctures are conical, not flat like with a knife. We also know

185

that the cutting surface was curved and the wound itself, though appearing clean, was somewhat ragged. All consistent with a large animal claw."

"Wait a minute—the wounds were perfectly straight. There's no way an animal could have made a cut that precise across the neck—"

Nagumo had his hands up in front of him. "Easy, Jack. I never said an animal did it—I only said that it was done with an animal claw."

Ransom hoped that the redness he felt climbing up his neck didn't show. That was twice this day that he'd made the wrong assumption and been nailed on it. Mercifully, Nagumo continued.

"Now the claw mark theory would fit those marks that were on the bedroom floor, and we also found a few animal hairs in and around both bodies. We should have an I.D. on those tomorrow. At first glance it looks like someone's trying to make us think that an animal is responsible."

"But you don't think so?"

"No way. For one thing, like you said, the wounds on the throat are too symmetrical. Also, there were no additional lacerations on the bodies of the type you would normally associate with somebody trying to fend off an animal attack. And then there are the bite marks . . ."

Nagumo furrowed his brow and looked for a moment at the ceiling, apparently deep in thought. Ransom didn't recall seeing any bite marks on the victims, but he also didn't want to put his foot in his mouth again, so he just listened.

"But even the bite marks don't concern me as much as the time of death. Now, your people have it estimated at two to three days ago, but it's more like four or five. Your boys apparently turned the place upside down last night, but they couldn't find any internal organs anywhere. And that's why the time of death is so interesting: it looks as though the organs were . . . bitten away."

"Aw, Christ, Doc."

Nagumo's hands went up again. "I know, I know, but that's the most positive evidence we have that it wasn't an animal. The teeth marks are, in fact, similar to those of a dog, but the bite configuration is all wrong. The shape of the occlusion suggests a human did it."

Ransom leaned back to mull this over but Nagumo continued.

"So what I'm thinking here is that the murderer probably isn't trying to cover anything up, not deliberately, anyway. Maybe he just likes to kill people that way. What do you think?"

"Right now I'm more interested in what you think."

"Okay, if we suppose he's not trying to throw us off the track by making it look like an animal, I can only conclude that he's acting out some sort of fantasy. Maybe he really wants to *be* an animal. Hell, maybe he thinks he already is one. Remember, we have the hairs to consider, and we know that the Edisons didn't have any pets. Also, an animal claw is only sharp at the tip, and these appear to have been artificially sharpened down the length of the claw.

"So maybe this guy dresses up in a hide to make the kills. He gets a hold of some animal claws, files them razor sharp, and attaches them to his hands with gloves so he doesn't leave any prints. Then, for the *piece de resistance*, he rigs up a set of dentures made from dog teeth that fit over his own."

Ransom was nodding now. "And all the evidence you found supports something like that?"

"It's the only thing that even comes close to explaining it. Except . . ."

Ransom could see the hesitancy in his friend's eyes. "Except what?"

"Well as bad as all that sounds, that's still not the worst part."

Ransom was up on the edge of the couch, not believing it could get any worse.

"I told you before that they were killed four to five days ago. Well, all of the trauma to the body occurred postmortem, after the victims were already dead. But not just *immediately* after. The removal of the organs appears to have taken place over the entire five days prior to discovery."

"Aw, Christ. You mean this sicko was hanging around there after they were dead and chewing their guts out all week long?"

Nagumo nodded. "Some of the wounds on the woman may have even happened on the day you found her. No animal I know of would have stayed in the house that long unless it couldn't get out, and then you would have found it there. I've been doing this job for a lot of years, Jack, and I've seen some strange things in that time, but it's hard, even for me, to imagine how anybody could want to do something like that."

Ransom's hands were nearly shaking and the room suddenly seemed incredibly warm. And then he had a sobering thought: someone that sick could be almost impossible to catch. Aside from the hairs and the scratches on the floor, which fit in perfectly with Doc's scenario, the guy had left no evidence."

"Is all of this going to be in the report?"

"Report's not finished yet. I'm calling in an animal expert from Portland today to nail down the species on the claw and teeth marks. I should have the results for you by Wednesday—Thursday at the latest."

"Thanks, Doc."

The two men walked to the door and before Nagumo opened it he said, "Do you think this killing was random, Jack?"

"For all our sakes, Doc, I hope to hell not. If the killer's connected to the Edisons, we at least stand a chance of catching him. But if not, and he does it again, he could make the Decapitator look like the boy next door."

Ransom left the morgue in something of a daze. This could wind up being bigger than even he had imagined. If there were more murders, and no more evidence than what was left in this one, they could continue indefinitely. There was only one other case in recent Seattle history like that. The dozens of unsolved Green River killings suddenly came to mind and something akin to panic began to rise in Ransom's chest. He needed to catch this guy fast, for all sorts of reasons. If he used his influence with Nagumo, and could get the coroner's report stalled for a few days, they would have an entire week of grace before the media swooped down on them with a catchy name for the killer and unrealistic expectations for the police. Once the details of Nagumo's autopsy became public, the investigation was going to turn into a three-ring circus.

But that would be nothing compared to what would happen if the guy killed again. When that happened, the pressure would really be on, liberally applied by everyone from the governor on down. Unfortunately, Ransom was going to be the guy on the bottom of the pile. Add to that his ebbing confidence and Gorham's gong-ho attitude and things were looking scary.

Meanwhile, he still had a couple of other cases he needed to get information on, and after lunch he could hook up with Gorham. Back outside, a heavy drizzle had soaked the streets and Ransom breathed a little easier. For the moment, anyway, he could forget about the Edison case and be happily annoyed at the weather for the rest of the morning.

CHAPTER FOUR

It was a few minutes after 1:30 when Ransom returned to the precinct house. Gorham was waiting for him. Ransom told his partner what he had learned from Nagumo and for once Gorham was speechless.

"Doc's calling up some expert from Portland to take a look at the bite marks. I'll talk to him tomorrow and we should have something to follow up on then."

"What if it is random?" Gorham finally asked. "What if he hits somewhere else?"

"Doesn't matter. There's nothing we can do about that now. We've got until Wednesday before the autopsy report's ready and we need to do as much as we can until then."

Both of them knew that the best chance they had of catching the killer was during the next few days, while the trail was still fresh. Once the details of the murder had been released, they would face the possibility of copycats, peculiarly twisted individuals who, in Ransom's mind, rated almost lower than the original killer. Copycats killed for the thrill of it, to see how closely they could duplicate another murder, to see if they could get away with it.

In addition, the murderer himself would officially know that the police were after him. He would examine newspaper articles, and videotape the evening news to see what evidence he might have left behind. He would be much more deliberate next time; he would be more careful, and therefore, that much harder to catch.

"Any ideas on the message theory?" Gorham asked.

"Yeah, but none of them good. And now with what the Doc told me today, I don't know what to think. How about you?"

Gorham shook his head.

"Did you find out anything about the mother?"

Gorham pulled out his notepad and flipped it open. "I went to the adoption agency and talked with the guy at the front desk. He says the woman who runs the place is a Mrs. Lawrence, first name, Michelle. She only works in the afternoons so I made an appointment to talk to her today in about half an hour. I thought we could go over there together."

"Good."

The Seattle Children's Placement Center was the city's biggest private adoption agency. It was located directly south of the University District on Capitol Hill, an area well known for its diversity, claiming host to a thriving business district, numerous restaurants, and two colleges, as well as being the center of the gay community in Seattle. Ransom and Gorham pulled up to a large Victorian house that had been restored and converted into office space. Promptly at 2:15 they were shown into the office of Michelle Lawrence.

"I know. I was notified immediately. It's just terrible, terrible what happened to that lovely couple."

Lawrence was in her late fifties, a heavyset blonde who wore plenty of makeup to go along with her silks and jewelry. She gave the men a big egg-sucking grin as she motioned for them to sit in a couple of fancy claw-foot chairs.

The room was heavily decorated and looked more like a place someone would want to take pictures of than do business in. The plush white carpet was littered with small square Oriental rugs, while the walls were plastered with mirrors, photographs and various other hangings. Throughout the rest of the office, and strategically planted around her desk, were tiny tables filled with knick knacks and statuettes. The only description Ransom could put his finger on as he moved to one of the chairs was claustrophobic.

When Ransom sat down, his eyes were already watering. He was about to comment on the fact when he realized the source of the irritation: it was Mrs. Lawrence. She smelled as if she'd put on her perfume with a fire hose. Ransom decided at once that he didn't like her.

"Isn't it a little soon to be putting the kid in another home?" he said, his tone a little more accusatory than necessary.

"Just terrible. Do you know how many people are waiting for children to adopt, Detective? Hundreds," she said, without waiting for an answer, "in this city alone. Millions of couples across the country are yearning for a child, but through no fault of their own they—"

"Yes, I think we get the picture."

She looked stunned for a moment and then smiled.

"I understand you picked up the kid from Bay Med early this morning."

"A hospital is no place for a baby, Detective. It was just so fortunate for everyone concerned that we had a family who was willing to take the dear child on such short notice."

"Is that standard procedure, for a kid to be adopted so soon after something like this?"

"Oh, the child hasn't been adopted. He's in a *foster* home now, and he'll stay there until adoptive parents are found for him. After all, we can't keep him in the office, now, can we?"

Ransom merely nodded while Gorham diligently recorded every word in his notebook. "Now, what about the Edisons? Were they the adoptive or foster parents?" Ransom proceeded.

"Oh, they were foster parents," she said, smiling so hard Ransom thought she was going to crack her mask of makeup. "The dear child went home from the hospital the day he was born to live with Mr. and Mrs. Edison."

"That was only last week," Gorham piped in. "Isn't that rather unusual?" Ransom made his displeasure obvious.

"Oh, heavens, no. The mother had come to us at the beginning of her pregnancy, and the Edisons had been picked out several weeks before the little child's arrival."

"Hold on," said Ransom, resuming command of the questioning. "You just said you had a thousand people waiting to get a baby, and in all those months you couldn't find anyone to adopt it?"

Lawrence's phony smile drooped a little. "Well . . . this was a . . . *special* case."

"What's *that* supposed to mean?"

"It means the case was *special.*"

Ransom's eyes bored into hers, but he said nothing.

"It means," she finally went on, "that all of our prospective parents carefully screen the birth mother before agreeing to adopt. The first step involves a complete background check on both the mother and the father and then, if all goes well, a face-to-face meeting. All of this takes time. We—"

"What was wrong with her?" Ransom thought he saw her eye twitch.

"Whatever do you mean?"

"There must have been something wrong with her if no one wanted her kid. Now, what was it?"

"Well, uh . . . she was, uh . . ." Ransom waited. "Disfigured."

"Come on, Mrs. Lawrence, what are we talking about here—a couple of hickeys, a bad nose job, dueling scar?"

She didn't say another word, quietly taking a Polaroid picture out of her desk. Gorham stood up and she handed it to him. He hardly took his eyes off the photo as he passed it to Ransom.

The distorted and hunchbacked figure in the picture looked barely human, at once repulsive and mesmerizing. It was a full-body pose, but Ransom didn't need a close up to see that something was very wrong. All of her extremities—arms, hands, feet, and legs—were grotesquely out of proportion with her body. Her face was large and uneven, with heavy lips and a jutting brow, and if not for the long hair and the dress, he could not have said what sex she was.

"We tried," said Lawrence, barely able to maintain her perfunctory smile. "Lord knows we tried. But no one would give her a chance. I believe her condition is called—"

"Acromegalia."

"Then you have heard of it?"

"Yeah."

"I must say, it's the first time I've ever come in contact with anything quite so . . ."

"Special?" Ransom put the picture in his pocket and continued the questioning. "Is this why the Edisons didn't want to adopt?" said Ransom.

"Oh, but they did—at least *Mrs._*Edison did. Her husband, however, flatly refused. In the end, they compromised and he said they would become the child's foster parents. He wanted to make absolutely sure that if anything went wrong with the child, they wouldn't be forced into keeping him."

Ransom nodded. "Just a couple more things before we go. First, we're going to need to see the adoption records, birth certificate, whatever you have on the kid. And we're also going to need any information you have on the natural parents. We have to question the mother and father, and anybody else who knew them."

"Oh, no, I'm afraid you won't be able to do that. You see—"

"Look, Mrs. Lawrence, let me make it real simple for you. Either you give us the records or I get a court order. Understand?"

Mrs. Lawrence wasn't smiling anymore. "What I was about to say, *Detective,* is that the mother was homeless when she came to us. We have nothing but her name; she didn't know who the father was."

"Even so, we'll still have to talk to her for—"

"She died on the operating table giving birth."

On the way back to the precinct Ransom didn't say much. He had made an ass of himself again. This case was turning into a nightmare. As Mrs. Lawrence had promised, the adoption agency had next to nothing on the mother except her name: Pamela Gerhardt. The only other information he and Gorham had managed to get was the kid's birth certificate and the name and address of the new foster parents.

He was dismayed to confirm the kid was, indeed, only a week old. Lawrence's testimony corroborated the fact.

"What did you say Gerhardt's condition was called?"

Ransom had stopped for a red light and Gorham was busily trying to finish up his notes.

"Acromegalia."

"How do you know about that?"

"Jesus, Al, don't you ever watch the late show? *Tarantula*, 1955."

"Is that another one of your movies?"

Ransom sighed as the light turned green, and then he pulled out into the intersection.

CHAPTER FIVE

Tuesday morning Ransom awoke to the sounds of Gregory Peck doing his best Josef Mengele in *The Boys From Brazil.* It wasn't very impressive, but the movie was. The ballroom scene had just begun and Ransom decided to watch it before taking his shower.

Mengele's plot to clone Hitler had just been called off; unfortunately, no one bothered to tell Mengele. So when one of his soldiers, who was supposed to be off in Kristianstad killing Oscarson, waltzed up to him on the dance floor and introduced his wife. Mengele flew into a rage and began to beat the hell out of the guy.

"Shut up, you ugly bitch!" Mengele yelled at the soldier's wife when she told him to stay away from her husband.

Ransom winced, but couldn't hold back a smile. "Ya gotta love those Nazis," he said to himself and hopped out of bed.

He and Gorham split up the work again that day. Ransom was going to take the picture of Pamela Gerhardt around to some of the homeless shelters and see if someone recognized her. Maybe someone had a grudge against her, or maybe Lisa Edison had been mistaken for Gerhardt—although with her disease, that seemed to be a virtual impossibility. Still, it was the only lead they had.

Gorham got the job of phone jockey: calling all the neighbors again and making sure there was nothing they had forgotten to put in their statements, as well as calling all of the Edisons' relatives to find out why anyone might want to kill them. They seemed pretty clean-cut—they would have to have been just to get the kid—but you never knew.

Ransom started on Roosevelt in the U-District. He showed the picture around, but other than mild repulsion and a few gasps, got nowhere. Next, he headed down to a Christian soup kitchen on Denny Way where he received a sermon along with head shakes and open-mouthed stares. It wasn't until he hit the shelter down on First Ave that he struck gold.

"Yeah. I recognize her."

Ransom was showing the picture to an old wino. The man was about sixty with dark dirty hair and a ten-day beard. His eyes were yellow and rheumy and his nose was riddled with burst capillaries. He was also wearing about three layers of clothes that had seen better days and smelled like piss.

"Could you tell me where you saw her?"

"Ain't never seen her."

The old man was sitting on a dirty mattress on the floor and leaning up against the wall, legs out straight in front of him. Ransom was squatting beside him.

"How can you recognize her picture, then?"

"Heard about her from a feller up in one of those skin shops. After I leave here with a shave and smellin' a damn sight better, I can walk into one of those places, pretty as you please." The old man flashed him a grin with brown, Nicotine-stained teeth.

"What exactly did you hear?"

"He said she was in some kinda live sex show. Course I never really believed him, but I nodded and smiled just the same. And now here she is," said the old man, motioning to see the picture again. "Whadda you know about that?"

"Do you remember who this person was you spoke with?"

The man looked at Ransom as if he had been speaking a foreign language, and then said, "I think he works there."

The porno shop was just two blocks up the street from the shelter. A small yellow sign above the door read *Adult Books* and the windows were blacked out for privacy of its patrons. Ransom grabbed one of the metal bars that ran the length of the door, and entered. The large room was filled with the requisite x-rated video cassettes, porno magazines, blow-up dolls, dildos, and leather goods. In the back he could see the entrance to the private video-viewing booths.

Behind the counter sat a Hispanic college-aged kid reading a copy of *Ulysses*. The wino had said that he should look for a balding white guy, but Ransom showed him the picture anyway. After getting over his initial shock, the kid shook his head. When Ransom flashed his badge and described the man the wino had mentioned, the kid nodded. The man's name, he learned, was Ned, and he was apparently the owner. The kid pressed a buzzer underneath the counter and a few minutes later, from out of the entrance to the private video booths, came the owner.

Ransom flashed his ID again and they went back to the man's office. The man who introduced himself as Ned Swaney was fiftyish, bald as Yul Brynner, but also about six foot four and not somebody you'd want to tangle with.

"No," he said, shaking his head vehemently. "Never seen her before."

Ransom knew that Swaney was lying. He hadn't even reacted to the picture—looked at it like it was somebody's graduation photo and that was that. It was obvious he had already known what she looked like.

"Look, Mr. Swaney. I'm not on the vice squad—never have been—and I'm not investigating you or your operation. I work the homicide division up in the U-District. This woman is indirectly involved in a case I'm working on and I just got through talking to someone who says you've seen her. Now, if there's any other way I can be straight with you, you just tell me."

Swaney frowned. "How do I know you won't tell your friends in the vice?"

"There's only one way, really. I take you out of here in the cuffs for obstruction of justice, and we go for a ride to the precinct. But before I book you, we go into an interrogation room and I sort of forget to read you your rights and then anything you tell me is totally worthless to vice."

Swaney's expression was so pained it looked as if he had been constipated for a week.

"Or . . ." said Ransom, "you can trust me."

"All right." Swaney, wearing faded brown corduroys and a green polo shirt, sat down at a desk that faced the wall in the small office they were in, and Ransom sat on a folding chair next to him.

"A few months ago this big Indian comes in—looks just like Chief Bromden—and I get a buzz from Kevin out front."

"*Who* did he look like?"

"The Chief, you know, from *One Flew Over the Cuckoo's Nest.*"

"Sure." That one had thrown him for a loop. He remembered the character, played by Will Sampson in the movie, but couldn't recall ever knowing he had a last name. Must have read the book, he thought. Probably borrowed it from "Ulysses" out there.

"So, anyway," continued Swaney, "he says he wants to talk to me, just like you did, except he doesn't have a badge. I bring him back here and he tells me about this private show he's hosting, you know—live sex."

"Hell, I get these guys in here every week telling me how great these shows are, but mostly what they are is bullshit. Personally, I prefer a videotape. You get a lot better view of the action, if you know what I mean."

Ransom nodded.

"But this guy gives me a little Polaroid preview, and so I start to get interested. Now, at most of these things they want a little cash at the door, but when I hear he's charging a hundred a head I start thinking that either he's got his head up his ass, or he's got something worth seeing. I don't mind plunking down a C-note every now and then, but I like to get my money's worth, if you know what I mean. So I ask him a few more questions and he starts to leave."

"Now most of these guys who come in here, you ask 'em to jump and the only thing they'll say is, how high? But this guy's walking away, so I know if the snapshots I saw were just a teaser that this show must be something special. So I went."

"Exactly how many months ago was this?"

"I don't know—let me think." Swaney scowled again trying to conjure up a date. "Must have been April," he finally said. "Tax time. I remember because my car was in the shop and I was thinking that it was going to be a real bitch getting down there."

"Where?"

"A house down by the airport. Shitty little place, but not too bad on the inside. There were a couple dozen of us in the audience."

"Do you remember any of the other people who were there?"

"Hey, come on. You think I go to these things so I can spend time eyeballing the other customers?"

"I just thought you might have talked to someone."

He scowled. "Nah."

"Okay, so what happened?"

"Well, they started with the standard stuff, you know—a couple of white gals with this Indian stud. Only the Indian was dressed up like an animal—"

Ransom's heart flip-flopped in his chest. "Wait a minute. Tell me exactly *how* he was dressed up."

"Well, he wasn't wearing a costume-like thing, you know. They were Indians. He had this skin over his back, like a cape, with the head still on it. I think it was a bear. That was on top of his head, and underneath it he was naked. It was supposed to be like this bestiality thing, and they made it look like some sort of ritual."

Ransom thought Swaney may have hit the nail right on the head. "Did you notice if he was wearing any type of claws on his hands?"

Swaney snorted out a laugh and shook his head. "I wasn't really paying attention to the Indian. Otherwise occupied, if you know what I mean."

"Do you know how many Indians there were total?"

"I don't know—maybe four or five."

"Was there anyone else there who looked like they might be in charge of the Indians?"

'I don't think so."

"Where does the woman fit into all this?"

"I'm just getting to that. They have a few more of those ritual-dance things and then old Chief Bromden comes out. Now I'm pretty big, but this guy's a couple inches taller than me, and he's hung like a horse. Jesus! He's got a hard on the size of a baseball bat and he just picks up one of those women and impales her on it. I swear to God if he'd let her go she'd have just hung there on that giant pecker.

"And while this is going on I'm thinking that this must be the end of the show and I'm getting kind of pissed off 'cause even though it was pretty good, I didn't figure it was worth a hundred bucks.

"But there's still more after Bromden's done: that's when they bring *her* out. And let me tell you I didn't know what to do then. I mean, this was carnival freak show time. She was buck-naked and there was no doubt she was a woman. That picture you have there is horrible, but that was nothing compared to seeing her in the flesh. Man . . ."

Swaney shook his head and took a deep breath, and suddenly Ransom felt sad for Pamela Gerhardt. He had only really thought of her in terms of a lead to finding the Edisons' killer, and now that the Indians had emerged as likely suspects, the reality of her situation hit him hard.

She had probably been a prisoner, and risked her life to escape from them. Pregnant and alone in Seattle, she had somehow made her way to the adoption agency. And in trying to give birth to the child inside her, a child whose father was in all likelihood one of her captors, she had lost her life. Then the Edisons had lost theirs.

He didn't know why the Indians had killed the couple and then left the baby, but he was sure as hell going to find out.

"Then they brought out the real ones."

"The real what?"

"Animals."

"Aw, Christ."

"You're telling me. I've been in this racket a long time and I've seen some videos of people doing it with animals, but this was *live*. They brought out a couple of dogs first, a Doberman and a collie. The collie was shaved so you could see everything. A few of the customers left at this point. I couldn't tell you why I stayed—I just did. After the dogs did her they brought out an honest-to-God goat, and at the end . . . I thought at first it was another dog—they had it in chains and the thing looked mean as hell—but it was a wolf, a goddamned wolf. No shit."

The sadness Ransom had felt for Pamela Gerhardt was gone now, and in its place was anger, a loathing he hadn't felt in seven years, since the Decapitator case. They should have taken their animal act on the road, thought Ransom. And perhaps they had. But one or more of them had made the mistake of coming back, and Ransom was determined to make them pay, not only for what they had done to a couple who was willing to take an orphaned child into its home, but for what they had done to the child's poor deformed mother.

"Thank you, Mr. Swaney. I'm going to need to use your phone."

"Oh, man, you're gonna call the vice squad after all." Swaney was standing now, his fists clenched and his neck turning red. "I knew I shouldn't have said anything. Goddamn it—"

"Sit down, Mr. Swaney!" Ransom stood, his eyes on a level with Swaney's chin, and reluctantly Swaney sat down. "I just need to make a call to my partner and then I'll be out of your hair," for now, he thought, because in reality Mr. Swaney was going to become very familiar with one of the interrogation rooms back at the precinct. They were going to need a detailed description of everyone he had seen that night. There was no need to tell him just yet, however, and he picked up the receiver and dialed.

"Goddamn it," Swaney moaned.

"Al!" he said, when Gorham answered the phone. "I got a line on the killer."

"Are you serious? Who is it?"

"I don't have time to explain right now. Do you have the name of the new foster parents for the Gerhardt kid?"

"Yeah. Irv and Deborah Jacobson. They live in the North End—"

"I need you to get over there right away. I think they're going to be the killer's next target."

"How do you know that?"

"The murders had nothing to do with the Edisons—the kid was the connection. Now, don't send a squad car, go over there yourself. I don't want them spooked. Just see if they're all right. Tell them anything, that there have been some robberies in the area, whatever, and to keep an eye out, doors locked, that kind of thing, okay?"

"Sure."

"Good. I'll meet you at the station in half an hour and give you the rundown."

"Half-hour, got it."

Ransom hung up the phone, ignoring the worried look on Swaney's face. His adrenaline was pumping, and he was feeling good. Finally, they had a solid lead.

CHAPTER SIX

"Well, well, what do you know about this? I'm honored you boys could find time to work me into your busy schedules."

Ransom and Gorham had just walked into the office of the precinct captain, Ray Elliot. Elliot was prone to sarcasm.

"We didn't really have anything to go on until today, sir," said Gorham, and Ransom instantly wished he hadn't.

"Bullshit! That's what the paper says, and I don't like reading about what my detectives have or don't have in the goddamn newspaper!" Elliot was also prone to speaking his mind. "What the fuck's going on, Ransom?"

"It looks like the connection between the murderer and the Edisons is the kid."

Elliot was leaning back in his chair now, looking at Ransom like someone would look at what he had just scraped off his shoe with a stick in the park. But the feeling was more than mutual.

Elliot was one of the "New Breed" of cops, handpicked by the mayor himself for his "War on Crime." The new "Get Tough" policy had, to date, produced more in the way of catch phrases than criminals, besides just plain pissing Ransom off.

Most of these "Warriors in Blue" reported directly to the mayor at monthly meetings with the commissioner in one of the swanky hotels downtown, and had more political aspirations than street smarts. Elliot was no exception. Ransom guessed by looking at the man that he had spent more time handling his blow dryer than his service revolver.

The truth was that Elliot had been to one of these little get-togethers yesterday morning and had made himself scarce the rest of the day, most likely avoiding reporters. Elliot didn't concern himself much with day-to-day operations unless it was going to reflect badly on him; then he would ride your ass from here to doomsday to get the case solved.

Ransom frowned. This looked to be one of those very cases. "We found out today that the Gerhardt woman was part of what could be a white-slavery ring that was operating in the Northwest earlier this year. The ring leaders are Indians and some of the practices that were described to me fit the M.O. of the killings."

Elliot had brought out a small emery board from the middle drawer of his desk and was touching up his manicured nails. "Where did you find this out?" he asked without looking up.

"Owner of a porno shop downtown saw Gerhardt at one of their little performances."

He glanced up for a second. "The girl's dead, isn't she?" Then went back to work on his nails.

"Yeah. We'd like to have a couple of teams available for a stakeout on the kid's new home. We think that's where they might try to strike next."

"You can have one team, two men, and make sure they come from the night crew. You two can take the other shift."

"Yes, sir," said Gorham, dying to get into the action but unwittingly bringing Elliot's file-fest to an abrupt halt.

"And just what the hell are you doing to earn your pay on this investigation, Gorham?"

Gorham began shuffling through his notebook while Ransom stuffed his hands in his pockets to keep from ripping it away from his partner.

"Well," said Gorham nervously, evidently finding the page he was looking for. "I found the name of the attending physician on the birth certificate, a Dr. M. K. Harris. The baby was born at the Elliott Bay Medical Center so I called there first and they said that Dr. Harris was on vacation, Port Townsend. So I have someone in the department there looking for him right now. I figure he can fill out some of the detail—"

"Jesus Christ! Is that what this city pays you for—to sit around on your ass making a bunch of phone calls that aren't going to add up to shit? Ransom here is at least getting something we can use. Sounds like you're just pissin' in the wind."

Gorham stopped, folded his notebook shut and slipped it into his pocket. It wasn't fair and Ransom knew it. It could just as easily have been Gorham who had taken around that picture and talked to Swaney. Not all police work is productive, but you have to cover all the bases; you have to be sure that you follow every lead until it's dead.

Gorham hadn't even had a chance to say that he'd gone out to the Jacobsons' right away, and stayed until he could call in a couple of plainclothes detectives to take over for him. Ransom hadn't known about the phone call to the doctor until just now. He thought it was damn fine police work. And yet, here was Gorham, being berated by a guy who couldn't find his ass with both hands and a road map.

"Are you boys going to make this collar pretty quick?"

That was one loaded question Ransom was not going to answer. "We've got a couple of men out at the new foster parents' home. If they try to hit that place at all, we'll get them."

Elliot glared at Ransom. Ransom knew he hadn't answered the question, but Elliot seemed to sense he wasn't going to. "All right, I've heard enough. But I want this case wrapped up pronto—you got that?"

"Yes, sir," said Gorham, but Ransom was already heading out into the hall. Gorham followed quickly.

"And you keep me apprised—" Elliot managed to get out before Ransom finally shut the door. It wasn't a full-fledged slam, but it was hard enough to rattle the windows in Elliot's office, and just hearing the faint sound of cursing behind the glass brought a smile to Ransom's face as he and Gorham walked away.

Gorham, however, didn't have very much to smile about.

"He's wrong, you know," said Ransom.

When Gorham didn't respond, Ransom grabbed his upper arm and they turned, facing each other. "He's wrong, Al. You *know* that."

"I know," Gorham said grudgingly.

"You're a good cop, Al, and I don't want anyone convincing you different. Least of all an idiot like him."

"I know, Jack, but thanks for saying it." Ransom could see in his eyes that he knew. "I just can't figure out why someone like that is in charge here." Ransom understood now and nodded his agreement. "Why don't they make someone like you captain— you're probably the best cop on the whole force."

Ransom smiled, but out of respect for his partner, he didn't burst out laughing as he wanted to. He clapped his hand on Gorham's shoulder and they walked back to the squad room.

Ransom had made Lieutenant exactly seven years before, and then only because the Decapitator had warranted it. He knew that was all the further he was going to rise in this particular police department. It reminded him of the scene in *Lost in America* where Albert Brooks is all ready to receive a promotion and then his boss tells him he's needed "creatively." Somebody else who is not as clever, and therefore "more the executive type," gets the promotion instead.

Ransom knew the streets, knew his precinct. He knew how to talk to people and get the information he needed. He was invaluable to the department right where he was, and they would lose all of that if they stuck him behind a desk. And except for having to deal with people like Elliot, that was okay by him. He liked the streets just fine.

They walked back to their adjoining desks and sat down. "Did they seem all right?" Ransom was speaking of the Jacobsons.

"Yeah. I only talked to him at first—they're older than the Edisons—and then she came to the door with the baby."

"And?"

Gorham perked up a little. "You were right. He looks a lot older than a newborn. If they get a hold of the doctor in Port

Townsend maybe you can ask him about it. I probably won't be here."

"Have you decided which shift you want on the stakeout?" Ransom asked.

"Nights."

This time when Ransom smiled, Gorham smiled back. They had already discussed contingencies for the stakeout, Ransom guessing accurately that Elliot would only spring for one team to help them watch the Jacobson house. With two teams they could each work twelve-hour shifts, but Ransom and Gorham decided to split their shift in half. Ransom had priority and had chosen the six to noon shift. The team from the night crew would take noon to midnight, and Gorham, the midnight to six shift. They both knew that Gorham's shift was the most likely time that the killers would strike.

"All right, you can have nights, but you make damn sure that you call for backup if you see anything. I don't want you getting yourself killed just to prove something to that asshole Elliot.

Gorham was already nodding. "I promise."

In his kitchen that night Ransom sipped on a cold Heineken and leaned against the counter as he waited for his dinner to cook. After work he had picked up a couple of salmon steaks and some potatoes from the Pike Place Market along the waterfront, and they were nearly finished baking in the oven. He ate them at the kitchen table while drinking another beer and reading the evening paper.

With the dishes drying in the rack over the sink, he retired to the front room and picked out a video to watch. He extracted the Jack Arnold classic *Creature from the Black Lagoon* from the shelves and fed it into the mouth of his VCR, then relaxed into his easy chair. As Julia Adams did her synchronized swim routine with the Gill Man, Ransom's mind was inexorably drawn towards the investigation.

What were the Indians trying to tell him? Were they angry that Pamela Gerhardt had died? And if so, why were they taking their revenge on innocent foster parents? It still didn't make sense. Putting the kid in the woman's body must have something to do with motherhood, but why gut the man too? Maybe the removal of the internal organs was some native custom Ransom wasn't familiar with. He shook his head. As close as he believed they were coming to catch the bad guys, there was still something he wasn't seeing, some crucial piece of evidence that was missing.

Swaney had given him what information he could about that house where he had seen the sex show. Undoubtedly, they would get better directions at tomorrow's interrogation. Once they nailed down the address, they might be able to trace back through rental agreements or receipts and get a line on the ring itself. Then there was the Port Townsend police; they had yet to return the call on Dr. Harris, though Ransom wasn't quite sure where that might lead.

Ransom yawned and stretched in his easy chair. He had been putting in some hard hours on this case and he was tired. But he was also angry, and he wanted to catch those bastards so badly he could taste it.

When the movie was finished he ejected the cassette, popped in something else without really looking, and headed off to bed.

CHAPTER SEVEN

A bloodcurdling scream nearly rattled the windows in Jack Ransom's bedroom and he instinctively reached for the shoulder holster that was heaped on his nightstand before he realized it was just Una O'Connor. She was racing down the stairs in *The Invisible Man* and screeching for her husband after realizing that Claude Rains wasn't all there.

The classics revival was likely to go on until he solved the case—especially after his flashback of Stacey—nothing more violent until then. He propped himself up and turned the sound down with the remote control while he woke up the rest of the way. He had set his "alarm" earlier than usual because he had to relieve Gorham at six. After he showered, shaved and dressed, Ransom ventured a peek out the front window and his heart skipped a beat. It looked as if the clouds were breaking up. Dare he even hope for sun? He buttoned up his overcoat, grabbed his umbrella anyway, and walked out to the car. Ransom's Wednesday-morning stakeout from six to noon would have been uneventful except for one thing: the sun was out. God, it was glorious. He felt better than he had in weeks and the shift was a pleasure—window rolled down, crisp cool air drying out the mildew in his Skylark, topped off with a thermos full of hot coffee and a couple cinnamon Danishes. All in all, a fine morning.

Neither of the Jacobsons left their well-kept, two-story house that morning, but they probably had little reason to. Ransom had brought along copies of the latest guardianship papers to peruse while he was waiting, and they showed that the Jacobsons were retired. Both in their mid-fifties, she had been successful real estate agent while he had been a pastor of a nondenominational church, and several years ago they had taken an early retirement. Except for their ages—and that was possibly why they couldn't adopt—they were shoo-ins to get a kid, he thought.

Promptly at noon, a dark-blue van pulled in behind Ransom. He rolled up his windows, boosted the volume a touch on his police radio and filled in the two detectives before heading back to the station. Gorham had taken last night's shift after having been up all day, and was undoubtedly getting some much-needed rest right now. They would touch base later on.

Ransom drove over to 1-5 and cruised south with his elbow cocked out the open window. He took the 45th-Street exit and made his way through one of the most densely populated sections of the University District. This case had been taking up a lot of his time, and he realized now that he needed to get back out on the streets and check in with his people—snitches, businessmen, small-time crooks, folks who found it in their best interest to stay on the good side of the local law enforcement officers. He didn't want them to forget about him. But more importantly, he didn't want them to think *he'd* forgotten about *them.*

Ransom parked in the lot outside the precinct house and stood outside his car for a few minutes, hesitating. He hated to leave the beaming sun for a stuffy squad room, but it was more than that. As much as he disliked the idea, once inside he was going to send two uniforms downtown to pick up Ned Swaney for questioning. It was not going to be as pleasant an afternoon.

After hanging up his coat and sitting down at his desk, Ransom reached for the phone to call Doc Nagumo and see how much time he had before the autopsy report was released. But as soon as he touched the receiver, the phone rang in his hand. He picked it up.

"Yeah."

"Hello. I'm trying to reach Detective Gorham."

It was a woman's voice, and Ransom thought that he was either having one monstrous attack of déjà vu, or he actually recognized the voice.

"My name's Ransom. I'm Detective Gorham's partner. What can I do for you?"

"This is Dr. Harris. I was contacted today by the police in Port Townsend and they told me you needed to speak with me."

"Yes." Now he had it, and he felt a sudden rush of adrenaline course through his body. Dr. M. K. Harris, he realized, was Marian Harris. That was a name he hadn't thought of in years, twenty-five to be exact. They had been something of an item back in high school, but drifted apart during their senior year. And by the time Marian went to college back East while Jack attended the local community college, it was a done deal.

The last thing he could remember was that she had said she was going to study psychology. And now she was back in Seattle. At least this part of the investigation might go a little easier. He'd had his fill of pain-in-the-ass doctors who thought they were too high and mighty to answer a few questions from a lowly civil servant.

"What's this all about?"

"Marian? Is that you?"

"Oh, my God! Jack?"

"Yeah," he said with a laugh. "I didn't know you were back in Seattle."

"I didn't know you were a cop. I mean, I thought I recognized your voice, and then your name. I was scared to death when the police came by and said the Seattle Police wanted to talk to me."

"It's good to hear your voice again."

"What *is* going on, Jack?"

"I'm working on a case, and I wanted to ask you a few questions about Pamela Gerhardt."

"Who's that?"

"You delivered her baby—a boy—about a week and a half ago. I know you must remember her: she had acromegalia."

There was a notable pause before she responded. "What about her?"

Ransom sat up straight now, wondering why Marian was being so evasive. "I understand she died giving birth."

"Yes," she said, her guarded tone suddenly ebbing away. "There were complications due to her disease—they call it acromegaly now."

"Sure. I was just wondering if she confided anything to you about anyone trying to hurt her or her baby. Maybe the father?"

"It was an emergency case. I'd never seen her before that day. Come on, Jack, tell me what's going on."

"Well, the foster parents of the Gerhardt baby were found murdered a few days ago."

"Oh, no! What happened?"

"I really can't say right now."

"Do you know who did it?"

"Yeah, we have a pretty good idea."

"Good . . ."

With business out of the way, their reunion came to a standstill and neither said anything for a few seconds.

"It really is nice to hear from you again, Marian. What are you doing in Port Townsend?"

"Oh, just taking a little vacation. I don't know. I've been working so much lately. But what about you? Still playing the sax?"

Ransom laughed. "Not since college."

"That's too bad. I always thought you were really good."

"I didn't think you ever noticed."

Silence. And there they were. It was as if no time had passed at all and he was back to accusing her of neglect. When it dawned on him that he still had a few more questions to ask her he was mortified. "Hey, I'm sorry . . . I just . . . Look, Marian—"

"How about dinner?"

"Dinner? What—"

"Yes. I just realized how much I'd like to see you again. I'll understand if your wife doesn't want you too—"

"Oh, I'm not married."

"Well, even better. What time do you get off work?"

"Five."

"Great. I'll take the ferry over to Edmonds and meet you at . . . how's six?"

"I'd like that a lot," said Ransom, gradually overcoming his surprise. "I think I'd like that a hell of a lot."

For the rest of the afternoon Ransom was so preoccupied with Marian he could hardly keep his mind on work. He finally did make the call to Nagumo. The report was, in fact, ready, but he was able to beg himself another day. It would come out Thursday afternoon: tomorrow.

After that, Ransom spent a couple of hours grilling Swaney, but his heart just wasn't in it. And besides, Swaney didn't appear to know any more than he had a day before. But he wasn't going anywhere just yet. Ransom left orders that Swaney was to go through every mug book they had to see if he could spot one of the Indians.

Back at his desk, Ransom was thinking about going home early when a call came in from Gorham.

"Hey, you still sound sleepy." You just get up?"

"Well, uh . . . actually I was down in SeaTac all morning. I found the house."

Ransom just about dropped the phone. "Aw, Christ, Al. What the hell are you doing? You're not a one-man task force on this thing."

"I know. I'm sorry—"

"You've got to be back on the stakeout at midnight. You can't afford to be nodding off if these guys come back to do the Jacobsons—"

"Yeah, I know, but listen to this. The house is owned by a small independent bank down here, Valley Savings. Anyway, they foreclosed on the thing last December and it's been empty ever since. They didn't know anybody had been in it until I talked to them today."

"Are you sure it's the right house?"

"Absolutely. I talked to the department down here and they've sealed it off already."

In his mind, Ransom was drooling over the possibilities. "If their fingerprints are still in there . . ."

"That's exactly what I was thinking. Should I get our guys down here to dust?"

"I want you to go home right now and get some sleep. You hear me?"

"Yeah."

"You let me take care of the rest, okay?"

"All right. I guess I'll see you in the morning?"

"Sure. And Al?"

"Yeah?"

"Good work, you lunkhead."

Gorham laughed and then they hung up. A few phone calls later, it was suddenly quitting time.

By the time he walked out to his car, Ransom was nervous as a teenager going on his first date. He drove home and grabbed a quick shower and a shave and was up in Edmonds at quarter to six. They had agreed to meet in the Safeway parking lot across the street from the terminal where cars are ferried back and forth across Puget Sound to Kingston.

The unseasonable warmth of this morning had lasted all day and it felt more like an evening in July than November. But the dark sky was mottled with fast-moving clouds, and Ransom thought that the conditions looked ripe for a thunderstorm. He watched as the cars filed off the boat and before long a black BMW pulled in alongside his Buick.

He stepped out of his car and walked around to hers. The windows were tinted and the first thing he saw as the driver's door opened was a smooth white leg in a black pump. This was followed by a second. The rest of her emerged all at once and nearly took his breath away.

The gangly but gorgeous teenager he had dated in high school had matured into a woman of stunning beauty. Marian's lithe body was cocooned in a shimmery black dress that swept around her hips, gracefully cupping her breasts and then tapering into thin straps over her bare shoulders. She gently pushed back one side of her shoulder-length blond hair behind her ear and flashed him a smile.

Then she surprised him by throwing her arms around him and kissing him. His own arms fell naturally around her body and it was just like old times. No—better. They decided to leave their cars and walked arm in arm the few blocks down to the restaurant. Sailor's, on the waterfront, was the spot Jack had picked out. It was a fairly posh place, and he had always enjoyed coming here on dates before, but now . . . Somehow it didn't seem elegant enough for Marian.

As they sat across from each other, lights dancing off the water outside the window as well as off the deep blue of her eyes, he marveled at her soft self-assurance. It was undoubtedly her most attractive feature.

". . . but for some reason Loren got it into his head that he wasn't a real man if he couldn't make more money than I did. We were getting in fights about it all the time and then one night he hit me."

"Aw, Christ."

"I had my lawyer draw up papers the next day and . . . Well, that was three years ago and now I'm happily divorced."

"And you took back your maiden name?"

"I'd never changed it. His last name was McFeely, and the thought of being Marian McFeely was just too . . . I don't know. Too alliterated." They both laughed and Ransom felt happier than he had in years.

Though he thought about Stacy, he didn't bring her up as they ate their meals and shared a bottle of wine. Ransom talked about being a cop, and Marian about being a doctor, and at some point during the evening he couldn't believe he had ever let her get away. Even though it hadn't really been his fault, he regretted it, now more than ever. She had wanted to be popular and hang around the in-crowd. She hadn't wanted to be seen at his band functions and had eventually stopped coming altogether. It had hurt him. To Ransom's wounded teenage pride, his only recourse had been to stop attending her functions; no more pep rallies and no more parties. Eventually, the relationship had just withered away.

Ransom paid the check and they walked back outside holding hands. The wind had kicked up and the night was cooling off. She clung to him and he to her. He didn't want it to end.

"Would you like to come over to my place for a nightcap?" she asked as they reached their cars. Apparently she didn't want it to end either.

"I'll follow you," he said, and Marian gave him a big, open-mouthed smile.

She led him down Aurora into Seattle and then west across town to a large house overlooking Shilshole Bay. They ran together up to the front steps in the whipping wind and he heard her laughing as she unlocked the door. Once inside they threw their arms around each other and kissed breathlessly. His hands ran up and down her body, and he thrilled to her somehow new and yet familiar form.

Finally, she pulled off his jacket and kicked off her shoes. Ahead of him in the dark, Ransom could see an open kitchen and to the left, a plush living room. She took him by the hand and walked over to the couch and this time they were reunited in proper fashion.

Her skin was soft and white, barely revealing her age, and it took his breath away. Her stomach was still smooth, and her breasts full and firm. She might not be the young cheerleader he had made love to in high school, but Jack Ransom had never been more turned on in all his life. The years had taken their toll on him, however, and he felt awkward for a moment with her bearing all his weight, but she didn't seem to mind and before long, neither did he. Their sex was fast and furious and when they thought they were through they laughed and hugged each other tightly.

Then they picked up their clothes and ran up to the bedroom. The night was still very young.

CHAPTER EIGHT

Ransom glanced nervously at the clock on the nightstand: it was already ten-thirty and he would have to relieve Gorham at six. He couldn't remember having a night like this, ever. It seemed they had made love constantly from the moment they had come through the door. He hadn't planned on any of it, though, and he began to wonder if it was assumed that he would stay overnight or not.

He looked down at the blonde head of hair on his chest and felt the warmth of Marian's body next to his. His left arm was running down her back and he squeezed her close to him. A few seconds later she reached down between his legs and squeezed him back.

"I need to be at work pretty early tomorrow morning," he said, letting the statement hang in the air, not really knowing what to expect.

Marian slid her body up on top of him and kissed him long and slow. When she finally pulled away she said, "What time should I set my alarm for?"

Ransom smiled, dilemma resolved, and answered, "Five-thirty."

She reached over with one hand and worked her magic on the clock, then slid back down beside him. "It's just like old times, isn't it Jack?"

"No."

She looked up at him, her soft round face in confusion. Then he laughed. "It's a hell of a lot better than it ever was in high school."

Marian turned on her side now, her smiling face propped up on her elbow, her body pressing against his. Ransom was pleasantly aware of her breasts against his skin and he found himself becoming aroused again.

"Remember when we used to go over to your house?" she said.

"During lunch period?"

"Or assemblies, or any other chance we could get."

"Sure."

She was absent-mindedly running her hand across his chest as she spoke. "I was so glad that both of your parents worked. My mom was home all day."

"What about that time my folks came home for lunch?"

"Oh, my God, that's right. We had just barely finished getting dressed and we were still sitting on your bed."

"We didn't even hear them come in."

They both laughed.

"Did they ever say anything to you about that?"

"Nope. A couple of other times my dad really chewed my ass, but not that time."

He looked over at the clock again: it was quarter to eleven.

"I set it for quarter after five," she said, and kissed him on the cheek, "just in case you don't want to get up right away."

This time he rolled over on top of her and they made love again.

It was ten minutes to twelve when Ransom finally got around to asking Marian what he had forgotten to on the phone. "How old does a baby have to be before he sleeps on his side?"

"Is this about the case you are working on?" Her voice sounded flat and distant again, as it had on the phone when he'd first mentioned Pamela Gerhardt.

"Yeah."

She waited a beat and then spoke. "Well, they don't begin to roll over until they're about three months old. I suppose it could be anytime after that."

"Was it a pretty big baby?"

"Not particularly. I think it was around seven pounds. Why are you asking me all these questions about the baby? Is there something you're not telling me?"

"Take it easy," he said, but she didn't and he began to think maybe there was something *she* wasn't telling *him*. Ransom propped himself up against the headboard with a pillow and Marian sat up beside him.

"It's just that something's been bothering me, that's all. When we found the baby at the murdered couple's house, it was sleeping on its side. And when I found out it was only a few days old, I thought it was kind of strange. I mean, it didn't look like a newborn when I saw it. It looked a lot bigger."

When Ransom turned to Marian, her face was white. "Hey," he said reaching for her. "What's wrong?"

He put his arm around her. She was trembling. "How were they killed, Jack?"

"Marian, please—"

"No, Jack." Her forehead was wrinkled with pain, her eyes pleading with him. "You have to tell me how they were killed."

"You know I can't tell you in the middle of—"

"It was an animal, wasn't it?"

Ransom's blood ran cold as Marian's words echoed in his brain. "What the hell's going on here, Marian? What aren't you telling me?" Suddenly Ransom was acutely aware of his nakedness. In his mind he had changed from lover to cop; his body, however, remained terribly underdressed.

"I didn't go on vacation because I was overworked. I left because I thought I might be losing my mind. I think there's something wrong with that baby, Jack."

The tremor came again and he gripped her tightly. She drew in a deep breath and hitched out a sigh. Ransom stroked her hair. "You're okay now," he said. "Can you tell me what happened?"

She pulled away from him and pushed her hair out of her face. "I was on call that day in obstetrics. She was sent up from emergency. The mother hadn't even gone into labor when they brought her in, but she was suffering from severe internal pain."

"Who brought her in?"

"I don't know; I assume it was the people from the agency. When I examined her I was concerned that the advanced stage of her disease might interfere with the delivery, but she checked out fine. Acromegaly really only effects the extremities, but I wanted to be absolutely sure. Her pain intensified, though, so I decided that since she was well into her ninth month we'd do a C-section right away. That would put us in a better position to determine what the problem was without the baby to worry about."

She stopped for a moment, as though she were catching her breath, and then continued, "I was just about to cut her open when the damn thing . . ."

"What?"

Her eyes became steeled now and she sat up straight, naked above the covers. "I was just standing over her, ready to make the incision . . . and the damn thing just cut its way out from the inside."

"Aw, Christ."

"At least that's what it seemed like. I looked up, but everyone else thought *I* had made the incision. It wasn't until after I delivered the baby that I saw the teeth."

"What?"

"Teeth. I swear to God, Jack, the kid had a mouth full of 'em. And they weren't just baby teeth, either—they were like . . . God, I don't know—some kind of animal fangs."

Ransom tried to hold her against him again but she shrugged him off. "Do you realize what you are saying, Marian? The kid's in a new home now, and I'm sure if it had teeth like you say, someone would have noticed—"

"They retracted!"

She looked angrily at him now, for not believing. But how could he? This wasn't some freak mutation out of a horror film. He had seen the baby with his own eyes. Sure it looked a little bigger than it ought to be, but it was still just a baby. It wasn't the star of *It's Alive* for Christ's sake. "Did anyone else see this?"

She shook her head. "No one. I had just delivered it and I was turning around to hand it to one of the nurses when I noticed. I damn near dropped the thing on the floor, it startled me so badly, but by the time the nurse took it from me it looked normal. Nobody else was paying attention because the mother had gone into arrest. We worked our asses off trying to save her but she was too far gone. She died on the table."

They were silent for a moment and then she pulled the sheet up over her exposed breasts. "I know you probably think I'm crazy, Jack, but I know what I saw."

"Look, why don't you come over with me tomorrow morning and you can take a look at the baby yourself."

"That's not good enough. Tell me what happened, Jack."

Ransom could only shake his head.

"Do you want to know why the mother died?" said Marian.

Ransom just stared at her, positive that he didn't.

"I think the baby had been eating her internal organs."

This was the point where he was supposed to think that her cheese had slipped off her cracker, but of course he knew something she didn't know. There was a little matter of the bodies, he told himself. Sounds like we have our man—or boy, if you prefer—doesn't it?

Now, wait a goddamned minute! His imagination had been running rampant but he was able to rein it in for a moment. He'd had enough biology in college to know that what she was saying was impossible. So what if all the evidence fit. It was too fantastic. There was no way the kid could have done that.

And then he thought of the locked doors and the

(wolf)

excavated body cavities.

(it was a goddamned wolf)

He was becoming confused, thinking about what Swaney had told him, but the he remembered Doc's report and blurted it out without thinking. "Wait a minute. Doc said it only *looked* like an animal had killed them."

"Oh, my God." Marian covered her mouth with her hand. "What did it do? Bite their throats out?"

"No they were slashed." Ransom was in a daze, answering her questions without realizing he was doing so. Swaney had said she'd had sex with a wolf. The pieces, as supernatural as they might be, were now falling into place faster than he could control. No fingerprints. Scratches on the floor. No forced entry.

"What else?"

"Their stomachs were—" And then he realized what he had been saying and stopped. He looked into her eyes and knew, for the first time since the case had begun, that he was frightened.

"I'm a doctor, Jack. What happened to their stomachs?"

"Their insides . . . they were all eaten out."

"And now the kid looks a whole lot bigger than an infant, right? Oh, God, Jack, we have to get over there and stop it."

"Aw, Christ, Marian. We don't know

(oh, yes you do)

for sure."

"So let's find out."

"It's after midnight."

"And if everything is all right we apologize profusely, and I make an appointment to see a shrink. That or a good eye doctor. But if that baby is killing people to stay alive, then it's going to kill again, and watching it from the outside of the house isn't going to do a damn bit of good."

Ransom didn't want to believe what she was telling him. He did not want to believe. And yet, inexplicably, there was no doubt in his mind that it was true.

"All right. Al should be on duty by now. I can go over there and check things out. Will that satisfy you?"

"I'm going with you," she said, and before Ransom knew it she was out of bed getting dressed.

"Absolutely not. There's no reason for you to come along."

"Oh, yeah?" She already had her underwear on and one leg in a pair of faded jeans, her breasts still gloriously naked. "And if one or both of them is lying on the floor with half their throat missing, are you going to be able to keep them stable until the ambulance gets there?"

She shot the other leg into her jeans and Ransom climbed out of bed, resigned, and began to dress.

CHAPTER NINE

The wind nearly pulled the door from Ransom's hand as he and Marian stepped outside. It was much colder now than when they had met up in Edmonds. He put his arm over her shoulders and they walked quickly to his Buick. Thick, boiling clouds had amassed overhead and Ransom heard a faint rumble of thunder.

The Jacobsons lived only a mile or two away from Marian's place, up above Carkeek Park, and he and Marian were silent as the car slipped through the dark residential area of the North End. Occasionally, a flash of lightning would flit above the clouds, preceding another, ever-closer clap of thunder.

Ransom pulled in front of Gorham's green Pontiac and killed the engine. "Now, I want you to stay here in the car." He could see that Marian was about to protest and he took her hand in his. "I promise you'll get to see the baby—I just need to talk to my partner first. If everything's fine, I'll wave you up."

"And if everything's not fine?"

"I'll come and get you personally."

She gave him a kiss that lingered even as he was getting out of the car, and then he began the long walk back to Gorham's car. Al wasn't going to be very happy about this and Ransom wasn't sure he could blame him. His window was rolled down when Ransom walked up to it.

"What gives, Jack?" He could see Gorham was a little steamed. "If someone's watching you're gonna blow the stakeout."

"I've got the doctor who delivered the kid in my car up there. She told me a few things that I have to check out."

"She?"

"Yeah."

"Well, what did she tell you?"

Gorham hadn't mentioned the kiss, so it was unlikely that he had seen it. He was probably running a make on my plates, Ransom thought with amusement.

"It's nothing to worry about, but I want to make sure. I'd like you to stay covered. With any luck I'll be out of your hair in a few minutes."

Gorham rolled up his window without answering and Ransom turned toward the house. Dead leaves scraped along the dry pavement and swirled around his shoes. He looked in both directions down the darkened street and headed across.

Ransom reached the front stoop and hesitated. He really hated to wake people up in the middle of the night, but he didn't suppose that either he or Marian would get a decent night's sleep if he didn't. He grimaced and then rang the doorbell.

No one answered and he stepped back to peer in the windows, but all the shades were drawn. He knocked. Still no answer. He beat on the door with his fist and this time heard a loud noise from inside the house followed by more silence. Instinctively he drew his weapon. He heard a car door open and prayed it wasn't Marian, then turned his head to see Gorham coming up the walk.

"What's the matter?" his partner whispered once he was beside Ransom.

"I've got a bad feeling about this one."

Ransom turned the knob while Gorham pulled out his own piece. It was locked. He backed off a couple of steps and yelled: "Police, is anybody home? Mr. and Mrs. Jacobson?"

Nothing. He nodded and Gorham aimed his weapon at the door, then Ransom reared back and kicked the door as hard as he could next to the knob. He felt the deadbolt splinter the frame and after he had recoiled he hit the door with his shoulder and it popped wide open.

Both of them froze with their guns out in front of them, but they were greeted only by a thick, stuffy odor emanating from the house.

Ransom took a quick look around and then said, "Let's go."

It was dark inside but his eyes adjusted quickly. Ransom pushed through the living room toward the back of the house while Gorham detoured through the kitchen on the right. His guard was up; the stench was unmistakable. Three days ago he had smelled the same thing at the Edison house: death.

When Ransom pushed open the bedroom door, he instantly turned his head to retch. Gorham came up quickly behind him to flip on the lights and they both pulled out handkerchiefs to cover their noses and mouths.

Lying on the bed was a man with wispy, white hair, wearing only pajama bottoms. He was totally gutted; it was just like before. The sheets around him were caked with dried blood. One arm dangled off the side of the bed while the other clutched at the ragged tear in his throat; his eyes were fixed open and strips of withered flesh hung from his cheeks.

On the floor next to the crib was a woman with dark hair. She was naked. He wounds were similar but had obviously occurred much more recently, her entrails were still glistening, spilling onto the bedroom carpet.

Gorham waited by the door while Ransom stepped over the woman to look into the crib. He nearly lost his footing, slipping on the blood around the body, and had to grab hold of the railing to catch his balance. When he looked inside, he found himself staring right into the unblinking eyes of the baby. It was covered in blood like the two adults and at first he thought it might be dead, but then it silently closed its eyes, rolled over on its side, and went to sleep.

"Stay here," Ransom ordered as he passed Gorham in the doorway. I'm going out to call this in.

He rolled out onto the stoop and took a great gasp of fresh air. Stumbling down the steps, he caught his balance and broke into a run toward the car. Marian was standing outside the driver's

227

side looking toward the house. "What's going on?" she asked worriedly.

Ransom's hands were on the hood, his head down between his shoulders. He was trying desperately to regain his composure. The boys down at the lab would not appreciate it one bit if one of Seattle's finest barfed all over their crime scene. "Same as before—" was all he could get out before Marian bolted for the house.

"Goddamn it!" Ransom yelled to himself, and then shouted to her, "Marian, get the hell back here!" But she was already through the door. He turned to run after her but only made it to the middle of the street. Suddenly he wasn't in Seattle anymore. In his mind he had been transported to another place, a small, brightly lit bathroom, blood on the floor, and his wife's hand around his service revolver.

Gorham turned when he heard the door, expecting Ransom, and was almost knocked over when a woman pushed past him and into the bedroom. Stunned, he watched as she headed straight for the crib and stuck both arms in as though she were going to pick up the child.

Of course, he thought, the doctor. Her name was Harris. She was muttering incoherently but Gorham stayed in the doorway, assuming that she was examining the child. But the longer he watched her, the more it seemed as if something wasn't quite right. For some reason he couldn't take his eyes off the doctor's arms. Exposed by the short-sleeved shirt she was wearing, they were flexing but she wasn't lifting the baby out of the crib. Gorham took a hesitant step into the room, then another, before he realized what was happening. She wasn't picking up the baby; she was trying to kill it!

Gorham ran up behind Harris and grabbed her by the arm, but she startled him by turning and pushing him hard on his chest. The unexpectedness of it sent him sprawling to the floor. He was horrified to see that she quickly went back to strangling the baby. Determined now, Gorham jumped to his feet and cold-clocked her in the back of her head with the butt of his revolver. He watched Harris fall to the floor, her body glancing off the dead woman and rolling onto the blood-soaked carpet.

The Gorham looked over to see if the baby was all right, but what he saw instead was a pair of taloned hands curling around the bars of the crib. He took a step back and raised his gun as the tiny head of the infant peeked over the top rail, its eyes narrow and piercing as it stared down at Harris. The skin on its bald head looked almost blue, and throbbed as blood pulsed through the distended veins that knotted the baby's skull. Suddenly its face began to distort, the lower jaw dropping, allowing for the eruption of huge, jagged teeth. Saliva dripped from its chin as it looked toward Gorham and then back down at Harris.

Gorham watched, frozen, as small bumps appeared all over its skin, and he nearly stopped breathing when each of them seemed to impossibly elongate. As they continued to grow, he understood, and before long a dense covering of hair had sprouted over its entire body. It was breathing heavily, eyes moving back and forth between Gorham and the bodies on the floor. Then it reared its head back, a bone-chilling cry bursting from its throat, climbed over the railing, and dove onto Harris.

Gorham's hands started to shake and he had trouble aiming his gun. The thing sliced open her clothes and began to gnaw its way into Harris's bowels when she came awake and started screaming.

Sweat from his forehead stung Gorham's eyes and his first shot went wide. The second one hit the thing in the leg. But its reaction was not what Gorham had expected: it cried.

Except that it wasn't the cry of a mutated beast; it was the heart-wrenching cry of a child. It looked up at Gorham with tears streaming down its blood-streaked face. Gorham rubbed his eyes and looked again: the teeth were gone, the hair was gone; it looked . . . normal. The wailing made Gorham panic. He threw down his weapon and ran to the child

"Oh, God, what have I done?"

But as he reached down to take the infant into his arms it suddenly leapt at him, a tiny hand lashing at Gorham's neck and deftly severing his carotid artery.

Gorham took a quick step backward. He could feel the hot blood pulsing from his neck through his fingers as he tried to stop the bleeding. He looked for his weapon but couldn't see it. He took another step back and faltered, falling hard to the floor.

The thing, now fully metamorphosed, began crawling toward him. He tried to scream but found that he couldn't. Gorham noticed that Harris had stopped screaming; she had either lost consciousness or was dead. Gorham's hands felt thick and slimy, unable to stop the steady flow of blood. He kicked and flailed, but it only made the blood flow faster from his neck.

He couldn't hold on any longer and let his head fall back onto the floor, the monster inching ever closer to him. The last thing Al Gorham heard was a shot ringing out from the doorway.

When Ransom's mind returned to Seattle, he was on his hands and knees in the middle of the street, a pool of vomit on the road beneath him. He couldn't stand up yet, but he knew what had to be done, and crawled to his car to call for backup. Afterward, he just sat in the car, the door open, his hands shaking, wondering if he should be inside with Marian. Gorham can handle it, he told himself. At this point Ransom didn't think he would be able to go anywhere.

The two shots from Gorham's gun, however, prompted him to action. He was out of the car in a flash, his gun drawn. He stopped at the front door to listen, and that was when he heard Gorham fall. He lead the way with is revolver, arms extended in front of him, to the bedroom. The shot was almost instantaneous.

Within a second he had seen Marian lying unconscious next to the woman, his partner's blood flowing across the floor, and the tiny, slavering animal that was crawling on top of Gorham. There was no hesitation.

The bullet entered that animal's head just above the left ear, and exited the other side along with most of its brains and the right half of its face.

It was dead—Ransom knew that—but it wouldn't stop moving! He was ready to fire again when he saw it wasn't really moving after all; it was changing.

Razor-sharp claws slowly withdrew into the ends of its fingers. Coarse, matted hair seemed to sink back into its body. Huge, jagged teeth retracted completely into its mouth, and face and limbs began to shrink into the form of a dead infant. Ransom couldn't believe his eyes; it was the kid. But he hadn't shot at the kid; he'd shot at an animal.

Before he could react any further, cops began streaming into the house. "Get a goddamn ambulance," he ordered automatically. "These people are hurt!"

Suddenly it was hard to breathe; his clothes felt too constraining. He wanted to go to Marian and hold her in his arms but he was afraid she was already dead. He was also afraid of another flashback. Ransom broke out in a cold sweat. His bowels had liquefied.

Panting, he ran outside to escape his growing claustrophobia. It seemed like minutes before he realized that the clouds had finally unleashed their burden. It was raining again.

CHAPTER TEN

". . . and you expect me to peddle this happy horse shit to Internal Affairs?" Captain Elliot asked incredulously.

Thursday morning had not been one of Jack Ransom's better mornings. Not by a long shot. In addition to killing a monster that turned out to be a baby—or maybe it was the other way around—both his partner and the woman he now realized he was in love with were in the hospital. Gorham was in critical condition. Marian, thank God, was much better off.

And as if that weren't bad enough, he was having to explain his actions to his precision-coiffed captain. All in all, it was turning into one shitty day.

"That's what happened."

"Bullshit," Elliot said, flipping Ransom's newly finished report on his desk. "What I've got here is some kind of fantasy tale. Now, I want to know what really went on in there."

'Gorham can back up everything. I pretty much got there after it was over."

"Bullshit!" Elliot's face was red and he was pacing behind his desk. "You don't just go into a house—without a search warrant, I might add—shoot a one-week old kid in cold blood, and then say you got there after it was over. Now what the hell really happened?"

Ransom was not up for this. He hadn't slept all night, waiting at the hospital for word about Marian and Al, and early this morning he'd come over to write his report. It was already 8:00

a.m. and he was exhausted. There was no excuse for shooting a kid, but he hadn't, and he was damned if he was going to make something up.

"I told you what happened. It's in the report. Now, when Gorham gets out of the hospital—"

"Stop jacking me off, Ransom. Gorham's a goddamn vegetable; he ain't ever getting out of the hospital. But your ass is gonna be in fuckin' jail if I don't get some answers, pronto."

Elliot sat down in a huff. If he doesn't watch it, Ransom thought, he's going to blow a hair follicle or something. Elliot glanced down at his nails, then briefly at the top of the drawer of his desk, as if contemplating a quick file but then opting against it.

"Listen to me Ransom, because I'm only going to say this once. I'm not taking this shit to the commissioner, you read me?"

Ransom only stared.

"You want to know what I think really happened in that house this morning? I think you and Gorham got a little excited. The Jacobsons had just been murdered, after all, and under the circumstances it was quite understandable that you two were a little keyed up.

"And then when your partner went down, well, who could blame you for being somewhat erratic? I think what you actually saw was a dog sniffing around the bodies. In your excitement you shot at the dog and accidentally hit the kid—"

"That's a goddamn lie—"

"Shut the fuck up and listen, Ransom, or I'll have you in a cell so fast you won't even remember how you got there. Let's not forget you've got a murder rap hanging over your head for the time being. And we've got you cold on it. This little fairy story you've concocted might get you to the funny farm instead of the big house, but you'll still be locked up. I have a reputation to uphold and I don't plan on going down with you. I think if you go back to your desk and make some slight revisions, you might just be surprised at how quickly this thing goes away."

"Are you telling me to perjure myself?"

"I'm not telling you anything, and I'm not promising you anything either. I'm just giving you the wisdom of my experience." Elliot took a breath and continued at a lower volume. "Let me put this another way, Jack. You can go ahead and turn in this report if you want to, as is. I won't stop you. But consider this. Are you aware of what happens to ex-cops in prison?"

Ransom nodded. "But you might be able to prevent that."

"Very perceptive, Lieutenant. Now, I just happen to have the coroner's report on the Edison murders right here on my desk. It should fit in quite nicely with your revisions. I had a little talk with Nagumo this morning and it turns out it was a dog that killed them, most likely a pit bull."

"What the . . ." Ransom stood up and took the report from Elliot's hands. "He said it couldn't have been a dog. He said there was no way."

"Well, it looks like he brought in some kind of expert who says it was."

Ransom had evidently underestimated the kind of pull that Elliot actually had in the department, and suddenly a horror not unlike that he had faced this morning bloomed full in his mind in the form of Seattle Police Commissioner Raymond P. Elliot. Ransom let the report slip from his fingers onto Elliot's desk and sat back down, his head in his hands.

"Look, Ransom, I really don't give a rat's ass if it was a dog or the goddamn Tasmanian Devil—that's not the point—but Internal Affairs is going to want to know what you were shooting at. You and Gorham both put a round into the kid. Now, as far as Gorham's concerned, it's academic, but if you don't toe the line on this one I'll run right down to the D.A.'s office today and get him to prosecute you unless we can come to some kind of agreement—"

Ransom didn't even raise his head when the knock came at the door. "What?" yelled Elliot.

A uniform stuck his head in the office. "We just got a call from Bay Med. I thought you should know."

"Yeah?"

"Al Gorham died about ten minutes ago."

Elliot looked at Ransom but he still wasn't moving.

"Okay, thanks."

The uniform shut the door and Elliot turned back to Ransom. "Hey, I'm real sorry—I know how close you two were. But you don't have any choice now. The Harris woman was unconscious, and now Gorham. There's no one left to bail you out, and I'm afraid that if you don't—"

Ransom mumbled something that Elliot didn't quite catch. "What was that?"

Jack Ransom straightened up in his chair and then stood. He pulled his badge out of his pocket and his service revolver from his holster, and placed them on the desk. Then he looked Elliot dead in the eye and repeated his statement: "I said, I quit."

Ransom stopped just long enough in the lobby of Elliott Bay Medical Center to get some flowers before going up to see Marian. He knocked once and pushed open the door without waiting for an answer. She was sitting up in bed and gave Ransom her big open-mouthed smile. He came up and kissed her and sat down on the bed while she called the nurse to have the flowers put in water.

She had a bandage on her head where Gorham had hit her, and the sheets covered the bandages on her stomach from where the monster had slashed into her while she was unconscious. The wound had broken the skin but there were no internal injuries. She didn't remember any of it and Ransom thought that was probably for the best. He would be having enough nightmares about that thing for the both of them.

Then he told her about his meeting with Elliot, but not about Al. That could wait for another time.

"Those bastards," she said. "He really tried to blackmail you?"

Ransom nodded.

"What are you going to do now?"

"I don't know. I haven't thought that far ahead." He stood up to pace. "Jesus, Marian, I hope I didn't make a mistake by quitting. I was filling out my report this morning and I started doubting it myself, wondering if I just hallucinated the whole thing. It's just so damned unbelievable. Maybe Elliot was right."

"Come here, Jack," she said, and he sat back down on the bed. "You're forgetting one thing—I saw it, too. And I'll testify to it in court if I have to. I'll be there for you."

"Thank you," he said. "But I don't think it will ever get that far."

"Why not?"

"Well, now that I'm not on the force, Elliot will probably get some flunky to write up his report just the way he wants it. I don't think he wants to go to court any more than I do."

"So that's it?"

"I'm pretty sure."

"No investigation?"

"I doubt it."

Neither of them spoke for a few minutes, and then Ransom finally said, "How are you feeling?"

"Fine. Better, now that you're here," Marian took his hand and after another silence she said, "Jack, I know this probably isn't the greatest time for you right now, but last night—before . . . you know—it meant a lot to me."

He was going to respond but she shook him off. "I want to say this all at once. I know it was a long time ago, but what happened in high school—I'm really sorry about that. I know it was my fault."

"No, it wasn't."

She smiled and continued. "I said it twenty-five years ago and last night I realized—you made me realized—that I still love you."

She squeezed his hand but it felt to him like she was squeezing his heart. "I love you, too," he said, and he put his arms around her and held her close. He kissed her and when he pulled back there were tears on her cheek. "Why are you crying?"

"I'm just happy—that's all. Do you think we can make it work this time, Jack? I'd really like to try."

"I think that's a great idea," he said. "As long as we don't meet up with anymore offspring of Lon Chaney, Jr."

With that her face lit up. "Even a man who is pure in heart, and says his prayers by night, may become a wolf when the wolfbane blooms, and the autumn moon is bright."

Ransom's mouth dropped open as Marian intoned the verse from *The Wolf Man,* and he stared at her in amazement, feeling a love for her stronger than any he had felt before. "Yes, indeed," he said, laughing as he gave her another kiss. "I think that's one hell of an idea."

EPILOGUE

Arriving at work in the basement of Harborview Medical Center, Emily Richards was not a happy woman. She'd been with the county coroner's office for three years now and she was still on the night shift. Predictably, she was the only woman in the department.

Maybe they thought they were doing her a favor—the night shift was not responsible for doing autopsies, only checking in bodies—but Emily hadn't gone into pathology to become a glorified secretary. Almost as soon as she had come on tonight, just after twelve, she was told that three bodies were coming in.

Great, she thought. She would have to take pictures, vacuum the clothes, take samples of anything found externally, and write up paperwork, while somebody else did the autopsy in the morning.

The three bodies came in around twelve-thirty: a man, a woman, and a small child. That sobered her up fast. It always made her sad when children died. It didn't seem fair, no matter what the circumstances. And whenever it happened, her problems seemed unimportant in comparison.

Emily supervised as the three bodies were wheeled in, still cocooned in their black zippered body bags, and each was deposited on one of the eight autopsy tables. She was told to take extra care and pay close attention to these because a police officer had been involved. But as far as she was concerned, the death of a child merited special attention every time.

After the medics had gone, she was alone again. The department was always cutting back, especially at night. There wouldn't be anyone in to relieve her until nine. Emily sighed as she locked up the doors to the office, and then put on her pager and started off to work. She quickly changed into her scrubs and grabbed a camera, along with a couple of extra rolls of film. She was checking over the camera as she stepped into the autopsy room, when a noise froze her in her tracks.

"Is someone in here?" There was no answer. But before she took another step she heard it again. It sounded like . . . No, it couldn't be.

Emily took a few more steps and realized the sound was coming from the far coroner of the room, so she made her way slowly in that direction. When she rounded the last table, her heart went out to what she saw. I *was* a child. It was a small boy, naked, standing alone in the coroner. He had his head buried in his shoulder and he was crying.

"Oh, my God. How did you get in here?"

She rushed over to sweep him up in her arms, but as soon as she neared him she saw what looked like blood on his skin. What was going on?

"Where did you come from, sweetheart?"

Emily stopped when she reached him and bent down. She didn't want to startle him. "It's okay, someone's here now."

Then he turned and looked at her and Emily froze. The entire right side of the little boy's head was nothing more than a bloody pulp. She wanted to scream, but she never got the chance, because those bloody smiling fangs were the last thing Emily Richards ever saw.

Bride of Blood Feast

Back in the days when I was writing fiction I was under the illusion that if I could produce more than one work in a series editors would know that I was serious and would then be more likely to publish my works, knowing that I had it in me to write follow-ups. That's how *Bride of Blood Feast* came to be, but not why. Once DimeNovels! closed shop I was stuck with a hundred-page horror novella and nowhere to even submit the thing. Since the main character, Jack Ransom, was into movies, I began to think that if continued on with the original idea and produced a trilogy—with *Son of Blood Feast* rounding out the series—I could publish them together as an anthology that would be big enough in terms of pages to justify the publishing costs.

Still, I didn't want to take time away from my other, more serious, writing so I decided to write the sequel out in longhand during my free time. I was working at a bookstore at the time and I purchased a small five–by-seven spiral notebook, and whenever I went for a coffee break around the corner to Starbucks, I took my notebook with me and wrote. Part of the idea had probably come from reading John Grisham's introduction to his first novel, *A Time to Kill*, in which he talked about his belief that if he were able to write something on the order of a page a day—that's all, one page—that by the end of the year he'd have over three hundred pages of manuscript. Seemed like a good idea to me.

The idea of the new partner for Jack Ransom came from my favorite of the Dirty Harry films, *The Enforcer*, while the actual character of Kay Wells was based on mystery author Patricia Cornwell, who I was privileged to meet and correspond with briefly in the course of my work at the bookstore. But the going was slow, and I certainly wrote much less than a page a day. The entire process took a couple of years, between 1993 and 1995. But by then I was committed to writing mystery fiction and the thought of finishing the third volume was not very enticing. *Bride of Blood Feast* is the last piece of horror fiction that I ever wrote, and I feel it is the most well written story in this collection. One would hope that would be the case. Including both of these novellas in a book of all my short horror fiction seemed the best way to sum up that first chapter of my writing career.

BRIDE OF
BLOOD
FEAST

a horror novella

For Marianne

If I must die, I will encounter darkness as a bride, And hug it in mine arms.

William Shakespeare
Measure for Measure

"That wasn't the end at all. Would you like to hear what happened after that?"

Elsa Lanchester
The Bride of Frankenstein, 1935

PROLOGUE

Marian looked down at the scar on her stomach. Still bright pink and tender, she didn't think she would ever get used to seeing it there. Then she reached down to touch it and she was suddenly somewhere else. She wasn't in her bedroom anymore, and she wasn't sitting on her bed. The towel that had been draped around her was gone, too. Though she had come out of the shower only moments before, Marian now found herself outside.

Darkness surrounded her, the only illumination coming from the full moon. Beneath her bare feet she could feel the soft earth and dead pine needles. When she looked down she discovered that she was still naked. Though the night air was cool it was not cold, and felt good against her skin. Her nipples were hard and gooseflesh rose on her arms.

Marian surveyed the area around her: a densely undergrown forest. She was in a crouched position but felt natural and not uncomfortable. What she noticed the most, all around her, were the smells.

The scent of pine and sap and decaying leaves were each clear and distinct in her mind. She could also detect the smells of other animals nearby in the trees and underbrush, but instinctively she knew that was not why she was here. She found she could also train her heightened sense of smell on herself and picked up the musky scent emanating from between her legs as well as something else similar to it in the air. She moved.

Marian was running now, faster than she would have ever thought humanly possible. She was weaving her way through the trees instinctively, her night vision excellent, enhanced by the moonlight filtering through the branches of the towering evergreens above her. When she heard the sounds she came to a dead stop. She listened for a moment and determined that there were two.

Marian moved slowly behind the trunk of a large pine. Their smells were stronger now, and more defining. Two, a man and a woman. She could hear them walking through the woods together. Marian's heart was beating fast, her breathing coming in quick gasps, almost a pant. She could smell them, strong and warm, and saliva began to run from her mouth. She was hungry. She moved again.

As she neared the couple she could feel them, feel their heat, feel their presence in her brain as her senses registered them. Her breathing became even more rapid as she raced silently through the forest toward them. The hunger in the pit of her stomach was growing. When they finally came into sight, she slowed and walked for a while beside them.

They were holding hands, heads down, both of them watching the ground to see where they were stepping in the dark. Then Marian's legs began to quiver, not from fright she realized, but with an almost sexual excitement. Her body, she now understood, moving with a will of its own, was preparing for the kill.

She had run out ahead of them and hidden in the undergrowth and they were nearing her now, heading straight in her direction. She could feel the moisture dripping down her legs, slicking the skin of her thighs as she adjusted her position. She felt as if she were on the verge of orgasm.

Marian bent low, a growl suddenly welling from deep within her throat. She bit it back and hunkered down, her legs like compressed coils, waiting to spring. When the couple was finally beside her, she pounced.

Marian was on fire as she struck the woman first, sending her sprawling into the soft loam of the forest floor. The man turned and froze, and in that instant of hesitation she lashed out and his throat began to bleed. He wobbled slightly, his eyes white and wide with fear, and then he fell to his knees, his hands groping wildly at his neck. She would return for him later. First, there was the woman.

As Marian looked down on her, the woman was trying to crawl away on her back. She was crying, and for some reason this made Marian even more excited. The woman's fear seemed to penetrate Marian's body in waves, and the moisture between her legs felt as if it were running like urine, but she knew that wasn't possible. Finally, when it became too much to bear, Marian reared her head back and screamed, her lungs bursting, expelling a seemingly endless supply of oxygen. And when her screams had stopped, her energy spent, she simply stood over the woman, panting. All that was left now was the hunger.

It was fast and furious, her body suddenly on top of the woman, her mouth at the woman's throat. She was biting and tearing, the thick coppery-taste of the blood warm on her tongue. She gulped down the chunks of raw bloody flesh, not bothering to chew. Marian couldn't stop herself and she found that she didn't want to. Her hunger was still strong, demanding more, and when she was finished with the woman she turned her attention toward the man.

He had crawled off some distance but the smell of his blood was easy to distinguish and slowly she followed the trail. The desire was not as strong for him. He was merely food. When she found the man he was lying face down near a tree and she rolled him over, feeding slowly and more deliberately than with the woman. Her hunger diminished with each bite until the blood in her mouth began to taste cold and gritty. Her heart rate began to decrease and she sensed it was time to leave.

Instantly she was off, her legs pumping, her hair flying wildly behind her. Branches and twigs whipped and tugged at her skin but did no damage. She ran until she was exhausted and collapsed in the brush. Her naked body was covered in a thick stringy sheath of blood. In vain she tried wiping the sticky substance off her stomach, but it merely spread the blood around.

When she took her hand away to look at it, she was back in her bedroom. Marian was shivering. She was still sitting on her bed, towel bunched around her hips. Her skin was wet, sheened with sweat, but there was no blood. Her heart was beating wildly against her ribs, and her legs felt too weak to stand. For a long moment she could do nothing but sit.

When she had recovered sufficiently, Marian sucked her lungs full of air and screamed.

CHAPTER ONE

Jack Ransom was sitting at the corner table of The Continental in the University District when he saw the two of them walk in. He was just finishing up his breakfast—a feta cheese and tomato omelet, Greek fries, and wheat toast—and was taking a sip of coffee when they spotted him and walked over.

"Jack," said Jim Razor, turning a chair around and sitting down, his arms resting across the back.

Razor looked even younger than his thirty-three years in his trademark letterman's jacket, a blond, blue-eyed version of Michael Landon in *I Was a Teenage Werewolf*. Razor's partner, Chet Burgher, who reminded Ransom of the doughy, latter-day Peter Lorre, stood uncomfortably in a suit and tie, hands in his pockets, shifting his weight from foot to foot in an almost subliminal dance step.

"Jim, Chet," Ransom acknowledged. "You boys like a cup of coffee?"

Razor shook his head. "Nope, we're just here to talk."

Razor and Burgher were homicide detectives with the Seattle Police Department's University Precinct. Up until two weeks ago, Ransom had been one, too.

"Come on, Chet," Ransom said, pulling out the chair beside him. "Take a load off."

Burgher cleared his throat first, then sat down. "Thanks, Jack."

They were silent as Ransom sopped up the last of the cheese and butter on his plate with a crust of toast. "All right," he said, after popping it in his mouth and washing it down with a slug of coffee. "What the hell do you guys want?"

"It's not what we want," said Razor. "It's what the department wants."

Ransom was immediately skeptical. "Yeah?" he responded guardedly.

"They want you back."

From the pocket of his jacket, Razor produced Ransom's service revolver and shield and set them on the table. The very items Ransom had set on his captain's desk fourteen days earlier.

Ransom glanced down at the table briefly before turning his gaze back to Razor. "You can tell Captain Elliot, for me, that he can go fuck himself. Any department he's on is too small for me."

Razor smiled and looked over at his partner. Though it didn't happen often, Burgher smiled back.

Ransom sipped his coffee and frowned. "All right, enough bullshit. What the hell's going on?"

"Elliot's gone."

The words stopped Ransom as he was lifting the mug to his lips, and he set it back down. "What do you mean, gone?"

"Gone. As in Phoenix."

Ransom didn't want to, but he couldn't help himself and broke in a grin. Raymond Elliot had been the worst captain Ransom had ever served under.

In the course of Ransom's final investigation—an investigation that also resulted in the death of his partner—he'd shot and killed a small boy. In exchange for not being investigated in the shooting, Ransom had quit.

It wasn't because he necessarily wanted to be investigated. He simply hadn't wanted the case go uninvestigated. He wanted an autopsy on the kid. He wanted to be sure he hadn't been out of his mind, that there really was a rational explanation for what he'd done. He wanted to reassure himself that he was still a good cop.

But Elliot wouldn't allow that. Elliot didn't want the negative publicity. Elliot wanted to sweep it all under the rug. What Elliot offered, if Ransom didn't comply, was a swift and speedy indictment for murder.

Every day Ransom waited for the federal marshals to appear at his door. They never came. And now Elliot was gone. Ransom looked again at his revolver and shield on the table. "What about the shooting? Isn't there going to be an investigation?"

Razor was already shaking his head. "Nope." His face was serious now. "That's why they want you back."

"What do you mean?"

"The day after the shooting, when the morning crew at the morgue came in to start their shift, they found a woman who was working there the night before in the corner of the autopsy suite. She was dead."

Aw, Christ." Ransom felt a cold chill seep into his bones. He almost didn't want to ask. "Was it—"

"Yep. Same M.O. as the cases you were working on, with one exception."

"What's that?"

"They took the kid this time." Razor shrugged. "Needless to say, without the kid's body, there's nothing to investigate."

Ransom suddenly felt a rush akin to panic begin to flow through him. His mouth took on a salty taste and he thought for a moment that he might lose his breakfast back onto the empty plate in front of him.

Razor and Burgher had discovered the bodies that began the initial investigation, a couple found disemboweled in their home along with a child who was still alive. They had asked Ransom to take over the case.

"What about my report?" Ransom asked, hoping but not believing that it still existed.

Razor and Burgher both smiled at this, and Razor said, "That's why Elliot got canned. The body of the woman at the morgue was discovered a little before nine. Naturally, the medical examiner's office notified the chief immediately."

Razor chuckled and continued. "Two hours later, about eleven, Elliot himself walks into the chief's office and hands him a report on the investigation taking credit for solving the murders. In light of recent developments, the chief didn't have much of a choice."

If that was good news, it was the only good news. Under different circumstances Ransom would have been celebrating along with Razor and Burgher, but he couldn't. If the woman at the morgue had been murdered in the same way as the others, there could be only one reason why: the killer was still on the loose.

But Ransom also realized something else. Without the existence of his original report, he was the only one who knew what had happened on his last investigation, and he was also the only one who could hunt down the killer. The department had come to the same conclusion, but for different reasons. Ransom had no choice. He reached across the table and picked up his badge and piece.

"All right," yelled Razor, turning the heads of nearly everyone in the place. The two detectives stood, and Razor clapped his hand on Burgher's shoulder. "See, I told you he couldn't live without us, Chet."

Ransom stood up and laid enough money on the table to cover his breakfast and a tip, and walked out with the two other detectives toward the front door. "So, who's in charge with Elliot gone?"

"Oh, yeah, I almost forgot to tell you." Razor was beaming. "This is the best part. Guess who's next in line for captain?"

"Come on, Jim. Just tell me."

"Robert Baldwin."

"Bobby?"

Razor nodded as the three of them spilled out onto University Way. Ransom was actually buoyant himself at the news. He may not have known what would happen on the rest of the case, but the investigation was going to be a damn sight easier than the last time.

"Bobby Baldwin," he said with amazement, more to himself than to the other two detectives.

"You want to ride with us?" asked Razor.

"No. I'll meet you back at the precinct," said Ransom. Then he turned north and headed toward his car.

"Congratulations, Bobby." Police Captain Robert Baldwin looked up from the file he was reading and grimaced. "Nah, don't give me none of that shit. This job is a bitch and you know it."

Ransom laughed as he walked into the new captain's office and gave Baldwin a firm handshake. Though Robert "Bobby" Baldwin was a couple of inches shorter than Ransom, his body seemed, proportionately, twice as big. Baldwin was black, weighed about two-twenty, and had the body of a fullback, which he had been before becoming Ransom's roommate at the police academy. Baldwin had been a star running back at the University of Washington, even playing a couple of seasons for the 49ers back in the seventies.

He'd been released because they said he wasn't big enough to play pro ball, but looking at him now Ransom couldn't have imagined how they'd come to that decision. Baldwin was barrel-chested, with thick muscular arms and stocky powerful legs. Even with his short-cropped salt and pepper hair, the man still looked strong enough to play.

Baldwin sat behind his desk, the sleeves of his white shirt rolled up to his elbows, tie loose and collar unbuttoned. He looked as if he were nearing the end of a long grueling day. Ransom looked at his watch: it was only nine a.m.

"Where'd they finally track you down," asked Baldwin, "The Continental?"

Ransom nodded. His favorite breakfast spot was as well known in the precinct as his aversion to inclement weather, and he doubted whether Razor and Burgher had done much tracking. "I was kind of surprised to see Jim and Chet in the daylight. Are they still on nights?"

"Nah, with you and Gorham gone, there were two spots open . . ."

The silence that followed spoke for itself. Al Gorham had been Ransom's partner for two years, up until he'd been murdered by the monster Ransom knew must still be at large.

Baldwin busied himself with papers on his desk. "I didn't see you at the funeral."

"I didn't go."

Baldwin gave him a look of genuine concern. "How you doin', Jack? Really. You holdin' up all right?"

"Yeah. Thanks, Bobby. I'm doing fine."

Baldwin sighed. "Good, 'cuz I got one or more fuckin' psychopaths on the loose, guttin' people and stealin' bodies, I was kinda hopin' you'd be able to catch 'em for me."

Ransom smiled. "Yes, sir."

Baldwin raised his eyebrows, his white teeth beaming back at Ransom from his dark face. "I don't remember you bein' this respectful before, Jack. Keep it up."

"What did Elliot's report say?"

Baldwin flipped open a file on his desk. "Pack of wild dogs it says here. Pack of shit if you ask me. Claims you were shooting at one when you hit the kid."

Ransom shook his head. "It wasn't a pack, it was one animal. And it wasn't a dog, it was a wolf. Gorham and I had a line on the group of Indians that own it. I think they were after the kid when we hit the scene. The wolf was still in the house."

"Well, it looks like they got the kid this time. Report says he wasn't taken from the first scene. Why was that?"

"We never found out. We think they were trying to leave us a message with the first killing, maybe planning to get him back when they killed again. We just didn't catch on to it in time."

"I hate to ask you this, Jack. But how did you ever wind up shooting the kid?"

Ransom hesitated. "Do I have to answer that?"

Baldwin locked eyes with Ransom for a moment and, in answer, asked another question. "You really think it was a wolf?"

"I *saw* it Bobby."

He nodded. "Okay, what's your next move?"

"We had a line on the house that the Indians were living in, but I'm going to sit on that for the time being. Right now I want to start with the woman who was killed at the morgue."

"Okay," said Baldwin. "I've got authorization to reinstate you at your original rank and pay. All we have to do now is hook you up with a new partner and you can get rolling."

"Wait a minute, Bobby. I want to work this one alone."

"I can appreciate that, Jack, and if it was up to me you would. But the department says you don't, and as long as the department is signing my paychecks we're both gonna do what the department says. Any other questions?"

Ransom wasn't very happy about this. It took time for partners to develop trust in each other, and right now he didn't even trust Bobby enough to tell him the truth. There was no wolf, and there were no Indians—though there had been at one time, but they weren't directly responsible for the murders.

There was no way that Ransom would be able to tell the rookie he would inevitably be partnered with any of it. Not without sounding like a raving lunatic.

"No, no questions about that. Do you want me to start today, or wait until tomorrow morning?"

"This afternoon. You're on swing shift."

"No way, Bobby. You know I work days."

"You mean you *used* to work days. Now Razor and Burgher work days. You and your new partner—who you're going to meet back here this afternoon at three-thirty—are working swing shift." Baldwin smiled, letting Ransom know he was on his side, but that he was still the boss.

"Jesus, you're a hard ass."

"That's what they pay me for."

"Nah," said Ransom, adopting Bobby's speech pattern. "Don't give me none of that shit. You know they don't pay you diddly squat."

"You can say that again, my friend. You can say that again."

CHAPTER TWO

For Dr. Marian Harris, the halls of the Elliott Bay Medical Center had taken on a distinctly different feel. Normally she walked down the corridors with a quiet confidence, secure in the sounds and smells of the obstetrics ward. But that had been nearly two weeks before—before she'd been here as a patient.

Only now did she realize that it had started even earlier than that, within these very walls. She shook her head, trying to clear her mind. It's all over, she told herself. It might as well have been a dream. But the scar on her stomach would be a permanent testament to the reality of what had happened.

Thank God it's dead, she though. At least that's what she'd been told. Marian had been unconscious when she'd received the wound on her stomach. The police had come in the nick of time and shot him before he could kill her. She should have been happy that that had been the end of it. So why didn't it feel like it was over?

It was that damn dream. She'd been having dreams all week, but nothing as vivid as this morning's. She'd been so drenched with sweat that she'd had to jump back in the shower again. It had all seemed so real. And yet, how could it be a dream if she'd been awake? It was as if she had actually been there in those woods, and killed that couple. It was horrible.

"Oh, Dr. Harris."

The voice suddenly snapped Marian back to the present. "Yes?" she said. It was the duty nurse.

"I'm glad I caught you. Could you sign this drug requisition so we can start an IV on Mrs. Patrick?"

"Let me see the chart first."

As Marian looked it over, the nurse babbled on about which doctors hadn't shown up yet and which patients were in dire need of attention. Finally, Marian signed her name—M.K. Harris, not Marian—and headed off toward the doctors' locker rooms.

Maybe the strangeness she felt was simply due to the fact she hadn't been here in a while. She had taken two weeks of vacation while she recovered, but after all she had been through Marian felt as if she could use another. It seemed too soon to be back, much too soon. There was nothing she could do about it now, though. Besides, it was her own fault.

Marian had lobbied long and hard to be put in charge of medical student rotations. She liked things done her way on the obstetrics ward and the only way to prevent sloppy or incompetent training was to do it herself. Since a new rotation was starting this week, it was either be here or leave it to someone else.

Marian walked into the locker room and began removing her clothes, averting her eyes from the scar as she dressed in her scrubs. Ever since she'd first put on the blue cotton uniform, she'd felt ridiculous ever after walking on the ward in a skirt and a lab coat. And in addition to being infinitely more comfortable— especially in emergency situations—she'd discovered that people tend to regard her more seriously when she was in her scrubs.

She gave herself a cursory look in the mirror. Not bad for forty-six, she thought. Her shoulder length blond hair had some grey in it, and there were lines around her blue eyes, but her body was trim and she felt good. All in all, she'd take it.

After tying back her hair, Marian left the lockers and headed around the corner to the doctors' lounge. Milling around as she walked in were eight medical students from the Maynard School of Medicine, a private school connected, literally, with Bay Med.

She took a clipboard from the nurse who had just finished a brief orientation, and looked it over. "Okay, which of you are first-year students?"

Two young women who looked impossibly young to be in medical school, and one intense young man raised their hands.

"You three won't be expected to answer questions on rounds yet, but we will have some work for you later on, interviewing patients, taking vitals, same thing you've done in the other rotations."

The other five, second- and third-year students, stood around self-assured, confident in having been through all this before. The two first-year women were predictably standing in the back. But the young man was standing in front of everyone, perfectly still and intent on every word that Marian was saying.

She didn't realize until after she had broken eye contact with him that her hand had gone unconsciously to the scar on her stomach. She pulled it away a little too quickly and drew the attention of a few of the students. Ignoring curious looks, she continued.

"Now, I'll expect the rest of you to familiarize yourselves with the patients I'll be treating, and be ready with answers. And while we don't have many deaths or emergency situations here, I'm sure you'll find that this rotation isn't any easier than the others you've been through."

Marian could feel him looking at her, but she didn't want to make eye contact again. The name on his tag read Sanger. She glanced down at the clipboard and saw that his first name was Andrew.

He had black hair and brown eyes. That, and his bronzed skin, made her think he might be Hispanic. Though he was slightly built and looked to be no taller than her own five-six, his presence somehow exceeded his physical form.

"Are there any questions before we begin rounds?"

Unexpectedly, Sanger raised his hand.

"Dr. Sanger," she acknowledged.

He smiled at her, a brilliant flash of white teeth, then looked down at the floor as he shuffled his feet. Now, he looked like a first-year student.

"You can call me Andy," he said when his eyes met hers again.

And have you call me Marian? Not on your life, buddy. It was a common ploy of students in any year, to ingratiate themselves with the female doctors and nurses.

"I'll call you Dr. Sanger, and you'll call me Dr. Harris. Any deviation of that protocol in my rotation and the guilty party will find themselves explaining their actions to the dean. Your question, Dr. Sanger?"

"Yeah. I just wondered how you felt about stupid questions." That elicited a laugh from the rest of the students. "I mean, about first-year students asking questions on rounds."

"As long as it's relevant, I don't mind. And while we're on the subject, I expect all of you to ask questions. If you're too proud to think you can learn anything from me, you probably won't. You're here to learn, and I expect you to learn."

Marian took a quick look at her watch. "If that's all, we'd better get going."

"Thank you, Dr. Harris," said Sanger.

He was smiling at her again. Marian looked him squarely in the eye, then simply nodded and turned to head out the door.

CHAPTER THREE

Ransom was back at the precinct by 3:00. Captain Baldwin was still in a meeting and Ransom took the time to look over the squad room. He had worked here for so long that it seemed like a second home to him. But things were different now.

He looked out over the sea of desks, their tops ladened with files, reports and a myriad of other papers. His desk, for the moment, was still empty. In a way, it had been a relief to come back. He'd thought seriously during the past week about retirement. For a lot of reasons it seemed like the thing to do. He'd also thought about getting another job, but he'd never expected he'd be back here again.

A few minutes later he heard a familiar voice behind him, "Ransom."

He turned. No one was there, but the Captain's door was wide open, and he walked inside and took a seat.

"Wells should be here any minute now."

"Wells? Is that my new partner?"

"Yeah, K. Wells," Ransom heard Baldwin say.

"K.? Jesus, doesn't this guy have a first name?"

Baldwin looked up from his paperwork and frowned. "Yeah, *she* has a first name and it's Kay."

"Aw, Christ, Bobby. You can't team me up with a woman."

"If I didn't know you better, Jack, I'd think you actually believe you have a choice."

Ransom was out of his chair and leaning over Baldwin's desk. "Please, Bobby. You can't team me with a woman."

"Why not?"

Both men looked up to see who had asked the question. It was a small blond woman with a badge dangling from a chain around her neck. Ransom turned away and closed his eyes. Baldwin only leaned back in his chair and grinned.

"Good question, Detective Wells. I was just about to ask that one myself. Jack? Care to enlighten us?"

Ransom turned around and watched Wells as she took a seat. She looked to be around five-two. Petite, he thought. She was wearing faded blue jeans, white tennis shoes, and a polo shirt beneath and unbuttoned navy sweater. Ransom's trained eye could just detect the shoulder holster beneath the left arm of her sweater.

She had short, strawberry blond hair, incredibly blue eyes, and she looked all business. Ransom took a breath and sighed. "It's nothing personal, Wells."

"Oh, just general sexism. That's good to know. I'd hate to think you were singling me out—"

"Hey look. It's not what you think."

"We're not talking about what *I* think—"

"All right," said Baldwin finally, and much to Ransom's relief. "You two can get acquainted later. First thing I want to do is square away some of the details. You still want to use your car, Jack?"

Ransom nodded.

"Okay, make sure you request a voucher today and have it in by the end of the month. Wells, you'll be riding shotgun." She nodded curtly and Baldwin continued.

"I don't know how much time this investigation is going to take, but you two will be on rotation as well. That means you'll be assigned to other cases in addition to this one. Now, the press knows about the two couples but we haven't verified that the cases are related. They also don't know about the woman from the morgue, or about the kid's body being taken.

"I don't expect you to check in with me every hour, but if you get something I'd like to hear about it. Jack, you'll have your old desk back. Wells, I think you're already settled in out there. So, if there's nothing else . . ."

Wells was up and out the door, but stopped short when she heard Baldwin speaking.

"I don't want any problems with you two, Jack."

"Hey, come on, Bobby."

"Find a way to make it work, that's all I'm saying. Now, get out of here."

When Ransom stepped out of the door Wells was waiting for him in the hall. What could he say? He hadn't had a chance to explain himself, but he didn't feel like getting into it in the squad room. The chip on Wells' shoulder was almost visible. In the end, he opted for the all-business approach.

"I'd like to take a run down to the morgue and check out the latest victim. Any objections?"

"Let's go."

It was bad enough that neither of them spoke on the way downtown, but Interstate 5 was a parking lot. Ransom's Buick idled in one spot, where the highway arched over Lake Union, for nearly ten minutes. He didn't carry a light bubble for the roof, and now he was beginning to regret it. Finally he was able to edge onto the Mercer Street exit, hook around Seattle Center and the Space Needle, and drive into the heart of town toward the south end, where he had to go back up the hill past the freeway again to get to the hospital.

The morgue was located in the basement of the Harborview Medical Center, and Ransom walked with Wells to the office of the chief medical examiner, Richard "Doc" Nagumo. His secretary buzzed them in immediately.

The Chief Medical Examiner had been known as "Doc" for as long as Ransom had been on the force. Nagumo had also assured Ransom that the bite marks on the first two victims could not have been made by an animal. In fact, he was adamant that they were of human origin. But by the time the autopsy reports came back, it appeared he had changed his mind.

"Jack," he said when the two cops entered his office. "I'm glad you're back with us."

"Thanks. Doc, this is Kay Wells, my new partner."

Nagumo was his usual starched self: white shirt, blue tie and grey slacks cloaked in his pristine white lab coat. "Detective Wells," he said, shaking her hand. "Pleased to meet you."

Since Nagumo had been working on the case with him before he had quit, Ransom cut to the chase. "I need to take a look at the woman who was killed here last week."

Nagumo shook his head. "Too late. I had to release the body a few days ago, but it's the same as the others." He gave a knowing look to Ransom. "Exactly."

"Have you still got the pictures?"

"Yeah. Let me get the report for you, too."

Had their meeting been different this afternoon Ransom might have told Wells, *You might not want to look at these*, or even asked her to step outside for a minute so he could chew Nagumo's ass for changing his findings on the autopsy report of the first set of murders. As it was, Ransom said nothing as Nagumo splayed the full-color eight-by-ten glossies across his desk.

For the first time that day Wells did something human: she gasped. "My God," she said. "Who the hell did that?"

"*What* did that, you mean," Nagumo answered.

"Huh?"

"A dog did that, not a person. It was just like all the others."

Ransom glared at Nagumo and the medical examiner averted his eyes. Two weeks ago, he had sworn that it *couldn't* have been an animal.

Ransom took a look at the pictures and felt a wave of déjà vu. The M.O. was exactly the same. The woman's throat had a gash across it that went almost down to her spine. The clothes over her abdomen had been torn open and she had been completely gutted. The killer had removed all of her internal organs.

265

"You're saying an animal did this?" Ransom asked. The implication was not lost on Nagumo.

"I had an expert on bite marks up here from Portland after the first murders." A thin sheen of sweat was apparent on Nagumo's forehead. "Though I was skeptical at first, the evidence he found proves it."

Ransom intensified his glare. "A dog?"

"In all probability."

"Has the report been released yet?"

"No. The family are the only ones who know. Since it happened in here, the media hasn't been informed."

"They've had enough mileage out of the two sets of double murders," Wells added.

"Can you send a copy of the report over to me, Doc?"

"Sure, Jack."

Normally Ransom had to do everything but run the damn copy machine himself. Nagumo's acquiescence must have meant that he was attempting to make it up to him.

"Would you like me to make some copies of the photos, too?"

"Yeah," said Ransom, as long as the generosity was flowing.

On the way back to the precinct Ransom and Wells were silent again, so he ventured some small talk.

"You doing okay?"

"What, those pictures?" Wells didn't turn to look at him. "I'm a big girl now, passed my police exams and everything. They even gave me a gun. Want to see it?"

"No."

Ransom looked over at her when they reached the next stop light. She was still looking stonily out the windshield. "Yeah," she said. "I'm doing just fine."

As he pulled into the intersection Ransom took a look at his watch. Seven more hours to go. It was going to be a long shift.

CHAPTER FOUR

When Jack Ransom let himself in the front door he heard a faint but steady tolling that sounded like a gong. When the noise stopped abruptly, he smiled. As Ransom climbed the stairs he removed his jacket and loosened his tie.

A quick glance at the TV in the bedroom verified that it was *The Changeling* he had heard. George C. Scott was on the screen in his pajamas looking up the staircase of a huge Seattle mansion in Ransom's favorite haunted house movie.

"What in the world happened to you today?"

Ransom turned and smiled. Then he threw his jacket on the bed. "Didn't you get my message?"

This time it was Marian's turn to smile. "Yeah, but it was a little cryptic, to say the least."

Ransom had been living with Marian Harris for the past two weeks. High school sweethearts, the two had become reacquainted during the case Ransom had been working on—was still working on, technically.

"I didn't want to give it all away on the phone," he said. "They gave me my job back."

Marian sat up and muted the TV with the remote control. "Jack! That's great! What happened?"

"They fired Elliot."

Marian laughed. "Oh, my God. Why?"

"Somehow the commissioner caught wind of how he was running things, and the little dictator got called on the carpet.

Anyway, the new captain is a friend of mine and he wanted me back."

"Why are you so late?"

"That's the bad news. In my absence, Razor and Burgher were moved up to day shift. I'm stuck with swing shift—three to midnight."

"Oh, Jack." The disappointment in her voice was obvious.

Ransom crawled across the bed to Marian. As they kissed he pulled down the sheet and caressed her skin through the silky materials of her nightgown. A few minutes later he felt her hands tugging at his belt, and they both took time out to quickly undress.

Their lovemaking was the best that Ransom had ever experienced—except for high school, but that had been with Marian, too. The night he'd brought her home from the hospital she'd asked him to move in with her. He didn't have to think it over.

For one thing, he was still in love with her. Their break up all those years ago had been hard on him at the time; he'd done a lot of things wrong. But with the confidence and maturity that both of them brought to their relationship now, the past two weeks had been unforgettable.

And for another thing, he was out of a job. Ransom had promptly given notice at the house he was renting and moved what few furnishings he had into the basement of Marian's spacious North Seattle home.

And, as if their relationship didn't have enough going for it already, Marian was as much of a horror film fanatic as he was. She insisted that he set up his TV and VCR in the bedroom, and even cleared a space against the wall for Ransom's bookcase where he displayed his collection of video cassettes.

She oohed and aahed as they unpacked the boxes, and they talked about their favorite scenes and actors. Ransom had a special penchant for the German silent films of the twenties, while Marian was a staunch advocate of the Universal films of the thirties. Before they had finished putting away all of the tapes, they had made love right there on the floor among the boxes.

He felt bad about not telling her the real reason for his being rehired. But he couldn't bring himself to do it. That baby had been the cause of severe emotional strain—not to mention the physical trauma—for Marian. He knew she wasn't sleeping well at nights, even though she denied it. And he was damned if he was going to do anything that might further inhibit her recovery.

With any luck, he could track down the kid. Then everything would be over and he and Marian could get married—they hadn't discussed it, but he felt it was inevitable—and live happily ever after. At least that was the way it happened in the movies.

Ransom was lying back on the bed afterward, Marian snuggled up to him with her head on his shoulder. "I didn't get a chance to ask you how your first day was," he said.

"That's okay. First things first."

Ransom turned and kissed her on the forehead. "So, how was it?"

"It was strange in the beginning, especially after being a patient, but once I fell into the routine it wasn't too bad. I've got a new rotation of medical students, so that should keep me pretty busy. How was your first day?"

When Ransom chuckled and shook his head Marian propped herself up on her elbow and looked at him. "What is it?"

He sighed. "I've got a new partner."

"Don't you like him?" she asked playfully.

"I wish it was that simple."

Now she sat up full. "Jack, you'd better tell me what's going on."

"I like my partner just fine, but I'm not sure that *she* likes me very much."

Marian looked at him intently, the corners of her mouth giving only the slightest hint of a smile. "Should I be jealous?"

"After what just happened in this bed? What do you think?"

"I think I'm damn lucky you came into my life again, and I'm not about to lose you this time."

Ransom pulled her close and kissed her. "You took the words right out of my mouth."

———————— ✦✦✦◆✦✦✦ ————————

Later that night Ransom awoke to find Marian thrashing around in bed. He turned and put his arms around her, holding her tightly against his body. When she came out of the dream, he released her so that she wouldn't wake up completely.

Eventually she began to sleep quietly. Her blonde hair laid spread out on her pillow, looking grey in the darkness. Ransom buried his face in it, breathing in the smell of her. Then she stirred again and he rolled back onto his pillow, looking up at the ceiling, thinking.

If Marian was still having bad dreams when she thought the person who'd tried to kill her was dead, he didn't even want to think about how she would react if she knew he was still alive. She was the most important thing in his life right now, the only thing. And that meant that his life depended on finding that kid . . . and killing it once and for all. It was nearly an hour later before Ransom finally fell asleep.

CHAPTER FIVE

Ransom awoke the next morning to find Marian's lips pressed to his. She was just heading out the door and, as he'd requested, she woke him up before leaving.

He sat up and rubbed the sleep out of his eyes as he listened to her black BMW pull out of the driveway, then walked in to use the bathroom. When he returned to the bedroom he began pulling videos from his shelves. *Rosemary's Baby*, *It's Alive* one through three, *The Brood*, and just for the hell of it, *Altered States._*

He slipped the last of these into the mouth of the VCR and turned on the set. Then, after shrugging on a robe, Ransom walked downstairs to make some coffee. As soon as he reached the bottom step his phone rang.

"Yeah."

"Jack? This is Razor. Sorry to call you so early."

"That's okay. I was up."

"Good, because Pearson and Davis found two bodies in Ravenna Park this morning. Chet and I stopped by to have a look. They're yours, Jack."

"You, sure?"

"Just like the Edisons."

"Okay, I'm on my way."

"You want me to call Wells for you?"

"No, I'll do it from here."

"All right, but you'd better get over here fast if you want to see them. Nagumo's already at the scene."

"Aw, Christ. You tell him to wait for me."

"I'll do what I can."

Ransom broke the connection and hesitated slightly before hanging up the phone and running back up to the bedroom to dress. He felt like hell for not calling Wells, but things were happening too fast. He needed a chance to talk with Bobby first. If he could be assigned a different partner, it would solve everything.

Dark black clouds roiled in the November sky as Ransom climbed into his Buick Skylark and headed east toward the University District and Ravenna Park.

Once he reached 15th he took a left onto Cowan Park. After flashing his badge to the uniformed officer at the entrance to the park he drove down the dirt lane that circled back underneath the 15th Street Bridge and into the bottom of the Ravenna Park ravine.

It wasn't much of a park as far as Ransom was concerned, several trails winding through a hundred-foot deep gash in the earth that was about a quarter of a mile long. Filled with trees and undergrowth, it was the perfect site for a murder. He'd only driven fifty yards in when he saw the two blue-and-whites, two unmarked cars, Nagumo's wagon, and an ambulance.

Ransom parked and stepped out of his car. A small stream ran the length of the ravine, making the ground swampy and wet. A makeshift bridge of tree branches and mats from the patrol cars had been erected so that the men could get from the access road across to the crime scene.

He flashed his badge again and walked past the uniforms toward the detectives. They were standing in a grove of trees that were surrounded by the skeletons of winter denuded undergrowth.

"What happened?" said Ransom.

A large black detective, Larry Pearson, took a step toward him. "Woman over there was jogging with her dog. The dog sniffed out the bodies."

"Well," came a voice from behind him, and caused Ransom to turn. Nagumo was just ducking under the yellow crime scene tape. "Maybe I can get on with my investigation now."

"Take it easy, Doc. I'm conducting an investigation of my own here." Nagumo frowned, but before he could say anything else Jim Razor called Ransom over to where two white sheets lay on the ground. The two motionless forms were about twenty feet apart, but both had been well hidden beneath the dense scrub brush that filled the ravine.

Ransom lifted the first sheet and had no visible reaction. It had become all too familiar: slit throat and excavated body cavity. The killer was back in business. He walked over and looked at the second body as a formality. One male, one female, the same pattern again.

Ransom went over to where Razor and Burgher were smoking. "Have you talked to Pearson and Davis about giving me the case?"

"Already taken care of. Cap' says you get any case you want."

"Good. I want this whole place cordoned off for at least twenty four hours."

"The whole park?"

"Yeah. I don't want anyone through here destroying evidence. And that includes Nagumo."

"Jesus, Jack."

"Do I have the authorization, or not?"

"Yes, but—"

"Then do it. Who's the best evidence team they've got downtown?"

Burgher coughed into his fist and said, "That would be Unglaub and Thurston."

"I want them out here until they find something I can use. I need a break on this case, fast."

Ransom noticed that Razor had slowly begun to grin.

"What's so funny?"

"Uh, Jack, did you ever call your partner?"

"Why?"

Razor shook his head. "Because she's headed this way and she looks pissed."

Ransom turned around and was suddenly face to face with an extremely angry looking Wells.

"So, were you going to tell me about this, or was I supposed to read about it in the *Times* tomorrow?"

Ransom tried to remain calm. "Listen, Wells, I just got here myself. I didn't have time to call—"

"Cut the crap, Ransom. I don't know what the hell's going on here, but I'm going straight to Captain Baldwin when we're through and ask to be reassigned."

Beautiful, Ransom thought. Maybe if they both wanted out, Bobby wouldn't be able to refuse. "Unglaub and Thurston are coming in from downtown," Ransom informed her. "After that, we can go."

Wells walked past him over toward the bodies. Burgher had wandered off during the confrontation, but Razor was still standing close by, a grin on his face a mile wide.

"What?" Ransom yelled.

"Nothing, Jack. Just watching you and your partner at work. Fascinating."

Ransom walked away and climbed into the front seat of his car without another word. What a mess. Because of Elliot, he was two weeks behind on the case. And now this thing with Wells. For the first time since his death, Ransom let himself think about his old partner, Al Gorham.

Gorham started out as a young rookie, like Wells, but had worked under Ransom for over two years. He'd been obsessive and single-minded, a bachelor who never went on dates. And then there was the fact that the man had never seen a horror film in his life.

Ransom shook his head. In his own way, Gorham had been as frustrating as Wells was now. But he also had been one of the most conscientious and hard working cops on the force. And in Ransom's nineteen years on the force, the best partner he'd ever had.

A single tear rolled down Ransom's cheek and he instinctively wiped it away. The more he thought about Gorham, the more he realized he hadn't really given Wells a fair chance. He'd been so intent on getting rid of her that he had no idea what kind of cop she would make.

A knock on the passenger window brought him out of his thoughts, and Ransom leaned over and unlocked the door. Wells climbed in beside him and said, "Okay, let's get this over with."

Ransom started the car and backed out slowly. Once they'd reached Roosevelt he broke the silence. "Listen, Wells. Before we see the captain, there's something I want to say."

"I think you've said just about enough."

"No, I haven't—"

"What else do you want from me? I'm talking to the captain. I thought that would make you happy."

Ransom immediately pulled over to the curb, even though they were only a block from the station house. He shut the engine off and turned to her. He was not angry, but he was stern.

"Wells, I don't care what you think of me personally. That's none of my business. But when we're on the job, that's different. I've been on the force over twenty years, and whether you think so or not, there's a lot you can learn from me. Not only that but, at least for the moment, I'm still your partner. Your *senior* partner. Like it or not, because of that I should already have your respect. I shouldn't have to earn it."

Wells just stared at him, fire burning in those piercing blue eyes. Then she turned and looked out over the dashboard. Her mouth was tight and her hands were clenched, but eventually she began to nod.

"You're right," she said, and turned back to Ransom with her hand extended, fierce determination still on her face. "I'm sorry, Lieutenant."

It was all Ransom could do to keep from laughing, but he did manage to shake her hand. "Please, call me Jack."

She hesitated for a moment and then her expression softened. "My name's Kay."

"Thank you, Kay."

Ransom wasn't sure what to say next. He wanted to tell her why he couldn't be teamed with a woman, but he didn't want to come off sounding like he was making excuses. The only way to do that, though, was to tell the truth. And what was the point if they were going to split up anyway?

"Kay? The thing that did this . . . that killed all those people—"

"You mean the dog?"

"It was no dog that did this, but let me finish. I don't know if anyone told you, but the thing that did this also killed my partner."

"What happened?"

"I want to tell you, Kay. I'd like you to know what really happened before you ask the captain to be reassigned. But I need to ask you one thing first."

She had put her leg up on the seat and turned her body to completely face Ransom. Her concerned expression seemed genuine. "Okay."

"No matter what happens later, what I tell you now does not leave this car."

Her forehead wrinkled and she nodded.

"The thing that did this is human, but not a man. The last time I saw it—about two weeks ago—it looked like it was only a year old. I think it's grown since then, though. That's how it was able to leave the morgue on its own.

"The woman I live with, Marian Harris, is an obstetrician at the Elliott Bay Medical Center. She delivered the baby and saw its teeth and claws. It killed its own mother getting out of the womb. It's killed three other women and four men. It nearly killed Marian.

"The last time I saw it, it had just killed my partner. I put a bullet in its head and blew nearly half its face off. Apparently that wasn't enough because it's still alive. If we meet up with this thing again, there can't be any hesitation. It has to be taken apart."

"What makes you think I'd hesitate?"

"Marian tried killing it, but Gorham stopped her. I think that maybe Gorham died because he couldn't shoot it. It looked too much like a kid. That's the reason, the only reason I objected to having you as my partner. I need to know that you'd be able to kill this thing if you ever saw it, without hesitation."

Ransom stopped then and looked out the window. Wells was deep in thought. The story was total lunacy, and he expected Wells to say as much before she asked to be reassigned. That was why what she said next surprised him.

"Who was the mother?"

"Some runaway, we assume. We think she'd been the prisoner of a sex-slavery ring. We know she had some sex with animals, but that still doesn't seem like a satisfactory explanation for how this thing was conceived."

Wells shook her head. "Jesus, Jack. You say you saw this thing?"

"Me and Marian both. It looked like a perfectly normal baby, but it's able to change shape seemingly at will." Ransom sighed. "I haven't even told Marian it's still alive."

"Why not?"

"It almost killed her. She's still having nightmares about it, and I don't want her to worry. That's another reason I want to get this thing as fast as I can."

Wells sat back. "It's just so . . . unbelievable."

"I know. That's why I initially wanted to work on this case alone. I wasn't sure a new partner would believe me. Or worse, they might think I was nuts."

"Yeah, it sounds like something right out of *Werewolf of Paris*."

Ransom was stunned. He had always prided himself on his encyclopedic knowledge of horror films, but that was one he'd never heard of. He assumed Wells had the title wrong and corrected her. "You mean *Werewolf of London*?"

She wrinkled her nose. "Not that god awful movie? No, I'm talking about the novel, by Guy Endore."

"You read horror novels?"

"Every one I can get my hands on."

Ransom smiled broadly. "So, tell me about this novel."

As she related the plot to him, about a child who begins to realize that he turns into a wolf at night, Ransom gradually recognized the plot of the movie based on it. "That's *Curse of the*

Werewolf, with Oliver Reed. Except they set it in Spain instead of France."

"Leave it to Hollywood to ruin a perfectly good book."

"This one was made in England."

Wells shrugged. "It's still just a movie." Then she smiled back at Ransom, who was still beaming.

"So," he said, starting up the car and pulling out into traffic. "Do you still want to see the captain?"

She looked over at him and slowly shook her head. "No. I want us to catch this thing, whatever it is. If you still want my help."

Ransom nodded as they neared the precinct house. "Absolutely."

CHAPTER SIX

Once she had managed to get over the first-day jitters, Marian felt glad to be back at work. She was happy for Jack, too. He'd seemed so lost after he'd quit. That, in addition to losing his partner and looking after her, had made for a rough couple of weeks.

But Jack had a new partner now, and he seemed to be in good spirits. For Marian, however, things were far from perfect. The dreams she'd been having were beginning to invade her waking hours, especially when she was at the hospital.

The dreams she had during the day were very different from the ones she had been experiencing at night. They were more like flashbacks, and somehow that was almost more frightening. After a deep breath she shook off those thoughts and tried to get her mind back on work.

Marian had rounds coming up in a few minutes, and a pretty big crowd now with the addition of the new medical students. She pushed herself off the bench in the doctors' locker room and headed out into the trenches.

Though most weren't of the life-threatening variety, the obstetrics floor at Bay Med had as many emergencies as any other ward. The women she saw had all of the usual medical problems that were encountered in any normal population, with one major complication: all of her patients were pregnant. Most times she thought it was probably more challenging; instead of one patient, there were really two. Two lives to be responsible for. But she enjoyed the challenge, even thrived on it.

There were times, of course, when it made her miss having children of her own, but that was the choice she'd made. Though some might have said it had been made for her, she knew that wasn't true. She'd had options and, consciously or unconsciously, never found the time to pursue them.

It wasn't until she was thirty-five that she and her ex-husband, Loren, first tried to get pregnant. After having no success for a year, Marian had herself examined and it was discovered that both of her Fallopian tubes were blocked. She immediately set up a consultation with another obstetrician, but an emergency on the ward that day postponed it.

After that, Marian just never seemed to get around to making another appointment. Work kept her busy. She had stopped taking birth control pills, and felt better than she had in years. And now it was too late. She was divorced, forty-six, and even though she was with Jack she didn't know whether they would still be together a year from now, let alone whether he wanted kids or not.

When Marian reached the end of the hall and rounded the last corner, she was taken aback by the throng of doctors waiting for her. The crowd parted as she walked through, and then fell in step behind her. She turned confidently into the first room and rounds were underway.

Later that evening, a few minutes before seven, Marian was heading to the locker rooms to change. Twelve hours of work was plenty, and she would still have time to unwind before Jack came home.

She was just about to take the top of her scrubs off when a breathless Dorry Williams came bursting into the room.

"I'm sorry, Dr. Harris, but there's an emergency and I can't find another doctor."

So much for unwinding, she thought, and stood up. "Okay. Let's go."

Marian was a little surprised that Dorry hadn't found anyone on call—and wondered how hard she really tried—but she was absolutely shocked when she saw Andy Sanger waiting outside the patient's door.

"What are you still doing here?" She hadn't meant to sound short; it just came out that way.

"I wanted to see if I could help."

She wanted to tell him to get lost but, looking around, Marian could see that Dorry was right. The ward looked deserted.

"Okay, but stay out of the way. I'll let you know if I need any help."

He nodded and flashed that irritating, but oddly magnetic, smile at her.

Once inside, Marian was able to size up the situation quickly. The woman, who had just been admitted, looked no more than sixteen. Dorry informed her that the girl was already six centimeters dilated, and a cursory ultrasound had determined it was a breech birth.

"Get her started on an IV drip," she told Dorry. "4ccs Lidocaine." Then Marian bent over the girl. "Susan, do you have anyone here to help you through this?"

The girl shook her head.

"Dr. Sanger?"

When he appeared at her side, she directed him toward the girl. "Susan, this is Dr. Sanger. He's going to hold your hand and talk you through the procedure."

"Am I going to lose my baby?"

"No," Sanger stepped in before she had a chance. "Dr. Harris is going to take good care of both of you."

Though she was mildly irritated at this premature guarantee, Marian was forced to turn her attention to the emergency C-section she would have to perform. "Dorry, I want you to get me an anesthesiologist and a scrub nurse, stat. I don't care if you have to raid the ER."

After Dorry had left, Marian turned to Sanger and said, "All right, let's get her into the OR."

—————————— ✦✦✦✦✦✦✦ ——————————

Two hours later Marian emerged from the operating room drained and tired, but happy. The operation had been successful, and Susan was now the mother of a five-pound baby girl. The baby appeared to be in good health, but it was a bit underweight. Marian was going to keep her under observation for a couple of days just to make sure there were no complications arising from the mother's drug use.

Marian was leaning against the wall when Sanger came out of the OR. Once Susan had been given the epidural Sanger seemed to do much better. He'd been supportive and had refrained from making any more asinine guaranties about Marian's ability as a surgeon.

He'd also stayed out of her way. And if anything earned rookie points in her book during an operation, it was that. He turned to her in the hall, about to speak, and she braced herself for another of his stupid comments.

"Dr. Harris. I'm really sorry about telling Susan that everything was fine before. I didn't realize how serious it was."

That was a surprise. Marian leveled her eyes at him and said, "If you want to guarantee your own work, fine. Just don't speak for another doctor."

"Okay," he said, with what looked like genuine sincerity. "I'll remember that."

"Remember that you still have a lot to learn. Otherwise, you did fine."

"Thanks."

As Marian turned and headed down the hall toward the locker rooms, Sanger kept pace behind her in silence. When he finally spoke, it was with a throaty resonance that she had never heard in his soft voice before. "Do you think you'd have the energy to have a drink with me tonight? I know it's late, but I'd really like to talk over some things with you."

Marian's immediate instinct was to say no, but before she could get out the word she remembered that Jack wouldn't be home until after midnight. "What's that?" she asked instead.

"Just that my major in college was embryology. And after watching you tonight, I've been thinking about specializing in obstetrics."

Marian allowed herself a grin and shook her head. If he'd been unsuccessfully trying to ingratiate himself with her before, he was certainly pressing the right buttons now. And yet, even with that, she had no idea why she heard herself saying, "Sure."

At a small bar called Damon's, up on 34th, Marian found herself engrossed in conversation with a medical student in a way she'd never imagined possible. Andy Sanger was something of an enigma. He appeared to have a vast understanding of medicine, but very little else. In some ways he was incredibly immature, while at the same time he had the most self-assured presence of any man she'd ever met.

"So what I thought I could do," he was saying, "would be to come in on weekends and free evenings to take patient histories and help out wherever I can. All I have to do is check it out with my freshman advisor and make sure it fulfills all my volunteer requirements."

Marian popped a few stray olive slices from the pizza they'd shared into her mouth. Then she swallowed the last of her beer and said, "That sounds fine to me." It was almost midnight and Marian yawned as she reached for her purse. "Have him give me a call and we'll set it up. But right now I have to get home."

He reached over and set his hand on her arm. She thought at first that he simply wanted to pay, but when she looked into his eyes she knew it was something else. In her mind she knew it was wrong, and yet, as he leaned toward her she felt as though she wanted him to kiss her.

When their lips met, she expected to recoil immediately. Instead, she didn't want him to stop. When he pulled away and took out his wallet, there was no remorse in his expression. He thumbed out some bills onto the table and stood so that she could slide out of the booth.

In a daze, Marian walked to the door with Sanger. He said goodbye as though nothing had happened, saying he would see her in the morning for rounds. Then he left.

Marian sat and stared out the windshield as the car warmed up. After several minutes she wasn't even sure it had ever happened. Had he really kissed her? She shook her head and pulled out of the parking lot. All she wanted now was to get home to Jack.

That night Marian dreamed again of killing.

CHAPTER SEVEN

"Silver bullets?" Wells asked.

Ransom was drinking coffee at his usual table at The Continental. Wells had called him a half-hour before, all excited about making the ID on the couple in the park. But Ransom had news of his own.

He'd decided the day before that they should hold all of their discussions about the case outside of the squad room. The other detectives might not be too comfortable with their talks of werewolves and—

"Silver bullets," Ransom repeated. "How the hell do I know? The thing is, I know that regular bullets aren't going to kill this kid. Silver ones might not either, but I'd feel a lot better if we took the extra precaution. If the legends have any truth to them at all, it could be the only way to stop it."

Wells was shaking her head, but more to herself than Ransom. "I can't believe we're really taking this seriously. Isn't that going to be expensive, though . . . silver?"

"Just leave it to me. As long as you're not using them for target practice, you shouldn't need more than a few rounds."

In fact, that was what Ransom had been doing all morning. He'd taken a roll of silver quarters he'd had down to an ammunition maker he knew. It had taken until nearly two, but now Ransom placed six silver .38 slugs on the table in front of Wells.

"That was fast."

"I told you—I want this thing bad."

Wells smiled as she scooped up the bullets and slipped them into the pocket of her jeans. When the waitress came around to refill Ransom's cup, she ordered coffee, too. It wasn't until she had taken her first sip that Ransom said, "So, you made a positive ID on the couple?"

She shook her head.

"But I thought—"

"It wasn't a couple."

Ransom leaned forward and let her continue.

"The initial ID's we had last night from the identification in their pockets were correct. That's what I followed up on this morning." She took out a small black notebook from her jacket and began to read.

"The male was one Frank Slater, 47, Caucasian. The female, one Glenda Tucker, 33 . . . Black."

"What?"

"She was very light skinned. I don't think any of us at the scene were looking too closely because we saw what we wanted to see, a white couple."

"This changes everything."

Wells nodded. "And from what I can tell after talking with the families, the two of them never really knew each other."

"What do you mean, 'really?'"

"I'll get to that later, but here's the most interesting part. I talked with Nagumo this morning—thanks for introducing me, by the way—after he had finished with the preliminary autopsy. He says that they weren't even killed at the same time. He says the woman was died twenty-four to thirty-six hours earlier."

"Two separate murders."

"Bodies dumped in the same place."

"Dumped?"

"Oh, yeah. I also talked to Thurston and Unglaub. They didn't find anything. The only thing they could say for certain is that the victims weren't killed in the park—there wasn't enough blood. The murders took place somewhere else."

Ransom sat back and ran his hand through his hair. This completely changed the M.O., and for the life of him he couldn't imagine what it signified. He took a sip of coffee and looked over at Wells. "So, where does that leave us?"

"There is a connection between the two."

"Okay, so why wait to tell me about it?"

"Because, after what you told me yesterday I wanted you to prepare yourself. I don't think you're going to like it."

" . . . What?"

"When I said before that they didn't really know each other, they almost certainly knew *of* each other. They both worked at the same place."

"Where?"

"Bay Med, Jack. The Elliott Bay Medical Center. Slater was a doctor, Tucker was in housekeeping."

Suddenly Ransom had to set his cup down when he realized the significance of this. His hands were shaking and it wasn't from the coffee. "Aw, Christ."

Wells stood up while Ransom dug out a couple of dollars for the coffee. "We have to—"

"Tell Marian," Wells said.

Ransom stood and slipped on his jacket. "Yeah. Nice work, Wells."

"Do you think this thing could still be after her?" she asked.

"I hope to hell not," Ransom said as the two of them headed for his car. But in his gut, he knew it was true.

Ransom had been thinking to himself all the way across town. Wells finally broke this silence as they headed up the Magnolia Bridge. "What do you think the new M.O. means, Jack?"

He shook his head. "I have a pretty good idea, Kay, and I don't like the looks of it."

"What?"

Ransom pulled up in front of the hospital entrance and turned off the engine. Then he turned toward his partner.

"When I saw the kid, it had only been born a week before and yet it looked at least a year old. This whole time I've been going on the assumption that its growth pattern has been linear: one week equals one year. That would be our best bet to catch it. It's been four weeks now, not many places a four-year old is going to be able to hang out with no clothes and a bloody face."

"But you don't think that now?"

"No. For one thing, if those bodies were moved then this thing has access to some kind of transportation."

"You don't think someone could be working with him?"

"No. Gorham and I pretty much ruled that out on the initial investigation." Ransom sighed. "And then there's the trauma to the bodies. If he's not killing them where the bodies are found, he must have a place where he can take the victims. It would be a private place, a house or apartment, where he could take his time." He shook his head. "I think his growth is proceeding geometrically."

"Meaning?"

"He's at least twenty-five by now."

The two of them climbed out and headed in through the glass door of the entrance. As they approached the elevators Ransom turned to Wells and said, "I don't want her to know that this is the same investigation."

"Jack—"

"I mean it. I'm going to tell her about the murders, but this has nothing to do with the thing we are hunting, okay?"

She tried to persuade him with a cold blue stare, but Ransom stood his ground. "All right," she finally said, and he held the elevator as she stepped inside.

They rode up to the obstetrics ward with a male nurse in green scrubs and a woman in a wheelchair. Emerging from the elevator, they headed over to the nurses' station. "Dr. Harris," Ransom said.

A large nurse who looked like Cathy Bates in *Misery* frowned at them and said, "Who wants to know?"

Ransom flipped out his badge and leaned across the counter. "Police."

The woman's demeanor changed instantly. "Oh, uh, I think she's in—"

"Get her. Now."

"Yes, sir." A couple of the other nurses had stuck their heads out of an adjoining room. The nurse said, "Dorry, can you watch the desk while I go get Dr. Harris?"

"Sure."

While the first nurse waddled off down the hall, Dorry smiled at Ransom. When he returned it she whispered, "Are you Jack?"

He felt Well's elbow in his ribs before she walked off. Ransom sighed. "We'll be waiting over here." He motioned his head toward a waiting room that contained, among other things, a couple of expectant fathers. When Dorry nodded, the two of them walked over to the room to wait for Marian.

Luckily for Ransom, she arrived before Wells decided to say anything about Dorry. When Marian came into the room her brow was furrowed with concern. "Jack, what is it?"

"Can we go someplace private, to your office maybe?"

"Sure. I was just there. Why didn't you come down?"

From behind him, Ransom heard Wells clear her throat. He ignored it and walked beside Marian with Wells in their wake.

Once inside Marian's office they took seats in front of her desk. "Marian," Ransom said as she sat down herself. "Do you know a Frank Slater?"

"Yes. He's an obstetrician. He was on call last night, but he never showed up."

"He was found murdered yesterday in Ravenna Park along with Glenda Tucker."

She leaned back without saying a word, but her eyes never left Ransom's. "What happened?" she asked.

Ransom hesitated and he heard Wells say, "They were shot."

"I'm sorry. Marian, this is my partner, Kay Wells." They nodded at each other and Ransom continued. "Did you know Glenda Tucker?"

She shook her head, and again Wells picked up the slack for Ransom. "She was in housekeeping, a light-skinned black woman."

Marian nodded now. "Okay, I think I know who you're talking about. I just didn't know her name. This is incredible, Jack. Do you know who did it?"

He shook his head. "Right now we're just trying to piece together what happened, maybe figure out if there are any other connections between the two besides working here. Do you think they might have been seeing each other—"

Marian laughed. "Frank? I don't think so. He couldn't wait to get home at night. I know for a fact he was looking for a position in Kitsap County so he could live closer to home."

"He lived on Bainbridge Island?"

"Yeah."

Ransom looked at Wells and she nodded. "How about Tucker?"

"Mount Baker," she answered.

"Okay," he said. "But if you can think of anyone you might have seen with both of them, let me know."

Marian looked bemused and said, "What, this afternoon?"

"Or tonight, yeah. Call me."

Wells stood at this point and walked to the door. "I think I'll start interviewing the nurses and then go down to housekeeping. It was nice to meet you Dr. Harris."

"You too," said Marian, distractedly. Ransom merely nodded.

When Wells was gone, the two of them stood and Marian fell into Ransom's arms. "You're scaring me, Jack. What's going on?"

"That's what I'm trying to find out, hon'."

"You think someone at the hospital killed them?"

"That's what it's starting to look like, so I want you to do something for me."

"What?"

"Don't go anywhere with anybody. Even if it's your best friend."

"Jack—"

"I mean it. Don't go out for a beer, don't go out to lunch. Just get in your car and come home."

She pulled away and stepped back. "Is it that bad?"

"If I could rule out a few people and give you a list, I'd do it, believe me. But I can't right now. It literally could be anybody."

"Jesus, Jack."

"I'm sorry to make it sound so dramatic. What can I say? I'm worried about you."

Marian sighed. "Okay. Do you think I'm safe in the hospital?"

He shrugged. "Probably. Just be careful. And whatever you do—"

"I know. Don't go anywhere with anybody."

Ransom took a deep breath and trembled as he exhaled. Marian leaned against his chest and he rested his cheek against her forehead. Then her beeper went off.

She pulled his face to hers and kissed him. "I'll see you tonight," she said, and he nodded.

After he left Marian's office, Ransom interviewed as many of Slater's colleagues as he could find. None of them could offer much more than Marian had. He hooked back up with Wells shortly before five.

"I don't like it, Jack."

"It's not your call."

"If this thing's stalking her, she should know it."

"Let's just concentrate on catching it and she won't have too."

"That's fine, but—"

"Look, Wells, I appreciate your concern, but that's my decision."

"Yes, sir," she said, without attitude of any kind.

They were walking toward the front door when Ransom noticed that she had a computer printout in her hand.

"What's that?" he asked.

"I got a list of people who are assigned to the obstetrics ward."

"Hmm. What about people like the housekeeping staff, who work on every ward?"

Wells held out a large list. "I got a list of all the employees, too."

"That's a lot of suspects."

She shrugged. "It's a place to start."

"Yeah. If we knew who was working the last two nights, that would be better."

She held up a sheaf of papers. "Schedules for the nursing staff and housekeeping, as well as the doctor's rotation for this month."

Ransom stopped at the door and Wells turned to him. "Thanks, Kay. I haven't exactly been my best today, and you've been doing a hell of a job picking up the slack."

Wells smiled and repeated Ransom's own line back to him, "I want this thing . . . bad."

CHAPTER EIGHT

After an exhausting afternoon Marian went back to her office to do some paperwork before heading home. She had done as she'd promised Jack and had eaten lunch alone. Except that it had been more out of necessity than by design. There were reports to finish, schedules to make out, and she hadn't even looked at the medical student evaluations yet.

But even with all that pending, as soon as Marian closed the door behind her she walked over and laid down on the small couch in her office. She needed rest before she could trek down to the cafeteria for something to eat. She had only just closed her eyes when she smelled pine.

Marian immediately pushed herself up off of the couch, but found that she was naked in a bed of pine needles. It was happening again. She knew she wasn't dreaming; she hadn't even been asleep.

It was dark out. It was always dark in her dreams. And she could smell blood. Seemingly against her will, she began moving forward into the night. As she smelled her prey she slowed and crouched down behind a tree to wait. A few minutes later they entered a clearing and Marian's heart sank.

Stepping out into the moonlight were Jack and his partner. She wanted to scream at them, to scare them into running away. But the only sound she could emit from her throat was a low growl. Jack seemed to sense something and pulled his gun.

His partner followed suit and, unbelievably, Marian chose that moment to attack.

She screamed out as she approached them and they both turned to her. Then, just as she sprang at Detective Wells, they both began firing. Smoke and flames erupted as she felt bullets pepper her body. It stopped her short, but didn't stop her.

When she hit the ground, Marian sprang again and hit Wells in the chest. Her claws dug deeply into the woman's flesh as the two of them rolled onto the ground. Then, just as Marian was about to lock her jaws around Wells' throat, she felt a knifing pain in her chest like a red-hot ice pick.

She rolled over onto her back, whimpering as she saw Jack lean over her. The wound was like a fire in her body and she wanted it to stop. She wanted Jack to help it stop. He lifted his gun again and placed the warm barrel against her forehead.

The only fear she'd felt in the dream had been for the lives of Jack and his partner. But she was suddenly terrified for herself as Jack smiled. Then he pulled the trigger.

Marian jerked awake, still too frightened to be surprised that she wasn't alone. Andy Sanger was standing over her.

"Dr. Harris, are you all right?"

"What are you doing in here?"

"I was coming up to talk with you when I heard you cry out." He backed away as she sat up. "I thought something might be wrong. I'm sorry. I'll leave if you want."

"No, that's all right. Just give me a minute to get myself together. I was having a bad dream."

"It looked like it."

Marian shook off the singlet of fear that still clung to her, then walked over to sit behind her desk. After a couple of deep breaths she said, "What was it you wanted to talk about?"

"I don't mind coming back," he said.

For the first time since she'd woken up she really looked at him, into his eyes. What she saw there made the nightmare disappear. Her nerves calmed and her heart slowed and she felt herself relax all over. "Go ahead, Dr. Sanger."

"Please, call me Andy."

She sighed, and he said, "I'll still call you Dr. Harris."

She smiled and shook her head.

"I promise," he said.

"Okay, Andy. Spill it."

He drifted across the room to her desk and leaned down toward her. His eyes caught hers and peacefulness filled her again. "I want you to have dinner with me tonight . . . at my place."

She looked at him, but the incredulity wouldn't come. Unconsciously her hand went to the scar on her stomach. When she realized it, she pulled her hand free and set it on the desk. "I don't know, Andy. I have a lot of work—"

"I'll be here at six."

"Okay," she said, without knowing why.

"I'll see you then."

Even after he was gone, his hold over her continued. Only when she concentrated on her work did she feel free from his influence.

Marian pulled out the large manila envelope from the medical school and began to look over the student evaluations. They weren't due until the end of rotation, but she always liked to fill them out as the quarter progressed. Not only would the evaluation be more accurate, it wouldn't be so much work all at once at the end of the quarter.

Looking over at the cover sheet, Marian noticed a glaring omission. Andy Sanger's name was not among the students assigned to her. She reached for the phone to call Dean Spencer at the medical school, when a knifing pain in her abdomen doubled her over in her chair.

The scar on her stomach seemed to throb beneath her hand, and she broke out in a light sweat wondering what could be wrong. The clock on her desk said it was just after five. The dean wouldn't be in anyway.

As soon as she had the thought, the pain was gone. Andy would come to get her in an hour. Her feelings were complicated. Marian didn't want to feel the way she did, but she knew that once he was here the pain wouldn't be able to reach her. He at once compelled and repulsed her, but she felt powerless to resist.

She took a sheet of paper from her desk, filled out his name at the top, and added it to the evaluations of other students. Then she set to work for an hour.

"I can give you two, but that's it."

"Aw, Christ, Bobby."

Ransom and Wells were in Captain Baldwin's office. Ransom was pacing in front of he captain's desk while Wells stood quietly in the doorway.

"The only way we have of catching this guy is if he dumps another body in Ravenna Park. If we have enough men to cover the area, we'll get him."

"I told you, Jack. I can't spare the man hours."

Ransom threw up his hands. "I though you wanted to catch this guy."

"No."

Ransom stopped in his tracks and looked at Baldwin. The captain smiled. "I said I wanted *you* to catch this guy."

"Then give us the people we need. There must be a dozen ways into the park. We can't cover all that with four people." Ransom stared down Baldwin until the captain finally sighed and shook his head.

"I'll call downtown and see if I can authorize the overtime. But a dozen men is a hell of a lot of man power for something that's as iffy as the guy *might* be back to dump a body."

"It's all we've got right now, Bobby."

"I know. What I'm saying is, don't hold your breath. Until you hear from me otherwise, though, you've got Razor and Burgher for as long as you need them."

Ransom left the office and went back out to the squad room with Wells beside him. They'd just come onto their shift a few hours before and it was almost five-thirty. Ransom looked at his watch and sat down. Wells' desk was opposite, and faced his.

He was leaning back, eyes focused on his desk, when he heard Wells say, "Do you want to go to the park now?"

He looked up and shook his head. "I called them this morning," he said. "I told them I was going to ask Bobby, and they said they'd cover us at the park until seven."

"That's great."

"Yeah, well, you'd better prepare yourself for a long night."

"Are we staking out the park?"

He nodded. "From seven until daylight."

Wells didn't say anything, and Ransom went back to his own thoughts. A few minutes later he got up and said, "I'm going to take an hour. I'll meet you back here at seven."

"What did you want me to do until then?"

"Keep going over those lists of names," he said. "Whoever we're looking for has to be on there somewhere."

The Ransom grabbed his umbrella and his coat and headed out into the darkness.

There was a knock on the door and Marian's head lifted excitedly from her desk. It was almost six.

"Come in," she said.

The door opened and Jack walked in. Marian tried not to panic, even thought the dull throb began again in her abdomen.

"Jack. What are you doing here?"

He grinned. "I thought I'd give you a lift home."

The pain increased as she stood and hugged him. "That's sweet, but I have a patient in labor. I was going to stick around another couple of hours." She shrugged. "I'm sorry."

"That's all right. Just thought I'd take a chance."

She didn't know what to say. The pain was steadily increasing in spite of the lie about her patient. Jack looked at her funny, but before she could say anything the door opened.

Andy Sanger stepped forcefully into the room. "Dr. Harris. Your patient is going into the delivery room."

"Oh." She was suddenly confused. Marian looked to Jack and then over to Andy. It wasn't until the younger man took her arm that she allowed herself to be ushered out of the room. She looked back at Jack once—the concern on his face evident—before she passed over the threshold of the office.

At that moment flames seemed to engulf the door and she was suddenly in the woods running. But this time she was not alone. An animal was running along beside her.

Marian stopped to look down at her body. Her thin forelegs were covered in a thick coat of gray fur. Looking back at her flanks she could see that her whole body was covered with fur as well. The other animal was walking in circles around her, urging her forward.

He pushed his muzzle into her neck and she bolted forward. With two quick strides he was beside her again and the two of them were off running. On and on they ran over trails, through the undergrowth, and into clearings. It seemed to the animal Marian had become, that they had traveled many miles before they came to the cave.

He entered first and she followed. The two of them lay inside the warm earth, tongues moving back and forth in their muzzles as they panted, resting. A few minutes later he was up and circling the front of the cave.

Then he was back around her, smelling. She stood and walked out to the front of the cave with him following. She needed him, she needed him to have her, but she wasn't quite ready yet. She felt him climb on top of her and she moved away and headed back outside.

He followed, determined, and she led him to a meadow. Lit by the full moon it was almost like daylight in the grass. There they growled and bit, and she fended him off until she couldn't stand it anymore. Then she arched her back and allowed him to mount her.

As they coupled, the scenery around them began to subtly change. The brightly lit meadow shimmered and became a darkened room before changing back to a grassy field. At one point she looked down and her hairy foreleg became hairless and smooth. The smells changed, too, from animal to human and back again.

Then she felt it inside of her. Something traveled up her spine to her head, and then down again between her flanks. Marian cried out. She screamed and moved forward feeling him slip off her back. She turned to look at him, but he paid no attention. He was lying in the grass panting, his eyes unfocused. Then she ran.

Her four legs met the ground as quickly as she could move them. Her paws sure-footedly gripped everything in their path as they propelled her to safety. Eventually she crawled under a dense thicket of undergrowth and hid.

Her body shivered though she wasn't cold, and for a long time she stayed perfectly still, looking and waiting. Then she lay her muzzle down on her forepaws and let her eyes close. At last, Marian slept.

CHAPTER NINE

Ransom decided to wait in Marian's office. Maybe she would be done with her delivery soon enough for him to take her home anyway. He stood and paced for a while, eventually working his way around behind her desk. What he saw there made him reach for the phone.

"Wells," he said when he had her on the other end.

"Jack?"

"Yeah, listen, do those printouts you have there list medical students on rotation?"

"No. I don't remember seeing anything like that. Just people who are employed by the hospital."

The line was quiet for a moment as Ransom thought. "If I'm right about his age, our guy could be a medical student. What do you think?"

Wells said, "How do we get the names?"

"I've got them right here."

"Great. Give them to me and I'll try to track down addresses before you get back."

Ransom fished out the list from the papers on Marian's desk and read the males. But as he was putting the list back he saw a separate sheet of paper with a different name: Andrew Sanger. That was the kid he'd seen come in to get Marian. He gave Wells that name too and said, "Do that one first."

"Okay."

"I'll see you at seven."

He paced a little more, and finally went out to the nurses' station to see how long Marian might be. Dorry and another nurse were sitting there. Ransom said, "Do you know how much longer Dr. Harris is going to be in delivery?"

The nurses looked at each other and Dorry said, "I think Dr. Harris went home for the night." The other nurse was nodding. "She left with Dr. Sanger a few minutes ago."

Sanger.

Ransom was suddenly reeling. He felt as though everything had been vacuumed from his mind. He was empty and scared.

He took a few steps away from the counter, trying desperately to get his mind to work. Dorry rushed out and held his arm. "Are you all right?"

"Yeah," he said. It was the truth. He suddenly knew what he needed to do. "Listen, where does Marian park?"

"Huh?"

"Dr. Harris. Where does she park her car?"

"There's a doctors' lot that's covered, near the emergency entrance."

"Thanks," he said, and sprinted off toward the elevator.

Riding down, he knew it was too much to hope for. If Marian's car was gone, he could put out a call to have it stopped on sight. When the elevator reached the ground floor he ran down the hallway toward the ER. He had to ask one of the nurses where the doctors' lot was, and then he was outside looking through the rows of cars.

He found it in less than a minute. The doors were locked and Ransom stood there for a moment, thinking. Sanger must have taken her in his car, but where? His place, most likely.

If he'd dumped the bodies in Ravenna Park, it made sense that he lived in the University District. That didn't make it true, though. He had to find out where Sanger lived.

The sheet of paper on Marian's desk had no information on it, so he was going to have to find out on his own. He had a pretty good idea where to start, and headed back into the hospital.

Asking the same nurse again, he returned to the elevators and rode up to the third floor. From there he turned left and headed down a long hallway toward the Maynard School of Medicine.

Maynard was a private medical school attached to the hospital. Once he had reached what looked to be classrooms, he found mostly locked doors. Finally, a light led him to a room with a circle of students leaning over a black lab table.

Ransom burst into the room and made eye contact with the older man in the lab coat. "I need to get into the dean's office," Ransom said. "Or the admissions office or whatever."

The man stood and said, "I'm teaching a class here. I don't know who you are—"

"Seattle Police," Ransom said, his badge already out.

That even caught the attention of the few die-hards who hadn't deigned to look at Ransom when he'd entered. It also took Dr. Lab Coat down a peg. "Yes, sir. Uh, I don't think anybody's in the office right now—"

"Then why don't we just go to your office and call the dean, or somebody with a key."

"Of course. Uh, class . . ." he was flustered now. "Continue and I'll be back presently."

Ransom followed Lab Coat down the hall to a small office and wedged himself in between stacks of textbooks. He wasn't feeling very patient, but he appeared so for the doctor's benefit. He needed this call.

Lab Coat picked up the phone and hesitated.

"Call the dean," Ransom urged. "I'll take full responsibility."

That eased his mind and he dialed. "Dean Spencer? I have a gentlemen here from the police department. An officer . . ."

Ransom took the receiver and said, "This is Lieutenant Ransom, Dean Spencer." He looked pointedly at Lab Coat, who turned away. "I'm a homicide detective with the Seattle police."

"What can I do for you, Lieutenant?" said the voice on the other end.

"I need the address of one of your students and I need it now."

A brief pause was followed by, "Do you have a court order?"

"Someone's life is at stake, Dean, at this very moment. Using that, I can break into the office myself if I like, but I'd rather not do that. Now, if there's someone higher up on the chain of command that I should talk to—"

"No, that won't be necessary. I'll be there in five minutes."

"I'll be waiting for you."

Ransom handed the receiver back to Dr. Lab Coat and said, "Now, if you'll show me to the dean's office, you can get back to your class."

It was the longest five minutes of Ransom's life. It was nearing seven and he wanted to call Wells and tell her he would be late, but he didn't want to chance missing Spencer.

He didn't have anything like real proof that it was Sanger, but he didn't need it. The last time, he and Gorham had walked into an ambush. This time he was going in prepared to kill. If Sanger had even so much as touched Marian, Ransom was going to take him apart. Though he knew he would have to do that anyway.

He wasn't just going to kill the thing. He was going to make sure it didn't survive this time, even if that meant burying the pieces all over town. Ransom was checking the silver bullets in the cylinder of his .38 when he heard a voice behind him.

"It's not that bad is it?"

He turned to see a tall man in his sixties, with large facial features and grey hair. An older version of Rondo Hatton, he thought, and flipped the cylinder shut. "I'm afraid it is."

The man offered is hand. "My name's Don Spencer. I'm the dean."

"Lieutenant Ransom," he said, and shook the man's hand.

"I don't mean to be rude, Lieutenant, but—"

Ransom nodded and pulled out his badge. Once he was satisfied, Spencer took a ring of keys from his pocket and opened the officer door.

It didn't take long for the old man to fire up one of the computers.

"Okay," he said, "Shoot."

"Sanger. Andrew Sanger. I don't know what year he's in, but I do know that he's in Dr. Harris's rotation in obstetrics."

Spencer nodded. "That should be easy enough." He typed the name into the computer and sat back. Two seconds later he announced, "He's not in here."

"What?"

"No one by that name enrolled. Let me take a look at former student files." Again he typed, and again he came up empty. He turned to Ransom and held his hands out. "I'm sorry, Lieutenant. I can't find a single person named Sanger—male or female—in our files."

That was all he needed. Now Ransom knew that it was Sanger. The thing wouldn't have been able to enroll in medical school, and he wouldn't have an address either. It wasn't evidence, but it was the closest he was going to get.

Ransom could feel the panic well in his chest. He wasn't going to be able to get to Marian in time. Without being able to track down Sanger, he could only sit and wait. But that was one thing Jack Ransom couldn't do.

He picked up the phone and called Wells.

"You're just in time," she said. "I was on my way out the door to relieve Razor and Burgher."

"Forget that—I'll call them. Right now I need you at the hospital."

"Bay Med?"

"That's right. There's a covered lot by the emergency room entrance. I need you to stake out a black BMW." He gave her the license.

"What do I do when it moves?"

"I want you there to make sure it doesn't."

" . . . Dr. Harris?"

"Yeah."

"Jack? Who is it?"

"Did you ever get a line on Andy Sanger?"

After a brief pause, she said, "I don't know how you did it, but I don't care. I'll be there as fast as I can. How will I be able to—"

"I'll find you."

"I'm on my way."

Ransom hung up and immediately called Razor and Burgher off of the stakeout at Ravenna Park. Then he thanked Spencer for his time and headed back to Marian's office.

He looked over her desk carefully this time, trying to find whatever information he could about Sanger. He didn't have any luck. Ransom was rapidly running out of ideas, but he couldn't just sit and wait. Finally he pushed himself out of the chair and headed out to the parking lot to bring Wells up to speed.

The last person he expected to see at the nurse's station was Wells. "What the hell—"

"Jack . . ." Her face was white and she was put of breath, as if she had been running. When she reached him she put a hand on his forearm and gripped it. He could feel her nails digging into his skin through his jacket as she said, "The car's gone."

Her eyes opened on a dark, unfamiliar room. Marian sat up quickly and her head began to spin. She leaned over and stared at a spot in the carpet to keep her equilibrium and stayed that way until she heard someone enter the room. It was Andy Sanger.

"Where am I?"

"At my place," he said. There was no emotion in his voice or his features. He looked at her impassively for a moment and then sat in a chair opposite her. He was wearing only a robe.

"What am I doing here?"

"You weren't feeling too well when we left your office. It must have been the dream you were having. Since my house was right across the street, I thought I'd bring you here to rest. You fell asleep on the couch."

When Marian sat back she noticed that her clothes didn't feel right. She was wearing everything she'd had on when she left the office, but if she hadn't known better she would have thought they were someone else's clothes.

She tugged at her bra and stood up to adjust her skirt. It felt as if she had been dressed by someone else. Marian stopped and looked up. Andy hadn't moved from the chair he was in.

"I'm going home now," she said.

He simply nodded. "Okay."

She saw her purse by the front door and picked it up on her way out without looking back.

Once Marian was outside it took a few seconds to get her bearings. The house wasn't exactly across the street, but she could see the hospital. She walked across Magnolia Boulevard toward the parking lot and her car. A look at her watch told her it was almost seven.

When she reached for her keys her hands began to shake. Her purse dropped to the ground, spilling its contents, and as she bent over to pick them up Marian began to tremble all over. She fell against the car and slid down the door to the pavement, trembling all over.

Tears rolled down her cheeks as she searched for her keys. It was back. It hadn't died. She could feel it now. That was why she'd been having the dreams.

Marian pulled herself up off the ground, unlocked the car, and climbed inside. She drove out of the parking lot wiping the tears with the back of her hand, almost sideswiping a parked car in the process. But she didn't care.

She had to get to Jack. She had to tell him. He was going to have to kill it again.

CHAPTER TEN

"Let's go," Ransom said. "My car's out front."

Riding alone down the elevator, Wells asked him where they were going.

"Home," he said. "My place. If Marian's there, I have to make sure she's all right."

"What if she's not there?"

"We put out the word and every black BMW in this town gets stopped. Every one in the state, if I can swing it."

He looked at Wells. She swallowed hard, but she still looked strong. For the briefest of moments Ransom wondered if he'd done the right thing in confiding in her.

Once they were on the main floor the two of them ran through the lobby and out the front door. They jumped into the car and Ransom spun out on the wet pavement as Wells asked where the light was. When the tires caught, Ransom told her he didn't have one. She nodded once and they cruised to Alaskan Way and then up 15th through Ballard with Ransom weaving through traffic and almost hoping a patrol car would chase them so that they could clear the road with the siren.

Neither of them spoke as Ransom gingerly made his way between cars and through red lights, west on 85th, and down toward Shilshole Bay to his and Marian's house.

It seemed the closer they came to reaching the house, the harder the rain began to pour. When the two of them stepped out of the car, Ransom was immediately drenched. And though he'd always hated the rain, for once in his life he didn't care. The only thing he could focus on was the dark garage. He ran up ahead of Wells, cupped his hands over the wet glass, and looked in.

Ransom's knees almost gave out. He turned with his back to the door and leaned against it. Wells ran up, rain plastering her hair to her head. "Well?"

Ransom nodded. "It's here."

Wells took a step back and wiped off her face.

"Come on," said Ransom. "Let's get inside where it's dry."

The door was unlocked and Ransom opened in onto a darkened living room. His chest tightened slightly as he called out. "Marian?"

No answer.

He pulled his gun, and Wells followed suit. "Check down here," he whispered. "I'm going upstairs."

Without waiting for an answer, Ransom headed quickly up the carpeted stairs. Rainwater was still dripping off his hair down the back of his neck, but he refused to let it distract him. At the top of the stairs he switched his revolver to his left hand, then dried his right on his pant leg before returning it.

"Marian," he said in a normal voice.

No answer again, but he could see a dim light coming from the bedroom as he neared the doorway. His weapon up near his cheek as he leaned against the doorframe, Ransom was all set to go in when he heard retching from the bathroom. Quickly he darted his head into the open doorway, then followed his piece into the room.

It was dark and empty, lit only by the light from the bathroom. He heard the retching again and said, "Marian?"

"Oh, Jack," he heard her sob.

He holstered his weapon and ran into the bathroom. Marian was on the floor next to the toilet. A sheen of sweat covered her face, and tendrils of hair stuck to her cheeks and forehead. Ransom went to his knee and put his arm around her.

"Oh, Jack. I called and they said you weren't there and . . ." More sobs.

Wells appeared in the doorway. "Clean," she said, then holstered her piece and left them alone.

"I was worried," he said. "When you left with Sanger—"

"Jack." She gripped the lapels until her knuckles turned white. "It's him. He's still alive."

Cold fear washed slowly over Ransom's entire body. "Did he do something to you?"

"No, Jack. You don't understand. It's him. The baby."

He held her tight, wondering what to tell her. "The baby I killed before?"

She nodded into his chest. "I don't know why I think that, but it has to be him."

"Sanger."

She looked up at him, eyes wide and wet.

He said, "I'm trying to find out where he lives."

She pulled herself up on his jacket. "I know," she said. "Across from the hospital."

"Can you show me?"

"I'll try—" Suddenly it was as if Marian had convulsed. Her body curled into a ball and she moaned. Jack picked her up in his arms and carried her out into the bedroom. "Wells!" he shouted.

She was in the hallway and appeared instantly.

"We have to get Marian to the hospital."

"What about Sanger?"

"Marian knows where he lives. It's right across the street."

Wells led the way downstairs and shut the door behind Ransom. When he put Marian in the back seat beside Wells she was still sobbing. Ransom gunned the engine and drove back the way he'd come.

They had nearly reached Bay Med when he heard Marian whisper from the back seat. "Where are we going, Jack?"

"I want you to show me where Sanger's house is, and then we're taking you to the hospital."

As he neared the entrance on Magnolia Boulevard, Ransom could only see a group of doctors' offices across the street. "It's up a little further," Marian said.

Ransom drove at a crawl past the professional buildings and saw a row of expensive looking homes.

"It's the first one."

He stopped immediately and backed the car against the curb behind a screen of shrubs. "All right," he said, looking at Wells. "I want you to take Marian to the emergency room."

"Jack—"

"No argument."

"I can't let you go in there alone."

He looked into Wells' ice-blue eyes and said, "This is one of those times you're going to have to trust my expertise."

She just stared at him and he went on. "This isn't going to be a righteous shoot. Sanger isn't going to be armed, at least not in a way internal affairs will recognize. You're still a rookie, Wells. With any luck you'll have a long career ahead of you and I don't want it to start out with a black spot."

She frowned but he shook his head. The car was still running and he opened the door and stepped out. When Wells emerged he said, "After she's been taken care of, you can come back here. Whatever you do, though, don't call for backup."

"Jesus, Jack—"

"Do you have your bullets loaded?"

She nodded.

"Okay, get going."

Ransom stepped to the rear door before she could argue. He opened it and leaned inside. Marian grabbed him weakly around the neck and he expected her to tell him to be careful or that she loved him. Instead she whispered into his ear, "Kill it, Jack."

Then she closed her eyes and slumped into the seat. "Get going," he told Wells.

As the car pulled away, he unholstered his piece and headed up the walk of the house. The windows were dark. The rain that had let up on the way back began to fall again. Ransom took a deep breath and tried to keep his legs from buckling beneath him.

But Marian's words were still ringing in his ears. That, and the memory of Al Gorham's death, propelled him forward and up the steps.

The house was a two-story structure, white with red trim. It was one of the many expensive older homes in the area, heavily landscaped and immaculately kept. Silently, he twisted the knob on the door. It was locked, but the door moved a fraction.

That meant only the deadbolt was engaged. It wasn't going to be quiet, not by a long shot, but he didn't have time to sneak around the back. Checking the hinges, he saw that the front door opened inward. That was good.

With all of his weight behind him, Ransom lifted his foot and kicked at the door just to the right of the deadbolt. It didn't open, but he could feel the frame give. The next kick splintered the frame and he was inside.

Ransom didn't say a word. He brazenly walked through the front room with his weapon at his side. There was no danger of being shot, only that Sanger would catch him by surprise. Ransom was going to make sure that didn't happen.

He walked quickly through the rooms downstairs and then headed up to the second floor. The framed photographs on wall— of men, women and children—slowed him down for a second. Looking back down at the living room he could see a definite female touch to the decorating. Sanger's living in someone else's house, he thought.

More cautiously now, Ransom reached the top of the stairs and pushed open the first door on the right. Master bedroom, he saw, except that the mattress was on the floor. Everything else in the room seemed as though it had been tipped over and piled up against the wall, but Ransom didn't take the time to turn on the light and investigate any further. If Sanger wasn't in the house, Ransom wanted to know as soon as possible.

He went through the rest of the rooms just as efficiently. Until he reached the last. It was a child's room with a stack of bunk beds in the far corner. But it was the smell that caused Ransom to turn on the light.

In the middle of the room sat five large plastic trash bags. Ransom stepped back out into the hall and took a deep breath. Then he clenched his jaw tightly to keep the rest of his body from shaking. He knew what was in the bags, but he also knew he couldn't leave the scene without verifying it first.

Stepping back into the bedroom he turned on a light and looked around. He found a pair of scissors on a small child's desk and proceeded to cut one of the bags open. The plastic was thicker than he'd expected and it took a few seconds to get the blunt point through the tough material. Once it was through, though, he turned his head and nearly threw up.

He swallowed hard and returned to his work. As the opening in the bag widened, the stench of rotting flesh began to pervade the room. Then, as he hefted the bag to get a better angle with the scissors, the small eviscerated body of a young boy spilled out onto the carpet.

"Aw, Christ." Ransom turned out the light and left the room. He'd seen enough.

Now he went back through the house, turning on lights to see if there was any other evidence of Sanger. After taking a second to look in each room, he quickly turned the lights back off. If Sanger came back while he was here, he didn't want to spook him. They'd been damn lucky to find him, and Ransom didn't plan on losing him now.

But when he reached the master bedroom and flicked the switch, he froze. The entire room was covered with brown stains, instantly recognizable to Ransom as dried blood. It was everywhere, on the mattress, the carpet, the walls, even drops on the ceiling. There were other things on the carpet as well, small dark objects of the same color. Ransom didn't even want to know what they were. He turned the light off and went back downstairs.

He was going to have to get out of the house soon, so that he and Wells could set up a stakeout. But Ransom wanted one last look in the study he'd seen. He turned on the desk lamp, illuminating the shelves along every wall filled with medical texts. It didn't take long to find what he was after. Sitting on the desk was Sanger's schedule for the week. One look at it and Ransom fled from the room in a panic.

The schedule showed that every night that week Sanger was volunteering at the hospital.

Ransom was out of breath and soaked to the skin as he came storming into the emergency room. He'd run all the way from across the street and now he was flashing his badge at anyone who would look his way. Finally, he saw the nurse who had given him directions earlier.

"I need to find Marian Harris."

She looked puzzled for a moment. "*Dr.* Harris?"

"She was supposed to have come in here a few minutes ago. She wasn't feeling well."

Just then a doctor came through looking for a medical chart. The nurse said, "Dr. Denny, have you seen Dr. Harris in the ER tonight, maybe as a patient?"

He shook his head. "Not tonight." And then he was off.

"Sorry," the nurse said.

Ransom took another quick look around, just in case, and then headed for Marian's office. In the elevator on the way up he unsnapped the leather restraint to make sure his revolver was loose in his holster.

There would be almost no chance of him keeping his job if too many people saw him take out Sanger in the hospital, but he was out of options. His only desire now, was that Wells would be on her way to Sanger's house. With any luck she wouldn't figure out what was going on until it was all over.

Ransom's main concern was with Marian. He had to get to her and make sure she was all right. Once he knew she was safe, he could track down Sanger and end this thing.

Walking quickly past the nurses' station, he received curious looks from Dorry and the other nurse he'd seen earlier. When he reached Marian's office he grabbed the knob in stride and was inside as soon as he'd opened the door.

Marian was lying on the couch and Ransom went to her immediately. "Marian?" he said, but her eyes were closed. He put a hand on her forehead: it was hot.

"You shouldn't have brought her here."

At the sound of another voice in the room Ransom whirled around, drawing his gun in the same motion. At first he had aimed for the door, but seeing no one was there, his line of sight moved to Marian's desk.

Sanger. He was sitting in the dark, grinning. His shirt was unbuttoned and he sat back and met Ransom's gaze without flinching.

"Get up," Ransom ordered.

Sanger stopped smiling and stood up.

"Now, come around the desk slowly and stop by the door."

Sanger obeyed.

"Turn around and put your hands behind your back."

As Sanger complied, he said, "Aren't you supposed to read me my rights?"

"We'll get to that."

Ransom stuck his gun hard in Sanger's back, then he took his cuffs out from the case on his belt and secured them around Sanger's wrists. His plan was to get him back to the house and kill him there.

"Okay," he said. "Let's go."

"What about Marian?" Sanger asked.

"Let *me* worry about her."

Ransom pushed Sanger forward with the barrel of his gun, and the two began walking toward the nurses' station. By the time they had reached the central hub of the floor, there were four wide-eyed nurses behind the counter.

"Dr. Harris is sick," he said. "She's in her office. I want one of you to take her down to the emergency room—"

As he was saying the words, with Sanger in front of him, he heard the handcuffs fall to the floor. He had barely looked down when the body in front of him disappeared.

Ransom looked up to see Sanger running down the hall. He lifted his weapon and fired, but Sanger's body was already falling and the bullet went high.

Then he saw that Sanger hadn't fallen. His pants remained on the floor where he'd run out of them. The shirt came next, and Ransom could see the animal Sanger had become, rounding the far corner of the hallway.

He'd just recovered in time to get off another shot and this time he hit his mark. A yelp echoed back to Ransom as the animal slid into the far wall. But then it was out of sight. When he reached down to pick up his handcuffs, Ransom saw Sanger's shoes right next to them.

He turned to the catatonic nursing staff and pointed down the hall. "Is anyone down there?"

Dorry slowly shook her head. "The operating rooms are down there. They're empty right now."

He wondered exactly what they'd seen, and if they could back him up, but it didn't matter. "Please," he said. "Someone help Marian." He had a job to finish, and Jack Ransom took a grim step forward down the hallway.

Past the pants and shirt, he found a bloody smear on the floor where the animal had taken a round in the leg. But that meant nothing at this point. If it could survive a head shot from a regular bullet, it could certainly live with a silver one in its leg.

The drops of blood led down the hall to one of the operating rooms. He looked inside. The room was dark. Ransom searched for a light switch but couldn't find one. And there was no more time to look.

Ransom knew that hospital security would be there any second. He had to do it now. With his left hand he opened the door and light from the hallway spilled into the room. He held the .38 in front of him for several seconds, then looked down and lowered the doorstop with his foot. Now, with both hands on his revolver, he entered the operating room. The drops of blood looked black on the floor. They glistened in the slanting light and led around the back side of the operating table. Ransom thought he could hear breathing other than his own as he stepped forward. The room was bigger than he'd expected and it seemed as though it took a long time to cover the few feet he had to go.

When he reached the table, he backed away and moved around behind. Quickly, he swept the gun around and prepared to fire. But there was nothing there.

And then, as if it had materialized out of thin air, the wolf appeared above him, coming over the top of the table. Ransom barely had time to lift his gun before searing pain in his wrist caused him to drop it.

Suddenly it felt as though he were being smothered. The flash of teeth and heat of the animal's breath were the only things that registered. That, and the intense pain in his chest as the animal's claws ripped into him.

Pain shot through his body like electricity. His skin was slick with perspiration and blood. The animal's fur was wet and Ransom couldn't find anywhere to grip. Then he felt a slash across his throat. He couldn't breathe, and blood began welling out of his mouth.

He was lost now. The world seemed to tilt on its axis and Jack Ransom was sliding down toward some distant pit, to be swallowed up whole. Darkness and light reversed itself. The growl of the animal roared in his ears like the ocean then faded into white noise.

He had come prepared to kill the beast, not to die. But in his final moments he let go of all that and began to turn his thoughts to what lay beyond.

Before him was a light, blinding in intensity. He shut his eyes and yet still it was there. And in his ears, through the white noise, he could hear the sound of a cannon, muffled but distinct. It fired once a second for six seconds. And the last thing Jack Ransom thought before he died, was that he could smell cordite.

The minute Marian Harris opened her eyes she knew: he was dead. Dorry entered her office a few moments later, but by then she was sitting up. Her head felt clearer than it had in the past two weeks.

"Where's Jack?"

Dorry looked stricken, saying nothing. Marian stood and walked out of the room with Dorry trailing behind. When they reached the nurses' station there we cops everywhere. Through the crowd came Jack's partner, Detective Wells.

"Where's Jack?" Marian asked.

Wells took her aside and said, "He's in pretty bad shape. All the doctors here say it was lucky that he was in the operating room already or he never would have had a chance."

"What about . . ."

Wells nodded. "He's dead."

Marian sighed with relief and began to walk toward the operating rooms.

Wells was beside her in an instant and took her arm, stopping her. "Where are you going?"

"I have to be in there with Jack. Even if I can't help, I have to be in there with him."

Wells nodded, but before she could walk away Marian asked, "Are you sure the thing's dead?"

Wells smiled grimly this time. "Yes, ma'am."

EPILOGUE

It was nearly two weeks to the day after Detective Kay Wells killed Andrew Sanger—in defense of her partner, the police report said—before Jack Ransom could thank her in person. His throat had been severely wounded, but fortunately none of his vocal cords had been damaged.

Unfortunately, nearly everything else had. In addition to deep lacerations all over his chest, the artery in his right wrist and the carotid artery in his neck had been severed and had pumped out his blood as fast as his heart could manage. As Wells had told Marian, if he hadn't already been in an operating room, he surely would have died.

After arriving at the hospital Dr. Harris had insisted on being taken to her office. Wells dropped her off there with the intention of meeting Ransom back at Sanger's house. Evidently she had passed him on the elevators, because as soon as she reached the emergency room, a nurse there told her that Ransom had already been through a few seconds before.

She heard shots just as the elevator disgorged her onto the obstetrics ward, and was calling for back up before Dorry could even finish telling her what had happened. With help on the way, and her piece unhoslstered, Detective Kay Wells ran to back up her partner. Her *senior* partner.

Mere seconds after Wells pumped six silver bullets into the wolf that was attacking Jack, the emergency room staff arrived and began working on Ransom. As per her orders, they ignored the naked body of Andy Sanger that was lying next to him.

That night, after Jack was in stable condition, Wells met with Doc Nagumo at the morgue. She reminded him of what had happened the last time, suggesting that he leave the bullets in the body and cremate it as soon as possible. By the time Jack Ransom was sitting up in bed and thanking her, the being that had called itself Andrew Sanger no longer existed.

"You disobeyed my orders," he said to her in a raspy voice.

The smile she was wearing widened, and her blue eyes no longer looked icy.

"Thanks for saving my life."

She shrugged and then stood as Marian entered the room. "Next time," she said, leaning close to him, "If you leave me in the dark, I'm going to let you die."

Ransom's laugh turned to a wince, and his hand went to his throat as she left the room. Marian kissed him and sat in the chair next to his bed.

"How are you feeling?"

"Like I've been through a meat grinder."

"Other than that, I mean."

"Good," he said. And then he looked over at her and met her eyes. "Why?"

She was half-smiling and half-grimacing. "I'm not sure how to say this, because I never expected it to happen."

Ransom pushed himself up in bed as much as he could manage and turned toward her. "What is it?"

She sighed and said, "I think I'm pregnant."

Ransom's jaw dropped. " I thought . . . I mean, I didn't think, I just assumed that you . . . I mean—"

"I didn't think I could, Jack. I haven't been on the pill, or used anything else, for years. When Loren and I had been trying I found out I had blocked Fallopian tubes so I figured it wasn't possible."

Ransom sat back, grinning.

"I want to keep it, Jack."

He turned quickly and felt the pain in his throat. "Of course. I think this is fantastic."

"I was hoping you would."

He nodded.

"Then you don't mind being a father?"

"Mind?"

"It's not going to be easy," she said. "I'm not exactly in my prime child-bearing years."

"I think you'll do just fine, as long as I can help."

"You'd better."

Ransom took her hand. "Then what do you say we get married?"

"You're proposing?"

"Exactly."

She hesitated, and for a moment Ransom was awash in uncertainty. Then she nodded. "Yeah," she said. "I think I'd like that. I'd like that just fine."

Even at that moment, as Jack Ransom was proposing, blood deep inside Marian Harris's womb was being diverted to the placenta, through what would become the umbilical cord, to the embryo growing there.

The being inside of her was perfect in every respect, and for the next nine months would continue to grow inside her. Ultrasound and amniocentesis would confirm that it was a boy, and her obstetrician would be satisfied with his progress.

But what wouldn't show up on those medical procedures, what Marian couldn't feel in her womb, was what happened every month. At nights during the full moon, while Jack slept next to her, the fetus in her body sprouted tiny fangs where its teeth would eventually be, and little slivers that looked like claws from the ends of its tiny fingertips.

About the Author

Eric B. Olsen is the author of six novels in three different genres. He has written a medical thriller entitled *Death's Head* as well as the horror novel *Dark Imaginings*. He is also the author of three mystery novels, *Proximal to Murder* and *Death in the Dentist's Chair*, featuring amateur sleuth Steve Raymond, DDS, and *The Seattle Changes*, featuring private detective Ray Neslowe. In addition, he is the author of *If I Should Wake Before I Die*, a book of short horror fiction.

Today Mr. Olsen writes primarily nonfiction, including *The Death of Education*, an exposé of the public school system in America.

Mr. Olsen currently lives in the Pacific Northwest with his wife.

Please visit the author's web site at http://eric.b.olsen.tripod.com, or contact by email at ericbolsen@juno.com.

Printed in the United States
By Bookmasters